Fish, Blood and Bone

By the same author
**Bombay Ice**

# Fish, Blood and Bone

## LESLIE FORBES

God made paradise
And redeemed man.
To each man He left
A living through his work.
Some are fitted to do damage,
Others are good Christians,
Others, card in hand,
Gamble to support themselves.
And I can be grateful
That I am a maker of saints.

*Florencio Caban Hernandez,*
*Puerto Rican* Santero (*Saintmaker*)

Weidenfeld & Nicolson
LONDON

First published in Great Britain in 2000
by Weidenfeld & Nicolson

© 2000 Leslie Forbes

A CIP catalogue record for this book
is available from the British Library.

Typeset at The Spartan Press Ltd,
Lymington, Hants

Set in Minion

Printed in Great Britain by
Clays Ltd, St Ives plc

Weidenfeld & Nicolson

The Orion Publishing Group Ltd
Orion House
5 Upper Saint Martin's Lane
London, WC2H 9EA

*To Gavin Jones, Sally Cameron and the gardeners of Devons Road, Bow, in whose miraculous community garden this book is rooted, and to the participants in the Wellcome Trust Sci-Art project of 1997, in particular Heather Ackroyd, Dan Harvey and Howard Thomas, whose ephemeral 'green' art and science I grafted on to mine.*

# Acknowledgements

Special thanks to my editor, Rebecca Wilson, to Terry Trickett and Laurence Smaje, who devised the visionary Sci-Art project at the Wellcome Trust, which introduced me to many of the ideas in this book, to Rosie Atkins, for sending me to the Cameron Community Garden in the first place, to Audrey Ellison, whose unpublished work on the search for new useful plants was of tremendous help, to Len Fisher, Harold McGee and Tony Blake, for their comments about cancer, chlorophyll and flavour chemistry at the Erice Conference on Molecular Gastronomy, and to Andrew Thomas, listener and groundbreaker.

This is a work of fiction grounded in fact. To my knowledge, there is no green poppy like the one described in this book, although its healing and narcotic properties would not be impossible. There was a famous nineteenth-century 'Two-headed Bengali Boy', whose skull is held by the Hunterian Museum in London. This story is not his. The facts regarding Jack the Ripper, however, are well documented, and the Indian pundit Kintup did exist: I have borrowed many of his journeys, far more extraordinary than any recounted here, for Arun and his father. I have also taken liberties with the discovery of the Tsangpo Falls. Details were lifted from true accounts of the period and combine real explorations described in Derek Waller's book *The Pundits*, in Frank Kingdon-Ward's dramatic *The Riddle of the Tsangpo Gorge*, and in accounts of the National Geographic team who explored the gorge in 1998 and discovered some 'Lost Falls' (if not mine).

Oliver Rackham's classic *The History of the Countryside* (Phoenix 1997) was a great inspiration, as were Richard Mabey's *Flora Britannica*, Martin Booth's *Opium, A History* (Pocket Books 1997),

Stephen S. Hall's *A Commotion in the Blood: Life, Death, and the Immune System* (Little, Brown 1998), R. D. Laing's *The Divided Self* (Tavistock Publications 1959), *Dead Men Do Tell Tales* by William R. Maples and Michael Browning (Mandarin 1996), Susan Orlean's *The Orchid Thief* (Heinemann 1999), the diaries of Marianne North, *The Quick and the Dead: Artists and Anatomy* by Deanna Petherbridge, *Mapping an Empire* by Matthew Edney, *Calcutta* by Geoffrey Moorhouse, *Memoirs of a Bengal Civilian* by John Beames, *The Plant Hunters* by Charles Lyte, *The Language of Genes* by Steve Jones and the essays of Oliver Sacks.

# Fish, Blood and Bone

# Contents

# I BONE

# Jack's Garden

# 1

IT IS THAT time of evening when the setting sun seems to rise again and saturate every colour in one final luminous shower. I am lying on the grass with my arms spread like someone about to dive, or a stone angel fallen from a grave. Tower blocks loom above this cemetery of a garden, oversized tombstones in shades of grey, yet from the ground all I can see is a mosaic of green leaves and cobalt blue sky, both colours so intense from their last benediction of light that it is impossible to tell which colour is near and which is far away. Then the tree leaves begin to rush in at me. I am falling through them, diving through them, at the same time being pressed into the ground by their weight. Composted, buried under more greens than I can name or count, I loop the loop down a double spiral, one of those funfair rides that leaves you feeling sick – call it The Big Helix, a long coiling bridge or tunnel linking two stories a hundred years apart.

*It began in a garden, and ends in one: Jack is dead; I killed him.*

Thinking back to the night before Sally's murder, I remember trying to listen to the trees. It was one of Sal's crazier theories: concentrate hard enough and the trees' whispers will resolve into words. Another theory involved a compost invented by Rudolf Steiner. 'He said . . . wait a minute . . . Don't laugh. He said it had "the power to reunite the earth with its severed soul".' She grinned, knowing the occult phrase sounded funny recited in her tarmacked accent. 'Good, innit?'

'The only Rudolf Steiner I've heard of was a philosopher who set up a sort of alternative school system. Same guy?'

'Dunno. But my bloke was worried because the planet was sick "both in spirit and in soil" – look, I copied it into my garden book. The cure was to make a compost out of a stag's bladder stuffed with yarrow flowers, a pig's gut stuffed with dandelions, the skull of a goat filled with oak bark, a bunch of nettles wrapped in moss and a length of cow's intestine filled with chamomile.'

Her language was always full of pulpy, mulching words, but at this gothic recipe I burst out laughing. 'What do you do then, Sal, add an eye of newt and boil it up under a full moon? Could be pricey these days, given the cost of newts. Aren't they an endangered species?'

When I teased Sally, the ardent conservationist, the vegetarian, for her bloodthirsty soil, she told me that every butcher in London used to have a garden where they buried the stinking guts so they wouldn't cause offence, and if you tempered these with lime the result was a good fertiliser. 'The earth is full of blood and bones,' she said. 'You just can't see them now. It's all the same colour.'


'Will you want to claim anonymity if you are called as a witness?' asked the detective who took my statement the morning after Sally's murder. He was a big man, uncomfortably poised on the very edge of my sofa as if he were afraid of getting dog hairs on his Stay-Prest trousers.

'What happens if I do?'

'It might mean the Crown Prosecution Service disallowing your testimony.'

'Then I won't.' Although if anyone could claim anonymity as a birthright, it was me. Anon: the name you see next to countless poems, paintings, Christmas carols – and crimes, anon, anon, anon.

'You're sure?' his female colleague pressed. 'You will have to stand up in court . . .' A pause before she added what none of the cops who questioned me has put in words. 'And there's no guarantee the men who did this won't get off. They'll have your name. They have your address already.'

'I'm sure.' The idea of my identity – of *me*, Claire Fleetwood – being important, even dangerous, is an odd one. I am such an ordinary person. Not brave. Not at all sure that I want to face those men in court. But a public testimony seems the only way to take control of my life again. Otherwise, the men who left Sally in the street will have won. Their assessment of me that night – young, small, girl, *no threat* – will be correct. I'll be consigned to the big compost heap: People of No Consequence, Anon.

Since the murder my brain has been on a circular track that keeps shunting me back to that point when I went over the wall and saw . . . what did I see? I've told it to so many different faces whose features were arranged to imitate sympathy, appropriate sadness, whatever people think they should look like in the face of violent death. For my official witness statement I had to give a general synopsis first, then break it down stage by stage. All the details:

> whether it could have been a robbery I interrupted
> if she tried to defend herself
> how long they hesitated after I called out
> the shape of the blood running out of her

Then the cops read it back to me and I had to initial any change I'd made, a story repeated so many times that the telling has become the event. Maybe that's why the police make you do it, to fix it, the way I fix my forensic photographs with chemicals. Unless you fix them, they keep getting darker and more obscure.

'How did it happen?' The question they all ask. Could I have stopped it? The question I ask myself.

'It was dark – 10.30 on a warm April evening.'

'The twentieth, that was?' asked the detective recording my statement.

'Yes. I was taking pictures of the *Helleborus orientalis*.'

'Hellebor–?' The policeman questioned the unfamiliar name as if it were a suspect.

'A flower,' I told him. 'From the East.' Fleshy, dusky blooms the colour of unripe plums and bruises. What was I thinking? Maybe just enjoying the pure sensuous pleasure of warm night air like a silk scarf on my skin, the smell of life in the damp earth, the fishiness of my fingers as I brought them close to my face, remnants of the Fish, Blood & Bone fertiliser I'd sprinkled on the garden, *my* garden. It's a new sensation for me, feeling tied to a place. For the first time in my twenty-eight years I've put down roots, and it's the physical act of digging, of literally getting dirt under my nails, that has had this effect. The recent pictures I've been taking at home reflect this new interest, a break from my daily work as a forensic photographer.

Part of my brain slides away here and tries to move a few feet down the line past the uglier pictures. Another side zooms in, adjusts the focus. The side with a different agenda, one of those ghouls who drive slowly past road accidents.

Feeling again her hand cooling in mine. Her skin turning waxy as hellebores.

A spring night. Warm on my skin, a night that smelled of broom and wet ferns. Like my brother Robin when he came back from three days' fishing. Like Sally and Mr Banerji when they came in from working in the garden, bringing a smell with them of washing hung outside to dry. I didn't put that in the statement. It's not relevant to the careful cataloguers from the CID. No one needs to know how Sally smelled when living. Her last smell was sticky and sweet. Blood and urine.

The CID man looked up from his notes. 'Where were you when you first heard the cries for help?'

'I was in the garden taking pictures. I had unscrewed the camera from the tripod to get closer, strung it around my neck for safety. The garden wall, about seven feet in height, separates me from the almshouses.' And on the third side from the patch of weeds, flowers, broken bottles, used condoms and syringes that lies between the wall and the street. What Sally calls – *used* to call – the Front Line. I cleared my throat, as if by doing so I could clear the memories along with the unshed tears. 'Gradually I became aware that someone had been crying, calling out for help for several minutes.'

'It seems to have taken you a long time to notice.'

I stared at him, working out the motive for his comment. 'Have you walked down that street? My friend – Sally – she called it the Front Line, for a good reason. It's supposed to be an extension of the back central garden belonging to the house I live in. In fact, it's not a garden, it's a battlefield where we wage war on vandals and hookers and junkies and the people who think their dog's shit smells better than my flowers.'

I would have given up the first time they snapped off the climbing vines and trampled on the seedbeds. It was Sally who kept the garden going. She found the steel-blue thistles whose stems were too tough to break easily, and the rose with a name – *Blanc double de Coubert* – as tissuey as Sally promised its clove-scented blooms would be, with branches armoured in a thick hedge of spines. She bicycled off to a churchyard last year and took seeds from the tough old hollyhocks growing there, so that later this summer we would have a phalanx of them, marching shoulder to shoulder against the marauding hordes. Sally stored up in her head like seeds all the garden aphorisms she had ever been told. 'Mr Banerji says gardening is the art closest to giving birth,' she'd say. 'But spring shouldn't get all the credit because every garden starts with a little death. Mr Banerji believes in the cycle of reincarnation. I guess I do too.'

Of course, these weren't the kind of things the policeman wanted to know.

'Sally – this would be Sally Rivers, the dead girl?' he asked.

'Yes.' Every garden starts with a little death. 'I thought it was just another car radio thief. I don't know when I recognised her voice, maybe at my dog's first barks.' Then I was running, holding the camera against my chest to stop it bouncing. Got to the gate and heard the impact, the soft thump against it, and in that moment I realised I didn't have the keys with me. We had only just started locking the gate. I heard Sally's voice and ran down the wall to the trellis, started to climb it, the stupid suburban trellis that Sally pleaded with me to buy from the stupid garden centre, still holding my camera (why didn't I drop the camera? would I have been faster, could it have made a difference if I'd dropped it?). Pulled myself over the wall and saw them: three figures, one falling, being held, fallen, an arm up to protect her face, one man holding her while the other hit. He was using this club thing, not a knife – 'A truncheon, would you call it?' the detective interrupted, and I nodded. I'd forgotten I was speaking aloud. A truncheon, that was the word. A word with a wet crunch in it.

'I shouted. The big man looked at me. He hesitated for a second. Our eyes met. Then he got on with it.' No anger in his face. His job. What he does for a living. 'I slid down the side of the wall . . . and then – I don't remember. They were running past me under the streetlight, two biggish men –'

'And you're how tall? Five foot two?'

'Five-one. They were well-dressed, beefy. Expensive trainers.' Men you could stand next to in a bar without feeling nervous. The kind of men put on this earth to protect us, the weaker sex. 'Then I heard sirens, I think. Someone called the police, the ambulance. I was holding her hand, telling her she'd be all right.'

Keep breathing, Sally, don't stop breathing. There's someone coming, Sally, you're going to be all right. And meanwhile a great petal of blood slipping past me like Sally's shadow. Sally's eyes rolling back. She's hiccuping for air. Her hand loosening, cooling, the blood getting sticky. Still no ambulance, although I see the police and I'm swearing at them, shouting for the ambulance while they pull on their latex gloves. I remember the gloves, how long it took to put them on, how thin and transparent the gloves were. 'The ambulance came. It took about twenty-five minutes, I think.' By then, I couldn't tell if it was Sally's hand holding mine or mine holding hers. We were both sticky from the blood running down inside the sleeve of her plastic coat, where she'd held up her arm to stop them hitting her face.

All the time my dog Russell was barking and barking. I could hear him scratching at the garden gate, then throwing the full weight of his terrier body against it. Sally was his friend too. She saved bones and toast corners for him.

They took her away. I made the nicest policeman promise to

tell me what happened to her. But he didn't. I was just a friend, not family. Other things on his mind. I didn't hear what happened until the next morning at six when I went out to see the street blocked off with yellow tape. By then it was murder.

She died in the early morning of the twenty-first of April, a few hours after getting to Emergency. A small girl. Aged eighteen, about my height, puny, not the product of weekly feedings and mulchings during her prime growth period. She had multiple stab wounds in her side, a broken arm where the truncheon blows had missed her head, several broken ribs. Her head was smashed in and her left hand, the one she wasn't holding up to protect her face, was pierced through the palm. She was holding on to the rose, they said. It troubled me that she'd died before it flowered. Clove-scented, she'd promised.

'I should have stopped them,' I said to the CID man.

He shook his head. 'She'd been stabbed before she got to your gate. We found traces of blood around the corner and smeared along the cars where she'd staggered into them. The stab wounds alone would've killed her, let alone the blows they used to finish her off.'

'I should have gone with her.'

'Nah – it's amazing she lived as long as she did.'

I wasn't amazed. She was a small girl, but tough as weeds.

After the forensic people had completed their work that day, they hosed down the scene. I guess the blood wasn't a good advertisement for our neighbourhood, which the council claims to have cleaned up. The police clean-up job was just as inadequate. A pale red stain remained, like the watercolour of a fallen petal. Beside it was one of the policemen's crumpled latex gloves, the thumb poking out from under an empty cigarette pack so I thought at first that the glove was a discarded condom. We get a lot of those tossed into the bushes around here. Now I can't seem to get rid of that collage – the bloodstain and the latex. The seventeen stab wounds in Sally linked to a different form of penetration.

When the CID man asked me whether I thought that the attack on Sally might have been a robbery which got out of hand

I knew exactly how to put the worst slant on it. They suggested that the men might have been 'driven to violence', as if violence were a place you got to faster in a car. But I knew how to give them premeditation in the right language to stand up in court. Truth is, I'm not so sure. Did they hear me call out, hesitate, and then return to the killing? Whatever. I don't want justice now, or repentance for their sins, I want revenge. I want someone to blame for the things that happen to us.

'From what you've told us it doesn't seem that this was just a random killing,' the policewoman said before she left, trying to comfort me. Randomness you want to avoid at all costs. A random murder could happen to anyone.

# 2

THE NIGHT OF Sally's murder, one of the cops had to break in through the gate for me using some device that opened the lock with a flick of his wrist. Russell immediately threw himself against my legs, chasing his non-existent tail, growling fiercely and keeping an eye on us to see if he could raise a laugh.

'That's his standard joke,' I said.

'Great dogs, Jack Russells. Now, you sure you'll be OK? I know you're used to the odd corpse, but reactions are different if it's a friend.'

'I'll be fine.'

The policeman looked beyond my dog's dervish act to where the garden stretched away like a promise. 'You own all this?' he asked, with a note of grudging admiration. In the moonlight the house and garden had a magic that covered up the dry rot, rising damp, subsidence.

'Not exactly own,' I told him. 'It's in trust.' My trusty house.

'Still,' he said, glancing around at the huge yew tree and the old bench under the pergola and then sizing me up to see if my small stature suited the grandeur of such terrain. 'Well, someone from CID will take your official statement tomorrow about what happened.' He didn't offer help again. Anyone of my age who lived somewhere like this had already had all the help she deserved.

I relocked the gate and packed the photographic equipment into the house, my body by now so heavy that I barely had the energy to undress before climbing into my sleeping bag on the striped silk sofa. Russell promptly jumped up next to me, turned around precisely three times and curled himself into a neat circle like a spotted Cumberland sausage, nose tucked firmly next to testicles to protect them from unseen but always expected attackers. I'd adopted him from the Battersea Dogs' Home in 1984. It was my first year in London, shortly after my brother's death. All the other abandoned dogs had been whining and pressing their damp doggy wistful noses against the wire, desperate to charm, while Russell had sat back on his haunches with a look in his clever brown eyes that said: 'We're the same: small, brown, wiry. I can live anywhere, eat anything – or nothing; we belong together.' I knew nothing about dogs, and when the Battersea manager muttered the words 'Jack Russell', I assumed that it was the name of my new dog. Jack had bad connotations for me, so I called out 'Russell' instead, and he trotted briskly over as if he had known all along that we had this urgent appointment. He always gave the impression of being a small dog with high ambitions.

I find myself using Sally's murder as a memory check these days – the night before, two weeks later . . . I remember that it was the morning after Sally's death I went back to camping in the big front room, my cooking reduced to toast with a veneer of Marmite spooned from an ancient jar of my great aunt's that probably dated from the Jurassic period (Marmite being one of those substances that I believe lasts for ever, closer to lichen than to food). It's the sort of gypsy life my family has always lived. The Fleetwoods never put down roots. We weren't gardeners or tillers of fields. We did not have a 'home team'. When I was a kid we were always on the move, always going somewhere: somewhere else. Maybe that explains why my first cheap camera was used to take pictures of fixed or slow-growing stuff: rocks, trees, plants unlikely to stray far from their source, as well as the precise wire insects my younger brother Robin made out of thread and wire for his fly-fishing. Both of us were attached to precision (except, in Robin's case, when it came to sex).

Our English father, by contrast, was an imprecise man, unattached in all senses. A part-time actor who dragged Mum and us in a caravan back and forth across America in search of his big break, he claimed to have no history. 'I'm an orphan,' he would tell us, 'perfectly suited to the United States, a country with no history.' He talked about North America as if it had begun with the Ford car or the Declaration of Independence at the earliest, implying that all the Sicilians and English Quakers and Russian Jews who had turned up on the continent before and since had abandoned their individual histories, left them behind on a dock in the Old Country like overweight luggage. History was not transportable, if you believed Dad; it had to do with heavy, medieval shit – family armour, castles, a thousand years of class war. Wiping out the native people of America doesn't really cut it by comparison. Like a sense of irony, history was supposed to begin and end on the other side of the Atlantic. When I finally made it to England, to the Other Side, I found that Dad's view of history as immovable was common to most Europeans. It only occurred to me recently that he might have preferred it that way, or that he could have something to fear from digging up his own roots.

He had dropped out of a London drama school in 1958 to follow my American mother to the States, both of them early converts to Jack Kerouac, the Billy Graham of the open road. I think Dad always hoped to turn me into a daughter who was as wild and beautiful as Kerouac's women. Seeing my books of photographs one day (I called them 'still lives'), he asked if I knew the French word for a still life. '*Nature morte*: dead nature, Claire. Not composition but decomposition.' Memento mori: a reminder of death, that's what he called my work the day he dissected my still life, my lack of animation.

He never really forgave me for being a Plain Jane instead of a Claire. The kind of face you pass in a crowd, that's me: light brown hair, long nose; a bit governessy, with bright hazel eyes and olive skin. A short-ass Joan of Arc before the Voices gave her glamour. Not at all what my stoned beatnik parents had in mind when I was conceived one moonlit night in 1959 in a motel outside San Francisco. But Robin, born just ten months after me, he fitted his name. A bright child in all senses, a charming, would-be actor like Dad, he charmed his way into one too many pairs of pants and died of AIDS in 1984, the fly-fisherman gone badly adrift.

# 3

IT'S SURPRISING WHAT is possible after a shock. You listen to the weather as if it matters ('Dull becoming murky' reports the BBC, summing up my mood). You laugh, make jokes, think about what to buy for supper. Then someone says they're sorry to hear your friend is dead and you're gone: tears, the works. It's because you don't really believe it. They're not dead, they've moved to China. They're not dead, you've had a fight and are temporarily out of touch.

Four days after Sally's murder, I went into the office as usual. Chalked on the blackboard over my boss's desk (still decked with a dusty garland of Christmas cards) were the weights of various organs and bones taken from corpses examined the previous day, with one of my boss's typically cryptic messages written underneath: 'URGENT – SEND BRAIN TO PADDINGTON LAB!' I worried a little about the exclamation mark. It suggested someone had left the brain lying around unclaimed for a while, like Paddington Bear; forgotten the office brain, just as they'd forgotten the office Christmas cards.

Those of us employed at the Carrington Forensic Science Unit, a private laboratory dealing largely with historic crimes and deaths, used the word 'office' ironically. Our place of work looks more like a Milanese designer's kitchen, all stainless steel tables, industrial ceramic fittings, galvanised metal lamps and soup tureens. Fortunately, most of the unpleasant smells are removed by the clear plastic odour hoods fitted over the tables and sinks by my boss, Dr Valentine Sterling (Val, we call him – he's not a hearty kind of guy).

Until Val hired me, forensic anthropologists took their own

photos or used photographers from the police scene of crime team. But he'd always wanted to train someone from scratch, and at the point we met I was so exhausted from working nights to get the money to go to art school during the days that anything seemed preferable. Road sweeper? I would've licked roads clean I was so tired. Then along came the eminent Dr Sterling to give a lecture, saw my photographs of mole skulls and offered me the position of photographer in his lab. It seemed ideal for a person with my peculiar interests and skills, forensic anthropology being a profession where the stability of one's subject is pretty much guaranteed.

My boss is in his late fifties, completely bald except for an ecclesiastical collar of silky white hair around his golf-tanned skull, and very stooped from bending his long skinny frame over so many old bones. Glancing up from under his shaggy eyebrows during the examination today, he had the appearance of a heron about to spear a fish. 'I thought I told you to take a week off.'

'Yeah, well . . . it feels better to be working.'

'So I gather,' he said drily. 'I heard through the police grapevine that you volunteered to take the scene of crime photos of your friend Sally, and when that offer was rejected, you turned up at the pathologist's to do the post-mortem pictures.'

I'd forgotten how many friends Val still has from his days as a police pathologist. 'I . . . I wanted to make sure correct procedure was followed.'

'It's never a good idea to get involved in the autopsy of someone you know. Impairs the judgement.'

My judgement might have been impaired, my vision was not. I could still picture Sally on the night she was murdered, her pockets stuffed with envelopes of seeds: poppy, foxglove, hollyhock. A handful of seeds in her pocket but just the single one inside her, the medical examiner told me. A sprout of four months. Ill-fertilised, fallen on stony ground, but tenacious. 'She looks too young for motherhood, let alone murder,' the examiner said. 'Not much more than a child herself.'

'She was older than she looks. Nineteen next month.'

'Do you know who the father was?'

'I didn't know there *was* a father, apart from her own.' If you could call Derek Rivers a father.

Val was giving me his fishing crane look again. 'So you didn't trust the medical examiner's office to get the details right?' He, more than anyone, knows how important detail is in forensic photography. Crime scene technicians like me are trained to take pictures from angles that keep the essential bones and organs in focus, something the untrained FBI man who photographed John Kennedy's wounds did not do, which is one of the reasons why JFK's death has remained a mystery. Dr James Humes, the pathologist who examined Kennedy, left out many details that would have helped later investigators, because, as he stated, the complexity of the fractures and fragments taxed description, 'and are better appreciated in photographs and roentgenograms'. Bone fragments in X-rays can be very revealing. X-ray photos – roentgenograms – are the first things Val taught me to take. 'Röntgen was a German physicist,' he told me. 'Discoverer of the X-ray in 1895. First real breakthrough in our field.'

On the advice of colleagues at the C. A. Pound Human Identification Lab in Florida, Val has me operating a miniature X-ray machine stocked with the extremely sensitive film used for mammography. Because there's no danger of cancer occurring in dead bones (although, since the discovery of DNA testing, no bones are truly dead), our X-rays involve long exposures of up to fifteen minutes, with results that are far more detailed than those in doctors' surgeries. We can turn solid bone into silvery shadows as transparent as moths' wings. Capturing phantoms on film, Val calls it; a ritual I like, precise as a tango, reinforcing the belief that to reduce life's disorder to manageable routine you just follow a recipe, a list of ingredients. Making risottos and real coffee is enjoyable for the same reason: there are rules to follow, something I never had as a kid growing up in a hippie community where control was lacking. We were all out of it in our family the way other families were out of essentials like milk or toilet paper.

That's why I knew this work would suit me from the moment I first watched Val shine his hot beam lamp through an historic ante-mortem X-ray, one of the murky ones taken with the shorter exposures necessary when a subject is still alive. 'The skeletons in our closet,' he says of these images, opaque until he pierces their shadowy caverns with his beam of light. It is as if he brings the ghosts to life, drags them out of the past to interrupt our modern stories with their own. He calls himself a cellular archaeologist excavating molecular remains. Mysteries from the past: those are what get his juices flowing, and although I am loaned out occasionally to the local cops if they are short of a scene of crime photographer, Val assists them only when they find old bodies that need dating. He is most proud of the plot of ground behind our laboratory, another idea from Florida, his 'Bone Garden', a collection of corpses buried in moist peat, dry sand, wood, lead-lined boxes, plastic bags, packed in ice. We dig up the remains at regular intervals to photograph and measure their varying rate of decay. The first time I was involved in one of these shoots, a couple of years ago, I asked Val what he thought about to distract himself from the smell. 'Golf,' he replied, 'I think of golf.' I caught him today, absentmindedly practising his golf swing with a long femur that he uses for teaching. The groove or scar was still evident where the knee bone used to be separate from the femur, a sign that it had recently united at the time of its owner's death. An epiphysis, the separate element is called. It begins to fuse with the thigh bone as growth progresses, until finally there is not even a groove to indicate that the single bone had once been separate.

'You should go for a walk, play some golf,' Val was saying now.

'*Golf*?' To me, a golf club is one step removed from a zimmer frame.

'Well, maybe not golf,' he conceded with a small smile. 'Although it's a good sport – long walks, plenty of fresh air. That's what you need now. Get your mind off things. What ever happened to that boyfriend you had?'

'He got fed up with my line of work.' A lot of guys are put off by it. Formaldehyde isn't exactly up there with Chanel Number 5 as an erogenous scent.

'Well, you should get out more – raving, or whatever my daughter calls her odd parties.'

'Raves,' I said, trying not to laugh. 'And I don't think I'm up to a rave just yet.'

He's always trying to fix up dates for me with the younger generation of morticians and pathologists, his pet themes being: I don't mingle enough with friends of my own age, I need to take long walks, I read too much (the wrong kind of books). In the past he's been known to accuse me of being an autodidact, which sounded like one of those unreliable eastern European cars made out of old bicycle spokes and reject Aeroflot engines. Then I looked the word up and found it to mean 'of or by oneself, self-taught, self-invented'. That's me, all right. In the journal Robin called my Book of Lists I copied out some intriguing auto words:

*autochthonous*: indigenous; a blood clot originating where found

*autoecious*: a parasitic fungus completing its life cycle on a single host

*autotoxin*: the product of an organism's metabolism which is poisonous to the organism itself

*auto-eroticism*: sexual gratification obtained without the involvement of another person

One problem with being an autodidact is that there are these great blanks in your knowledge. The Magna Carta is one example, which I missed on the way to Hollywood, where my Dad had been promised a role of a butler on a movie set in England. I never quite made it to the Corn Laws, either, let alone their Repeal. But that's not to say Robin and I weren't educated. In and out of new schools between one term and the next, we picked up our education from the portable library my parents considered essential for their life as a permanent road trip across America: *A Wildwoods Field Guide and Cookbook* (my mother's favourite recipe for hash brownies marked in chocolate thumbprints), *Mrs Grieves's Modern Herbal*, the Gormenghast trilogy, the complete Tolkien, Shakespeare and Dickens. Mum was keen on myths, magic and mechanics, Dad went for travellers' tales and murder. As a result, there are parts of Kerouac that I will always confuse with *The Reader's Digest Encyclopedia of Car Repairs*. One thing I do remember very clearly is Dad's obsessive collection of books and old newspaper clippings and magazine articles about Jack the Ripper (the last word in randomness, a universal bogey-man shared by half the world). As part of his repertoire, my father had a one-man show called *Jack's Back!* which he performed often enough for Jack to take on a broader meaning for Robin and me. 'In England, Jack was always a name for anyman,' Dad would say as he began his act, 'and any man has the capacity for violence, every man Jack of them.' Jack-off, jackass, a knave. Jack of all trades, especially murder. Alone together in our family's caravan, my brother and I read ripping descriptions aloud, memorised all the victims, all the suspects – from the mysterious 'Indian doctor' ('They say I'm a doctor now *ha ha!*') to Montague Druitt, born into a family of suicides and the insane, whose mother tried to kill herself with an overdose of laudanum. For us, the bogey-man was always a Jack – under the bed, behind a cupboard door, in the dark space under the trailer, waiting to grab you if you didn't hit the ground running when you had to use the outhouse on nights the caravan's plumbing failed.

Val's next question interrupted my reminiscing: 'And did you learn anything from your pictures of Sally?'

'I guess. I learned that a lot of damage had been done to her before the killers got anywhere near.'

I thought Jack was long gone – Jack be nimble, Jack be quick – into the realms of legends and nightmares. A will-o'-the-wisp, just one more Jack from a long line of violent Jacks in Dad's one-man show (Jack 'Leather Apron' Pizer who bullied whores, Jack the Painter who was hanged at Portsmouth yardarm, Little Jack Sheppard who died at Tyburn, Sixteen String Jack Rann the highwayman hero of penny dreadfuls, Spring-heeled Jack who assaulted women and children). Yes, Jack was buried, it seemed, until one fine day last year I got a call informing me of an inheritance from a relative I'd never heard of. And Claire Fleetwood suddenly gained a history, more history than she had ever wanted.

# 4

YOU COULD SAY that I've got Eden's number. I know where it's at – longitude and latitude, that is. An exact location, half way between The Angel tube station and a former plague ground. There is more than one angel in the neighbourhood, as it happens, a fact which struck me the first time the estate solicitor showed me a photo of the gates leading to my new front door: a large iron angel raising its wings above gold lettering that read 'Eden Dwellings 1889'.

'Not as portentous as it sounds,' Frank Barrett said, appreciatively rubbing his hand over his clean-shaven cheeks. 'It refers to a park in Calcutta where Magda Ironstone, the woman who set up the estate, liked to walk. Oldest cricket ground in the world. Named after the Eden family, well-known –' He caught himself. 'In British circles, that is. Sorry, you're American, aren't you?' He tapped the angel with his finger. 'Looks as if it's poised to fly, doesn't it?'

'Or dive.' I attributed my iron angel's glum expression to its perch not far from the sites of the Ripper murders. Clearly, the angel had been off duty those nights.

'Very desirable property,' the solicitor went on. 'Even in our uncertain economic climate.'

His comment was a reminder that I wasn't the only thing on the move. It was just a few days since Black Monday, the largest one-day fall in stockmarket history (start of a Second Great Depression, people were saying), and a week after Britain's Great October Storm, which had uprooted fifteen million trees and left a legacy of broadened vistas – including mine. And like so many other seeds lying dormant under the tree canopy until then, I was destined to flourish in the storm's wake.

Frank Barrett moved on quickly to inform me that the property left in a legacy to me by Magda's daughter, Miss Alexandra Ironstone, consisted of the larger central block in a group of late nineteenth-century almshouses in London's East End.

'Almshouses?' I asked.

'Originally, almshouses were charitable foundations for housing the poor and elderly. In the case of Eden Dwellings, they were for women – specifically those who had "fallen on hard times". The almshouses attached to your house are still on long-term lease to the original families for whom the trust was set up.'

'There must be some –' I had to stifle an impulse to tell him that there must be some *mistake*, you must have the wrong *name*, this is the kind of thing that happens to *other* people, not to me. The only time I won any form of lottery it turned out to be split a hundred ways. I got about five dollars, tops. 'I don't understand,' I began again. 'Is this something to do with my Dad growing up in an orphanage?'

Barrett looked bewildered. 'An orphanage? Surely not.' He consulted his notes. 'Let me see . . . we were to trace the family of a man called William Fleetwood, who was born in 1889 in India. His son, Colin – your father, Colin Fleetwood – was born in 1939. I *think* Miss Ironstone referred to him as her nephew – or was it adopted nephew?' He rubbed his cheek again, the opposite direction. Still no disobedient hair follicles. 'The family connection is rather obscure, I'm afraid. I know that Colin's parents – your grandparents – were killed in the Second World War, and that he lived with Alexandra Ironstone from then until he was eighteen. We were told to find out if your father had had any daughters. Your mother gave us your address.' He looked up at me, smiling uncertainly. 'I suppose you might be a great niece of Alexandra's?'

I shrugged. 'It's all news to me. I never heard of any Alexandra Ironstone or William Fleetwood.' The words came out drier than they felt. I was listening to this crisp-suited little guy with vanilla-fudgey skin, a man who knew more about my family than I did, and I was thinking: why the Hell did Dad keep all this a secret? And how much, if anything, did Mum know?

'We couldn't manage to trace your father, Miss Fleetwood. Neither could your mother, apparently.' Barrett said this in a sympathetic voice, embarrassed by my family's evident carelessness.

'Yeah, well, he sort of disappeared ten years ago.' Somewhere on the road to another missed opportunity. He was probably in a nameless motel right now, smoking dope and feeling sorry about losing his family so casually. 'Dad was what you might call a travelling player.' I glanced down the list of the Trust's managing body. 'It says one of the trustees is a Jack Ironstone. What's the connection?'

'He is the only child of Miss Ironstone's brother, Congreve.' Barrett looked apologetic. 'I'd like to fill in more details about your father's side of the family, Miss Fleetwood. But I'm afraid that while our firm has always handled her family estate, Miss Ironstone did tend to keep herself to herself. She lived to be a hundred and two – and bright as a penny till a few days before she got sick! What else can I tell you? She was born in 1885, moved to Calcutta, came back here with her family in – let me see . . .' he checked the dates, '1888 or '89, and –'

'What about her father?'

'Rather tragic circumstances, actually. Famous case at the time: he was shot and kidnapped – believed murdered – from Eden Dwellings in November 1888. By the time the police got there he had disappeared. Never found the body, never found who did it. Nasty business.' He peered over his glasses to see how I was taking the history lesson.

'Jack's year, 1888. The Ripper.'

'Ah. Yes. Indeed.'

'I still don't see why this Alexandra Ironstone would leave her house to the daughter of an adopted nephew she hadn't seen since he was eighteen.'

Barrett frowned slightly at my tone. 'They were rather

24

*colourful* families, the Ironstones and the Fleetwoods,' he offered by way of explanation, 'with unusual ideas for their time. But nothing to be ashamed of, I'm *absolutely* sure, Miss Fleetwood.'

Barrett had one of those accents that used to make me feel very self-conscious about my own flat mid-America voice. Sneh sneh sneh, I say, snick snick snick; the sound scissors make shearing off thick hair. My father always managed to cover up his Englishness with a transatlantic patina, but without his actor's skill at mimicry my grasp of this new language has not been entirely successful. Even though I've learned to say knickers when I mean underpants, people still remark, 'Oh, you're *American*' every time I open my mouth. As if American is a synonym for no culture, no history, the wrong vocabulary. I pronounce flower with an er in it, God with an awe. Although inside me there's a different voice, refined and full of ironic insight, it always comes out *awe, er, um*, and instead of 'Absolutely!' I say 'You bet!' (a New World stress on the element of risk). In England, a less extreme landscape, people seem more sure of their footing. They're always saying 'Absolutely!', an expression Val has taught me to avoid. Nothing is absolute, he says. Not rock, not bones, and especially not truth.

Barrett was wearing an encouraging smile. 'Magda Ironstone, née Fleetwood, was an extraordinary woman, you know, born into a very distinguished family of planters in India.'

'Tea planters?'

'Opium.' He coughed and hurried over that one pretty quickly. 'In later life she became a well-known botanical explorer, set up dozens of charitable foundations. She established Eden Dwellings as almshouses not long after her husband disappeared.' His round face drooped tactfully before shifting back into its former jovial upright position. 'Your legacy is as extraordinary as the woman who set it up, not least because Magda's will states that her property is to be passed down only through the female line. And this includes the families resident in the almshouses. When the female line runs out, the trust transfers to the next male heir, and in the event of there being no progeny, the trustees are empowered to choose suitable families as occupants.'

'Who would have inherited if my father hadn't had a daughter? Dad?'

A slight pause before his reply: 'I'm afraid that I am not at liberty to say.'

To make up for this lapse he laid some recent photos on the desk between us. All they proved was that my stake in Eden would be overlooked by some of the most notoriously violent council estates in London. 'The original house was built in the late seventeenth, early eighteenth century,' he said. 'It was bought by the Ironstones, who turned it into this more substantial house forming the central block – your block – of the current building.'

He sketched the gothic outline with his finger. 'Magda Ironstone took it over in the late 1880s and added these almshouses with rather fine porches. As you can see from the plan, the almshouses form a U-shaped terrace facing a central garden at the back of the block. Or they *would* have faced it except that some time before the listing of period houses this inner wall was constructed to give each of the houses, with the exception of yours, its own small garden. Still leaves you with about half an acre to yourself, which Miss Ironstone let run a bit to seed until one of the young tenants, Sally Rivers, offered to take it over. Sally's father, Derek, is the caretaker looking after the estate buildings. His family have been residents there for generations.' He went on to mention complicated legal ramifications, the difficulty of contacting me etc. etc. I took in not much more than the fact that this castle of a house, this garden the size of a small park were mine as long as I wanted them. All I had to do was live there. Why would I want to leave? Claire Fleetwood, Heiress: I tried the phrase out in my head. Dad would be shitting himself if he could hear me.

Barrett passed me some photocopies of the few original documents his firm held, one of them the Ironstone family tree. I wondered if these names were the origins of Dad's battered trunk of costumes, left behind with us when he moved on.

Mum's wardrobe was stored in it as well, and as kids, my brother and I had invested it with the whole weight of our rootless, feckless history. We'd try on platform shoes in silver lamé, a felt stetson and a belt made of rattleskin with the bullet-hole still visible where the snake had been shot, draping ourselves in the remnants of those castaway lives and imagining cousins who had shaken their hips to the saxophone bleat of an age that had come to a bad end before they did. If you put your nose to that sheepskin jacket you could smell wild pony dung and the smoke of a campfire. Maybe a big Edwardian woman gone to seed had lured her husband back to bed by covering her ample curves in this silk nightdress the colour of shells.

That hefty trunk of fictional relations, dragged with me all the way from the States, was balanced now by the papery weight of the Ironstone family tree, a real history denied by Dad. Reading it gave me a curious feeling of familiarity – call it déjà vu, a sensation I've heard can be explained scientifically: two hemi-spheres of the brain temporarily out of sync, one side of the brain receiving input a fraction of a second after the other. My theory is different: it's that old funfair loop-the-loop, the Double Helix, a spiralling gene train closing the gap between past and present, the passengers within yelling distance but never quite touching.

Our genes have long memories – why shouldn't certain scenes speak to us in familiar voices? OK, maybe not voices; they went out with the Middle Ages – overlaps in our genetic memory, then. Lots of things are genetic that no one has explained. Like when Mum used to say that she knew if Robin was going to phone, which for a long time I put down to LSD trips repeating on her. Lately, I've started to revise my thinking. Why couldn't there be things we know without reading or hearing them, memories that are part of us, that we're born with, just as we're born with a talent for music or golf?

I squeezed my eyes shut and tried out the names on the Ironstone tree to see if any of them sparked off genetic bulbs, but apart from those green lights you get on your eyelids from having stared too long at the sun, the only thing to dawn on me was that its sparse branches indicated I had sprung from unproductive stock. Still, at least its main trunk was a name on which you could strike a match: Luther Ironstone.

◆ ◆ ◆

**Verdigris**: *a blueish greenish crust formed by atmospheric corrosion.*

*Oh Luther, don't beat our son so. No good can come of such beating.*

*It was the Congreves what killed her (though she'd plenty of laudanum about her): them splints dipped in sulphur what they use for lighting fires, them we call Congreves or Lucifers. We found her eating them, like the girls on the streets do when they want to end it all. They say she's been off her head since surviving the horrors at Lucknow, where the savages performed the most awful indecencies on the ladies. Sitting in her muck with the little lad solemn as an owl beside her.*

*He's always down there. Every night I hear him at his measurings and lists, that 'Acquisitions' book of his father's. All those lists can't be healthy, I tell him. But his mantra of the dead and dissected is powerful: liver, heart, vulva, womb. I show him my watercolours, he counters with the flayed bones in Veneziano's sixteenth-century Allegory of Death and Fame. The resurrection of bones, he calls it.*

*Ma fire killt Fa Boygir cry Ma see hearear speke Ma fire killt Ma*

*He is the ghost in the weeds. He was born under a black sun, the occidental sun. The accidental son, the unwanted, the wrongly chosen. To dive for ever, that's what it is to be me.*

*The earth is full of blood and bone, he said, his hands dark and wet from the earth – and from something else as well. 'It is our duty to order and arrange it.'*

◆

I'VE ALWAYS BEEN a list-maker: roads travelled, words to learn, books I mean to read, other people whose brothers died of AIDS (making us a new clan, a tribe). Maybe it's because my education was so patchy that lists became a way of filling in the missing links. That's why I like recipes, especially the kind where each ingredient appears in the order it is used.

'Frankly, I can't see the difference between a good risotto recipe and blank verse,' I'd said to Val the day before meeting Barrett.

'An indication that you are trying to reduce life to the level of a risotto.'

Well, why not? Next to DNA, a family tree is the ultimate list, the list of your own ingredients, the recipe for how you were baked. *Luther Ironstone*, I read in Barrett's office, born 1819 in London, died 1886 at Canal House in Essex. Married in 1849 to Emma Congreve (b. 1830, d. 1857). Survived by one child, Joseph Alexander Congreve Ironstone, born in 1850. So Joseph's Mum died when he was seven, in 1857, the year of the Indian Mutiny. Or do they call it the Sepoy Revolt now? The First War of Independence? Joseph's wife, Magda, must have seen her own fair share of horrors too, if she was witness to his shooting. Violent times, although the Ironstones did well out of them, as Barrett proceeded to tell me.

'Luther Ironstone left India not long after his wife died,' he said, 'bought a property from a thriving butcher's close to the Regent's Canal and from the butcher himself won the tender for the company's huge bone pile, then parlayed this into a contract with a Deptford fertiliser factory.'

This is the framework of my story, I thought, the skeleton I am fleshing out.

Barrett, reciting my family history, spoke with real passion: 'The bones were shipped east down the canal to the Ironstone works in East London, and there by Luther's patented process they were combined with various chemicals that doubled their efficiency as manure. He was an early convert to the work of Baron Justus von Liebig, you see, Miss Fleetwood!'

'Bit of a bone man yourself, are you Mr Barrett?' I was probably one of the few clients Barrett had who would know about Liebig, the German chemist who discovered that adding sulphuric acid to bones made the phosphate in them water-soluble, more accessible as fertiliser. He also invented the soluble bouillon cube.

'Actually, I'm rather keen on the history of garden ceme-teries!' Frank, suspecting that his pet subject had sent waves of dinner guests to sleep, was an information vampire hungry for a new listener. One of those masterminds on the quiz shows, only thirty seconds to suck the juice out of a subject before the gong goes: *Next Contestant.* 'You know that the English led the way in producing bonemeal? Our supplies of bones were always limited, so it was necessary to import on a massive scale. Fortunes were made in shipping bones from Europe. At one point the British were selling 40,000 *tons* of bonemeal a year, an output which led von Liebig to accuse England of vandalising the battlefields of the Crimea and Waterloo in her eagerness for garden bones. "England is robbing all other countries of the condition of their fertility," ' Frank quoted Liebig in a stirring baritone. ' "Already from the catacombs of Sicily she has carried off the skeletons of generations. She hangs around the neck of Europe and sucks out its heart blood." '

Graves were fertile ground for all my family, it seemed. In the nineteenth century, a time of rapid suburban expansion both in India and Britain, Luther's father had reasoned that you couldn't lose by betting on an increase in death. Already involved in the new cemeteries being built in Calcutta, he visited London from India and discovered new frontiers. The earth of graveyards and crypts and pauper burial-grounds in over-crowded city centres was beaded with bones. 'Like blanched almonds in a fruitcake,' he told Luther.

'Putrefaction contaminated whole neighbourhoods,' said Frank.

But improved the soil.

So Luther's Dad became an early investor in England's garden cemetery movement, one of his century's great economic booms. Sparked off by the passing of a Bill to establish cemeteries away from churches, futures-trading in cemeteries became so profitable that shares in the General Cemetery Company soon doubled in value. The gilts of their time.

I was just one more in a long line of bone gardeners.

'The Ironstones were rather looked down on in those days,' Barrett explained. 'Whereas today they would be celebrated as conservationists, enabling gardens to be built out of the city's rubbish and waste.'

On the way back to my flat I practised saying 'rubbish' instead of garbage, part of my gradual metamorphosis from an American with no history into an historic Brit. That night I drew in a new branch on my family tree: the Fleetwoods, floating next to the main trunk, but not yet grafted. More like a lost tributary whose junction with the main river was still unmapped.

# 6

I MOVED INTO Eden Dwellings on the thirtieth of October 1987 – not quite Hallowe'en, although the event is written in my book of lists next to a Polaroid of the Jack whose last night out is All Hallows' Eve, before he vanishes back into the earth with all the other ghosts and ghoulies. Jack-o'-Lantern, a will-of-the-wisp: something misleading or elusive that deludes people who try to follow it across the marsh from this world into the next. A perfect allegory for my new home.

Beautiful old houses do exist in the East End of London, but moving day proved that mine wasn't one of them. The approach to Eden was down echoing canyons of post-war highrises with no claim to architectural charm. Urban rock faces, that's what they were, and about as impenetrable: the species who inhabited these tower blocks appeared either wary or predatory, with a tenuous grip on their vertical habitat. Eden Dwellings, dwarfed between the escarpments of concrete (despite its own nineteenth-century pretensions to grandeur), seemed too ornate to have been built in stone. Its intricate contours were more suited to plexiglas – a castle mould from a Dungeons and Dragons kit, say, lacking only the warning to parents that children under five should not play here. In Chicago it would have been a Cattle Barons' Conference Centre, a Playboy Club.

I was expecting to be greeted by a vacuum-packed Nosferatu, at the very least, so it was a pleasant surprise when the door was opened instead by Sally Rivers. With her shiny brown hair parted in the middle and her neat, heart-shaped face, the caretaker's daughter might have passed for the heroine in a Victorian melodrama (even that description – 'the caretaker's daughter' – had a penny dreadful ring to it). She'd have to trade her jeans and Doc Martens for sprigged muslin or whatever Dickens' girls wore, but otherwise Sally had the look: a triangle of big dark eyes and startled expression, pointy chin, rosebud mouth.

Then she opened it. Her teeth might be good, but her language was riddled with the cavities of East London's missing vowels and consonants. Not quite Eliza Doolittle, but definitely another new dialect to catalogue – in Sally's words, 'You don't get sumfink for nuffink.'

'Big, innit?' she said of the house, while I clocked the beginning of a bruise circling her left eye like a shadowy monocle. 'Dad's sick,' she added, to explain his absence, and clapped her hand over the eye. This junction of bruise, father and lie was a pattern it didn't take long to learn.

Russell immediately pushed past her and darted down the hallway, his nails skidding on the floorboards. 'Cheeky bugger!' Sally said admiringly. We followed him more slowly, entering a huge living room filled with what looked like the detritus of forty years as a bedsit. Every flat surface was covered in old newspapers, magazines and packaging, like one of those museums of local ephemera, minus the charm. Furniture had long since lost its function: an armchair served as a receptacle for romantic novels, a brocade sofa held a collection of handbags made out of a zoo's worth of reptiles and exotic mammals, still more or less identifiable, including one constructed from an entire armadillo, its stomach overflowing with scent bottles. 'For the last few years Alex didn't budge from 'ere,' Sally explained, as if it were her own relative's mess she was apologising for. 'She was very frail. And almost blind.'

Alexandra had cooked as well as slept in this room, it seemed: an electric stove rested on a sideboard bulging with the carbuncles of carved fruit, the sideboard's varnish protected by a newspaper announcing the death of Winston Churchill. Passing decades were recorded in the changing graphics on an array of Colman's mustard tins and bottles of Camp coffee, with the classic Camp label depicting a standing, turbanned Indian bearer holding a tray of coffee for a seated British officer giving way in the sixties and seventies to a more politically correct version, the Indian's tray retouched out (although he still stood *behind* the officer, I noticed; he didn't slouch around in jeans, smoking dope and exchanging recipes for chutney).

A big window on to the garden let a flood of sun into the recesses of the room, even through the thick film of London grime, and for a millisecond some trick of the luminous light and the old flawed glass conjured a figure out of the shadows. Russell barked, a cloud shuttered the sun and the figure turned into a hatstand bedecked with two absurdly feathered hats of an earlier generation.

I turned back to Sally. 'What about the kitchen?'

She pulled a face. 'Stone Age. Not even an electric oven. All the cookery books are stuck together with damp. Spiders the size of rats.'

Following my guide down a dim corridor lined on either side with miniature glass greenhouses, all empty, I heard from her that these were 'Wardian cases', named after a nineteenth-century inventor who had put a caterpillar to pupate in a sealed glass jar with some dirt, and a month later found a tiny fern springing up. 'Alex told me that botanists took up the idea and started shipping plants in them.'

'What happened to the caterpillar?'

She had to think about that for a few seconds, her three-cornered face even more pointy, before admitting that she didn't know. 'But rats or seawater sometimes got in and killed the plants, often enough that people started calling the cases Wardian coffins because so few specimens arrived alive, know wha' I mean?'

Halfway up the stairs to the next floor I felt pressing down on me from above the weight of clutter felty with dust, rooms of other people's bad choices in wallpaper, gloomy furniture carved out of extinct tropical woods. 'Maybe I should've looked at the garden first.'

Sally stopped. 'I guess . . . I guess you'll want to do the garden yourself?'

'Don't worry, Frank Barrett told me what a great job you've

done: the garden's yours.' At the next set of doors I peered past a sinister Victorian armoire into several big rooms where the twentieth century had never been allowed to intrude. 'Also, the Trust allows some money for upkeep. You can have that if you like.' When I glanced back to see if she'd heard me I saw that two spots of red had appeared in her cheeks.

'You serious?' she asked softly.

'I'm surprised they've never offered it to you.'

'They . . . it's my Dad: 'e gets it.'

'Does he work in the garden?'

She shook her head.

'Then I'll see the money goes to you.'

'Claire?' Sally was still in the corridor. 'If I order things, use the money to buy plants, I mean – can I give your address? I've got all the catalogues. It's just . . . my Dad wouldn't like it if they started delivering to our 'ouse . . .'

'What catalogues?'

'Garden mail order catalogues,' she said impatiently. 'Mr Banerji from one of the alms'ouses gives them to me.' Sally followed my eyes to the walls of books ahead of us. 'And Alex used to let me borrow garden books,' she added quickly, reaching into her pocket to pull out a small volume. 'That's the last one.' The title was just visible: *Annals of the Royal Botanic Gardens, Calcutta, 1888.*

I told her to keep it. 'Is this all there is, Sally?' Every room was packed, as she proceeded to show me, from the attic of old trunks to the library of damp-stained books on botanical exploration. I'd stepped into a position as museum curator. Nothing could be further removed from my roots, where Dad's most treasured possession, next to his dope, was a rock criss-crossed with veins of white that he called 'The Map of an Unknown Country'. Maybe this was it. 'D'you think I could store any of this stuff in the cellar, Sally?'

Her grimace made me smile. Something nasty in the cellar: it was so in keeping with this place. 'I dunno,' she said. 'Snails get in from somewhere and you find clusters of them on the walls like mushrooms. And there are pictures . . .'

'Family pictures?' It struck me that I hadn't seen a single family portrait.

'Naaah – 'orrible pictures.'

It wasn't really a cellar, more a series of sub-basements that probably once served as utility rooms: a single, crusted window level with the garden's grass, four or five grimy little chambers lit by low-wattage lightbulbs off a narrow central corridor. In the second room were the kind of rough pine cupboards you'd find in a Victorian kitchen, along with several expensive-looking collector's cabinets in close-grained dark wood, and hanging between two of the cabinets was a framed image that from a distance resembled a maze, or the coils of internal organs in a type of anatomical figure known as an écorché, with the skin of a human body flayed away to reveal its musculature. On closer inspection this picture proved to be nothing more gruesome than an engraving of the Leiden Dissection Theatre bearing the inscription *Know Thyself*. I'd seen similar images at London's Hunterian Medical Museum, where the anatomy teacher at art school had often taken our class to draw. Beneath it, on a pine shelf you'd expect to hold a teapot or a bag of flour, was something more curious: an old polychromed carving of a pregnant woman, smiling brightly as she used her hands to peel back the skin of her stomach like a bloody flower, exposing a foetus as perfect as a child's doll. The foetus was loose, intended to be removed so that one could investigate the woman's interior. It was a beautiful piece that my anatomy teacher would've loved, although I could see why Sally might find it disturbing.

'It's all right, Sally. These are just works that were used by doctors and artists so they could understand what makes us tick. Nothing sinister.' This was not strictly true. Some of the old anatomical drawings clearly made the link between dissection and punishment, maybe because until the nineteenth century most of the cadavers freely available for dissections were hanged criminals, their bodies deliberately carved up in public as further humiliation.

I wandered back into the small first room, empty barring a sink. 'This would make a good darkroom, if I blocked the glass up and installed a fan-heater to get rid of the damp. Maybe you could help me set one up some day?'

'A darkroom? Wha' for?'

'Printing my pictures. I do close-ups of bark and stone, that sort of thing.'

'That your job?'

'No, it's a hobby. I work as a forensic photographer.'

'A *wha*?'

'Pictures of dead people, but mainly of old bodies.'

'You solve murders?' She sounded both horrified and delighted.

'My boss does, sometimes – when a person has died in mysterious circumstances and only the bones are left. I just take pictures, although occasionally my shots help to identify the victim of a fire or a train accident. But Dr Sterling likes to say he maps all the angles and triangles of the human terrain. He uses instruments similar to these artists – to measure skeletal structure, that kind of stuff.'

Before we went back upstairs I couldn't resist opening one last plan chest, its brass name plate bearing the title 'Old Bailey'. Inside, a flat wooden box lay to one side of a cardboard artist's portfolio. Sally looked over my shoulder as I examined the drawing of a woman with her neck awkwardly bent. 'Is she sleeping?' she asked. I pointed to a declaration on the inside of the portfolio informing us that these mezzotints had been purchased from Jones & Sons of Clerkenwell, and were taken from a series on 'Heads of Murderers' by William Clift. The woman whose dislocated head had caught our attention was Catherine Welsh, hanged at the Old Bailey in 1820 for the murder of her baby son.

I remembered that Frank Barrett had given me the photo-copied cutting from a London newspaper about Joseph Ironstone, written at the time of his disappearance. He was said to have been 'a noted collector who saved his passion for photography'. Was this his collection? I closed the portfolio and opened the wooden box, which was divided into velvet-lined compartments. A refined version of my brother's fly-tying boxes, it was probably meant for gem stones – except that this collection was unlikely to fetch high prices at any antiques fair. The compartments held teeth, half-moons of yellowed nail-clippings, curls of faded hair, each numbered and matched to the name of its contributor in the lid. A Wardian case of specimens preserved in their own microclimate.

'I think I'd like to see the garden now, Sally.'

# 7

WE WENT OUT the back door on to a raised deck over-looking the central garden, and down some stairs, almost immediately submerging under the colour green. Swimming through the wet leaves, I followed Sally's mossy shadow along a path crowded by bamboo stems as thick as men's arms. More bamboo pushed through the shattered roof of a glasshouse buried among trees with leaves too big, too rubbery for this climate, and from a dry concrete pool, brown-edged, a silent lotus fountainhead rose. There were heavy sweet smells unnatural for October, ferns like ostrich plumes, ferns with fronds split on the ends and frizzed like old ladies' perms, ferns the size of my palm, each stalk ruffled and pliant as sequinned elastic. I could hear the rustlings of unseen burrowing creatures and a gate creaking in the distance. 'It's the big bamboo,' Sally said, stopping to listen. 'That's the noise it makes in the wind. Strange, innit?' It was a place where you could hide with ease, where things had been hidden, I was sure, and lost; a garden like a premonition, one of those tangled places you recognise from dreams and darker fairy-tales. Not frightening exactly, but alien, ambiguous.

Beyond the shadows lay a more familiar space, a grassy courtyard divided by four narrow paths in a stone the slaty blue of deep water. The paths' crossing was marked by a well carved with the inscription: *These are the Gardens of Eden, enter them to live for ever.* Faint scrapings around the word 'live' indicated where the stonemason of a previous century had tried to erase his own spelling mistake. Originally he had engraved 'dive', and traces of the 'd' still remained. *To dive for ever.* I closed my eyes and saw a photograph tucked into one of Dad's books: two children in a pony cart, behind them a garden full of secrets. *My* garden, except that glimpsed through this graphite curtain of black bamboo there should have been a Hindu monastery.

Dad had made a joke of it when Robin found the picture. *Jack's garden*, he'd called it, laughing when we asked what he meant. I haven't thought about that picture for years. Why did we never press Dad for an answer? You always think you'll have time for the questions later, but lots of times people die with the important ones still unanswered.

'This formal part of the garden is the remains of a much older one,' Sally was saying. 'Based on Persian principles, Mustafa told me.'

'Who is Mustafa?'

'Another one of the residents. A paradise garden, 'e says, and in Turkey and Persia the crossing paths would be water.' Wa'er she pronounces it, the glottal stop a bridge.

'The wild part seems more like paradise.'

'Eden after the snake, Jack says.' She blushed.

'Another neighbour?'

'Jack Ironstone, Alex's nephew.'

'You know him, then?'

'Jack used to visit Alex a lot until last year. Then they 'ad a fight. Alex was always fighting with people.'

'Not with you, though.'

She shrugged and turned away quickly.

Maybe there is magic in all overgrown walled gardens, anywhere that the wild pattern of things has begun to scribble its graffiti, but I believe Sally's was unique. Overlooked by the kind of bleak inner city estates dreamed up by politicians and accountants who never factored green into their equations, buried in a ferroconcrete wilderness where even the grass looked violated, a skinhead pelt of brown, Sally's single stripe of garden seemed like a reversal of those lost Mayan cities found in remote jungles: all that remained of London's primordial rainforest after the Parking Lot Wars.

'I wasn't responsible for the big trees and bamboo and that kind of planting,' Sally explained. What her friend Mr Banerji called the bones of a garden – the well, the hedges, the paths – had been here for as long as anyone could remember. 'But after Alex showed me pictures of Indian gardens in her library I got similar stuff from Mr Banerji – and from Fatbwa – and started planting it.'

'Fatbwa?'

She pointed through the foliage to the garden gate of almshouse number five. 'Fat boy, that's what 'is Jamaican friends call 'im because of 'is size. But Fatbwa's not fat at all.' She grinned. 'Fuckin' gorgeous! And 'e grows fuckin' 'uge vegetables and tropical flowers.'

'In that space?' Each individual garden was about the size of a rug. Yards, we'd call them in the States.

She began to weave the pattern of the estate, reeling off names and biographies of her fellow residents as she described the gardens I had seen briefly from my deck: Fatbwa's blazed with colour; Arthur's had a rabbit hutch, a goldfish pond and various mossy constructions Sally said were hedgehog dens; Mustafa the dry-cleaner's was a mosaic courtyard with a cobalt blue wooden table and chairs transplanted from a souk in Istanbul; Mr Banerji's was the lush green of a rice paddy; Mrs Patel's was strung with washing lines on which hung transparent curtains of rainbow-coloured saris, a stageset for an Indian dance performed by her chorus line of plastic flamingos; the Whitelys' sprouted rows of bright Woolworth's flowers, a barbecue and a deflated children's paddling pool; Sally's family at number one had a violent metal garden of rusted bicycles, anonymous car wreckages, chains.

We walked past the remains of espaliered fruit trees, aged attendants for a huge yew which had spread out from a hollow core and welded itself together in rusty wood, like those bark-coloured metallic rivers you see crossing ancient peat land-scapes. *Runnelled*, I thought, a *runnelled* trunk, wondering where the word came from, not knowing if it was the right one, except that it reminded me of rivers and channels running together, like the yew's trunk. A brooding silhouette, the tree had lower limbs propped up arthritically on the small tombstones of long-dead pets. Or I guessed they were pets, unless the owners had names like Gripper and Prince.

'But this is the best bit,' Sally said, taking me over to admire three pens of rotting leaves not far from the yew tree. 'My compost heaps. Everything 'as always grown like weeds in this part of the garden – probably because of my compost leaching through into the ground.' She quickly adjusted her expression to imitate humility. 'I mean *yours.*'

'No, definitely yours. Looks like garbage to me.'

'That's because it's full of lots of organic stuff. Chicken feathers, for instance. I get those from the butchers and shred them in a machine Nick made for me – Nikhil, Mr Banerji's grandson.' She plunged a garden fork into the centre of one pile and the mixture released a damp vegetal fart. 'And I always add nettles and comfrey, because they are 'igh in nitrogen to speed up the rotting process.'

'Is our high priestess of organic gardening chanting her litany to the god of compost?' asked a soft, slightly foreign voice behind us.

Sally turned. 'Nick! This is Claire. She's moving into Alex's house.'

One quick glance at Nikhil Banerji was enough to confirm that my inheritance was looking up after all.

# 8

I SOON FOUND out that Banerji was used to people staring, first at his literally breathtaking beauty, then at his hand. He was fine-boned in a way people are who grow up on fish and green vegetables instead of steak and milk, with skin that had the sleek, translucent sheen of hard caramel. You could imagine it tasting sweet. In fact, all his surfaces looked edible, from his shoulder-length, licorice-black hair to his right hand. When I put mine out to shake it, his mouth twisted in an uncertain smile, then he gave the hand a strange flip of the wrist to turn it palm up. Apart from the rudimentary shape, no effort had been made to disguise the limb's artificiality. It was bright pink, the texture of barley sugar, a bizarre contrast to the metal rods visible within its plastic palm. Banerji's face stretched into an outright grin at my stare. 'Does it embarrass you?' he asked. 'My state of the art prosthetics?'

'The articulation is amazing, Nik-um—' I stumbled over his name.

'You may as well call me Nick. Everyone here does.' He turned the wrist and flexed his fingers as if they were newly acquired cookery hardware.

'How far does it extend?' At his little huff of amusement I apologised quickly. 'Sorry. It's just that I'm interested in structure, in how things work underneath.'

He shook his head. 'I don't mind. I too am fascinated by this phantom limb of mine.' He pulled up his sleeve and stretched it out, palm down this time, a priestly caste of android conferring a blessing.

The limb extended to just below his elbow.

'I lost it – although it was a case of lost and found, in fact – in a moped accident. The hand was completely severed just above my wrist, and the radius – that is the bone in the forearm extending from the humerus to the thumb side of my wrist – was smashed so badly as to be irreparable.'

He offered the plastic gel of his hand to feel, tension in his muscular upper arm giving to the artificial addition a feeling of reality and ownership. 'Tell me,' I began, and hesitated as he narrowed his eyes.

'Tell you what? Please don't stop now.'

'You said your "phantom limb" – are you referring to the sensation that the old limb is still with you?'

His smile reappeared. 'Yes. I see this exaggerated hand, or sense it, whenever I remove the plastic one.'

Phantom limbs were not uncommon among people who had had peripheral amputation, he explained. Most amputees suffered from them. 'And many doctors believe that without these phantom records of absence, these "sensory ghosts", as they have been called since the nineteenth century, no amputee can use an artificial limb. So if we lose our old ghosts, they must be resurrected.'

While many phantom limbs appeared smaller than their prostheses, his phantom was much larger, connected to him by long spectral tendons of pink flesh like stretched skeins of chewing gum, a magnification that he'd been told might be linked to his accident. 'It happened on a busy street in Calcutta when I was twelve.' An exhausted rickshaw driver, over-burdened with passengers, had failed to see Nick's father on his moped with his wife and the boy behind, and swerved into them. Nick, falling, had put his right hand down to break the impact – into the path of an oncoming taxi.

The car braked, but not soon enough.

'I watched my hand disappear under its front wheel. The car's impulse carried me forward several feet, breaking the bones. I remember no pain, only the strange dislocating sight of my hand disappearing behind me, no longer attached.'

Yet, by a miracle, there was an ambulance near enough to

stop Nick bleeding to death, even while he screamed for his hand, lost among the feet. 'A cry went up, I remember so clearly: "The hand! The hand! Find the hand!" And the crowd surged first to one side and then the other while I tried to raise my head from the stretcher carrying me to the ambulance.' A slight tremor in his voice was the only indication of how painful he found the memory. 'Finally they brought the thing to me. I didn't recognise it at first, flat and bloody like a surgeon's discarded glove. Too dirty to be of use. Yet I still felt curiously attached to it, as if it were tied to me in a way not immediately evident. They put it in a jar of formalin at the hospital and I kept it next to my bed where I could look at it floating like some strange sea creature, and feel its combined absence and presence at the end of a wrist I no longer possessed.'

A neuropsychologist had told him that his phantom might eventually telescope back into its stump. 'Even disconnect and fall away. But I think I would miss it, that last, tenuous link to the place I was born. Does it sound absurd?'

'No, it makes sense.' I was thinking of Robin, who ran away to New York when he was sixteen and left Mum waiting impatiently for his return. Mum magnified the lost Robin's importance until he remained for ever the late guest at dinner, the missing commentator, the better story. By the time we found him again the story was over. Lying in the hospital bed he seemed curiously flattened, as if the supporting bones had been crushed like Nick's hand. Deboned, as a chicken is for stuffing.

'It seems that areas in our brain which formerly got input from the lost limb continue to be activated,' Nick said. 'The disconnected cells send out erroneous information indicating that the limb is still present. It makes us lopsided.'

My thoughts about Robin, running parallel to his comment, were cut short by his next question: 'So, Claire, is your profession linked to this interest in structure?'

Sally piped up: 'She photographs dead men's bones.'

At the melodramatic words Nick raised his eyebrows.

'I work with a forensic anthropologist,' I said. 'A man who

specialises in studying the human skeletal system. He provides information to everyone from pathologists doing autopsies to historians investigating claims that the remains of Akbar have been found in an unmarked grave outside Delhi.'

'And have they?'

'What?'

'Have the remains of Akbar been found in a grave outside Delhi?'

'Sorry, I . . .' I was fascinated by the way Nick used his hands in an almost Italian manner – or must have done, when he had two. His right hand still conducted those sweeping Neapolitan gestures, except that now there was a missed beat in the music, a hesitation in notes being transmitted. No longer than an intake of breath (the way he *almost* pronounced the 'h' in Delhi), it moved me like a jazz song played in a minor key.

I dragged my mind back to his question. 'Why, you interested in Akbar?'

'I'm interested in the remains of things. Or used to be.'

'And now?'

He picked up a stick and traced a foursquare outline in the dust, an 'N' at each corner with a circle in the middle, like a rough plan for Sally's paradise garden. 'I've transferred my affection to the chlorophyll molecule,' he said, adding the letters 'Mg' to the circle. 'Here at its heart it has a magnesium atom, easily detached with the application of heat, the reason green vegetables turn yellow when overcooked.'

'You're a scientist?'

He shook his head. 'An artist – with an interest in science. Which I put down to this arm of mine.' He pushed back his right sleeve to reveal the metal inside. 'Most of the magnesium we eat is stored in our bones, as you are probably aware. In a neat twist, my bones are made entirely of magnesium alloy.'

Imagining him sculpting with only one hand, I asked what kind of art involved chlorophyll. He smiled at Sally. 'Hasn't our gardener told you? I work in grass. I'm an artist obsessed with the colour green.'

'A grass artist.' I tried not to sound disappointed. Next he would tell me his work was conceptual, a word that art school had led me to distrust.

'You should see the work Nick does,' Sally said.

'Mmm,' I said. 'Sure. Some time –'

'Come – now.' Nick took my hand in his artificial one so firmly that I suspected him of wanting to see me flinch.

The space he lived in with his grandfather was a dollshouse compared to mine, four or five tiny box rooms with walls that he had turned into a gallery for his rows of surreal green photographs. The pictures looked like grassy Turin shrouds or X-rays of the Green Man. Apparently triggered by our movement, one image released a strange pulsating rhythm. I shook my head. 'What is it? I can't work it out.'

'A soundtrack from one of my installations. Grass pushing up through soil, amplified 10,000 times. The pictures are bad imitations of the actual pieces, where the grass is grown vertically in a darkened studio and then exposed to light so it produces varying degrees of chlorophyll. You can get a tonal range of greens equivalent to the greys which develop in black and white photographs.' He pointed to the face of a man yellowed by lack of light. 'Green disappears when grass is under stress. Eventually the plant dies.'

'How did you come up with the technique?' I asked.

'It was Sally.' Sally smiled, pleased with her contribution. 'She left a ladder on the lawn and when she moved it a few days later I noticed it had left a reverse shadow where the grass underneath had been so starved of light as to become etiolated. I have learned that plants as they are dying switch on a gene which degrades their chlorophyll so that they lose colour and fade away, like humans.'

Nick's images of grassy snakes and turf goddesses and Hindu temples sprayed with mud and grass seed to sprout vertical green rugs, all of these would die back when their supply of nutrients was used up, he explained. His photographs recorded the living canvases fading with time to the dun and gold of late summer. 'I'm interested in the point at which plants emerge from darkness into green and then disappear again,' he said. 'The narrow bridge between life and death.'

How did he manage a sentence like that without sounding as if he was on a pulpit? 'Have you tried paint?'

'Not paint,' he said sweetly. 'But fungus, red mites, spiders. Two years ago I grew a rug of barley on the floor of the Palais de Chaillot in Paris and then let loose a thousand locusts to eat it.'

'A plague of locusts,' I said. 'Very biblical. Nice for the caretaker who had to clean up.'

He frowned, momentarily repentant. 'Still, my locust phase has passed. Now I want something more fixed.'

'Why grass, if you want your work to survive? Why not Astroturf?'

He thought his obsession with grass, the backbone of British gardens, came from his own roots in a country that for much of the year was too dry and too hot. Grass in India tended to be brown, only briefly green – at the time of the monsoon, or when someone could afford to waste precious water on irrigating it. 'Green thus becomes an even more potent symbol of wealth and privilege.'

Whereas in Britain and the States the lawn was a green security blanket: my patch; my plot; my slice of the Arcadian dream. That weekly punctuation mark Robin and I never had: the day Daddy mows the lawn.

'I am working with a geneticist, Christian Herschel,' Nick went on. 'He believes that he will be able to switch off the genes that normally get switched on as plants begin to die. If he can do that he will be able to slow plants' ageing process. Even stop it altogether. He calls his new grass Eva-green.'

'Must be a rare species, a geneticist interested in grassy photos,' I said.

'I was introduced to him through Alex's nephew, Jack Ironstone. Jack and Christian are studying chlorophyll at UNISENS, the big pharmaceutical company. Some of the research money is coming from golf courses, tennis clubs, grassland commissions, some of it's a gamble by UNISENS to develop a new drug using chlorophyll, a molecule they believe may help in protecting the immune system. My work is a lucky offshoot.'

'What's he like, Jack Ironstone?' I asked.

'They're related,' Sally pitched in.

'Sort of cousins,' I said.

'Jack is an interesting fellow. A bit of a loner.'

Later that day I managed to get out of Sally a rough CV for Jack Ironstone (Eton, then Cambridge; biochemist by profession and botanist in his spare time). It didn't interest me as much as the fact that Jack was a family contact who could fill in some of the missing lines in my story. Nick gave me Jack's home and work numbers and over the next few weeks I left a couple of messages for him, but he didn't phone back. Once, Jack's secretary told me he was in India pursuing his experiments with chlorophyll. Another time he was in Bhutan researching something to do with orchids. For months the man I would come to see as the key to Dad's past remained a 'distant relative', tantalisingly elusive.

# 9

UNTIL A FAR less innocent explanation for Jack's friendship with Sally emerged, I put it down to her ability for making things grow.

She had a green thumb with people as well as plants. We often stopped in at the almshouse belonging to Mustafa, a small, dapper man with a bandit's moustache who informed me on our first meeting that Sally was responsible for the mint he needed for Turkish tea. Watching his wife pour this scented liquid from a samovar into etched glasses, I thought how very exotic it seemed, with the silver samovar sitting permanently under a series of sepia photographs of villas on the Bosporus. I had never drunk tea from a glass before, nor met any dry-cleaners like Mustafa, whose air of grave intelligence came from a different century than my own, not just a different continent.

When I mentioned to him on a later visit that his work seemed to make him happy, Mustafa replied that his happiness was because of his beliefs. 'Islam?' I asked, imagining all Turks to be Muslims.

'Existentialism. My father was Christian, like many dissenters in Turkey. So much that is creative comes from dissenters, rarely from fundamentalists. I am an existentialist, Miss Fleetwood. That is what makes me happy in my work.'

'I see.'

Sally giggled. She could tell I was bluffing.

'I was won over to existentialism from the first moment of reading Camus.'

'Ah.' I wondered if there was a dry-cleaning connection.

'But you must not confuse existentialism with nihilism,' he added.

'No, no. I'll try not to.'

Sally, a welcome visitor at most of the almshouses, soon made me part of the community. She introduced me to Fatbwa, from whom we collected exotic seeds, and to Arthur, a long-time Eastender in his late sixties who asked me to leave bowls of milk out for the hedgehogs. Arthur's giant pet rabbit, George, put the fear of God into Russell. 'Did you see the size of that rabbit's balls?' Sally whispered as we left.

But in all the time I lived at Eden, my friend never invited me into her own house. The raised voices coming from it every night after the pubs closed was reason enough, and her reticence when questioned soon taught me that if I pressed too closely she would simply clam up. Like the residents of many other closed communities, Sally had a dislike of outside interference into family affairs. She was a village girl at heart, happy to pass on her insider's knowledge: the best bagel shop in Columbia Road, the cheapest supermarket in Brick Lane, Fatbwa's gift for growing superior marijuana, a greasy spoon where the artists Gilbert and George could be seen taking all their meals. She even pointed out Percy's 'Bag-it with Maggots', a twenty-four-hour maggot vending machine where local canal fishermen put in coins to get live bait.

'They're so desperate for maggots?' I asked. 'Like, maggots are a twenty-four-hour addiction?'

She grinned. 'You can't bag the biggest fish with stale maggots.'

'Maybe we could run a sideline. There's no shortage of maggots in Val's bone garden. But what are they doing in there all day together, those maggots? In a vending machine, I mean.'

'Praying no one comes along to stick that fifty pence in the coin slot, is what.'

Sally was friends too with Mr Silver, who had run the electrical goods shop on Commercial Street since 1945 – WHY GO TO THE MOON WHEN YOU CAN GET EVERY-THING ELECTRIC AT SILVER'S? For pocket money Sally helped him to write captions in the elaborate window displays that had made him locally famous (handheld mini-fans and pocket alarms, steel locks, *Powerful miner's headlight can be used as table lamp*, light bulbs with various filaments in the shape of crosses and Stars of David). Why didn't it strike me as strange for a teenage gardener to have composed such captions as this:

CRIME CRIME CRIME. Every day you hear so many stories of mugging and rape, or on the underground vicious attacks. You never hear after-effects of these attacks on the victims. Must be unhappy experience FOR A LONG TIME. This pocket alarm might help in your hour of need!

Apart from these local excursions, Sally was interested in the world outside only as it related to plants. She convinced me to buy specimens of the Himalayan blue poppy called *Meconopsis baileyi* by wooing me with tales of its romantic history. From her I first learned about Colonel Bailey, the Political Officer who had noted its presence in eastern Tibet in 1913.

Plant hunters: those were Sally's idols. Other teenagers fell in love with lead guitarists, she had a crush on the adventurers and spies who had braved the Himalayas in search of rare flowers. In her head was a garden filled with lost plants: a 'long ago garden' she called it. The trophies she coveted were not her heroes' sweaty underpants or autographs but just the reverse, a group of unsigned botanical watercolours, hand drawn copies of originals that had been painted by anonymous Indians at the Calcutta Botanic Gardens in the nineteenth century. The man who commissioned this paper garden was Sir William Roxburgh, whom she described as the 'the fuckin' God of Indian botany'.

'They're called The Roxburgh Icones.' She wrote it down for me, complete with capital letters and that odd spelling. As close as she got to holy relics, Kew Gardens their reliquary. 'When my school took us to Kew the custodian let us touch them,' she added in a hushed voice normally reserved for Fatbwa's enviable torso. A great treasure trove of the world's botanical treasures, all on paper.

We made a pilgrimage to see these paper icons last January, and what really struck me was the fact that Sally's heroes had not signed their work – not the copies, not the original masterpieces still held in Calcutta. It was the great age of taxonomy, a time when the Linnaean System for classifying plants was being widely adopted, yet Roxburgh's iconic Indian artists were completely anonymous. They had copied everything down to the last watermark, up to and including the printed plate numbers, but had left no names, no history.

'Kind of ironic, isn't it?' I said to the custodian at Kew. 'These scientists obsessed with classifying the *plants* of India didn't bother to do the same with the men making the record?' It worried me, because list-makers were my kind of guys.

Sally's affinity with the early plant hunters and painters came from having forged her own sense of identity out of Magda Ironstone's botanical library. In it, we found a drawing showing a layout of the original orchard planted at Eden, and by cutting up photos from Mr Banerji's bulb and seed catalogues and matching them to a wish list drawn from plants seen among Roxburgh's icons she put together a crazy collaged paper garden for us. One night, after a book on period gardens gave her the idea that ghostly traces of Magda's planting might still be revealed, Sally managed to convince Fatbwa to shine his car headlamps through the back gate and across the lawn while I took pictures.

'This crazy, girl!' he said. 'What we doin' here?'

'The parchmarks that emerge in grass after spells of drought 'ave given much valuable information about early garden layouts,' Sally read aloud. 'Seen from above, these often show the overall pattern of lost gardens.'

The next morning I asked Sally what she wanted to do after she left home, wondering if she hoped to become a landscape architect, or maybe to follow in the footsteps of botanists like Roxburgh. She was on her knees carrying on with the digging we had started the night before. 'What do I wanna *do*?' she echoed, rocking back on her heels as if the question had never occurred to her.

'Yes: *do*. Your wildest dreams.'

'I'd like to see the real Roxburgh pictures, know wha' I mean? Find out more about the artists.' She thought for a minute. 'Jack said once there was a Rivers working for the Ironstones in India and 'e 'ad something to do with plants. A doctor, Jack said 'e was.'

'Jack said that?' Filing away Jack's comment for a later date, I didn't mention that Rivers was hardly an uncommon surname. 'So this is the extent of your wildest dream? No profession, no trek into the Himalayas to find a new plant?' I thought of the alternative: 'Or marriage, kids, a house of your own?'

'Of my own?' She stared at the muddy impressions where her knees had been. 'We've always lived 'ere. My Mum's family lived in number two. Dad's family always lived in number one.' Two imprints, history joined at the hip.

'What do you mean, *always*?'

'Always, like forever.' She picked up a handful of earth and held it out to me. A pink worm expanded out of the dark soil, coiled in on itself and dropped back on to the ground. 'What you see at first is a kind of uniform brown muck, right? But if you look closely you find it's made of cat turds, dead leaves, yellow London clay and ground up old factory bricks and horse shit, some dead beetles and rotting chicken bones, a few seeds that might sprout in fifty years, a bulb or two, a chestnut those ratty squirrels buried. You find little broken pieces of blue and white china down deep, below the topsoil. Really thick and old, maybe a 'undred years old, Arthur says, and 'is grandad used to drive a 'orse and cart round 'ere.' She squeezed the soil tightly and let it fall in a clump. 'Sticky. It's the clay.' She grinned. 'I'm a sticker too. Never thought about leaving, know wha' I mean?'

Self-taught, like me, but with broader gaps in her knowledge, Sally was proud to be the first to introduce me to Magda Ironstone's illustrated diaries, a life's worth of journals that Alex's mother had dated only by month, not by year, as if she wanted to extinguish the difference between one spring and another. I remember Sally rolling Latin words on her tongue like pebbles while she pored over a painting in one of these books:

''*elenium autumnale*: common name 'elen's flower. Magda says that its Greek name is beautiful because "it aligns flower and classical 'eroine, while *autumnale* signifies both its flowering season and its discoverer's nostalgia for classical culture". '

'*Helianthus exilis*,' I read over her shoulder. 'The exiled sunflower.'

Under her own careful pencil sketch Magda had written: 'How many surveyors lost their lives or their health in the service of our map, each one affected by loneliness and the effects of climate? Even the formidable Everest finally suffered a crisis, "an abscess at my hip and another at my neck, from both of which fragments of decayed bone have repeatedly been extracted".'

I won't say I could hear her voice then, Magda's voice. I won't say it because all my life I've struggled to avoid the kind of fey spin on events preferred by my trippy parents, their passion for clairvoyance over clarity. Then again, Swedenborg was a scientist and he still had visions, he had long chats with angels. Is it so strange that I hear colours, shades of green?

◆ ◆ ◆

**Sap Green:** *a bright kingfisher green made from unripe berries.*

*Fragments of my past like Everest's bones within me. I feel them when I move. You want me to judge your action, he is saying again, to be your judge and jury, condemn or forgive what you did. Be your own judge. Weigh the colour green, he says. Put it on the scales before and after it fades to yellow, measure what is lost. Even scientists are near-sighted or far-sighted, he says, we suffer from peripheral vision and colour blindness. How can we claim objectivity, omnipotence? How examine what is not there? And yet the missing element, the one we take for granted, the discarded, the unobserved, may prove to be of more importance than what is seen and contained.*

*He studied the colour green the way other men studied classical architecture, trying to break it down into separate fragments long before there were instruments delicate enough to discern its pillars*

55

*of nitrogen and pediments of carbon, its mysterious central column of magnesium.*

*He was my love, my life, my green thought in a green shade. The element I lost.*

◆

# 10

IT TOOK ME a long time – too long – to realise how strange it was for a girl from a family like Sally's to have been given unlimited access to Alex's library. Maybe I was so slow on the uptake because I felt like even more of an interloper myself, a mall rat from the wrong side of the Atlantic whose family had never stayed anywhere long enough to acquire such things as library cards.

'Looking back,' I'd said to the CID officer who took my statement after the murder, 'it seems that Sally was trying to tell me something important in the weeks before she was killed. To do with her father.'

'Derek Rivers?' The officer started to look interested. 'What about him?'

'I think he stole something from my great aunt's . . . from my house. Or –' I was trying to frame Sally in the best light. 'Maybe she was . . .' Stealing. Maybe Sally was the thief. 'She said I should change my lock, that Alex had often forgotten to lock her door and it wasn't a neighbourhood where you should leave your door unlocked. Things could go missing, she said.'

'Did anything go missing?'

'While I was there, I don't think so. My dog would've barked. But before . . . the place is practically a museum, and I don't think there was an inventory after my great aunt's death. Plus, she was apparently quite deaf in her last years.' I didn't tell him about all the books Sally had 'borrowed' from Alex. Put on the list of things that were difficult to explain: anything so indistinct as my friendship with Sally and its unspoken limits.

The officer stopped writing. 'Where's the link to Derek Rivers?'

'He has a key to my house, because he's the caretaker. And he came up to me after Sally's murder and asked if she had said anything to me about him.' I shrugged, admitting the weakness of my argument. 'He was very aggressive.'

'Had you changed the lock?'

'I forgot.' I was trying to remember when Sally had mentioned about changing the lock. It was early spring this year, one morning when I went out into the garden at dawn with Russell. Wading through the shallow waves of mist that lapped the bamboo, I imagined an Eastern landscape, a dreamy, liquid place, wet and snaky. I think I was secretly hoping Nick would appear and find me looking picturesque. He was probably asleep. Russell, snuffling happily at the base of a new fern, suddenly raised his head and barked at the yew tree. Not a warning, more of a welcome. 'What is it, Russ?' It wouldn't have surprised me to catch that leafy dinosaur in the act of metamorphosis. The hollow inner core was as satiny as mother-of-pearl, mottled with green and white algae like the weed and barnacles on a big old whale rolling in the sea.

There was movement inside the trunk. Slowly, stiffly, someone was rising from sitting to standing. 'Sally?' She had one hand on the tree's verdigris hide, in her other a blanket collaged with leaves and moss. 'Sally! Did you sleep inside the tree last night? Your Mum'll be worried about you!'

'Mum stayed the night at a cousin's,' she blurted out, the clear implication being that Sally would have been alone with her father in the house.

I suspect it wasn't the last night Sally slept inside the tree to escape Derek Rivers's drunken attention, if the flattened leaves and twigs I found from time to time were any evidence, although it was the only time that she was careless enough to let me find her. That morning I managed to draw her into the kitchen, the one corner of this house stamped with my personality. A few of my photos of Mr Banerji's market stall were pinned to the wall, bunches of dried herbs hung on a shelf

58

holding Indian spices from the local Bangladeshi grocery stores and there was a jam jar filled with early blossoms on the pine table. In my first week here Sally had helped to shift the two-burner stove from Alex's front room to the kitchen, and I put a pan on now to scramble eggs with toasted poppy seeds and chillies, the way Mum used to do. Watching me stir spices into the sizzling butter, Sally told me that her mother had an Indian bread recipe using poppy seeds. 'From Dad's family. We should try it some day.'

'So your Dad knows about this Indian connection Jack mentioned?'

She shrugged, uncomfortable at my sudden interest.

'Does your Dad have any more facts about the history than Jack does?'

'Not really. He says we're maybe related, the Rivers and the Fleetwoods, or maybe the Ironstones, that's all I know.' Her closed expression of 'thus far and no further' brought my questions to an abrupt end. She put the end of her finger into the bag of spices, peering closely at the tiny shot-grey seeds that stuck. 'Did you know these come from opium poppies? The company Jack works for uses opium poppy seed oil to make perfumes. The seeds are tough enough to wait a hundred years before sprouting.'

I asked her what she felt about the old names for poppies we'd found in Magda's library – redcaps, thunderflowers; implications of violence to come – and she blew on her finger so that the seeds vanished into my aunt's room. 'Old wives' tales.'

I think that was the morning she tapped the lock and remarked casually about having it changed. 'I could get you a good deal from Mr Silver's shop.'

It was Nick's grandfather who forced the situation between Sally and her father into the open. He knocked on my door one Sunday to complain: 'Really, this shouting and thumping is not at all acceptable.'

'You mean the Rivers, Mr Banerji?' The night before there had been a real uproar when Sally's father got home from the pub.

'And now she has not showed up to help. Normally she is coming early every Sunday morning to take my plants to Columbia Road, and for this, as you know, I am giving her a small commission or her choice of plants. Not to show up without informing me is most unlike her.'

Beneath his March Hare fluster he was genuinely worried. I knew how much he loved Sally. 'Have you been to her house?'

'No, no. I have not your authority. It is no business of mine, he will say. I don't like to interfere. Not living so close. He will accuse me again of eavesdropping and busybodying. And my grandson is away setting up a big exhibition.' The implication: Mr Banerji was alone and vulnerable while I had the invisible backing of Eden's trustees.

I hesitated, reluctant to ask the obvious question. 'Do you think I should talk to Mr Rivers, Mr Banerji?'

His kindly face was anxious but relieved. 'Shall I come with you?'

'No, I don't want to get you in trouble. I'll be fine. But if –'

'Yes?'

'If Rivers gets funny, could you call Fatbwa?'

As much to fool myself as Rivers, I donned a pair of heavy boots that added an inch to my height. Shit-kicking boots, although I'm not a shit-disturber by nature. Putting Russell on his lead, I went around and knocked on the Rivers's front door, my heart matching my fist's thumps.

Rivers came to the door unshaven, smelling sour. I was accustomed to seeing him outside, his brick-shaped body dressed in army surplus gear. Without the combat hat and camouflage jacket, he seemed older, shorter, blotchier. But more impressive. There were bunches of neat muscles filling his white T-shirt, unexpected in such a heavy drinker, and under his shaved pelt of hair the bones in his head were clearly visible and constantly working, full of suppressed energy, as if, like some small, fierce animal, he was using his life up faster than the rest of us. Or other people's lives. 'Little Sally is busy helping clear up,' he said, trying to shut me out. But Russell, spotting his friend Sally down the hall behind her father, wedged his sausage body between us, and Rivers had to open the door again.

'Sally!' I called. 'It's me, Claire. I have some work for you.'

Rivers told me she'd done enough work for me and who did I think I was coming between a man and his family and he had a good mind to.

'To what, Mr Rivers?' Fear made my eyes feel as if they were attached to long strings of chewing gum like Nick's phantom hand. *To hit me*, I thought, *the way I suspect you hit your wife and daughter.*

He stepped forward, and I could feel as well as smell the heat of last night's beer on his breath. And something else – rotten teeth, maybe, or the stink of some condition not yet diagnosed. He started calling me a bitch and saying he had as much right to this property as I did if only people knew. 'Think you're lady of the fuckin' manor! Ask that cousin of yours, he'll tell you!'

'Jack Ironstone? He'll tell me what?'

His eyes got shifty. 'And that fuckin' Paki Nosy Parker can fuck off too!'

'Mr Banerji? But I thought –'

'Fuckin' Pakis!'

'I thought you –'

'And 'is fuckin' wanker grandson!'

'But I thought you were so proud of your Indian heritage, Mr Rivers?' Russell was barking and growling while I dragged on the lead.

Rivers lunged with his foot. 'Keep that fuckin' rat out of my sight or I'll –'

I picked up the struggling, snapping Russell. 'Go ahead and hit me, Mr Rivers.' Not knowing where the courage came from. 'Hit me and I'll have the social services and the Eden trustees down on you so fast your head will spin.'

He looked as if he would. Then Mrs Rivers was beside him, putting her hand on his arm, telling me he wasn't a bad man, just worried by work, and please don't call the socials, Miss Fleetwood, because Sally's fine. 'Socials' was how the social services were referred to by people round here. The emphasis put on the word made it sound like a disease.

Sally wasn't fine, though. Her eyes dull in a bruised face, she raised her hand with a gesture that made me ashamed of my reluctance to confront her father. Stepping out of reach of Rivers's fists, I said as steadily as my voice would allow, 'I know what you've been doing, Mr Rivers, and so do other people. We're watching you. Remember that. And I certainly will go to the socials tomorrow unless Sally is back in the garden.' My hands were shaking when I finished speaking.

Sally came back. But she shook her head when I questioned her and asked me not to tell the socials for fear of her Mum losing the house. Her mother crept around Eden like a whipped dog, muttering about Rivers having been out of work for years. For a while, Rivers stayed clear of me and kept the noise of his embattled family to a minimum. But it was not his last run-in with Sally, judging by the old bruising on her corpse found by the pathologist. Rivers had simply stored up his frustration and violence like a bank account, let it escalate and run up interest. Then he'd had a spending spree on his daughter.

# 11

'THAT'S IT?' THE CID officer asked. 'The sum of your suspicions about Rivers?'

'Yes . . . no. There were Rivers's night visitors, as well.' I was starting to connect all the events of that spring. 'The first time I noticed them was a night in March.'

I woke to hear Russell growling, his nose as close to the windowsill as his pint-sized stature allowed. He's afraid of the dark, so it was only to appease his feelings that I picked him up and looked out the window, where the moon clearly lit two men standing by my back door, one white, one black. Some instinct made me clamp my hand over Russell's muzzle to stop him barking, and I held it there until the men moved off into the bamboo. They reappeared seconds later by the gate to Sally's house, the gate opened and they disappeared inside. There was nothing more to do. My garden gate wasn't locked. They hadn't broken in. What was worrying me? 'It was their silence,' I said to the CID officer. 'If they'd been loud or drunk they'd have been less threatening.'

'Did you report them?'

I could see he only asked the question for form's sake. After all, what was to report? 'No, I . . .' Unable to get back to sleep after the night visitors, I decided to do some printing in the cellar, where Sally had helped me to build a small but perfectly adequate darkroom. Recently I'd started doing collages with pictures of Sally gardening double-exposed on to botanical studies taken with a hybrid X-ray camera developed by Val. The new camera could penetrate plants deeply enough to bring out layers of greys whose richness seemed almost green. In one collage the veins of a leaf were eerily fused with Sally's raised hand, in another her fingers extended along the parallel of a growing tree, her bony foot emerged from the yew's mossy limbs. That night, filled with a sense of foreboding, I began a more sinister series, juxtaposing flower studies and images of Sally on to forensic photographs that reminded me of Picasso's women or Henry Moore sculptures, everything in the wrong order, holes in the wrong places.

I was using photographs I had taken of specimens in the cellar that might have featured in a Victorian freak show, in particular of a child's skull with a smaller skull growing out of its anterior fontanelle. The faces were turned in opposite directions, the smaller, imperfect skull appearing upside down and back to front. Its label read: '*Craniopagus parasiticus.* Skull of Bengali child with two heads, aged four yrs, believed to have been badly burned as infant.' I overlapped the image almost seamlessly with a page from Magda's diaries: 'Vegetable Teratology: until recently, exceptional formations were considered as monsters to be shunned, as lawless deviations from the ordinary.'

When I'd finished printing the collages I looked through the cellar's cabinets and found a scrapbook containing pictures of orchids and poppies, neatly annotated in a hand recognisable to me now as Joseph Ironstone's: 'Artists and anatomists have always sought what divides our species from more rudimentary forms, paying particular attention to bones (the scaffolding of vertebrates). But I seek to define the invisible, a definition of humanity and inhumanity – what I call Self versus Non-Self.'

*Self versus Non-Self.* I felt as if the man who had written that a century ago had reached into my brain's dusty crannies. It was one of the many terms I'd picked up before Robin died, while scanning every book and article for information about the immune system. Impossible not to learn a little about cancer at the same time, because it was research into cancer retroviruses that first led to the discovery of AIDS. And you can't read much on the immune system and cancer research without coming across the term used by Joseph Ironstone.

*Self versus Non-Self:* one of the great problems in cancer research. Why doesn't our body's immune system recognise tumours as Non-Self? Why does it tolerate them? How does a cancer cell disguise itself as an erratic uncle rather than a deranged monster, thus protecting itself from destruction by the immune system? How does it jump our genetic traffic lights, buck our internal police?

Part of the answer lies in cancer's mastery of disguise. By reactivating genes used in foetal development, tumours manage to trick the immune system into 'tolerating' errant cells. Cancer specialists speak of 'breaking the tolerance', referring to the process of forcing the immune system to overrule this forgiving familial relationship, to recognise the tumours as a threat.

I had questioned Sally only once about her father's visitors, who came in twos and threes that spring, usually well after pub closing time, and always through the central garden. She shook her head and quickly lowered her eyes. 'Why put up with him?' I asked, spurred on by her stubborn silence. 'Why stay, Sally?' Trying to break the tolerance, force her to see her father as the threat.

'My Mum,' she said, finally meeting my eyes. 'She feels sorry for 'im because 'e sees this caretaking as a bit of a comedown.' Sally hunched her shoulders at my disbelief. 'Anyway, Mum won't leave 'im and I'm not leaving without her.' She muttered that he wasn't so bad, just when he drank.

I didn't tell the CID guy all of this. Nor did I tell him my theory that Derek Rivers was a kind of virus infecting our neighbourhood. But whatever I said was enough for the detective to give me a funny look, and when he asked what Sally's response had been to my questions I was so unnerved that I made the mistake of telling him. 'Dad's not so bad,' Sally had repeated. 'If it ever gets really 'airy, I can always stay in Fatbwa's spare room.'

My friendship with Fatbwa had been a lot more cordial since he'd realised that I wouldn't 'rat 'im out to the trustees' (as Sally put it) about his occupancy of Eden. His lease, like that of many of the other residents here, wouldn't have stood much scrutiny. The tenuous legal connection involved a girlfriend (since moved on) who was said to be the descendant of a run-away slave from Bristol rescued by Magda Ironstone. Renamed Hope, she had become a worker for the Trade Unions with Annie Besant, and later, a pillar of Hackney's Baptist church. 'A gospel singer,' Fatbwa said. 'In the music biz like me.'

Fatbwa, an independent music journalist with a razor wit, had this relaxed West Indian thing he did with his voice, teasing me with it when he thought I was getting too uptight and rule-bound, which was most of the time. He'd let the vowels saxophone out round and soft, the consonants take care of themselves. None of those bunched-up nervy tight-assed 'oi' and prissy little 'th' sounds. He did the jazz talk when he was tired, at ease, like an athlete slipping into bedroom slippers after a hard run. I've heard him on the radio sound completely different, his 'weekday voice', he called it: edgy-grammared, stockmarket-sharp, no way anyone would know he felt homesick for a place where his mother barbecued for thirty people every Sunday while his father wrote manifestos on democracy.

One day I told Fatbwa about the night visitors, on the off chance he knew them. 'Why don't they use the Rivers's front door, that's what I want to know.'

He put down the article he was writing and took off his glasses. Over his shoulder I could read the unlikely by-line Redge Ashworth.

'What you smilin' at?' he asked.

'*Redge?*'

'Don' gimme a hard time 'bout my name, girl.'

'Actually, I was smiling at your ability to write in one accent and speak in another. Like me.'

'Like lots of us.' Still focused on the problem, he asked, 'Rivers bin havin' hisself night visitors, has he? Bes' you stay well clear, girl. You don' wanna mess wit him an' his mates. A real mean bunch.'

'In what way?'

'We talkin' slots, slits, slashers, plenty o' dope. Then he got hisself some friends wit' mutual interests in de Yardies.'

'Scotland Yard?'

Fatbwa snorted with laughter. 'These Yardie don' come from no highlan' glen, girl, excep' maybe in our blue blue mountains of Jamaica.' He kept his vowels Caribbean-slippered for my amusement, but his face was as serious as he ever allowed it to be. 'I'm tellin' you, don' mess wit dese bwas' (letting the boys hiss out with stagey melodrama; but still a warning). 'Real badasses. Yardies into drugs big time.'

My wry glance at the hedge of marijuana plants bordering his neat vegetable patch earned me a deadpan look from Fatbwa. 'These purely medicinal by Rivers's an' his friends standards. Purely medicinal. Anytime your medicine chest need fillin', come to me. But stay clear o' Rivers. Bolt your door and stay inside when his friends come callin'.'

'What about Sally?'

He shook his head. 'Sal's a sad case, though I told her, like I'm tellin' you, anytime she in real trouble, she can always come to me. She stays for her Ma. An' Mrs Rivers too beaten down to notice. Grateful Sally take the heat off her.'

'What do you mean, Sally takes the heat off?'

He shook his head again, and said it was none of his business, Sally would tell me in her own sweet time.

'Should I call the police?'

'Tell 'em what they don' already know? Arthur knew Derek as a boy, says he was always a right bastard. Police know Rivers's a scumbag. Everyone know it. Trouble is to catch him.'

# 12

TODAY, THE POLICE sent along an artist from a specialist operation called the 'SO11 Facial Imaging Team'. He held out his business card by way of identification, the line immediately under his name testimony that Scotland Yard doesn't lack a sense of the postmodern: THIS CARD IS NOT PROOF OF IDENTITY.

His was a low-tech operation all round. Instead of the PhotoFit library of easily manipulated photographic images familiar from American cop shows, this artist was equipped with a sketchbook and charcoal. He was also very bad at capturing a likeness. First we tried to establish the face shape of the only man I had seen clearly, then hair and relative ear position, for which I had a series of 'standard' line drawings to choose from. When the artist had sketched these, producing an image that was only vaguely human, we began on details (eyes this shape, nose that, mouth wide or narrow, brows bushy or smooth), all chosen from ring binders displaying mugshots of convicts supplied by an American forensic bureau.

'The problem is, all these men look like criminals. And American criminals, at that,' I said, after two hours trying to pick out my murderer from among the rapists and child molesters and junkies. 'The man I saw looked ordinary.'

'Ordinary? In what particular way?' He picked up his charcoal again.

'How can you look ordinary in a particular way?' I asked impatiently. 'He was anonymous. Like me. Medium height, medium brown hair, medium features.'

He sighed. 'We often find this. The problem is that not all criminals conform to our image of them.'

Together we stared at his bland, badly drawn caricature of Anyman. 'Would you like some coffee?' I asked, for want of anything more useful to say.

'No. I don't like to drink while I'm working.'

'I said *coffee.*' But he shook his head and told me that coffee kept him awake at night. 'You sure it's the coffee?' His encyclopedia of criminals leered up at us. I should talk.

After he left, I went down into the cellar again, where I've spent hours lately searching for the missing links between Joseph Ironstone and Claire Fleetwood. I want photographic proof, shared physical attributes, but no photos of either Fleetwoods or Ironstones have turned up, a strange omission for the remorseless cataloguer Joseph, who kept these drawers full of nail clippings and teeth and curls of hair. Without the benefit of my century's most relentless aid I'm forced to build a collage of spare parts in the manner of that police artist, invent a face to fit Joseph's private obsessions. His books have taught me that we shared our interests with the greatest list-maker of all time, Carl Linnaeus, the Swedish guy who invented the most famous system for classifying plants. On a tour of Sweden in 1747 Linnaeus noted in his diary that farmers were using churchyard soil for their cabbage patches. He wrote of human heads turning into cabbage heads which in turn became human heads, 'In this way we come to eat our dead, and it is good for us.'

Linnaeus wasn't the only plantsman with an interest in dead men's bones. The seventeenth-century Dutch botanist Frederick Ruysch devoted most of his life to preparing wax-injected anatomical specimens. For his *Thesaurus Anatomicus* he arranged plants and skeletons with dismembered limbs in macabre tableaux of life very like my photographs – and Joseph's too, I learned, when I found a hidden portfolio: photographs at last, but not of the family. Like me, Magda's husband had produced images that mirrored Ruysch's, and in Joseph's collage of growth and rot there was something deeply disturbing but also wonderful. I come from a country where ageing is unacceptable and violence is sexy. Getting old and dying is considered to be a lifestyle decision, an option for the weak-willed. Don't get old, get a facelift! Don't die, freeze your sperm! That's the American way. But violence is casual – drive-by, takeaway. Why are we obsessed with it? People always have been. Does witnessing violence make us feel more alive? George Stubbs cut up his first animal at the age of eight. What made him an artist, not a surgeon or a butcher? What stopped him from becoming a Jeffrey Dahmer, who moved onwards and upwards through the scale of murder from insects to cats, dogs, humans; killing, rotting and bleaching his chosen subjects and then photographing the results. Spray-painting the skulls to turn them into fetishes (so, an artistic leaning, a homicidal Damien Hirst), he wound up with something he could truly own, more than was ever possible with a living human: a series of printed images of mortality to be laid out with the skulls in a shrine to possession. The body as ornament, as altar. Apart from the final act, what made Dahmer different from Damien? Or from a collector like Joseph Ironstone, a photographer like me?

Over the last couple of days I have been drawn back constantly to the sad little double skull of a Bengali child, a reminder of the eighteenth-century German guy called Blumen-bach who spent his whole life classifying skulls (and acquired a collection so famous that scientific pilgrimages were made to his university to view it). Would he have wondered, as I do, if the two heads from that small body half-burnt in a fire shared a single brain, a single voice?

*Ma. Two heads? Burn fire fear killit Singilbrensingilvoys Fa. Boy girl? smile cry? see hear ears? speak? Ma. Whatsay? Ma. Wurds. Ma.*

Two days after the police artist's session, I found a book whose contents, largely a series of measurements, were listed next to what I presumed were the names of those measured. It was written in a cramped but legible copperplate, similar to Joseph's, but distorted. The first entry was Joseph Ironstone, the second, Magda, then followed two children, judging by their smaller skull size. The measurer dismissed earlier traditions of building up faces from an oval, and proposed instead a triangulation of human geography. Putting the book down, I picked up the calipers next to it and slipped them around my own skull. While jotting down my head measurements I heard Russell's warning bark and ran upstairs to see who it was. For a second my dog didn't recognise me. He turned from the door to bark at the shadow on the wall of my head, an alien insect in its caliper crown. 'Mistaken identity, Russell,' I said, and he wagged his stumpy tail at the familiar sound of my voice while maintaining a sceptical expression.

The man with his finger on my doorbell was another CID officer who wanted to know if I would mind displaying some photocopies of the police sketch I'd helped with. He gave my insect headgear a quick look, but didn't mention it. Presumably he's seen a lot stranger things in the line of duty.

I replaced the calipers before turning the lights out in the cellar, glancing down the old list to find that my head measurements exactly matched Joseph's. He must have been a very small man, not much bigger than his wife. What was he attempting to prove with all this measuring? What was I?

A few people seemed nervous at accepting the mugshot, as if that bland face could see through the photocopy process, but Derek Rivers's reaction was more aggressive than worried. 'You helping the coppers with their inquiries?' he asked, looking over the photocopied suspect with his muddy eyes. 'Little Miss Helpful. Always sticking her nose in where no one wants it.'

'I wasn't the only witness,' I said quickly. 'We're all trying to help.'

'You're the only one claims to have seen their faces. You're the only one stupid enough to help the coppers make one of these.' He shoved the picture so close to my face that I had to step back. For our own safety the witnesses weren't supposed to talk to one another about the murder. Of course, by the time the cops got around to telling us that, everyone had talked already. I watched Rivers now, trying to read his flat, bottomfeeder's eyes as he tossed the picture to the ground. 'Fuckin' lady of the manor! Why don't you just fuck off back where you came from before you get into trouble! Fuckin' Yank!' He banged the gate in my face.

Should I tell the police? Everyone here had watched for years as Rivers put on a good show for the trustees: the rough diamond, the working-class lad fallen on hard times. Salt of the earth, with his wife backing him up in the charade. No one wanted to risk getting involved with him. 'Derek's always 'ad evil friends,' Arthur warned me when I asked what I should do. 'Doesn't 'ave to be 'im that does you over, know wha' I mean?'

I spent the evening sticking the mugshots up around the neighbourhood, but by the time I left for work the next morning many of them had been torn down. A phonecall to the police produced the weary response that it wasn't an area in favour of police co-operation. 'Not if the crime is racial.'

'Why would it be racial? The men who killed Sally were white, not black.'

'You said there'd been black men visit the Rivers at night. And there's that big Jamaican bloke – he was a friend of hers. Maybe she had a white boyfriend who got jealous. The parents both deny these night visitors you mentioned.'

'Fatbwa had nothing to do with it! And the men at night – there were more whites than blacks – and they weren't visiting Sally; they came to see her father.'

'How do you know?'

'I . . . I just know, that's all.'

'Got a record, hasn't he, the Jamaican? Bit of a radical?'

'What have politics got to do with it? It's Rivers who's been threatening me!'

'Physically? Has he hit you?'

'No but – he's said things.'

'Verbals don't count.'

'Can't you warn him off?'

'Thing is, Rivers says you're a bit of a troublemaker. Says you took funny pictures of his daughter.'

72

'He *what*? But my pictures aren't . . . I'm a forensic photographer . . .'

'Still, I wouldn't want my daughter's pictures used like that. So you see, Miss Fleetwood . . .'

I saw all right. Even the police I'd worked with thought it was 'funny' for a woman to take the kind of pictures I took. I could imagine this station reading over my list of wild allegations about Rivers and drawing their own conclusions, just as they'd drawn them about Fatbwa.

# 13

AGAINST ALL THE odds, the police managed to pick up a suspect within two weeks of the mugshots going up, which made me think that they'd had someone in mind already. Very possibly the guy they've arrested is a known criminal. Maybe they found some incriminating evidence at the scene of crime. No one will say. All I got from the Witness Protection Unit was the information that the police driver taking me to the ID parade would be 'in civvies'. 'And your driver will phone before arriving,' the girl on the phone said. So he wouldn't be mistaken for one of these villains, I guess.

But no villain could have looked as uniform as the grey man who collected me, so grey it was hard to tell where his suit stopped and his face began. Driving with silent efficiency through the rush hour traffic, he parked his anonymous grey car just as carefully. We waited in it for twenty minutes, 'To make sure you don't meet the accused coming in,' he told me, letting words out of his zipper of a mouth as if he had to pay for each one. Then he took me into the station where two bored overweight cops ignored us. The driver made no attempt to explain who we were. I figured he'd grown up in one of those families where the parents said kids should be seen and not heard.

Shortly after us, a hard blonde in white stilettos arrived, her old-young face vaguely familiar as one of the hookers who worked the streets near Eden. After another fifteen minutes a stark naked woman walked in from the street and started screaming for Sergeant Brown. 'Where is he?' she shrieked. 'Where is he, the fucking cunt, the arsehole, the bastard! I'll give him filth on television!'

We all tried to blend in with the stains on the plastic chairs.

Eventually, a tired man appeared through a locked door on our left, draped a coat around the woman and escorted her out. I wondered if he was Sergeant Brown or Blue or White.

Twenty more minutes ticked by and an air of weariness settled over the room like dust. 'How long am I going to fuckin' wait here?' the blonde rasped.

'We'll get to your complaint when we can,' answered a man behind the desk.

'I'm not gettin' fuckin' *paid* for this, you know!' she added. 'I didn't fuckin' *ask* to be a witness!'

'What case are you – Rivers?' asked the bored cop, and made a note.

The grey driver shook some wrinkles out of his melancholy demeanour. 'Actually, this lady is also here as a witness in the Rivers case.' He sounded apologetic, as if the blonde and I, by agreeing to be witnesses, were getting in the way of procedure. Without us the cops could have filed Sally away in one of their beige filing cabinets and got on with more important things like the football pools.

The blonde slanted a worried look my way as one of the two cops made a phonecall. After another lengthy wait the naked woman's escort appeared and took us through to a room where three young Indian men were watching reruns of *This is Your Life!* on television. I recognised one of them as the resident of a flat above the corner shop opposite where Sally was murdered, a shop boarded up since a racially inspired firebomb months earlier. A sign above their heads:

NOTICE TO ALL WITNESSES ATTENDING AN ID PARADE

1 Please do not discuss the case with anyone whilst you are at the Centre.

2 Once you have viewed the Parade: when you return to the Witness Room once again do not discuss it with anyone.

3 If you make a positive identification a written statement will be taken from you before you leave.

4 Any questions please ask the ID Centre staff.

The room, painted a clinical shade of shiny green that I always associate with forensic uniforms, had the tedious yet sinister edge of a dentist's waiting room. On the wood-grained formica table was a stack of celebrity magazines from a year ago, and these I proceeded to leaf through without interest, trying to figure out why people already famous would choose to have their houses, weddings, holidays recorded by such bad photographers. The blonde wondered if anyone knew what time *Neighbours* started. No one did.

Time passed heavily.

'Know why it's painted green?' one of the younger Indian guys asked suddenly. 'The room, like? So it don't show the blood. Like hospitals.'

His friend said, 'What d'you mean it don't show the blood?'

'I read that somewhere: this shiny colour green don't show the blood so much.'

The other guy looked worried. 'What blood – why should there be blood here?'

For a few minutes we all silently considered why there should be blood here. Then the nervous blonde asked, 'They can't escape, can they? These witnesses? I mean, they can't, like, get in here and clock our faces, do us over?'

'Nahhhh,' said the first Indian guy. But he didn't look convinced. Frankly, I was sure we'd die of boredom long before the suspect got us.

After twenty-five minutes a beaky-nosed policewoman strode in, crackling with energy, and speaking in the snaps and pops of a lightbulb short-circuiting. 'Right. Sorry for the delay. Waiting for the suspect. To join the other people in the parade. Not obliged. He isn't. Not sure why they turn up. Suspects. Unless they think it would look suspicious if they didn't. So, who'd like to go first?'

Desperate for a change of venue, I put my hand up and followed the woman through an antechamber into a narrow room divided by a wall of glass. On our side was a policeman and the suspect's lawyer. The lawyer looked pretty criminal to me. Beyond the glass sat nine men on numbered stools. 'That side is mirrored,' said the policeman, 'so he can't see you. They sit there looking at themselves.' And his lawyer sits there looking at me, I thought, wondering how well he knew his client, whether they were drinking buddies.

I was warned to take my time, study each of the faces carefully, be absolutely sure before identifying any of the men. But I'd spotted him immediately. 'Could you ask number three to stand up?' I said to the sergeant, and there was a whispered protest from the lawyer, who had already given me a sharp look. He would know me again, even if his client didn't.

'Why?' asked the sergeant.

'Last time I saw him he wasn't sitting down,' I answered, as patiently as I could. 'Then he ran past me. I want to see his profile.' Due process was wearing me down. When the duty sergeant asked if I was *absolutely* certain that number three was the man I claimed to have last seen weeks ago beating Sally to death, I nodded, yes, that is the man. Number three, yes, I'm *absolutely* sure. And heard Val's voice in my head, asserting that nothing was absolute. Of course I wasn't sure. It was dark, he was running, I was upset.

Walking out of the parade hall into the second waiting room, I clocked the same sign warning witnesses to silence, same gloss-painted hospital green walls, same wood laminate coffee table and moulded plastic chairs. As if I had passed through the suspect's one-way mirror and made no differ-ence. 'You're right, it's identical,' the sergeant answered my question. 'Except for the Coke machine.' He sketched the layout for me and explained that in the middle was an invisible viewing room where the CID and legal eagles could watch witnesses viewing the suspects. 'The CPS – Crown Prosecution Service, what we in the police call the Criminal Protection Society – need to be sure you haven't been briefed on a suspect before going in there.'

We are all being watched, these days. We don't exist unless we've been recorded doing it on Dad's new Pentax or the family camcorder. We've got Walkmen for ears, TVs for eyes; soon we'll have latex skins. The condom world.

I waited while each of the other witnesses went through the ritual and joined us, everyone expressing relief at the ordeal being over, everyone secretly glad not to have spotted a killer in the line-up. 'Trouble is, they all look alike, don't they?' said one of the Indians to his friend, a mild joke at the expense of the white folk present. Only the blonde kept quiet. Her tense body language betrayed the same cold stillness I was feeling. Our eyes met, slid away, met again.

I had to make the first statement, back into the first Witness Room with the same CID man that I had seen on the morning after it happened. Now I would have to explain in more detail the role of Number Three, go through it all again. The officer kept probing, trying to make something solid out of an event that had happened at the wrong speed. He wanted to develop the whole picture, bring out the unexposed details at the edges of the negative:

Was he holding or hitting?

Did he hesitate?

How much blood? What shape, how far?

Before I left the station, the CID guy warned me again not to talk about the case. 'The second man is still out there, you know, and the man we have arrested says he was hired by someone else.'

It probably wasn't a good idea to spend the rest of the day in the cellar, even though I convinced myself that it was a form of family archaeology. The trouble is, the roots you dig up aren't always the ones you were hoping for, which is the conclusion I came to on discovering Joseph Ironstone's hidden library. Some books were relatively innocent: a translation from the German psychiatrist Richard von Krafft-Ebing's by now classic text, *Psychopathia Sexualis*, in which he explains his ideas about forensic psychiatry and sexual pathology, a book whose contents I knew only in the way that anyone familiar with forensic matters might. And at first there seemed nothing unusual in the choice of translation – a section on sexual crimes describing the ritualised slaughter and mutilation of women. Fairly mundane material in our era; in Krafft-Ebing's time it was revelatory, predating Jack the Ripper's attacks by several years. But it was the next books which made me feel uneasy, stories by the Austrian lawyer Sacher-Masoch, whose form of eroticism was subsequently named after him. De Sade was represented, as well, along with a collection of Victorian pornography in all its repressed undress: beefy men in leather masks with their testicles in clamps, grown men being spanked by bored-looking women in corsets.

It wasn't all pornography. Between the pages of one sad little pamphlet devoted to the whip was a crumbling English account of the execution in January 1870 of the multiple murderer Jean Baptiste Tropmann. A popular event: Tropmann was escorted to the guillotine by the Russian author Turgenev, one of the fashionable guests who had first consumed foie gras and punch at the prison director's reception. Apart from the main show, celebrity guests were offered the opportunity of lying prone in a position only hairs away from the blade as the executioner triggered its descent, lighthearted fun and games which Turgenev much enjoyed.

Joseph Ironstone must have been in India at that time, yet he'd marked the passage carefully. What had interested him? I wondered, not for the first time, what had happened to Joseph 'shot and kidnapped, believed murdered', as Frank Barrett had told me. Where did Joseph disappear to? Why was he believed murdered? I kept thinking of my father's old questions, the ones he used to pose to the stoned audience entertained by his Ripper one-man show:

Why did Jack stop?
Where did he go after the last killing?

Last night I suffered again from a nightmare that has been recurring since Sally's murder, the one in which Jack comes back, in all his gaudy glory.

*I'm not a butcher,*
*I'm not a Yid,*

*Nor yet a foreign skipper*
*But I'm your own light-hearted friend,*
*Yours truly, Jack the Ripper.*

The garden is a cemetery, the bamboo swollen to endless monstrous forests. I am being followed by Jack, or following him, forced to retrace a path leading to something I don't want to see or do. Graveyards, open tombs. Waking up in a sweat I wrote the dream in a notebook and this morning found the words: 'I'm earning mortuary miles. Like air miles. Travelling between mortuaries.'

Other people might be able to lose themselves in work, but forensic photography is not a field designed to let you forget mortuaries. When I dropped the X-rays for the third time in an hour today, Val sighed and asked me what was wrong. 'This is going to sound crazy, Val, but . . . but do you think the genes of our ancestors could haunt us? I mean, sort of like squatters who take over a house?'

I was worried he'd give me a lecture warning against the easy metaphors offered by science. Instead, he took the question seriously. 'In one way we are all haunted,' he said, pointing to a femur I was photographing. 'This bone shows the result of congenital damage, the life of a man's ancestors preserved in his skeleton. Surely that is one form of haunting?' He searched my face. 'Not yours, I gather.'

Stumbling at first, I tried to explain. 'This house . . . I don't know, it makes me feel as if I'm living inside someone else's brain, sharing someone's nightmares, as if all its collected bits and pieces are the brain's neurons and I have to make a connection between them but I'm missing a crucial bit of wiring or evidence.'

'The ancient Greeks had a word – anagnorisis: the recollection of a forgotten past. Terribly popular with chaps like Sophocles. Bit overrated theatrical device I always thought it.' Val, in his own gentle, circular fashion, was leading up to a less antique solution. 'Of course, we *can* be haunted by things we have done and only dimly remember we have done, if we remember at all,' he continued. 'Neurologists use the term "scotoma" to describe a gap in consciousness, a mental blind spot that may be caused either by a neurological lesion – in the sensory cortex of the brain, say – or by the psyche's attempt to deny items of conflict. Witnessing a particularly brutal murder might cause such an effect, I imagine, don't you? Or drugs – a man who kills his wife under the influence of the drug PCP, for example. Have you ever taken any drugs that might cause hallucinations? I've heard some young people find them very . . . enlightening.'

I told him I preferred to carry on in my own unenlightened fashion. 'My parents' experience put me off drugs. They always sounded so boring when they were stoned. But what do you think about Joseph, our common traits?'

'I think you should try spending less time in the cellar. Judging by what you've told me, it's not surprising you're having nightmares.'

'Very ironic from a man whose profession is dealing with decaying bodies. Anyway, it's dumb, these nightmares about the Ripper. Stuff I used to dream as a kid. Serial killing isn't even a form of murder I find interesting.'

'Implying that there's a form of murder you *do* find interesting?'

'Sure. Yeah. The one with a motive.'

'Random killing doesn't intrigue you?'

'No. It's sort of . . . I don't know . . . too much like what happens to us anyway.'

'You see God as a form of serial killer, then?'

I was doing a close-up of the abnormal bone formation on the foot of a man who would have had a limp from birth. 'A serial killer? No. I'm just not sure I like him much, that's all.' Trying to make a joke of it: 'Let's say that if I ever get a chance to meet the guy there's more than one bone I have to pick with him.'

Val finished extracting a fragment from the chest cavity before straightening his back to peer at me. 'I think you need a holiday. Perhaps a sabbatical.'

This house and its former occupants haunt me, it's as simple as that. I see Eden Dwellings as one of those congenital diseases passed down only through the female line, punishment for a crime I can't remember committing. I know there is something called a 'founder effect', where a gene for colour blindness or dwarfism, say, can be tracked back to a few founding ancestors. We can trace it because humans like to name things, file them in one category or another – to know where we're going, and how far we've come. I'm not alone in this; we're natural list-makers, the only animal with a name for each individual, and this obsession with genealogy makes it easier for us to trace our own roots, particularly in isolated communities like mountains, valleys or desert islands. All we are doing is following footprints in the sand until we find the Man Friday – or the cannibal – who made them. Or discover that we made them ourselves.

I want more than that. I want to tap Man Friday on his shoulder. Make him turn around, see if I recognise my face in his. I want to know if I am living in the house that Jack built.

◆ ◆ ◆

**Gangrene:** *localised death of tissue, from the Greek for a green growth on trees.*

*By night I walk the streets wondering why these mutations and degenerates continue to reproduce their monstrous babies. Malignant tumours feeding, evil cancers to be cut out cut out. Like this other head growing.*

*The river is a vicious brown eel. The pink sky flaked with dirty clouds, a raw skin stretched to dry over the city.*

*We rot here like fish. He was rotting. His bones weakening and his hair falling out. His teeth loose. Thin as his mother had been. Her eyes like smoke rings, hands like dry leaves.*

*A desire in him impossible to put into words or even into waking thoughts. Searching for someone who can read him and make him real, searching for his own species – on the river banks and in the seething stinking lanes where the men and women are black and smeared. Especially the women. My camera the only safety.* His *camera. An extra eye to capture someone I know –* he *knows –* is *waiting, following behind, later. Then he can rest.*

◆

# 14

TO KEEP THE nightmares at bay I followed Val's panacea for every ill and started taking long walks. Instead of golf clubs, I had Russell, who insisted on being carried if the walk lasted longer than an hour. At first we kept to the neighbourhood, returning home while it was light, then gradually I extended our walks into the dusk, pacing down the broad streets of large-scale buildings around Bank and Monument and Tower Hill, big names with space in them. Empty as canyons at night, they gave me a sense of freedom that brought to mind the open roads of America. I became a municipal explorer, a navigator of the wilder cityscapes. I wore thicker boots, crossed bridges, time zones, walked until I wore myself out. One day, I'd just keep walking and wind up on another horizon, in another life. I called it shadow walking, a way of fighting off my shadow self.

I soon learned that the process of evolving up or down happened more quickly in my part of town; even overnight – a forced eviction to make way for another restaurant, a Pakistani's wrong turning past a skinhead pub. Darwin didn't need to go to an island in the south Pacific to discover the origin of species. He could have studied the displaced Yorkshire miner begging on the Old Street roundabout, the random beak development of Whitechapel Jew and Bangladeshi Muslim, my own mutations in Jack the Ripper territory.

Jack had always meant money as well as murder here. He was the first serial killer given star press coverage, so Dad claimed, and the success of the Ripper in selling papers launched tabloid newspapers. Jack was an icon now, part of the English Heritage industry. A 'Ripper Walking Tour' passed my front door every week. Enamel signs on nearby pubs advertised: 'Jack the Ripper Last Seen Here'. On the White Hart: 'Who was The Ripper? One suspect was George Chapman who lived in the cellar of this pub. Or was Jack the mysterious Indian Doctor?'

One night about ten days after the witness parade, with Russell stopping me at every lamp post along Leadenhall Street, I found the old mantra of victims and locations coming back: *Martha, Polly, Dark Annie, Long Liz, Catherine and Marie*, learned by heart from my father's books, as other children learn the names and dates of the Kings and Queens of England. Where Marie Kelley was dismembered and strewn about her bedroom there was now a Corporation of London car park with twenty-four-hour security cameras that might discourage the stalker of a modern Marie. Who was it had chalked on one wall: 'Thursday Girl: 8.45'? Victim or criminal?

I stalked my adopted city trying to salvage the dry old bones under its raw new skin, trying to work out who or what killed Sally, seeing in the sprayed, stencilled graffiti a code to the build-up of suppressed resentment: PAKIS OUT; PV NERVE; HOUSES AINT LOVE; NO FORCED EVICTIONS; NATIONAL FRONT RULES; WARNING THIS BUILD-ING; TO LET TO LET TO LET. Along a row where 'Soup Kitchen for the Jewish Poor' was carved in stone above a doorway that led to elegant flats for the godless rich, up Brick Lane past the eighteenth-century Huguenot chapel which became a synagogue and is now a mosque, Hanbury Street off to the left, where Annie Chapman met the Ripper by the shadow of Christchurch Hall. Two Annies: in the same year, the same hall, the matchstick girls held their strike meetings (their matches tipped in phosphorus to strike the fire of British Trade Unionism) under the auspices of Karl Marx's daughter and Annie Besant. Phosphorus, which makes plants grow; the contradictory stuff of lighthouses – and will-o'-the-wisps. Down past the old Jewish cemetery on Brady Street (above the lane where Polly was ripped open), now locked for good. The sign on its gate – IF YOU REQUIRE ENTRY, PLEASE TELE-PHONE – sparked the thought: do the dead telephone when they require a grave? How do you catalogue a place like this? All of us compost, enriching the soil: like Jack's victims; like Jack himself, for all I know. In London, even the dirt has a claim on museum space.

Reaching the Angel underground station I decided to take the tube home, and tucked Russell under my arm to ride the escalator down to the platform. The Angel, one of those stations where passengers travelling north and south share a single platform, can get very crowded if trains are delayed, as they were tonight. I could travel either direction to pick up my connection, so when a southbound train came first I hopped on and sat down with Russell beside me, both of us facing the passengers waiting to head north.

The doors closed, the train moved off, shunted a few yards up the track and stopped with a jerk. A northbound train came and went. A new group of travellers arrived, including some waiting to travel south, who peered through our windows. That's when I saw him, the second man. Only ten days since I'd told the police that I wouldn't recognise him and believed it to be true. Maybe it wasn't him. He had his head down, reading a copy of *The Sun*. Maybe the bare tits on Page Three would stop him noticing me.

With the doors still shut, it was getting hot and stuffy in our carriage. Russell gave me a brooding look.

I couldn't stop watching the man, waiting for him to see me.

The doors opened a few inches and some people stuck their fingers in, pulling them out quickly as the doors shut again. Not him, though; no sticky fingers for him. He waited, very cool. But the noise must have made him look up.

I didn't get my eyes away quickly enough.

About six feet separated us, and a pair of glass doors. It might be all right, I thought. He wouldn't remember me in this context.

The doors opened again. Russell started barking and made a dash for the door.

The man clocked me. I saw it happen: the dog, the girl, the house.

He stuck his hand in the door, just as it closed again. And

snatched his fingers out like the people around him. Not so cool, then. But he kept his eyes on me while the train pulled out of the station.

As soon as I got home I rang the police. 'Did he follow you?' asked the bored cop on the phone.

'No, I told you. He tried to but –'

'The door slammed on his fingers. Mmmm. Did he make any threats?'

'No, I keep telling you, he –'

'He watched you.' In the background I could hear a voice call out, 'The *Northern* Line? He probably wanted her seat.'

'Yes.' My voice was getting smaller with every question and answer. 'But I'm sure – I mean, I know he recognised me.'

'How do you know?'

'The way he . . .' I trailed off.

'Stared at you. And you've never seen him round your house since the murder.'

'No, but he didn't know I'd recognised him then.'

'Remind me how he knows now? Or how you know it's the same bloke, given that it's been several months since you saw him? At night, and couldn't remember what he looked like the next day.'

'My dog.'

'Your dog barked at him. A Jack Russell. So he's never barked at a stranger before?'

'Well, um, yes.' *The lady with the funny pictures*, I could imagine them saying.

'What do you expect us to do?' He had a point.

Russell and I went round to Fatbwa's for the night and ate sausages with black beans and chillies. The next day a very sceptical CID officer turned up to take more details. After he left I went down into the cellar and started to destroy my 'funny' pictures of Sally, stacking as many of the photographs as could be cut in one go with her big garden secateurs. Dissecting the second batch of pictures, the secateurs slipped and I cut through the fleshy tip of my left thumb. I stared down at the little half moon of skin lying there, a piece of me no longer mine. At that moment the doorbell rang and dizzy with shock, I wrapped a cloth around my thumb and went to open the door.

Nick stared at the blood dripping down my arm and on to my blouse. 'My God, Claire! What has happened?'

'Do you know how to stop bleeding?' I said dully and held up my bloody hand, the fingers stretched out as if to put on a glove.

He took me in his arms without saying another word, cradling the back of my head against his shoulder with his good hand. I pressed my face into him, smelling the starch his grandfather used to iron his shirt and beneath it the salty sweat of Nick himself. He pushed a cotton handkerchief into my hand, but I couldn't seem to cry, although the tears were so close that my throat hurt and my shoulders heaved. After this dry heaving had subsided, Nick led me across the garden and into his grandfather's kitchen, where he and Mr Banerji bathed and dressed my hand. They fed me with spoonfuls of sweet milky tea tasting of cardamom and insisted against all my protests that I stretch out on their prickly green nylon sofa, an Indian woollen shawl draped over me. When I worried about Russell, Mr Banerji said, 'I will send Nikhil,' and told me to lie down again. I fell into a deep sleep, the first untroubled night I'd had for weeks.

In the morning I woke to see Nick lying on the floor, stretched out on his side with his good hand under his cheek like one of those sleeping Buddhas I've seen in pictures. He might have been made of stone. There was no slack and drape to him; the flesh had been chiselled to a minimum, just enough to fit snugly around his long, narrow muscles, cleanly defined as if by some profession used to regular hard labour. Not a tall man, but built on tall lines: wide shoulders, tapered hips. In repose, his face had the kind of once-removed beauty that you see out of focus in the papers. A face defined by detachment; an expert in it, having lost a hand. He had removed his artificial arm to sleep and the puckered, shiny texture of the truncated limb reminded me of a plucked wing, a strange contrast to his toffee-coloured skin. I was just admiring how the silky hair on Nick's chest circled round his brown nipples when he opened his eyes and grinned, all trace of the icon vanishing instantly. I sat up quickly and started to fold the blanket, feeling the heat suffuse my neck and cheeks. Even my ears and eyelids were glowing red.

He watched for a few moments, amused at my efforts. 'I'll make some sweet tea,' he said, rolling himself upright in one smooth curl. 'It is my grandfather's cure for everything.'

# 15

WHILE I WAS drinking my tea, listening to the contented sounds of Russell wolfing down the remains of last night's fish curry, Nick admitted that he had a confession to make. 'Collecting Russell from your house I sneaked a look at those pictures in your cellar, the ones you were intent on chopping up.' He paused, his expression half embarrassed, and held up a large brown envelope. 'I've put them in here. Apologies for snooping. But you know, Claire, they're very very good.'

I frowned and put the teacup down. 'What are you talking about?'

'They're good – really cutting edge. I could get you an exhibition at the drop of a hat.'

'Cutting edge? Are you being funny?' It didn't feel funny.

'Sorry, I didn't mean that the way it sounded. What I meant was that my dealer, Terry Flack, the fellow who usually shows my work, would love your stuff.'

It would've been difficult to be unaware of Flack's face and reputation. For several weeks after the sensational opening of his recent exhibition, 'Breakfast Serials: Icons for the 80s' (artwork inspired by the media's portrayal of violence – especially serial killing), Flack's elfin features had been inescapable in the press. Every cultural programme on the radio seemed to have echoed with his nasal South London bleat, a real pie-and-mash hash of vowels, and in keeping with his rag trade mentality, Flack too seemed fashioned: for the fame machine, for instant consumption; a man with a bar code indelibly tattooed on his shifty little soul. The last man I wanted to get a look at the inside of my brain right now. 'I'm not an *artist*, Nick. I'm just trying to get my dreams on paper.'

'Not a bad description of art,' he said. 'But if your nights are filled with some of the other images I saw, you should stay out of that cellar.'

My dreams, however, were no longer limited to scenes of violence. Now there was snow, vertigo, heightened colours. I reeled off the night images that came to me like intuitions, 'ice caves and rivers and gardens and extraordinary architecture, a feeling of being hunted – or hunting'.

'Sounds like a bad LSD trip. Still, if you're not interested in the Flack angle, there is someone else I have in mind.' He held up his good hand before I could interrupt. 'Don't worry, he's perfectly respectable. My tame geneticist, Christian Herschel, as it happens.'

'Why would he be interested in my pictures?'

'I'm not sure he will be. But I'd like to show them to him, if you don't mind.' He patted the envelope of my pictures next to him. 'At least it will keep these safe from your deadly secateurs.'

Feeling strongly that I had to make some changes in my life, clear out the dead wood, I started with an easy option and told Darren, my hairdresser, to give me a new look. He took this as carte blanche to sheer off my Plain Jane bob and bleach it wheat-coloured, an alteration that was truly startling. When he'd finished, Darren stepped back, blinked his urban fox's eyes and wiggled his snakeskin hips like a dog on heat. 'Darling, you look marvellous! Look at that lovely long Audrey Hepburn neck you've been hiding all these years.'

I nervously rubbed my newly exposed neck where his breathy voice tickled the hairs. 'You don't think it makes me look like a kind of medieval martyr? Or maybe Mia Farrow in *Rosemary's Baby*? You know, a sort of victim?'

'No, darling. Like the sweetest little urchin, only slightly prematurely aged.'

On the Thursday Nick phoned me at work to ask if Val would give me the Friday afternoon off. 'Christian will be in town for a conference tomorrow morning. I've shown him your work and he says he'd like very much to talk to you. What d'you say?'

Val, of course, was delighted, and asked hopefully if my time off was for a romantic long weekend. I couldn't resist teasing him. 'Actually, I'm taking up golf, on your advice. Trouble is, I don't have any clubs. Think I could borrow that putting femur of yours? The one you use for teaching about epiphysis?'

He shook his head at me. 'Get out of here, you scamp, and enjoy the sunshine!'

Nick arrived at my house with two men in tow. First through the door was the geneticist, Christian Herschel. About thirty-five, with a face that only TV companies would call 'ordinary', Herschel was not easily placed in the field of science. He was a guy you'd expect to see on TV advertising sporty family cars or mid-price bubbly wine on beaches with windswept women. Not ruggedly handsome enough for Marlboro Man – more of a middle-aged Bovril Boy. 'Nick mentioned your work to me weeks ago,' he said, his voice as smooth and confident as his suit. 'He told me it was astonishing, and now that I've seen it for myself, I can certainly concur.'

The man behind Herschel was a few years older, I guessed, very tall, with chilly good looks and longish black hair brushed straight back. He had a red scarf knotted and tucked into his collarless shirt like an old-fashioned cravat, a slightly incongruous match for a kneelength Nehru jacket that looked as if it had barely survived the Indian Mutiny. For a fortyish white guy to wear it required a degree of self-esteem and disdain for convention. He lit a cigarette and inhaled deeply, eyeing me critically through the smoke.

'I should introduce you,' said Nick, grinning at the smoker. 'Claire Fleetwood, this is Jack Ironstone, just returned from the land of elephants and maharajas.'

'Jack Ironstone?' I repeated stupidly. 'My . . . cousin Jack? I mean, Alex's nephew?' Unlike mine, his was a distinguished face, the narrow, severe kind you see in museum paintings of muscular rearing horses or executions. 'I've wanted to meet you for months!' I decided not to mention the messages I'd left at his office. Let him bring the subject up.

If Jack's smile was slower than Herschel's, a charm that made you work harder, his words were friendly enough. 'Like Christian and Nick here, I am a great admirer of your work.'

'Oh. Yeah. My work,' I said, more interested in my long lost family. 'Well, you better go upstairs to the library. It's the only place I've managed to clear any space for company. I'll get the tea. The library is the first door –'

'I know where it is,' said Ironstone, and led Herschel down the narrow path between the Wardian cases. I managed to scowl mock anger at Nick as he passed. 'Why didn't you tell me you were bringing Jack Ironstone!'

'Good surprise, hmm?' He ran a hand over my new hair and down my neck. 'You look amazing.'

'So what is it that interests you in my pictures?' I asked awkwardly, when we had all arranged ourselves stiffly on the bulbous horsehair sofas like people in a Victorian studio portrait.

Herschel held up the envelope of photos that Nick had taken away with him the other morning. 'May I spread these out on –' His glance ran quickly over the tables crowded with dusty Indian knick-knacks. 'On the floor, perhaps?'

Jack Ironstone's narrow face curved up with suppressed laughter. 'Dear Aunt Alex never did believe in minimalism.'

Carefully laying out ten of my less gruesome botanical images to one side of a tigerskin's jaws, Herschel began to question me closely about the process involved in using the new hybrid X-ray camera: was the camera portable? Would it and its film survive extreme changes in temperature? I answered as well as I could. When he had established to his own satisfaction that I knew my stuff, he turned to Ironstone. 'Well, Jack, what do you think?'

Jack lit another cigarette before answering. 'Oh, I'm happy to join the Claire Fleetwood fan club.' His careful scrutiny of me indicated that the membership was not necessarily paid up as yet. 'These botanical X-rays of yours are a revolution in a field that usually relies on illustration to get such detail.' He took a long drag on his cigarette, closing his eyes this time to savour it, then leaned forward to pick up one of the pictures and study the caption I'd written on it. 'Fish, Blood & Bone?'

'An organic fertiliser,' I answered automatically. Ironstone seemed to be waiting for something more, so I went on, 'Roughly equal parts nitrogen, phosphates, and potassium – potash, that is. It's called Fish, Blood & Bone, but when you take a handful of the stuff you can't tell the difference between one ingredient and the other. It's the same colour. I just . . . I think it's funny the distinctions people make between what's acceptable and what isn't. Like, putting handfuls of ground-up animals in your garden is OK but it's disgusting to take my kind of pictures, of bones and decay. Worms are OK but not maggots.'

'And why have you juxtaposed bark from a yew tree with what appears to be the charred remains of a skeletal hand?' Herschel asked.

Unused to talking about my work in terms of its meaning, I hesitated, checking to see if he was really interested. 'Well, we used to get potash for fertilisers by burning plants. Then you've got bone meal – calcium phosphate, the form in which phosphorus appears in the earth's crust.' Which means Sally was right about it being full of blood and bones. 'Fire reduces bone to its components like calcium carbonate – carbonised, you see . . . and photosynthesis is important to the carbon cycle, and then there are carbon copies . . .' I trailed off, imagining the expression on Herschel's urbane features if I tried to wow him with my excremental garden pitch: did you know that most phosphates are now reclaimed from sewage? And that one day we might be able to recycle them into Coca Cola as well as fertilisers? Would he be entranced by the role of phosphorus in building bones?

My internal dialogue was given a footnote by Ironstone's drawl, 'And phosphorus, considering its use on nineteenth-century match heads and its references to Lucifer, is appropriate to whoever was responsible for this person's demise.'

Herschel cleared his throat. 'Miss Fleetwood – Claire, I have a proposal of work. Nothing to do with the artistic merits of your photographs, I'm afraid, and everything to do with your technical skill with botanical subjects. Perhaps Jack would like to explain, given that you two are – cousins, did you say?'

'*Distant* cousins,' Ironstone affirmed, the distinction subtle but intentional, despite his pastiche of a smile. I wondered why he was so determined to emphasise that relative distance between us.

# 16

'WHERE SHOULD I begin?' Jack asked. He inhaled deeply on his cigarette, building up an expectant theatrical pause, then began to spin a tale of hidden valleys, opium, forests in the air, lost maps, so fantastic that it might have been lifted straight from my parents' gothic library, a Quest or Wonder Voyage to a fabled land in search of marvels. After five minutes I had to ask Jack to repeat some of the details because I suspected Nick and him of having concocted an elaborate joke at my expense. No, it was all true, my cousin insisted. A few years ago he had come across some nineteenth-century files about a lost cure for cancer. Buried deep in the Fleetwood archives, which the Indian branch of UNISENS had acquired when they bought their Calcutta property, these files proved to contain early research on the alkaloids of opium poppies, studies sponsored by Philip Fleetwood, Magda's father. 'Fleetwood had a long association with Calcutta's Botanic Garden at Sibpur – Sibrapur, as it was known then,' Jack said, 'and his records were beautifully illustrated, no doubt because he used Sibpur's botanical artists, who came from a long line of artists trained by William Roxburgh.'

*Sir William Roxburgh, God of Indian botany*: I could hear Sally saying it.

'The studies recorded a miraculous green opium poppy containing a mysterious new group of alkaloids about which we know nothing,' Jack said, and the more he talked, his delivery ironic enough to make the most implausible details seem almost probable, the more I could see my father in him. Under Jack's patrician manner he had Dad's glib, actorish way with a story, the circus grifter's charm that relished a gullible audience and could make you believe in any cardhand you were dealt – whether it came from a marked deck or the bottom of the pack. 'Our magic poppy was also extraordinarily high in chlorophyll, a molecule whose photosensitive properties our current research leads us to believe may help to target tumours and protect the immune system.'

I was listening very carefully now, immunity being a subject close to my heart.

Herschel took up the story. 'The strange thing is that Fleetwood was pursuing this research a hundred years ago – and the structure of chlorophyll wasn't even discovered until the early 1900s, when Richard Willstätter managed to fracture it into its individual components for the first time. Yet Fleetwood's studies indicate that the green poppy's alkaloids, combined with chlorophyll, might help to prevent cancer. One of his botanical chemists wrote that the poppy's resin when eaten induced a state of euphoric insomnia. "Lucid dreaming", he called it.'

A phrase that could be used to describe my feelings in Joseph's cellar.

'There's more,' Herschel continued, 'the makings of a real adventure. In Fleetwood's files, Jack found rough maps to the poppy's habitat. The flower was first discovered in a triangulation of the remote border valleys between Bhutan and Tibet, and was most common in or near Tibet's Tsangpo Gorge, one of the deepest and least known gorges in the world –'

'Site of the legendary – and never discovered – Rainbow Falls,' Nick broke in, 'once believed to be as high as Niagara.'

'Which is why we're calling the expedition Xanadu,' Jack said, a hint of laughter in his voice. 'Appropriate for an expedition into a lost valley, don't you think? Of course, in these days of satellites, there's no such thing as a lost valley. We can map Xanadu and Shangri-La quite precisely.'

I was thinking that distance became a relative thing – and so did maps – when we first extended our mode of transport beyond footpower. Going to Timbuktu, for example, no longer had such legendary connotations of hellish remoteness after its location was established as a long-haul destination for 'adventure' package tours. This flexibility of space, the deceptive reality of cartography, I've been aware of ever since reading that even minor roads on the British ordnance survey maps are drawn at a scale that would make them some fifty yards wide. For me it is an indication of how much mapmakers omit in order to take into account the fact that roads are where most people use maps *from*. Step off the beaten track, so to speak, and you have to rely on a different set of markers.

'Three to four months should do it,' Jack was saying. 'One month in, six weeks to collect and catalogue the poppy, if it exists, a month to get out.' He paused to observe the effect. 'Christian is keen to get you on board.'

'On board?' I felt drugged by their fairy tale. 'It's a dream –' I stopped, figuring I should keep my own lucid dreams to myself.

Jack smiled, this version further removed from the executioner's block. 'You like the idea of a trek into the wilderness? We all do.'

'But what exactly do you need me for? I'm no scientist.'

'We have enough scientific expertise,' said Herschel. 'What we need is a photographer to catalogue what we find.'

I turned to Nick. 'Aren't you going?'

Ironstone answered for him: 'Of course. The project is right up Nick's street. And he should be bloody useful, speaking a smattering of Nepali, as well as Bengali like a native. Of course, he *is* a native.'

'But I freely admit to having nowhere near your technical expertise, Claire.'

I asked Herschel why UNISENS would be interested in an expensive expedition to search for a flower with tenuous links to a cancer cure. 'Isn't your company largely involved in developing flavours and perfumes? That's what Nick told me.'

Before he could respond, Jack broke in, 'There's big money in it, that's why! You've heard of the Madagascar periwinkle? Did you know that the vincaline derived from its seed appears in Helena Rubinstein's most expensive anti-ageing creams? And that the periwinkle's alkaloids are used all over the world to reduce cancer tumours?'

'So why isn't . . . ', I started, intending to ask, why isn't everyone in Madagascar rich? I barely managed to keep the question to myself.

Harnessing nature was no cottage industry, Herschel explained. Dior allocated twenty per cent of their research budget to ethnobotany, the study of plant's active molecules, and they were only one of many companies competing for forest people's products.

'UNISENS has funded research teams to collect samples in the jungles of Madagascar, Bengal and Guyana,' Jack said. 'We work with tribal holy men – living plant librarians, men responsible for cataloguing the forest, giving every plant a name and use.' He had first-hand experience, having been on an earlier expedition into Guyana. 'It was like the dawn of man, a botanist's dream.'

'And in the virgin forests of Guyana alone we discover twelve new useful species a year!' Herschel added. 'If only one of the many products tested turns out to be a winner, it could pay for the next ten years of research.'

Virgin forests, lost horizons: they've always held more appeal for men than for women (who are usually happy to wait until there is a bus system). In my experience, men like to plant their flagpoles where no other man has gone before, they like to think they're the first to tell you things or do things to you, so I didn't let the three men know how much of this information I had learned already. It interested me that no one had mentioned the National Cancer Institute at Bethesda, whose plant collection to test thousands of plants for anti-AIDS and anti-cancer activity had proved so effective that hundreds of medicinal species were now at risk through exploitation by pharmaceutical companies. Nor had Herschel and Jack referred to the United Nations convention that some countries, including the States, had refused to sign, largely because it contained clauses requiring profits to be shared with the species' country of origin.

'Hasn't Madagascar's rainforest been all but wiped out because of the periwinkle?' I asked as mildly as I could, not wanting to dampen Nick and his friends' enthusiasm.

Jack shrugged off my comment. 'Balance that against results,' he said. 'Thanks to drugs derived uniquely from that Madagascar periwinkle, leukemia victims now have a 99 per cent chance of remission – Hodgkin's sufferers a 70 per cent chance. You think that should be stopped just because the drug makes millions for Eli Lilly a year?'

All I knew was that as fast as we discovered miracle plants we seemed to be destroying them. And that reservation about Xanadu wasn't the only hitch to my joining the expedition. 'Believe me, what you've told me *does* sound exciting – wonderful!' I began. 'But I should tell you . . . I have identified one of the suspects in a murder case and may be called as a witness in the trial.'

'Sally Rivers,' Nick said to Jack.

'I would have to check with the police before going abroad.'

Herschel leaned forward to fix me with his convincing Bovril brown eyes. 'You don't have to decide now. What we would like is for you to come down to UNISENS, meet the other member of the expedition, get a feel for our work. Ring me as soon as you have time to think about it.' He offered a firm smile like the handshake that closes a business deal. 'But don't think about it for too long. We plan to leave by jeep from northeastern Bengal at the end of September.'

The men stood up and moved downstairs, Nick and Herschel explaining that they had to get back to the conference. As they reached the door, Jack Ironstone turned back and gave me a smile more charming than Herschel's. Before I could lose my courage in the face of this tall, distant relative, I asked if he would like to stay for a few minutes. 'Sort of chat about family connections,' I said. 'I could make some more tea. Or coffee.'

'I'd be delighted . . .' His eyes panned over the tea tray I was carrying, most of the cups still half full of my watery brew. 'And I'd prefer coffee.'

I had planned to make the coffee and bring it back up to the library, saving myself the embarrassment of letting Jack see the squalor I lived in, but he had already strolled off down the hall and opened the door to the front room. By the time I caught up, he was examining the dresser where Alex's perfume bottles mingled with her ancient jars of Gentleman's Relish. I plugged in the kettle and tried to ignore the lingering smell of greasy bacon from last night's dinner. 'Do you mind instant coffee? It's all I've got.'

'Then that's what I'll have.'

Next to the two-burner stove, reinstated in the front room since Sally's death, stood three empty cans of Heinz beans. I reached over to dispose of them while Jack wasn't looking.

'The trust doesn't oblige you to live within the confines of Aunt Alex's limited imagination, you know,' he said, twisting his head to read the headlines of Churchill's funeral.

'Interior decoration is not really my thing.'

'What about the garden?'

'I haven't been out there much since . . .'

'Since what?'

I poured water into two mugs of Nescafé, using the action as an excuse to avoid Jack's inspection. 'Since Sally's been gone.'

'Americans have such strange euphemisms for death.'

I handed Jack his cup, into which he peered bleakly, as if suspecting it of being infectious. 'Hope you take it black,' I said. 'There's no milk, unless you like it in lumps . . . And it wasn't a euphemism. I still think of her as gone. Absent. On the road. Not dead.'

'I gather you were good friends.'

I walked over to stare out at the garden. 'You were friends as well.'

His footsteps behind made me turn to face him, and for what seemed a very long time we stood immobile, figures in freeze-frame with the action still to occur. Too close together, a proximity that made me feel uncomfortable. 'Friends? With Sally?' he said. 'What makes you think so?'

'Sally told me you were. At least –'.

'She used to help my aunt, and I saw her a few times at Nick's. Hardly a friendship.'

There was a long silence while I tried to think of something more to say. 'Didn't you tell her about the connection between her family and ours . . . mine?'

'What connection?'

'Fleetwoods and Rivers, Ironstones and Rivers – I can't remember.' His blank stare made me blush. 'Sorry. I thought . . .'

Russell, sensing some tension in the air, barked, and Jack leaned over to stroke him, which prompted my shameless terrier to roll on his back and wave his legs provocatively. Tickling Russell's fat pink stomach, Jack asked if I ever got nervous, 'living alone in this big house'.

'Not really,' I said, damned if I'd give him the satisfaction of knowing that I was frightened of everything these days. 'Fatbwa – the Jamaican guy who lives here? He's told me to call him if I get jumpy. And Russell makes a hell of a noise at anything suspicious.'

Jack looked puzzled. 'Russell? Oh, the dog.' Russell pricked up his ears at this second mention of his name and tipped his head to one side in an expression of studious inquiry. 'He's not exactly a Dobermann.'

'*Get him, Russell!*'

My cousin held up both hands in a gesture of submission as Russell reluctantly leaped up and barked. 'I grant you he has a large dog's bark.' Content with his performance, Russell sat down to lick his balls, graciously allowing Jack to pick up one of the books next to my sofa, the *Medico-legal Investigation of Death*. 'Nice bedside reading,' he said, pausing over the bookmark, a list I'd made of characteristics I shared with Joseph Ironstone. Then he added as casually as if he were discussing the weather, 'So, you've identified Sally's killers?'

'One of them.'

'Have you asked for anonymity? Nick tells me most of the witnesses have.'

'There doesn't seem much point. The men who killed Sally saw me come over the wall. They know where I live, who I am.'

'They don't know yet that you picked one of them out of a

lineup. Brave girl, to stand up in court and point the finger at a murderer who might get off.'

I wished people would stop saying that. 'The police have other witnesses. DNA evidence too. And other men may be implicated, more than the two I saw.'

'Even more reason not to be involved. The killers might trade someone higher up the ladder in return for a light sentence.'

I wanted to change the subject. 'Look, um . . . I really asked you to stay . . . I really hoped you could tell me something about my – our – family.'

'Yours or mine?'

'Are they different?'

He lit a cigarette. 'You know,' he said, the parentheses of lines around his mouth widening to allow room for a faint smile, 'I'm not entirely sure.'

'So you never knew my father, then.' I said it humbly, not expecting much, given Jack's evident lack of enthusiasm for the connection between us.

'Oh yes, I knew Colin, when I was a boy. But it's been – what, thirty years since I last saw him? Whenever it was that he moved to America.'

'I don't suppose . . . that you knew his parents?' I rushed quickly on. 'The thing is, I've tried to find out about the Fleetwoods, Magda's family. I've asked the estate solicitor and I've been to Somerset House –'

'You're unlikely to find anything there. Most of Magda's family were born in India. You might find reference to them in the Oriental department of the British Library, but I doubt it. Most of the family papers were destroyed.'

'In the war?'

'Oh, it was a war, all right.' He didn't bother to clarify his comment. 'I'm surprised you haven't checked in the library here. Magda left extensive diaries. Forty years or more of them. Didn't you have any luck tracing the family story there?'

'No, well . . . as you say, there are a lot of them, and they are a little cryptic. She was a funny old broad. Her botanical notes are

103

as precise as any scientist's, but the personal insights are enigmatic at best. I was sort of hoping you could provide some of the missing details.'

'What can I tell you?' He made an elaborate play of searching his memory, before serving up a very odd scrap: 'You must know that Magda held a series of exhibitions near here in the late 1880s?' At my negative reaction he continued briskly, like a man reading from a boring but worthy sermon: 'Her mission was to bring fine art to the working classes in the East End – an area largely famous at the time for the Ripper murders. It's hard to imagine who she thought the visitors to her gallery would be, given that most of the local population consisted of dredgers, watermen and other trades connected with the river, as well as slop-workers and sweaters, dog-thieves, shoplifters, prostitutes . . . Still, Magda's plan to illuminate these people's lives was so successful that she later built a permanent gallery – destroyed by a bomb in the War, sadly.' With no inflexion in his voice, he added, 'The bomb that killed your father's parents. Colin was a year old, I believe.'

'What . . . How do you know?' I asked, trying to conceal my anger and hurt at the way he'd sprung this story on me. Was this Jack's subtly superior way of telling me that Dad's parents too had been culled from the population of dog-thieves and prostitutes?

'Con told me. Congreve, my father: Magda's son, Alexandra's brother.'

'Magda's son was your *father*? How –'

'He married very late,' Jack interjected, forestalling my next question. 'And Alex adopted your father after the bomb.' His blue eyes rested on me for a moment, something hidden in them. 'You must know that.'

'No,' I said, unable yet to grasp the fact that Jack, in his forties, could reach out and span two centuries with his hands. What was that old song? I danced with the man who danced with the girl who danced with the Prince of Wales? Here was a man capable of taking a fine grip on history and waltzing with it, yet, like my father, he chose not to. Why?

'Didn't Colin tell you anything of this?' he asked.

I shook my head. 'But why didn't her solicitors inform me?'

'They probably don't know. Alex guarded the family secrets pretty closely. I can't tell you much more, except that your father had a violent quarrel with Alex and ran away to America when he was eighteen or so. Lots of people quarrelled with Alex, including me. She was a very quarrelsome woman.'

'But . . .' I started again. 'I've been looking for family pictures –'

'You won't find them: Alex burnt them all.'

'Because of the quarrel with my father?' It seemed pretty extreme, unless other members of the family had been involved, but what did I know?

His mouth twisted in that almost amused look again. 'No. It happened long before Colin turned up.'

There was a brief silence while I waited for more details that Jack didn't seem to feel the need to offer. His reticence might be no more than a reflection of a certain kind of English upbringing, I thought; maybe he lacked my American instinct to volunteer information and advice. Still, I couldn't help wondering if there was another Jack inside this careful construction. 'Isn't there anything you remember about Dad's childhood?' I pressed, suspecting my reluctant cousin of editing the facts in the same way he edited his emotions. 'I mean, you'd think that this garden would be a sort of paradise for a kid, yet Dad never talked about it.'

Except for Dad's old picture, I remembered suddenly, *Jack's garden*.

'Yes, childhood is supposed to be paradise, isn't it?' my cousin responded, and the matter of fact way he spoke made his next words even more chilling: 'But what if it's Hell, as it was for Alex and my father? Tracing one's roots then becomes a somewhat less attractive proposition, doesn't it?'

There wasn't a lot I could say to that, and the pointed look he gave his watch put a stop to any thoughts I'd had of quizzing him about Derek Rivers's hints that the Ironstones and the Rivers were connected.

He gave the room one more cursory glance before leaving. 'I get the impression that this house is more of a campsite than a home for you, Claire.'

'Yeah, well, my family have always been part gypsy, so this Xanadu thing should suit me. I've had a lot of experience camping.'

He laughed at that, a dry little bark that made Russell prick up his ears and furrow his spotted face in a frown, worried that he'd missed something. Jack's departure left me feeling the same way.

# 17

ON SATURDAY MORNING, spurred by Jack's comments, I resolved to make a stab at the garden chaos that had resulted from weeks of neglect. My resolution was slightly delayed by a storm that started shortly before lunch, one of those summer ones you can feel bubbling and brewing long before they arrive. I remember summers like this on the prairies, storms you could see as well as feel. There would be a dark swell on the flat horizon, impossibly distant and removed in time, and we would have to race it, aiming for the nearest motel, our trailer only weatherproof up to a point. I remember opening motel room doors and pulling chairs up to watch a storm that came out of that flat prairie like the apocalypse. 'Better than any movie,' my Dad would say.

This English storm didn't have the ferocity of those violent downpours, but by late afternoon its dogged persistence had cleared the air to leave it smelling sweet, and there was a shift in the light, a rusty summer glow that filled me with anticipation. Carrying my tools back to the compost piles, I began to hack away at the weeds, watching spiders scurry off as the stalks were reduced to a brown beard of stubble. My fork, plunged into earth that was the moist and crumbly chocolate of a good fudge brownie, released a smell that reminded me of something Nick had told me about the 'green' aromas in peppers and asparagus, five-cornered ring compounds also found in cocoa products and in barbecued meat and soil. For a while I thought about how strange it was that brown earth, however newly turned, should mirror something as intensely green as a pepper or as bloody as a steak. Then the rhythms of digging wiped my head clear of everything except this dirty green smell and the afternoon sun on my head. I must have been working for about an hour when I hit something so hard it sent a jar of pain through my shoulders. Moving the fork to one side, I tried again, and once again the fork shuddered and stopped. It didn't take long to remove a foot of soil and reveal some hardwood boards beneath it, but the process of clearing enough earth to lift them out and lay them to one side occupied me until seven o'clock, at which point hunger and a sore back forced me to take a break.

Coming back to the task at seven-thirty, I began to fork over the soil, this time throwing in buckets of manure and handfuls of Fish, Blood & Bone. What should have been a tedious process gave me an absurd feeling of satisfaction as the rich dark carpet of loam rolled back behind me. The work was slow, so it wasn't until just before dusk that I uncovered the first forkful of bones. Too long in the business not to recognise them as human, I stopped immediately, wanting to drop the fork, pack up and run, escape this feeling of being trapped in a house where each step forward led back into a history girded and strutted with the remains of other people's lives. Everything has always grown like weeds here, Sally had told me, and here was the reason. My own bone garden. Val had joked about this house on the occasions he'd come round, calling it my cloister. 'Like the cloister in a medieval convent where they find the walled-up bones of saints.'

I went into the house and retrieved a small trowel and a paintbrush and used these to clear some of the earth from the bones. What I'd found was a complete skeleton, an old one, it appeared, the size and shape of the pelvis indicating a man no taller than five foot four or so, a small man who had been on his knees before the bullet through his skull had pushed him backwards.

It was getting too late to take photos, and if my guess was correct about the age of the bones, there was no urgent need to call the police. Nor was I ready for more interrogation. I simply stretched plastic garden sheets over the site and weighed the sheets down with rocks to stop any foxes or cats digging it up, then rang Val at home. His promise to come over first thing in the morning filled me with relief. 'Have you informed the police?' he asked.

'They're old bones, Val, of no interest to the cops.'

'You can always learn something from bones.'

Rising very early to go out into the garden, I tried to imagine what it would be like to wake and see the wider horizon Jack Ironstone had proposed, without this boundary of tombstone-grey estates. The expedition would start in northeastern Sikkim, he'd said, a country with the best natural passes through the Himalayas to Tibet. Its original inhabitants had named the region Nye-mae-el: Paradise. Full of otherwordly flora and fauna: red pandas, blue sheep and poppies, snow leopards – and almost seven hundred different kinds of orchid, that strangest, most Martian of plants. All I had to do before getting to Paradise was to escape from Eden.

I started working on the burial site using big paintbrushes to sweep away as much of the earth as possible from the bones. It soon became clear that this man had not been laid to rest peacefully. There were three bullet holes – one through his right hand, where it lay next to his skull, one through his right frontal bone in the upper right of his forehead, which had exited through his lower left jawbone. As if the gun had been pointing down at him.

And he had not lain here alone. Below him was the evidence of other, older bones, in geological layers like stratified lime-stone.

Val arrived at nine, an ancient canvas rucksack over his shoulder, looking like the archaeologist he had been before getting interested in forensic anthropology. From experience I knew this rucksack would contain trowels, paintbrushes, tea-spoons and fine sieves, as well as several plastic dustbin liners and a roll of Kitchenpride Press 'n' Seal watertight sandwich bags, 'For Freshness and Convenience' of any smaller remains we found. 'The police are following shortly,' he said, adding that we had the rush treatment because they hoped for a connection to Sally's death. 'I told them that the Ironstones had a long history in the bone business.' At the burial site he began to stroll around, crouching down from time to time to mutter notes into his little tape recorder. 'No fly pupal cases, so we assume the subject didn't lie above ground after being killed, and was buried subsequently more than a few inches deep.'

'Can you tell anything from the three bullet holes?'

'Four.' Val pointed out a small fracture that I had missed on the man's right thigh bone. 'Judging by the angle, I think the first bullet hit here, while the man was standing, and passed through the thigh, chipping and fracturing the bone as it did so, bringing him to his knees.' He indicated the knee bones, set more deeply into the earth than the shoulders.

'He's fallen at an odd angle.'

Val nodded thoughtfully. 'He has his back to his killer, perhaps, when he hears something that makes him spin round. You see how the right thigh is well forward of the left and the bones of the feet are strangely twisted under the torso? Then, before he has time to face his attacker completely, the bullet through his thigh brings him down, and he braces himself with his left hand behind him as he falls – see how deeply embedded in the earth the left hand bones are.'

He leaned forward to examine the right hand. 'I am conjecturing, but I believe we will find that the same bullet passes through hand and skull.' He used a small paintbrush as a pointer to indicate details. 'See the angle, and the shattered bones of the fingers? He puts his hand – so.' Val looked up at me, shielding his face with his hand, the palm turned outwards. 'Perhaps pleading for his killer to stop. Or simply trying to protect himself. It's a natural, if rather pointless instinct.

'The second bullet then passes through his hand, enters here on the right and travels upward through the skull to leave this exit wound – a rather neat one, but for the bevelling of the bone surfaces and these slight fractures to the immediate skull area.' He stood up, brushing earth off his knees. 'As soon as we get this gridded up and photographed we can have a look for the bullets.'

His expression was pleasantly eager as he went to get his graph paper and wire. 'Excellent bones!' he called back, and returned, still talking, 'We might be able to keep this top skeleton for a teaching specimen.'

Starting at the skull's dome, we began to establish a grid system, pegging the ground around the site and stretching across fine wires between the pegs. 'Bangladesh was such a marvellous source for skeletons,' Val sighed. 'Now we have to settle for plastic – and even that's expensive. Over four hundred pounds for a plastic skeleton – not even deluxe quality!'

Smothering a grin at a complaint I'd heard many times before, I began taking pictures as Val worked. Luckily, my fork had struck at an angle, only shaving the edge of the skull. The earth around had protected it like a boxer's head gear.

'Have you got a water source nearby?' Val asked, getting out one of the mesh screens he uses on smaller sites to wash soil through.

I unrolled the hose and brought it within reach.

In a neat row next to him Val laid various sizes of spades and trowels, a couple of paintbrushes to brush away earth from the more delicate bones, and a few teaspoons. Working slowly and patiently, as he always did, he began measuring the position of the body and marking it on his pad of graph paper, like an artist sizing up a rough sketch to make a more monumental work.

A cop arrived about halfway through this process and had a look at the bullet we'd found. 'Probably from an old handgun of military make,' he said, content to trust Val's assurance that these bones were too old to be related to any unsolved crimes of the last fifty years. He left after we promised to send him a copy of our finished report.

'Interesting,' Val said, as he used one of his teaspoons to scoop earth away from the top skeleton's pelvic region. 'I want a close-up of this. The contents of the fellow's jacket pocket

remained intact until the fabric rotted and they fell through.'
When I'd finished shooting, Val took a closer look. 'What have
we got – a few odd old coins, a locket perhaps . . .' He spat on
its surface and rubbed away the dirt. 'Containing what might
be hair. And what appears to be an old chewing tobacco tin.'
He handed me a small, rusted box bearing the brandname
'Century'.

Prised open, it revealed thousands of tiny shot-grey seeds.
'Poppies?' I asked.

'Perhaps.'

He began sorting through the soil immediately below. A few
of the bones were from human skeletons, but most of them
Val suspected to be the remains of animals – cows, pigs, a lot
of horses. 'I wouldn't be at all surprised if we've uncovered
that butcher's pile you told me your relative Luther bought up.
A good place to hide your murder victim, wouldn't you say?'
He held up a heavy leg bone and pointed to the saw marks on
it. 'A butcher's cleaver made that, if I'm not very much
mistaken.'

We've photographed so many bones over the years that I
carry their hieroglyphics in my head. Just as hikers learn the
symbolic patterns used in a map to indicate mountains and
rivers, I can differentiate between the overlapping arcs of the
oscillating saw, the fine and straight cuts from a bandsaw, the
tiny squares produced by a hacksaw. 'But what about the human
remains?' I asked him.

'Apart from that top skeleton, they're jumbled up with the
animal bones. It's possible that the butcher's digging disturbed
an older burial site. Or the murderer's did!' He rocked back on
his heels to study the yew tree shading our work. 'You've heard
of the ancient tradition of burying bodies beneath a yew's roots?
Yew trees that predate the churchyards in which they grow are
often found to have ancient bones tangled in their root balls, the
earliest dating from about AD 1200, I believe. Most of the
human bones here would seem to be more recent, but there may
be a connection.'

I rested my hand on the mossy side of the hollow trunk,

where its bark flowed down in fingers of green into the earth. 'How old do you think this beauty is?'

'Impossible to tell. They lose their heartwood to fungal decay, as your tree has, at around five hundred years, and from then ring-dating is impossible. You find this typical formation of an outer cylinder of white wood supporting the canopy, while the exterior is repeatedly encased with the lava flow of new growth.' He said that yews, like banyan trees, had the ability to send down aerial roots, except that in the yew's case these were *inside* the hollow trunk, the tree regenerating itself from the heart out. Once the branches touched ground they would root, again like the banyan, and produce a family circle of clones.

'Isn't there any way of dating it?' I asked. My family tree.

'The only sure way is by records. Parish registers are good sources. The Domesday Book even mentions such trees. Occasionally you can date them from the age and position of the bones tangled in their roots.'

But the really ancient yews predated human records. In Scotland Val had walked around a huge, shattered leviathan believed to be the oldest piece of vegetation on earth. Perhaps 5000 years old, perhaps twice that, its twin trunks rose together from a united root system. The hollow centre of another yew he'd seen had widened as it grew so that its girth now measured fifty-two feet, yet of the tree itself no more remained than a wooden henge of silver tombstones. 'For all the world like our ancient rings of standing stones,' he said. 'And within this tree it's believed that the Druids used to gather just as they did at Avebury and Stonehenge. Yews have always been linked with death and rebirth.'

Using an axe to chop through some of the roots below the top dressing of whole bones, we found more remains, an ossified mosaic of splinters and flakes – and with this skeletal dandruff the birds arrived, delighted at the banquet of grubs and bugs we had turned over. We spent the whole day documenting my bone garden. When Val finally left, his rucksack full, I took a peanut butter sandwich to bed and wound up letting Russell finish it, while around me the house creaked and groaned as it settled into the London clay. Subsidence, they call it here, each house a sinking ship. I fell asleep planning my escape from the wreck.

# 18

THE UNISENS COMPLEX had the kind of corporate anonymity that is in itself an identity. Linked pods of low, white, rectangular buildings resembling a scattered handful of huge business envelopes yet to be addressed, the complex extended across acres of undulating countryside, each geographic ripple concealing another pod, and another, with the buildings' separate functions delineated by alphabetical signs: Block B, Block C2. Everything on the site was synthetic except for the trees, and they looked uneasy, dotting the site stiffly, scaled-up versions of the plastic plants in architects' models. It made even more surprising the transition to Christian Herschel's office, where personality was stamped like a monogram on a piece of expensive luggage from the great age of travel, with that same humidor smell of leather and wood polished by decades of other people's humility. I felt dwarfed by the walls of hand-drawn maps, records of an earlier empire's colonial takeover bid, by Herschel's framed citations and qualifications, by the scale of his desk, a walnut fortress perfectly suited to this room redolent of grand decisions and memberships in clubs that exclude women.

Both Christian Herschel and Jack Ironstone stood up to greet me, Herschel offering his wide TV presenter's smile, Jack slicing off a narrower version of welcome. I wished desperately for Nick as moral support, but he was long gone: off to India the previous week to install an exhibition in Delhi. After that he was travelling to the government opium plantations near Patna, in Bihar, the first stage of work for his major installation piece based on photos and sound recordings about the green poppy.

I wanted to plead a migraine and escape – and would have, if it hadn't been for the huge grin on the face of a man standing next to Jack. Introduced as Dr Benjamin Fisk, the final member of the expedition, he had the legs of a short thin man, the torso of a tall stout one, and a happily messy air that carried through from his Greenpeace T-shirt and his badly shaved peach of a face to his wispy but still plentiful greyish hair.

'Ben is a specialist in teratology from the University of Bristol,' said Herschel.

At the word 'teratology' Fisk started speaking fast: 'Don't worry if you don't know what it means, Claire. You're not alone.' His American vowels immediately made me feel more relaxed. 'A teratologist is a guy who studies the biology of congenital malformations. From the Greek *teratos* or *teras*, meaning monster. That's how you get teratology, which in addition to my form of cancer studies can also mean the mythology relating to fantastic creatures –'

'Ben is an expert on Tibetology and other comparative mythologies,' Jack said, damming the American's river of words. 'Excuse me, comparative *religions* – as well as being the country's leading expert on the teratoma form of cancer.'

'I do know something about teratoma,' I said cautiously, remembering Magda's diaries. 'If it has anything to do with vegetable teratology.'

Ben grinned. 'You bet it does! Both are monstrous mutations! Teratocarcinoma is a tumour resembling a monster or mal-formed baby, mostly found in the gonads. You could say that I've always been interested in *ball* games!' Herschel's wince at the bad joke had no effect on Fisk. 'A teratocarcinoma has cells arranged in tissues which may form primitive organs like spinal cord, hair, teeth. It happens when the genetic wiring short-circuits, endlessly repeating the same anatomical phrase. The most extreme forms of teratoma resemble embryos.' He paused for breath. 'I'm also an amateur botanist –'

Jack held up a hand with a traffic policeman's authority and gestured across the huge desk. 'Which is how Ben came to meet Chris, our chlorophyll expert.'

'The Green Man himself!' added Fisk, 'What a mythic troupe we are to set off on this crusade! The Holy Grail: that's what the press is calling the Human Genome Project, did you know, Claire?'

Val had told me about this Human Genome Project, an organisation involved in mapping the order in which the three thousand million DNA letters needed to make us human are arranged. I knew that to set up grid lines across this genetic map the HGP was using blood from closed communities like the Mormons, some of the largest extended families in the world. That was about the limit of my knowledge, but it was enough to make Fisk's comment puzzling.

'Ben's little joke, Claire,' Herschel cut in smoothly. 'The discovery of our poppy was linked to the Great Trigonometrical Survey of India in the 1800s, which Ben insists on equating with the Genome Project.'

'Like any mapping enterprise,' Ben added, 'so the mappers can control what they map. This time it's our insides. Geneticists are the twentieth century's answer to Victorian empire-builders.'

Herschel, his features rippling with controlled impatience, suggested that perhaps this discussion could be postponed until I had seen more of UNISENS. We were led through several indistinguishable rooms of modular furniture and flowcharts and soothing pastel carpets, where I got shocks off any metal I touched, into a laboratory densely packed with white-coated men. These men, Herschel explained, were intent on analysing 7000 existing aromas and flavours a year. 'All the information is stored in our molecular library to be accessed later if we find a particular molecule keeps cropping up in the human pleasure zone. We have the largest library in the world devoted to breaking down smells.'

'How do you break down a smell?' I asked. 'It's so ephemeral.'

'Come and have a look,' he said, guiding us down bleached corridors where smells were the paint on the walls, so volatile and invasive that they were impossible to contain in test tubes.

Vanilla pursued you into stainless steel rooms full of test tubes and electronic gadgets, pipe tobacco cropped up in the ladies' room, bananas slipped from under the door to the men's urinals. Herschel proudly showed me a rose trapped in a bell jar as if in an oxygen tank, pipes leading in and pipes leading out, all being pumped into a cartridge attached to a chromatography unit. An image of those shaved rabbits used for testing pharmaceuticals flashed into my mind, along with another memory, too far back to access, and I had the crazy urge to smash the jar and free the hostage (The first horticultural terrorist! The Flower Liberation Front!).

'This is what we will use on our green poppy if we find it,' Herschel was saying. 'Chromatography combined with a mass spectrometer, an instrument which breaks down molecules into fragments. Then we'll apply NMR –' At my dizzy expression Herschel stopped to search his brain for the idiot's guide to science. 'NMR: Nuclear Magnetic Resonance. Another technique for deciding what a molecule is.' He pointed to one pipe attached to the rose and continued. 'Imagine this flower as a car. This pipe lets air in, this other pipe pumps out the rose's volatile aromas, whose cells can later be read by chromatography or a mass spectrometer. Think of them as carwreckers' yards which break down the car into its separate parts, telling you if the car had five wheels, say, while NMR can tell you which wheel was spare. The problem is that NMR requires a substantial quantity for an analysis. And while we suspect that our green poppy's ability to boost the immune system depends on the freshness of its chlorophyll, the potent part of the poppy's chlorophyll might be as scarce as the molecule that makes fresh raspberries taste fresh rather than artificial –'

The more he talked, the more that other image, halfway between farce and tragedy, stirred on the edge of my consciousness.

'For comparison, imagine a raspberry the size of a swimming pool,' Herschel went on patiently, 'and the "fresh" molecule as a grain of sand dropped into it. Now let me show you our olfactometer – that's our sniffing outlet.'

Ben Fisk could barely contain himself: 'An olfactometer! Like the orgasmatron for synthetic orgasms Woody Allen had in – what was that movie, Jack?'

Frowning at the irrepressible Fisk, Herschel took us swiftly into a laboratory with sniffing outlets, where Fisk, Jack and I pressed our faces into clear plastic masks which channelled a pungent smell into our noses. Fisk roared, 'Roast chicken!' Jack, eyes half-closed, murmured, 'Butter browning.'

'And yours, Claire?' asked Herschel. 'All three are related.'

I'd smelled it a thousand times. 'Rotting flesh.' That point when the skin is so rotten it slips from our skeletons like cast-off clothing.

Herschel clapped his hand lightly on my back. 'Exactly! Butyric acid, the syrupy fat found in rancid butter – and also in corpses, as you point out. Of course, dead bodies also smell of methane gas, but butyric acids are the ones that make our stomachs churn.'

'What's the purpose of studying disgusting smells?' I asked Jack.

'So that our company can manufacture pleasant disguises for the unpleasant aromas,' he answered. 'Useful in a job like yours, don't you think?'

The bad smell still present, I thought, but buried. Again there was that twinge of a lost memory nagging at me like a mild back pain I'd lived with for a long time.

'We have an interesting laboratory in the basement,' Herschel said. 'Our "evaluation chambers", where Jack used to work before his remarkable discovery in Calcutta. He was an expert on disguising fetid smells.'

'Oh yes,' Jack said, 'I was an expert on all our least well-kept bodily secrets and every pungent molecule used to disguise them. I can play you multiple tunes on the theme of petty stinks – the yeasty scent of clean armpits, the Roquefort reek of athlete's foot.'

The evaluation chambers turned out to be air-tight glass cubicles resembling shower stalls, within each stall a toilet. 'This is a first for me, Chris,' Ben Fisk said. 'So what happens here in the toilet room? Your research team takes a dump and then sniffs it?'

'More sophisticated than that,' the geneticist said tightly. 'An excremental – if artificial – liquid is poured into the toilet and flushed away, and then we analyse which of our products remove the less acceptable aromas left behind.'

'An orifice of armpit sniffers!' Fisk roared, and leaned back so far in a great belly laugh that he accidentally knocked the button setting all the toilets flushing.

UNISENS held copyright on synthetic versions of cherry pipe tobacco, jasmine, coffee; they produced a spray that made you think bread was baking, and sold it to supermarkets who pumped it out of their air vents on to the streets to entice customers. A 'brown' smell, Herschel called it. The smell of colours, which was how many smells were classified, was Jack's speciality. He worked in a room devoted to green in every shade from apples to parsley. Most of the subtler shades were overpowered by the pyrazines, compounds so powerful that even though they were tightly sealed in vacuum-formed foam, they still filled the air with the pungent vegetal aroma of boiled cabbage and green pepper.

Ben wrinkled his nose. 'What a stink!'

'It's very strong, I agree,' said Herschel, 'like many of our more volatile compounds.' He showed us one of the company's classy leather travelling cases for sample products, its stoppered glass tubes containing chemical aromas or flavours in the form of clear liquids, crystals, the white powders of detergent samples.

'Ideal for drug-smugglers,' Ben Fisk joked. 'Not only do your employees have a legitimate reason to travel with white powder to and from Asia and the States, they are obliged to pay frequent visits to the opiates' source – and to travel with smells that would disguise the drugs from the most sensitive customs dog's nose!'

Jack remained silent through this exchange, until Herschel asked him to brief me on the poppy experiments, at which point his lean face lit up for the first time. 'Measurable delight,' my cousin responded immediately. That was what he'd found when he'd exposed tumorous lab mice to the increased sensory level of chlorophyll the Fleetwood botanists claimed to be present in the green poppy. And measurable delight is what Jack thought boosted the immune system, stopped the rot, broke the crab's back. 'How do you measure delight?' I asked.

By the dilation of a pupil, Jack told me, and the increased beat of the pulse. 'At first we thought it might be chlorophyll's photodestructive ability that was the key, but now we think the answer lies in the colour itself, the smell and flavour of green, in combination with an alkaloid extracted from the green poppy, which the notes said produced a state of lucid dreaming. We are still trying to analyse what alkaloid it was.' He glanced quickly at Herschel and away again. 'Of course, it's all theoretical until we find the poppy itself, but I've repeated the nineteenth-century experiments as closely as I can using a synthetic compound based on alkaloids taken from the opium poppy and mixed with chlorophyll and hexanal.'

'Hexanal?' Ben said. 'That's interesting.'

Hexanal was the fugitive fresh 'green' note in many vegetables and fruits, Jack explained to me. 'We've tried different experiments – injecting tumours with this synthetic compound, feeding rats on a high-chlorophyll diet, filling the air around them with pyrazines. Not all trials have been successful, but we found that a "green" atmosphere noticeably diminished levels of stress – and in a few mice the tumours went into remission.'

'But it's still too early to make any conclusions, isn't it?' I said. 'If you haven't tried this out on people?'

Herschel spoke up. 'Actually, Jack *has* done some trials.' He paused. 'In India.'

'I didn't know you'd got that far, Chris,' Ben said. He gave Herschel a shrewd look. 'Why India? Easier to get volunteers?'

Herschel shrugged off the comment. 'The trials are very recent, but in a series of experiments where fifty per cent of the test cases were given a placebo, the cases receiving Jack's compound are showing some improvement.'

'What about the others?' I asked.

Herschel looked blank. 'The others?'

'The ones who had the placebos. Have you kept in touch with them?'

'I imagine the pharmacist's assistant has. She's the only one with the patients' names. The scientists involved used numbers, to preclude any chance of fraud. Nothing unusual about it. Standard procedure with any form of drug testing.'

And then I had it. I'd fixed it, that aching, elusive image.

# 19

FIXED AND PRINTED on my retina: Robin with an oxygen mask on his face that made him look like Darth Vader, tubes in his nose, bruises up his arms where the IV had been stuck in him again and again as if he were some kind of addict. Or a rabbit in a test experiment. Robin, when he was still well enough to sit up and look out the window on to the hospital carpark, saying that he'd really like a walk in the woods. 'Some grass and green leaves. That and a smoke.'

The week before he died, he gave me a poem scribbled down with the help of one of the nurses:

*Here lies Robin, but not Robin Hood,*
*Here lies Robin that never was good,*
*Here lies Robin that God has forsaken,*
*Here lies Robin the Devil has taken.*

'My epitaph,' he grinned, and waved a languid hand at his hospital smock, the kind open down the back. 'Does it do me justice? I think it lacks a little je ne sais *quair*, don't you? But so handy for easy access.'

I turned over the paper with its poem and on the back of it there was a list of names. First names, nothing else: Calvin, Freddie, Adam, Mel, Carlo, Marcus, Juan, Jack, Jo-Bob, Kevin, Randy, Jeremy, Genji. Like those lists parents-to-be make when they're expecting a boy. A cross-section of all America's creeds and affiliations. 'Who are –' I started.

'What?'

'These. These names.'

'They're –' His voice sounded funny through the mask.

'They're what, Robin?'

'They're –' He took a deep, harsh breath.

'What do you want me to do, Robin – call them?'

'No.'

'You want me to call them, I can call them, Robin. I'm happy to do that.'

'No you can't.'

'No, really, I don't mind! I can call them, tell them that you're . . . that you've got . . . that they should, you know, whatever. Take precautions. I can call, Robin, but I need their phone numbers.'

He took off his mask. 'YOU CAN'T FUCKING CALL THEM!' A voice up from somewhere I don't know, a life I can't reach or share any more.

He put the mask on again for a long minute and when he took it off his voice was back to normal, or as close to normal as it got. 'You can't call them, Claire-bear, because they're all dead.'

They had been on the AIDS ward together, he said. Each agreed to take part in a clinical trial on a new immune-deficiency drug. Half were given placebos and died. Half lived. They didn't live long – a few months – or well, but they lived. 'It was all in the *strictest* secrecy, darling. None of us knew who got the placebo and who didn't.' The scientists doing the tests were given folders with study numbers, no names. Anonymity was necessary to avoid the risk of data being falsified. 'Lots of incentive to cheat, Claire. *Big* profits to be made from us naughty boys.'

After the deaths of those test cases who had received placebos Robin thought that it couldn't hurt to keep a record. 'The names of all the boys who auditioned and never made it to opening night,' he said. My brother, the drama queen, who never made it as far as off off Broadway, but still managed to perform his last big scene with real style. Even when he was dying, really sick unto death, he had to play Camille . . . I told him, 'Robin you *are* dying now, you don't have to put on this act.' I was so mad at him when he died, when he left me behind

124

for good. One minute he was here, the next he'd gone. He had – what do they call it? – *passed away*. As if he slipped past without me noticing. No goodbye. Passed on. Like a dress that no longer fits. One of the last things he said to me, I swear to God: 'Lipstick!' How do you pick up that baton and run with it? *Lipstick*: I mean, what was he hoping to cover up at that late date?

I must have been silent for too long, because I became aware that the three men were staring at me. 'Sorry, what did you say, Doctor, I mean Professor Herschel?' Which was it?

'Call me Christian or Chris, please. I was saying that you might like to see some of the background material that Jack has managed to find on this poppy.'

'Oh yes, of course.'

With the exception of one illustrated notebook written in a script even Ben couldn't identify (the closest he got was eastern Tibet), much of the work Jack had collected consisted of nineteenth-century technical drawings relating to trials done on opium poppies, first at the Fleetwood Factory and later at the Calcutta Botanic Gardens. A team of native artists and botanists had been responsible, all of them anonymous, Jack claimed. Which seemed odd, because I spotted the tiny initials 'AR' woven into the designs of the six watercolours I liked best. 'Who was AR?' I asked Jack, knowing that even without that almost invisible signature I would recognise the lively brushmarks of this artist again.

'AR?' said Christian. 'Where? I can't see it.'

'No idea,' Jack replied quickly. His abruptness suggested that I had wrongly accused him of something. 'They are part of a series of scientific drawings I tracked down while researching opium alkaloids in Calcutta.'

'But these aren't exactly scientific. Here you've got two different flowers from different seasons sharing a common root system.'

Jack approached my comment with a haughty look that I didn't think it deserved. 'The artists who emerged from Hindu and Mogul traditions in India, as these did, seldom distinguished between past and present,' he said. 'Or they didn't until they were retrained to suit their new British patrons.'

I looked closely at another of AR's paintings, even less scientific. A paper garden as fine as any Sally and I had seen at Kew, it showed the detail of a tomb almost obscured by green poppies.

'Burial place of the Mogul Jahangir's great love, Nur Jahan,' Ben said softly, dropping the comic mask he had been wearing all afternoon. 'A woman who rose to power through her husband's weakness for opium, and was as famed for poetry as she was for politics.'

'There speaks the teratologist,' said Jack.

Ben smiled. 'It's a wondrous tale, all right. Nur Jahan designed both Jahangir's tomb and her own, did you know? And on her tomb she had inscribed an epitaph she'd written herself, the one this artist has painted. A plea for anonymity.' He recited the lines slowly, as if he were composing them himself:

Upon my grave when I am dead,
No lamp shall burn nor jasmine spread,
No candle's pale, unsteady flame,
Serve as reminder of my fame,
And nor shall bulbuls' cries at dawn,
Tell all the world that I am gone.

'It's always a good idea to write your own epitaph,' Jack said.

Trailing behind my tall cousin on the way back to Herschel's office I was hoping to initiate some kind of personal conversation, but the only way to get him on his own was to follow him outside when he went for a smoke, a ruse that Jack seemed not to appreciate. He was even less pleased when I started asking how he'd first got interested in the opium poppy. He stubbed out one cigarette before answering, lit a new one. 'Opium has a long history in our family, didn't you know?' His taut face loosened slightly. 'Particularly on the Fleetwood side.'

'Could I find out more about the Fleetwoods in India?' I asked quickly, feeling like an irritating terrier snapping at his heels. 'I was thinking of maybe going there first – to Calcutta, I mean – to do some digging around before joining you in Kalimpong. That is, if I decide to hitch up with your expedition.'

'You might not like the Fleetwoods you dig up.'

'What do you mean?' It was the Ironstones who worried me, Joseph's side. But I couldn't say that to Jack. 'Most people are interested in their roots, whatever turns up.'

He dropped his cigarette on the ground and rubbed it out elaborately with his foot. 'Your father doesn't seem to have been, does he? And actually, I've felt oppressed by history all my life, the way other people are by the weather.' The expression on his face mocked my enthusiasm. 'Dig up the Fleetwood family tree, Claire, and what you will find is opium, opium and more opium.'

'But it's kind of exciting, the opium trade, isn't it?'

'You have a romantic view of it. Perhaps in a hundred years people will believe the same about the trade in heroin.'

'Yeah, well, heroin, that's different.'

'Is it?'

Jack said he could tell me all I needed to know about opium's roots, 'The roots of the Fleetwood family. It might save you some time.' He had the facts at his fingertips, so he claimed.

The facts: most of the artists and authors and poets (not to mention the farm workers and prostitutes) who gave us our romantic vision of the eighteenth and nineteenth centuries were at some time or other drugged to the eyeballs. We got their books on the school curriculum, but not their source of inspiration.

The facts: sales of laudanum were always heavy on a Saturday night in the Norfolk fens. In the nineteenth century, come Saturday, they were sure of a high old time.

The facts: soldiers came back from the American Civil War as morphine laudanum opium addicts. It got rid of the runs, not to mention the blood in their heads. They never told us that in the history books. Nor did they mention the summer of 1971, when army medical officers reckoned that up to 37,000 serving troopers in Vietnam were heroin addicts. Real Super Troopers. War memories of the ones who came back are full of black holes.

Try putting opium smoke under a microscope, Jack told me. It's possible. 'You find Xanadu.'

'What do you mean?' I asked him. 'You mean that what you're telling me has something to do with the expedition?'

'I mean that we're still not sure if it was the chlorophyll or the opium derivative that caused the measurable delight in Fleetwood's test cases. We don't know why the poppy research was terminated – whether it was because of Fleetwood's death in 1888 or for another, more sinister reason.' First, I had to understand about opium, Jack explained. 'Forget all its meconic, sulphuric, lactic acids, its blend of sugars and proteins.' What mattered were its alkaloids, chemicals so complex that it was amazing they were produced by simple plants like poppies; strange compounds, frequently hallucinogenic, often toxic. The reason for alkaloids' presence in plants remained a mystery. A means of discouraging animals and insects from feeding on plants, that was one theory. 'Yet some insects are able to metabolise highly toxic alkaloids,' Jack went on, almost smiling. 'Perhaps the insects even *need* the toxins to survive. It's a complicated symbiotic relationship.' Like humans' equally symbiotic relationship with alkaloids. Caffeine, nicotine, quinine, strychnine, mescaline, codeine: the list went on and on; beneficial on one side, harmful on the other.

'And then there's the Ironstone family favourite – morphine, from which we make heroin.' Jack didn't give me time to ask what he meant. 'What are the properties morphine shares with all alkaloids? It contains nitrogen – and it has a bitter taste. Study the history of opium if you want to know more about our family history, our bitter history. You'll find that I'm not the first member of the family to be employed in disguising bad smells. When the East India Company needed middlemen to ship the drug to China illegally – so that the Company wouldn't be, as its directors put it, "exposed to the disgrace of engaging in illicit commerce" – the Fleetwoods got in at the start. An early form of money laundering. Laundrymen, that's what they were, precursors to the arms dealers and pharmaceutical companies who protect our government today from getting its hands dirty.'

Bones on one side, drugs on the other. That was our inheritance, if Jack was to be believed.

# 20

I WATCHED THE summer fields of southeast England unroll past the train window like a new quilt on an old bed, a tamed landscape where 'green field sites' equalled potential for building developers, where every road implied the division of property: that's your tree, this is mine. In that wilder landscape Jack had described, we would have to wash in cold water, wear the same clothes for weeks on end; we would be climbing up out of subtropical valleys of giant ferns through ten thousand feet of rhododendron forests and into mountain passes where alpine flowers were miniaturised by lack of oxygen, then back down again into temperate meadows of apple and apricot and walnut trees. What would that high, thin air smell of, taste of?

Even more than the artificial air at UNISENS, it was the disturbing reminders of Robin that had made me decide to cut short my visit. After dinner, against all the men's protests – and despite the fact that my overnight visit had been arranged for the last ten days – I'd had enough of the hospital atmosphere and made excuses to leave. 'Worried about my dog,' I lied (Russell was still at Eden). 'He hates kennels.' In fact, although I liked Ben Fisk very much, and trusted that Christian and Jack were admirable scientists, there was something about the UNISENS expedition that didn't feel right to me.

It was one of those nights when you miss every connection. Delays on the Northern Line, 'due to a person under the train', as the loudspeaker put it ominously; desperate crowds at King's Cross, so many that it took three full trains going by before I could squeeze on; almost midnight by the time I turned the key in Eden's lock. Still, Russell would be glad I was back early.

I'd left him a light on and a meaty hambone from a butcher who was fond of him, and Fatbwa had promised to take him for a walk. 'Russell!' I called out, kicking the door shut and switching on the lights. 'Russell!'

A strange sound from the next floor, but no Russell. The thought hit me that he might be sick. I threw down my bag and ran up the stairs.

There were two men. I didn't recognise either of them, but I saw the hundreds of books they had pulled off the shelves and torn open to throw on the floor. I can't remember if I made a noise, turning and tripping and sliding back down the stairs. On my bum, on my knees, falling like nightmares from childhood, wanting to fly and being tied to the ground, earthbound while the Ripper gets closer, Jack gets closer, his hand reaching out, you wake up just before he gets you.

The fucking front door is deadlocked.

Turning down the hall. Three steps and that's when I screamed. Something is there, something bloody you see by the side of the road and turn away don't look it's too late to do anything change the subject kind of dead thing.

I didn't hear the man hit me.

'Russell.' I called out to Fatbwa when I regained consciousness.

'You were scared, hon'. It was jus' a big piece of poison meat those bastards brought for him, along with the towel it was wrapped up in. Russell was kickin' up such a fuss after you left that I carried him round here.' It was Russell's barking that woke Fatbwa and brought him running down his path and into the central garden. By then the men were gone. There was nothing to do but call the police and the ambulance to take me to casualty, where Fatbwa waited while the doctor X-rayed my head, and made sure that I was well enough to go home.

The police were still there when we got back, but they didn't hold out much hope of catching the men responsible. 'You must have surprised them,' one cop said. 'It's lucky in a way you came back when you did or the loss could've been much worse. Apart from your head. And luckier still that your b–' he was going to say 'black' but stuttered it into 'b-big friend scared them off.'

I wasn't sorry when Fatbwa insisted on spending the night in a chair next to my sofa. He was still asleep when the first lightning woke me and lit the room, bright as movie lights. I managed only one count before the thunder broke to roll across the roof. That first bolt must have hit something. The night was suddenly black, the streetlights knocked out. Russell started barking and Fatbwa's eyes opened wide. 'Shit! What the fu–'

Then again, that spectacular, unearthly light, a giant camera flashing everything to white. This time there was no pause before the hammer blow of thunder. I heard another crack and a wrenching, grinding, tearing sound from the garden. Before Fatbwa could stop me I was off the sofa and at the back window staring out to where the yew tree stood, the backbone of its trunk flexed. Our old leviathan was raising itself arthritically, poised to dive, and above it, falling back on to it, sprayed a white sleet of femurs, tibias, radii, skulls, jawbones, hips, ribcages, vertebrae. All the butcher's bones.

I sensed Fatbwa join me. Neither of us could look away. His fingers dug into my shoulder. 'Jesus!'

'That's enough,' I said, 'I've got the message, God. Or whoever's sending it. I'm outta here.'

'It is impossible to calculate the loss of our yew tree,' Mr Banerji told me, a man giving the land a voice, a list of its gains and losses. The yew was living history, he said, a relic that can't be collected and stored for posterity in a museum – at least not in our lifetime. No doubt some future generation will manage it ('Look, dear: that's a tree. We used to have them for shade before we invented malls'). You can't reconstruct a six-hundred-year-old yew tree. And how do you mourn it? What arboreal funeral home do you call?

It lay on the grass long enough to leave one of those phantom yellow shadows that Nick photographs. One day it was there, the next it was gone.

First the man from my London Borough Planning Control Division certified that Listed Tree number 3265 on his Conservation Survey could not be saved. Its roots had probably been loosened by the big storm last year, he said, and further loosened by the digging Val and I had done. Next, RMS Tree Services sent me a quote for removing it, which the solicitor had to approve. Finally, the tree surgeons arrived, quiet men who warned me that I would lose not only the tree but all the small ferns and wildwood plants around it. 'Don't like to cut a yew tree.' The older man shook his head.

'It's bad luck,' said his assistant.

I watched them amputate the smaller roots and branches one by one before the big saws started up, high-pitched as dentist drills, and the machine to suck the remaining roots out of the ground. It left a deep ragged hole like the bloody gap where a wisdom tooth has been extracted, the scar of our impermanent archive of – what did Jack call it? Measurable delight?

'Regular Sherwood Forest, this corner, wasn't it?' said the older of the tree surgeons as they were leaving. He added a bone of consolation. 'Some good news, though. We've taken a few yew cuttings for you. Should root, if you pot 'em up, keep 'em watered.'

'How soon will they be trees?'

'Oh, about the time of the second coming,' joked his younger partner.

A few weeks later I went to Mustafa to tell him that I would be going on a journey.

'That is good,' he said. 'You need a rest. Where are you going?'

'To Calcutta first, to trace some family roots. Then northeast, to join the Xanadu expedition I told you about, into some remote valleys of Tibet.'

'Remote valleys in Tibet,' he said, chewing the idea slowly to enjoy all its separate flavours, tracing in his mind the course of an open road with a final destination so distant as to be unimaginable. 'I should like such a journey.'

Moving on again, I thought, the story of the Fleetwoods: at home in airports, train stations, bus depots. I had tried to define 'home' as distinct from 'house', noting in my book of lists that a house could be sold, yet a home could not be bought. 'House' had more negative connotations. Homework got you further up the ladder of evolution, housework didn't. You could be houseproud yet homesick. You could housesit and still be homeless. You could be claustrophobic when housebound if you weren't a homebody yet still feel elated to be homeward bound.

Homespun. Homestead. Homeland. The home truth: Eden was a house of cards, a house of ill repute, a warehouse for the past in which I had been no more than a houseguest. Truth is, I no longer care if I lose my lease in this house. I want to get away from all the bones and melodrama, all those unexplained shadows.

'I have a favour to ask, Mustafa,' I said, holding out my spare keys. 'Would you look after my house? Fatbwa's taking care of Russell, but he's worried the cops might suspect him of burglary if he has the keys. And I don't trust Rivers.'

He took the keys and wished me luck on my journey. 'And with this search for the roots of your family, as well.'

Nick had sent a letter inviting me to meet him at the opium plantations near Patna, where Magda Ironstone was responsible for initiating her father's poppy trials. We're going to travel together downriver to Calcutta, then he will spend a few days in the city taking pictures of the Indian branch of UNISENS, while I explore the old Fleetwood Factory and the Calcutta Botanic Gardens. After that we will head north to meet the rest of the expedition.

Joining Xanadu seems to be a road I was meant to follow. My inheritance, Sally's death, her father's hints of an Indian connection between the Ironstones and the Rivers (the connection Jack had denied), the bones in the garden that led to the yew tree's uprooting: everything is pointing me in this direction. I can't get over the hope that there is a reason for all the random things that happen to us, a pattern, a plot.

# The Paper Garden

# 1

THE PAST IS an opium dream, Jack had implied, and I am living it, lucid dreaming of a past and present existing on the same plane, in the same time. It's a sensation common here in India, Nick says, reinforced by our journey's methods of transport – first in a battered and dusty train from the opium plantations of Patna to the city of Hooghly, then by steam launch past the old jute mills, their chuff chuff chuff now reduced to melancholy silence, and on down the Ganges' long vertical list of settlements and godowns and ghats. Vertical on my map, anyway, because this is where the river turns south to the sea. We live on a globe, but can't escape the ups and downs of maps, the verticality of history. Instead of the truth: history as slightly rancid soup, every ingredient leaving its flavour long after it's been eaten up, all the bacteria still festering.

Our trip down the Ganges, which changed its name to the Hooghly at some point unclear on the map, could serve as a record of the links between opium and Bengal's four hundred years of colonists. We stopped briefly at Serampore, where the Danes traded in opium and missionaries, and at Chandernagore, the old source for French opium shipments to Indochina, and at Chinsurah, burial place of the last independent Armenian prince, and at Bhadreswar, where all remains of its Prussian traders have vanished, and finally at Barrackpur, whose former British viceregal palace is now a police academy. Sliding in and out of river landings, the long repetitive mantra of suffixes slurring into the rumbling purr of the launch engine – *poregoreahwar-poregoreahwar*, a litany of almost forgotten battles won and lost (from pore to war, from gore to war). All in my head, I believed, until I heard a soft chuckle from Nick.

'What is that little song you are humming to yourself, Claire?'

I felt the blood creep up my neck until it reached my ears. 'Nothing, not a song. Just . . . these place names seem – I don't know. A muffled drumbeat.'

'That's an imaginary tabla, an Indian drum.' He stopped the tape recording he was making of the river long enough to snap a picture of my glowing ear. 'You should use that energy. It could heat several rooms in your house.'

Nick's suggestion that we travel this leg of the trip together was not a romantic proposition – not on his side, anyway, although I find it hard to feel strictly platonic about a man who looks like a god, even when the god has only one hand (after all, most of the gods you see are missing arms or a head). I've tried reducing the man to a list of molecules; the sum of his parts – and missing parts. I've tried to concentrate on the river and the sailing barges that he says mimic the rafts floated down from Nepal in the nineteenth century, destined to become packing cases for the opium trade. But my disloyal brain is connected to parts of my anatomy that exist entirely in the present and have no use for history. Both of us are measuring the watery yardstick of Bengal in our own way: he offers me the map of a country; I calibrate such trivialities as the distance of his sandalled foot from mine and the way that the damp patch between his shoulderblades spreads on his shirt with the river's humidity. He smells of coconut, but not in a cloying, beach vacation way. More savoury. I lean in, breathing deeply, and catch him giving me a quizzical look.

'What are you doing, Claire?'

'Ah . . . mmm. I . . . one of your buttons seems loose.'

It's a crush, I tell myself; you'll get over it, which is just as well, because he is clearly not interested and romance is not my field of expertise. With luck, the odd love affair turns into what geneticists call a 'balancing selective advantage', where a bad inheritance like the sickle-cell gene has good results, like a resistance to malaria parasites. In the aftermath of my first affair

I learned to play chess; recovering from another I became expert at omelettes.

I keep reminding myself that I'm here not only for the Fleetwood history but also in a way for Sally. Why has it taken so long for the idea to grab me, Sally's ambition to put a name on the unknown, to trace those anonymous Indian artists who catalogued India? That's my job, after all: putting names to unidentified skeletons. And Jack's attempts to discourage any digging into our shared history have developed in me a suspicion that has nothing to do with forensic anthropology, unless you count the feeling in my bones.

Hoping that I could fill in a few of the gaps in Jack's stories, I had carefully plotted out a long list of appointments for my five days in Calcutta. Nick took one look at this list now and started to laugh. 'You think you'll be able to do all this, Claire? The highlights of Calcutta, research, family connections tied up – all ticked off like a trip to the supermarket?' He mocked my letter from the librarian of the Calcutta Botanic Gardens, an invitation to examine 'The Roxburgh Icones', whisking it away from me to wave over the edge of the boat. 'This, for a start, means nothing,' he said, lifting the letter out of my reach and half threatening to let the wind steal it from his artificial hand. 'In India, you have to read between the lines. And every missing line is a missing story.'

I had to stretch across him, and as I did the boat lurched on a wave and threw me against his chest. He brought his good arm around my shoulders, holding me there, my eyes inches away from his. Breathing hard, I glared up at him, furious, 'Give me the fucking letter, Nick. It's not funny.'

Abruptly, he let go of me and dropped the precious invitation into my hands.

'Sorry, Nick, but it took me fifty pleading letters and a recommendation from Kew Gardens to get this far.'

A smile played around his eyes and mouth. I wanted to kiss him, not fight with him. He raised his eyebrows, 'I hope you brought them with you. There is nothing an Indian bureaucrat loves more than lots of official-looking documents waved under his nose. It is that much more of a challenge to put obstacles in the path of the person waving them.'

A botanical historian at Kew, a Bengali transplanted to London, had first contacted the Calcutta Botanic Gardens for me. 'Who will not remember long-ago gardens?' he asked softly, when I told him of my wish to trace some of Roxburgh's anonymous Indian artists.

'What did you say?' *Long-ago gardens*: it was Sally's phrase.

'Words written by a Chinese gardener hundreds of years ago.' He sighed. 'I do hope that the Roxburgh originals aren't lost for good, or even more damaged than when I saw them last. Watercolours, unlike oils, are so transient – some colours more than others.' Green was fugitive even in paints, it seemed. 'Volatile' was the word he used, a word that brought the colour to life, gave it an outlaw's unstable personality. A fleeting, fleeing colour. Volatile, *volare, vol*: to fly away.

The historian asked me to record for him the havoc India's climate had played on the collection. 'Although I know how much Calcutta dislikes interference from Britain, still, who knows, we may be able to exert some pressure to get the works preserved in better conditions. Oh, and by the way, the library used to have some rare photos of the period. Have a look at those, on the off-chance that your famous relative appears.'

With that lost paper garden in my head I stood beside Nick and stared out at the sluggish, khaki, slowly unwinding river. I was here to put a name on an unknown face, to make a Rivers connection, to link up the family tributaries from my lucid dreams. But who would dream this unpretty river, plain and thick and wide? Only an odd fish like me.

# 2

ACROSS THE HOWRAH bridge into Calcutta, the largest cantilevered bridge in the world, our taxi progressed by inches through traffic made up of rickshaws, taxis, trucks, overloaded buses, hand-drawn and ox-drawn carts, generations of beggars – and a less obstructive but equally tangible air traffic, the dense brown fug rolling unchecked out of vans buses factory chimneys coal-burning furnaces that made my eyes burn and left soot the size of mosquitoes on my clothes. A wry comment from Nick confirmed that he was not unaware of my discomfort: 'Welcome to Calcutta, where the air has the world's highest level of SPM –'

'SPM?'

'Suspended particulate matter – up to eleven per cent toxic particles, including benzopyrene, a suspected carcinogen. Welcome to the Tropic of Cancer. Of course, a lot of people here don't live long enough to die of cancer. Welcome to Calcutta, the British Empire's chosen location for a capital – and possibly the filthiest climate in India, so deadly that the early sailors christened the place Golgotha. Welcome to Calcutta, intellectual capital of India, where decay is an art form and only the ephemeral survives: graffiti outlasts the politicians it satirises, a crime persists like a bad smell long after the criminal is dead.'

What did crime smell like? Did it have a high quotient of benzopyrene? Had UNISENS run the stench through a mass spectrometer yet and filed its compound in the molecular library, as they had done with opium and its alkaloids?

Opium had obsessed me since Jack's history lesson six weeks ago at UNISENS. From him I'd learned that India is the only country in the world where the growth of opium poppies for the raw gum is legal. At the Government Opium and Alkaloid Factories in Ghazipur, near Patna, Nick and I had watched liquid opium being poured into wooden trays and spread out to dry under the sun, a method that Fleetwoods of two hundred years ago would have recognised. Formed into cakes, the opium was then exported to international pharmaceutical companies who would break it down into morphine or codeine. The process earned India a relatively meagre yearly sum of fifteen million dollars. 'If it were turned into heroin,' Jack had said, 'India could earn billions, pay off the national debt, solve widespread poverty, repair the roads. In Pakistan and Thailand illegal opium is what you might call a nice little earner for many a farmer's family who would otherwise starve.' An odd comment for a scientist to make.

The hotel was my choice. UNISENS was not paying for this leg of the trip and all Nick's relatives lived in England now, so I'd chosen a cheapish place off the Maidan in the old British quarter, attracted by its name. But if the Raj Palace had ever justified that title, it must have been two hundred years ago, at least, before a chain of alternating Armenian and English landladies had reduced any palatial grandeur to the kind of pension ominously billed in our Lonely Planet Guide as having 'plenty of character for the price'. More of a Bingo Palace these days, it was furnished in Low Seventies veneer and chrome, the Ionic columns painted a threatening puce that turned the guests' faces the colour of raw bacon. Nick swore that the current landlady, an Englishwoman who greeted us with glad cries of 'Darlings!', was really a eunuch in a wig. But I loved her and her hotel, which reminded me of places my family had stayed in New Orleans, the ones Dad used to call 'the United States of Tennessee Williams, home of the In-crowd: everyone a little *in*bred, *in*tense, *in*sane'.

'You look happy, Claire,' Nick said, when we were settled in the hotel restaurant with cold beers. 'If I didn't know better, I'd say you looked right at home.'

'Oh yes, this is my kind of place, all right. A cheap hotel where the landlady drinks too much and dyes her hair too seldom.' I was half-hoping he would deny it, tell me I had class and style and a unique beauty that only he could appreciate. Instead, he started to spin me tales of growing up here in Bengal, a country where the people were in love with food and art, relaxed in the knowledge that both were impermanent but infinitely renewable. 'Maybe that's why fish is such an important image,' he said, and wrinkled his nose as a plate was slapped down in front of him by a waiter with the flat-footed gait of a man used to crushing cockroaches underfoot without losing his grip on the frozen peas.

'Just between us, darling, we can't get the staff we used to,' the landlady had whispered to me on the way into the dining room. 'All Communists now.'

Inspecting his dinner, Nick insisted that the cook certainly had Stalinist leanings. 'I am sure there is a hotel somewhere on the Russian steppes even now mourning the loss of his culinary expertise,' he said, pressing the fishy rectangle on his plate until it collapsed into a greyish paste flecked with just enough long pale bones to be fatal. Shortly after that we abandoned the fish and retired to the garden bar.

He crossed one bare foot high on his thigh in a supple movement that made it seem as if he were sitting on the floor or a bed instead of a hard plastic chair, and slid his good hand under his shirt to scratch his flat brown stomach. I tried not to think about his skin. He massaged his instep and talked about fish as an art form, rice as a sculptural medium. 'Bengali women sprinkle ground rice on the floors of their houses in elaborate patterns of leaves, flowers and fruits that they know won't last the day,' he said. 'They call them "dust paintings", a celebration of impermanence. Maybe that's how I first got interested in ephemeral art.'

I reached for my beer, deliberately brushing his wrist with mine, wanting him to be saying this to me personally, not working through his own thoughts on the meaning of art and life with an audience of one.

What he said was, 'Women are more joyous about the act of decoration here.'

Decorative, that's women for you, I thought, giving up any hope of distracting him. Men are empire-builders; they like to leave their names on things: countries, mountains, works of art, their offspring. Women practise an eclectic, daily art: filling the countries with children to provide a work force, cooking (the way women are always cooks, seldom chefs), turning house into home. Mum used to decorate our trailer with psychedelic images that she thought reflected the spiritualism of the East. Later switching her allegiance from Asian mysticism to New Mexican shamanistic rites, holistic healing, magic crystals, she claimed to have astral travelled to visit me several times, cheaper than a round trip on British Airways I guess. She always had a good imagination. When Robin and I got bored watching Dad as a spear-chucker, Dad as the cuckolded husband with two lines in Act Three, Mum used to take us for walks and say 'Look at this piece of driftwood, it might be a dinosaur's bone.' She'd say, 'We may not have any money but we've never been poor.' Poor meant no shoes, no books. She didn't see that poor could be no history, no fixed address, permanent dislocation. We went where the jobs were, drove 500 miles in a day and night and saw the Wonders of America from a car window, the Grand Canyon by moonlight. History, in passing. She wanted to show us all the high and deep places she'd never seen while growing up in a flat town on a flatter stretch of yellow prairie.

And what did Dad want? What was he running away from all those years? I was here to find out.

# 3

ON OUR WAY to the Asiatic Society the next morning I kept taking pictures of the crumbling British-era mansions while Nick apologised for the city's state of decay. He acted as if his home town was letting him down. Maybe twenty years in England had altered his perspective in a way he hadn't expected. 'It seems kind of charming to me, Nick. Anyway, you're not personally responsible.'

'No. I know. But I don't want you to judge my city the way so many foreigners do.' He camped up a TV war reporter's voice, heavy on baritone conviction: 'We stand, in the ruins of the once great city of Calcutta, now an inexhaustible source of abnormalities, mired in blood and dirt, where life is cheap.' Putting his arm through mine to stop me stepping on the grinning wares of a street hawker selling false teeth, he added in his own voice, 'A cabinet of curiosities, to be dipped into for a thrill like pornography.'

'Give me *your* view.'

He started walking so quickly that I had to jog to keep up. 'I remember India as a country rich in everything. Death, corruption, injustice, certainly; but also culture, family traditions. Never one without the other. You and I live in a country where the extremes are kept apart: ghettos of senile grannies, ghettos of rich retired stockbrokers, ghettos of people who like miniature golf. In India the extremes slide into one another. It's more difficult to ignore your failures.'

By the time we reached the Asiatic Society, hidden behind a drab frontage on Park Street, I was dripping with sweat, and more delighted to feel the air conditioning in its dim interior than I was to see its formidable library of reference material. The lean-faced clerk regarded us blandly as I inquired about Magda Fleetwood and her husband, Joseph Ironstone. 'Where will you begin?' he asked, overhead strip lights flashing off one lens of his thick glasses. 'We have here almost one lakh of books –'

'That's a hundred thousand,' Nick murmured.

The clerk nodded. 'Including part of Tipu Sultan's original library.'

'Ah . . . I don't think there are any sultans in my family. Let me see . . . Magda was born here and lived here until 1888 or '89, before returning to England to die –'

'You are mistaken. Magda Fleetwood did not die in England.'

'I'm sorry, *what* did you say?'

His expression did not alter. 'Magda Fleetwood died in 1935 and was cremated here in Calcutta. By her own wishes there is a memorial plaque laid in her name at the Kalighat temple. It is in the Bengali script, of course, with which I assume you are not familiar.'

'I am,' said Nick.

Another compass flash off the clerk's glasses. 'Second plaque to her is in South Park Street Cemetery.' He pulled out a photocopied streetplan of central Calcutta. 'For Kali Temple you will require a taxi ride. Cemetery is walking distance. Here – ' His bony finger slid from the Maidan down Park Street to the crossroads with Chandra Bose Road. 'Cemetery was new in the eighteenth century, when Park Street was called Burying Ground Road and led to what was then southernmost edge of the white settlement, now roughly city centre. After only twenty-three years it was full to bursting and no more of the dead were admitted, excepting a few influential families like the Ironstones and Fleetwoods, whose tombs still had some space left, despite cramped conditions.'

Surprised as I was by his knowledge of Magda, I was more surprised at the secrets kept by my father (and Jack: wouldn't Jack have been aware of this, with all the time he spent here?). 'How do you know?'

'Because Magda Fleetwood's tomb is not far from the great

pyramid of Sir William Jones, founder of our Society. Concerning the woman herself, my familiarity is due to her involvement with the rise of nationalism in the nineteenth century, especially under the name she chose after conversion, Sister Sarasvati.'

'Conversion?'

'To Hinduism.' Our skinny sage locked his long fingers together in a steeple. 'She was much influenced by the teachings of Swami Vivekananda, famous disciple of Ramakrishna.' His clerk's brain demanded a category, 'Flourished 1834 to '86.'

'A kind of reincarnated Hindu saint,' Nick whispered to me.

The clerk dipped his head slightly from side to side as if his skull was loosely attached at the spine, a very Indian movement that I had seen Nick use only with his grandfather. 'Swami's monks preached essential oneness of all paths to reality,' the clerk continued, 'and expression of spirit in fruitful action.'

'Especially revolutionary action,' Nick added mischievously. 'Was Sister Sarasvati one of those girls like the Irish one – Sister Nibedita, the one who inspired so many independence groups in Bengal?'

The clerk nodded. 'A widow herself, Sister Sarasvati worked to organise female education and make arrangements for widows to earn a livelihood. She was interested in those poor women condemned to poverty because of the illegitimacy of the children whose fathers – *English* fathers –' he looked sternly over his glasses at me, 'whose *English* fathers had left them to their fate. In later years she was earning respect as ardent social worker at Kali Temple, which is why you find a memorial to her in Kalighat. She encouraged Bengalis to adopt a contemporary Kali, a destroyer of outdated imperial institutions.'

With Nick's encouragement the clerk agreed to browse through the Fleetwood and Ironstone documents and photocopy any bits and pieces that might be of interest. 'Thank you,' I said, surprised by his unexpected generosity. He didn't look like a guy who would give an inch. 'I couldn't begin to know where to look.'

His expression affirmed my statement of ignorance.

'Quite a girl, your Magda,' said Nick outside, picking his way carelessly over the torn pavement with some inner radar warning of the countless potholes that caught me unawares every time I took my eyes off my feet. 'Undoubtedly she would've been a Communist now, like so many in the civil service here.' I was grateful for the crowded street as he took my arm in his again and waltzed me through the traffic to South Park Street Cemetery, a brief electric contact that gave me a pleasurable buzz at our point of connection.

For anyone used to the cosy Gothic charm of Victorian graveyards, where grief is reduced to sentiment with the help of maudlin stone angels and saccharine poetry, South Park Street Cemetery was a tragedy of epic proportions, a neo-Classical city straight out of one of those surreal drawings in which all of ancient Rome's buildings crowd together on the same plane. Roofs sprang from floors in impossible perspectives, miniature Parthenons were dwarfed by vast cupolas, in turn overshadowed by towering obelisks and giant marble caskets. Nature, no respecter of the dead, had streaked the sombre tombs with blackish-green monsoon tears and the white shorthand of birdshit graffiti and pushed blood-red trumpet flowers through the roofs of Palladian villas like inappropriate plumes in sober homburg hats. The congestion in this necropolitan garden created an air of breathlessness considerably increased by the lack of logical scale. None of the tombs were less than eight feet high, most were two or three times my height. Jumbled as a box of oversized and mismatched chess pieces, each memorial vied with the next, monuments to their occupants' belief that if you couldn't take it with you, you could sure as Hell mark your port of embarkation.

Nick, wandering ahead down the main avenue, muttered to himself the inscriptions that caught his fancy, his voice trailing back to me like a roll call of the drowned from a phantom ship:

'*Avery*, who went to his last resort aged 18 years, buried in the Indian Ocean . . .

'*Anderson*, whilst suffering from a dangerous illness under which he sunk . . .

'*Savage,* who whilst in the Vigour of Youth and Exercise of every manly virtue was engulfed by malignant disorder . . .'

'Not to mention a woman who died from a surfeit of pineapples,' I added.

We found Jones's obelisk behind a cow that was placidly cropping weeds from a mock Grecian temple: *Sir William Jones, died on the 27th April 1794, Aged 47 years and 7 months.* Thinking about that time when life was measured in months, I read aloud, ' "Restored by the Asiatic Society 1 Jan. 1854," Presumably they mean the tomb was restored, not the man.'

'I don't know – this is India, after all. We are in the business of reincarnation.'

The Ironstones were installed nearby in a domed mausoleum trailing jasmine and convolvulus, an elegant summerhouse for the dead. But what caught my eye was not Magda's stone, it was her mother-in-law's lengthy inscription:

*SACRED to the memory of*
*EMMA CONGREVE IRONSTONE: aged 27 years*
*Beloved Wife of Luther Ironstone*
*who departed this life on the 31st October 1857*
*having suffered an inflammation of the brain resulting from*
*the sad and disastrous siege of Lucknow*
*Also to the memory of HILDA MARY aged 10 months*
*the beloved daughter of Luther Ironstone*
*who died on the 21st August 1857*
*from the sheer want of proper nutriment*
*during the siege of Lucknow*
*This tablet has been erected by the disconsolate husband*
*and father, and his only surviving son, Joseph*

'Joseph Ironstone,' I said. Collector, photographer, whose skull exactly matched mine. 'I never knew he lost a baby sister and his mother the same year.'

'To an inflammation of the brain, whatever that might be.'

'Think she went off her head as a result of losing her child?'

'Magda's memorial is over here, next to several more

Ironstones who died of inflammations of the brain. An unstable family. Jack better watch out.'

Together we read the inscription:

> *To the memory of Magda Fleetwood Ironstone, born 1854,*
> *who one evening in 1935, riding homeward from the residence*
> *of a friend was stricken by a sudden brainstorm*
> *and fell down dead from the horse which bore her*

Struck down, like her yew tree, if not by lightning.

A cricket ball flew through the narrow gap between the columns, to be followed shortly by a group of small boys in ragged shorts. 'Is this your family?' they asked in unison. 'We are sorry if our cricket-playing is disturbing them, Miss, but we are very respectful and we are keeping all bad people out and if we want to play cricket otherwise we are having to travel two hours on the bus.' They beamed at Nick. 'Sir! Sir!' they shouted, 'Are you a fast bowler, sir?'

He raised his plastic hand. 'Not any more.'

'Oh, bad luck, sir!' Accustomed to imperfection, their faces fell, but not far. India: you got the whole of existence in your face, unedited.

The morning sky was losing its light to the remains of an unseasonably late monsoon cloud as we left, and the cemetery's high perimeter walls, lined with a vertical crazy paving of headstones, were further shaded by huge billboards advertising a new 'American-style' cemetery: LUXURIOUS! SPACIOUS!

'Sometimes I think India is no more than a memorial to departed and arriving empires,' Nick said, reading the ads. 'It will never belong to us.' He didn't speak again until I stopped to snap a dead crow, flattened by the relentless traffic to a graphic black shadow against the road's red dust. Watching me carefully record the shot in my book of lists, he remarked, 'My grandfather used to say that each person who comes to the East seeking something will find it. But what he finds is a reflection of himself.'

It sounded like Mum's fortune cookie philosophy of the

sixties: Be careful what you dream, it may come true. A little crossly, I said, 'Right now I'm seeking an air-conditioned taxi, if that's OK with you, Nick.'

# 4

THE KALI TEMPLE was smaller than my guidebook made it sound, tucked away in a pretty, suburban street lined with photographic studios. We left our taxi in front of Mother Theresa's clinic next door and entered the temple grounds through a spiritual mall that felt both strange and familiar, with a great line in glass bangles, red flowers, phosphorescent gods and glossy pictures of Kali. Stately priests drifted through like gracious celestial shoppers, and dogs with puja marks on their foreheads lifted their legs against the steps of a temple faced in Victorian flowered tiles, the kind you see in English museum lavatories, an unexpectedly cosy effect enhanced by the weather having turned more Scottish than Indian.

Almost immediately, a guide took us in hand, a Brahmin priest from the temple. 'Even in 1972 I was assisting an American historian,' he said. Pointing out the temple highlights, he was an urbane and implacable purveyor of erroneous information whom all our protests failed to dislodge. Like a stranger met in a desperate queue for the toilets at intermission in the theatre, he knew we could not escape, even when I tested his patience by stopping for ten minutes to take pictures of a savage Kali with a gold body and a face painted in the black enamel used to cover up damage on rusty cars. 'Kali is sticking her tongue out in remorse for accidentally trampling on her husband Shiva,' our guide intoned, 'who has prostrated himself in her path to stop her destroying the world.'

I stared at the black and gold goddess with her necklace of skulls and she stared right back. She didn't look to me like a woman who would kill her husband by accident. This girl was out for blood. Murder in her heart. Ready to trample over any number of husbands to sink those sharp fangs into the guy responsible, the bad designer who late one Friday night, impatient for his drink with the boys, couldn't be bothered getting the blueprint for women right, didn't want to spend that *leetle* bit extra time finishing the fine tuning on his creation before he knocked off for the weekend. 'I'll get back to it on Monday,' he promised himself. He didn't, though, did he? We got stuck with periods, painful childbirth, menopause – a pretty package and a bad design, like an Alessi coffee pot with a spout that drips and a handle that burns you every time you pick it up.

Our cultural interpreter, pushing through the dogs and crows who were licking and pecking at the bloodied pavement, herded us to a fenced-off court where a goat had been killed that morning. Nick kept giving me these little face-audits, ducking his handsome head to stare into my eyes, checking for me to register shock or squeamishness. 'What is your impression, then?' he asked. 'What's that word of yours – *weird*? This must come high on your weirdness scale.'

Determined to keep a straight face, I said, 'You've obviously never been to a Texas road-kill barbecue. Or a drive-in Baptist chapel in Mississippi. Granted, where I grew up, scapegoat was just a word, not your actual slaughtered horned beast. Still, I've seen worse. I was expecting more beggars. My guidebook warned about them.'

The priest piped up, 'This is quiet period for beggars. Most tourists are coming to the temple to see goat being slaughtered. So you are a little late for beggars.'

'What – they knock off for coffee before the next rush, is that it?'

'Something like that, Miss, yes.'

Although he had not heard of Sister Sarasvati, he soon found an elderly priest to direct us to her memorial, a pale rectangle of worn marble among many others set into the pavement not far from the scapegoat's altar. Most of the inscriptions were worn to a faint Braille, but hers was still readable. 'Symbol in front of her name is meaning "The late so and so" in Bengali,' said the priest.

*Too* late, I thought, crouching to run my hand over the stone's surface and getting nothing from it barring some dust and dried goat's blood on my fingers. It occurred to me that fragments could break off the main temple of history and be lost so easily. Swept up, disposed of, they could disappear into the museum basement to be discovered later by some archaeologist who didn't recognise the vernacular and had no interest in their context. I figured this is what happened to Sister Sarasvati. She just didn't translate into the grammar of her time.

We had been no more than an hour in the temple, but when we entered the street again it was to find the former peaceful atmosphere charged with tension. Our taxi was nowhere to be seen and on the main road a barricade of stones and handcarts had been newly erected, bringing trams and buses to a standstill.

We could hear the reason for the blockade before we saw it – approaching from about a quarter of a mile off, a huge group of men shouting and waving placards. Nick turned to an old man wearing an immaculate white lungi and starched safari shirt. 'What's it about? A strike? A *gherao*?'

'Gurkha people from north Bengal wanting independent state of Gurkhaland,' the man replied, shaking his head. 'Independence is the curse of our time. Everybody today is wanting. Even my son wants. I say to him: *then* who is running our family business!'

He explained to us that the militant faction of the Gurkha population, the GNLF or Gurkha National Liberation Front, originally from Nepal, had long felt discriminated against by the majority Bengali population in what was now north Bengal. They were demanding a separate state and pressurising each Gurkha family from the border towns into giving one son to their cause. I noticed a fresh slogan – DOWN WITH IMPERIALISM! STAND UP FOR GURKHALAND TO-DAY! – scrawled on a wall emblazoned with the imprint of a drinks company claiming to be WINNERS OF THE ALL-INDIA MANGO COMPETITION.

'We have to get out of here,' Nick said, pulling me through the crowd back in the direction we'd come.

'What's a kerow?'

He frowned. 'A what? Oh, *gherao*. A very dangerous Calcutta refinement on Gandhi's technique of passive resistance by numbers. A crowd surrounds an individual and prevents him from any form of movement, not touching him but threatening him. Students do it to teachers, employees to employers. Men have been known to collapse from thirst while their captors watch.'

The crowd around us had started to shout slogans back at the approaching marchers. Nick put his good arm around my shoulder and drew me close. 'If I say run, you run – understand?' he whispered. 'That way – towards the temple.'

I twisted my face towards his. 'If you think you're going to get mowed down like some martyred guardian angel while I run off to safety, forget it!'

'Right.' Nick managed a nervous smile. 'A one-winged angel, won't do you much good with that crowd. So I'll run and you protect *me*. How's that?'

The protestors were no more than fifty feet away from us now, wielding their placards like sabres, and the crowd we were part of started to retreat, shoving to get away. A woman in front of Nick staggered and fell, tripping him, bringing him to his knees. I turned to help and felt the crowd pushing into me, buffeting against me like logs caught in the current. I put my hand down as I felt myself falling and had an image of Nick's lost hand, the cries he had heard. *The hand! The hand!* Suddenly our comic Kali priest was there, aloof now, not quite touching us, making an eddy in the tide that threatened to roll us under.

And then we were out of the street and safe.

We were both shaken by the experience, although by the time we reached the hotel Nick was insisting that the march was mild by comparison with most. 'This is the capital of industrial and political disputes. We have it down to a fine art.' Finishing his third gin and tonic, he put down his glass abruptly and asked our landlady if we might listen to the news on her radio, an apparatus that looked as if it were last used to broadcast the Battle of Britain.

The BBC World Service devoted very little time to the disturbance. In a country where disasters are measured in thousands of deaths, our riot was worthy of no more than a paragraph. 'They seem to be saying that the worst outbreaks of Gurkha violence are around Darjeeling and Kalimpong,' I said.

'That's what worries me. It's exactly where we're headed. I'd better try to contact Jack. He and the others should have arrived in Kalimpong by now.'

# 5

NICK JOINED ME in the hotel restaurant thirty minutes later, his face strained. 'I couldn't get through – not on the hotel phone, not from the STD booth down the road. The operator told me the Darjeeling and Kalimpong phone lines are down, whether deliberately sabotaged or because of the late monsoon they don't know.'

'We only have a couple more days here. The lines might have cleared by then.'

He tried again to reach Jack the next morning, with no luck.

'What should we do?' I asked.

'I don't know – carry on as we'd planned, I suppose. I'll try Jack from UNISENS. If the lines stay down, we'll just have to hope the Gurkha trouble blows over before we fly north.'

I think Nick wanted to appear calm for my sake, but it didn't help that in the taxi to the UNISENS lab he kept fiddling irritably with the windows and asking the driver to turn the air conditioning up and down.

'Both the Fleetwood Factory and the Fleetwood home were built here on the Ganges to the northwest of the city,' the clerk at UNISENS told us, pointing to a house in the near distance, its Palladian silhouette an elegant contrast to the lean, functional lines of the UNISENS laboratory, 'to be easily accessible for unloading chests of processed opium shipped down during autumn and spring on the river craft from Patna. UNISENS bought this property in the 1970s and the late Miss Alexandra Ironstone endowed to us all her mother's company documents.'

Skirting the laboratory building, he led us to a small museum display. 'Here you see what they were calling "Black earth" and also "Company's opium" because of its black outer skin and its link to the East India Company. Fleetwood family is like Jardine Matheson, the big multinational in modern London and Southeast Asian trading: both made their first fortunes entirely from opium.' His eyes had a slightly malicious twinkle. 'You know the first Mr Jardine was dying finally of a dreadful and agonising illness? Superstition says that all those dealing in opium will have sticky end.'

'The opium curse doesn't seem to have affected Matheson,' Nick said. 'He lived to be ninety, built himself a castle and a political career.'

The clerk nodded, not at all chagrined, and with a serene smile asked me what I was interested in. 'I'd like to browse the archives for 1885 through 1889,' I said. 'I'm looking for any reference to a William Fleetwood or . . . a family called Rivers. A Dr Rivers?'

Nick gave me a funny look. 'Rivers? Why Rivers?'

'Nothing. A hunch. Something Sally mentioned to me once.'

'You might wish to try first in the Clerks' Books of Mortality,' said the clerk. 'These record the deaths of all staff members who were working for the Fleetwoods at the time. And you, Mr Banerji? How may I be of service?'

'I'm here to take some pictures of the lab,' Nick said, showing him the letter of authorisation given us by Christian Herschel before we left.

My paper defeat must have been clear when the clerk returned an hour later, because he immediately asked if I had found any Rivers, the amusement in his voice unconcealed.

'Hundreds. But no doctors.' There was a Book of Mortality for every year the Fleetwood Company had operated from 1720 to 1890, when Magda sold it. I had opened one of the 1880s books, its pages riddled with worm hole, to see long lists of copperplate Rivers. 'It seems to have been the generic name for half the Indians who worked here.'

He rewarded me with a small smile. 'I too think this. Perhaps it was the joke of an English filing clerk unable to pronounce our names.'

'Why didn't you tell me before I started?'

He shrugged off my indignation. 'Because you did not ask me.'

'But –'

His eyes were imperturbable. 'You want more time?'

'No. If you could photocopy these for me, that would be very kind.' I gave him the few interesting sketches and documents I'd found. 'And tell my friend, when he's finished, that I've gone for a walk to the Fleetwood house.'

'House is closed, Madam. It was left to the nation as a museum when Magda Ironstone died and not one object has been disturbed since then. But sadly there is no money for security to allow visitors in.'

'I'm not planning to do a survey of it,' I said crossly, 'just to stretch my legs.'

The three-storey arcaded house rose out of its encroaching vegetation about half a mile off, and from this distance I could almost believe that it would prove to be intact. Fifty paces away, it became clear that if any eminent Victorian ghosts still strolled its colonnaded verandas, they had long since grown accustomed to communal Indian living: the Fleetwood manor had become a three-storey Bengali village. Flocks of goats grazed what must once have been lawns, washing was draped to dry over the balustrades and a stately white cow drifted under the grand portico, pausing just long enough to punctuate the entrance hall's marble floor with a series of mud brown commas. It was not a bad indication of what was to be found inside, where chickens, goats and cows roamed freely and several families of squatters made their homes. A young man happily led me up the sweeping circular staircase, padding barefoot past the vegetables in recycled oil tins that stood in for potted palms. 'Sister, look at this tower!' he said when we reached the flat rooftop, and mimed a rifle. 'Nineteen forty-seven partition riots. Many killing.'

He forced open the door into the top floor rooms and I wiped my hand across the dust-felted surface of a glass cabinet to make a window on to the collection of crumbling plant specimens and stuffed hummingbirds inside. Similar cabinets were stacked to the ceiling.

'You see more?'

'No, that's enough.'

Defeated and dirty, I leaned against the balustrade on the hot sunlit roof and wondered if this was what constituted a distinguished history for someone like me.

'Glass Palace!' The young man, sensitive to my mood, tried to cheer me up by pointing to the remains of a huge greenhouse resembling the sketches I'd given the UNISENS clerk to photocopy. 'Come!' We pushed our way through the overgrown garden past a sultry pond hidden under the canopy of palms, and woke up an ancient custodian, who seemed delighted by my arrival. The formalities consisted of him asking, 'Name, please?' To which I replied 'Claire Fleetwood' and received a bright smile. 'Miss Fleetwood! Such a pleasure you are here at last!'

'You were expecting me?'

'Of course, of course! This is the Fleetwood house.'

'Oh, I see. You didn't mean –'

'Please to be coming this way. At last you will see how well I have kept this for you.' There was clearly some misunderstanding, but there seemed no point in contradicting the man's false impressions.

Inside, the air was thick and sweet, a rain forest in glass walls, with palms above us pushing through the meshed metal roof like giraffes in a shrubbery and two giant clam shells filled with water for the bright parakeets swooping overhead. I heard shouts from the girls bathing in the river nearby, the muffled percussion as liquid traffic chugged past. 'I have been here man and boy,' the custodian said proudly. 'Nineteen oh eight I first came, with my uncle.'

'Tell me about this place – the Glass Palace, the young man called it.'

'This place? This place is where Mr Fleetwood made all his experiments.'

'Who worked here?'

He looked sly. '*You* know.'

I let that one pass for the moment. 'Are there any records?'

'Old records are lost or eaten up by white ants so long ago. Or they are with this new company that has come.'

'UNISENS?'

'Hah.' The soft Indian expression of acknowledgement, a word like a mocking laugh. 'This one sense nonsense company, hah.'

'Do you get many visitors?'

'No one is coming here. Not for so many years.' It didn't seem to upset him, this Rip van Winkle of the conservatory. 'But always we keep things in readiness for you.'

'I think you have mistaken me for –'

'*He* came, though. The other one.'

'What other one?' I was suddenly excited. Would Jack have come here?

My younger guide had long since left, but the old man's voice lowered as if there were listeners. '*You* know.' His face secretive and shrewd. 'Looking for you. But only the one time, my uncle said. So long ago.' He touched me with his dry, skeletal fingers, like a twig stripped of leaves brushing my arm. 'The one you loved.' Off his head, I thought, easing my way back through the jungle to the door, worried that this old man who had seemed so happy to meet me was going to reveal more than I wanted to see, the big brown snake who kept the parakeet population down.

A tangled path away from the glasshouse must once have led through the remains of a flower border, now swallowed up by plundering weeds which tugged at my clothes like the old man's crazy suggestions. I had hoped to find the pattern of that lost garden from Dad's photo, *Jack's garden*; instead there was chaos and disorder. Grateful to reach the ragged edges of the clearing where the Fleetwood house stood, I saw Nick waiting for me on a bench encircling a big tree by the river. 'Where have you *been*?' he asked.

'Sorry, I got a little carried away with exploring. What is it, Nick? You look worried. Is it about Jack?'

He looked taken aback. 'What do you mean?'

'You said you were going to try to phone him again from here.'

'I thought you meant . . . No, I didn't speak to Jack. The lines are still down.'

'You thought I meant what?'

He shook his head. 'I'll tell you later.'

# 6

NICK WAS EDGY and worried that evening over dinner, his humour not improved by having to share a table with a group of my fellow Americans, the kind that made me want to start speaking with a heavy Chinese or Russian accent. They went on and on and on about the horrors of Calcutta, the poverty, the beggars, the filth, the way 'somebody otta do something'. *Who?* I nearly asked. Like, Uncle Sam has done so well in LA and Detroit? After they left I said quickly to Nick, 'Look, I hope you don't think –'

'What? Think what?'

Hearing the hurt in his voice, I wanted to tell him how much I liked him and his birthplace for all the ways they weren't like me and mine. It was India's *difference* I found so attractive, Nick's ability to be confident and sensuous in a gentle way few American and English men were. The kind of things even Americans don't blurt out in public. I felt this awful, hopeless tenderness for him and the best I could do was to ask awkwardly, 'Do you ever get homesick in London for Calcutta?'

'Homesick?' A formal voice, as if I'd asked to see the resident permit in his UK passport. 'I get homesick for somewhere, but not necessarily here.'

A place where he had two hands, I thought, glancing quickly at his plastic hand and away. 'I'm sorry about those guys,' I said. 'What they said was . . . dumb.'

'Actually, I empathise with our departed friends' feelings about the poverty and corruption among Indians.' He had a fixed smile on his face that didn't bode well. 'Indians as compared with *Americans*, with all their united histories of exciting elsewheres. *Americans*, who, six months after they get their green cards, are ready to enlist in that spotlessly clean motel chain, America Inc., America the Limited Company, where all food is reduced to McDonald's, all cultures packaged into a bitesize Disneyland.'

· I opened my mouth and let it close again, telling myself that he was still speaking to that other, departed audience.

'Then these same Americans are drawn to the famous, the original, the extraordinary,' he said. 'And what happens when they find the extraordinary? They brand it, market it, chop it up into T-shirts. Give it a logo. Even their names – have you noticed how many Americans are Brad Brown Juniors or Darren Smith the Seconds? They turn their own names into chainstore trademarks. Not as many incarnations down the line as us and yet convinced that all their earlier incarnations had an epic quality worth preserving.'

I swallowed, still trying not to take his comments personally. The beer tasted sour. 'You've put a lot of thought into American defects,' I said, hating the wobble in my voice.

'Frankly, if America is so wonderful, I'm amazed Americans ever leave.' Suddenly penitent, Nick reached across the table and put his good hand on mine. 'I wasn't talking about *you*, Claire. I didn't mean to hurt your feelings.'

I eased my hand out from under his. 'No, you're just implying that I don't belong here. You're probably right. Still, here I am, hot and sweaty. I think I'll just head upstairs and see if any water comes out of the old world tap.'

He leaned back in the chair, deliberately putting more distance between us, and crossed his arms behind his head.

Carefully lifting my chair so that it wouldn't make a vulgar American noise, I left him and went to my room, where I sat on the bed for several minutes, feeling sorry for myself. Then I had a lukewarm bath in about an inch of rusty water, picked up my camera and went out into the noisy streets to do what I'm best at. When I came back an hour later, Nick was waiting for me in the bar, a little drunk and very apologetic. 'I'm sorry, Claire. I've been worried about this situation in Kalimpong, and then . . . It's Jack . . .'

'What is? What about Jack?'

He had difficulties arranging the words in an order he liked. 'I got talking to some fellows that work in the lab at UNISENS and they were gossiping, not really aware that I knew Jack . . . They think . . . that is, there's a rumour . . .' He kept stopping and starting like a car with a faulty carburettor.

'What kind of rumour?'

'A couple of the low level chemists were fired . . . the fellows said it was on suspicions of smuggling small quantities of heroin –'

'The way Ben suggested? In the soap samples?'

He nodded unhappily.

'How is Jack involved?'

'No one is suggesting that Jack . . . Opium I might just believe – Jack's an old hippy at heart and it would appeal to his sense of adventure. But not heroin.'

'So what's the link between him and the dismissed men?'

'Someone suggested that he'd been working at the UNISENS Calcutta factory when no one should've been there . . . at the same time these men were working.' He hurried out the next words, 'I'm inclined to see this as jealous gossip because Jack's an outsider, a Brit.'

Them and us again. 'That's it? The only accusation?'

'Oh, there were other tall tales, none of them worth repeating.' Whatever they were, they had made Nick uneasy. His finger was marking out a series of stripes in the table's dust. Strokes against Jack, I thought; prison bars locking him up. 'Jack's explanation for his late nights was that he was working overtime on his chlorophyll experiments and he needed to study the original Fleetwood records at UNISENS, which the company doesn't let out of their library.'

'That makes sense.' I managed to squeeze my face into a reassuring expression, tucking in the edges of my suspicions and slamming on a smile like someone forcing a bulky suitcase shut by sitting on it. 'Why did no one tell UNISENS UK?'

'For the same reason that they suspected Jack in the first place, I would guess, because he's a friend of the directors.'

'When were the men dismissed?'

He glanced up briefly, then back at the marks he had made in the dust, brushing away his dusty calculations, 'Late September last year.'

'How did the subject of Jack come up, if the incident happened a year ago?'

'Through my own vanity. They were teasing me about my work and I asked if they had heard of Jack Ironstone and Xanadu, hoping to brag a bit about my involvement with a serious scientific expedition – pathetic, really. Before I had a chance to mention that I was part of the team, one of the assistant chemists, a very unpleasant fellow, started making snide comments about Jack's real motives for heading up into the mountains. One thing led to another –'

He stopped speaking as the waiter appeared carrying a bowl of snacks, pale grey and slightly porous, like flakes of boiled bath sponge. 'What *are* they, do you think?' I whispered to Nick.

He sniffed the bowl that had been slapped in front of him with the usual grace and charm. 'I can't be sure, but I suspect pork scratchings.'

'Those bits of fried pig rind and fat the English eat in pubs?'

'An odd after dinner snack, I grant you, especially in a country with one of the largest Muslim populations in the world.' He popped one in his mouth and grimaced. 'But that's what they are. Pretty nasty.'

It seemed safe to continue my interrogation. 'Those men who were dismissed from UNISENS – can't they be traced?'

'One man is from northern Bhutan, one from Arunachal Pradesh, up on the Indian borders between Tibet and Burma.'

'Aruna –' I stumbled over the name.

'Arunachal Pradesh, one of the northeastern hill states. A bit like the Golden Triangle in Burma – lots of remote uplands inaccessible to political intervention. Populated by highly independent and semi-nomadic hill tribes for whom, so the fellows at UNISENS claim, opium is a much appreciated new economic source.'

*A nice little earner*: Jack's phrase came back to me. 'If they're semi-nomadic, how do they find time to grow opium?'

'Slash-and-burn jungle clearings. The UNISENS chemists say one of the sacked men comes from tribal people who trade the raw opium to itinerant Chinese smugglers posing as Tibetans or Bhutanese. Then the smugglers sell the stuff on to drug merchants who process it into heroin. Except that in this case, it is one of the men at UNISENS processing it.'

'Couldn't we question the dismissed men or their contacts? They can't have been operating alone.'

Above us the crows called out, '*Y'WAH? Y'WAH? Y'WAH?*', following our conversation keenly, a convention for hard-of-hearing undertakers.

Nick sounded just as incredulous. 'We're not private eyes, Claire! At any rate, the opium gangs are rather respected in this part of the world. The fellows at UNISENS talk almost with envy of Khun Sa, the major supplier of opium in the Golden Triangle – and the fellow who's probably responsible for most of the heroin sold in New York. He's established an opium-financed mini state with schools, hospitals, local industries. He levies his own form of taxes on smuggled teak and precious stones, and prides himself on being a collector of rare Asian orchids –' Nick broke off as the Raj Palace's landlady drifted through with her nightly pink gin.

'Terrible shame about the orchids,' she paused to confide in us. 'Oh my dears, one used to look up into the trees of Bhutan and see orchids lighting up their branches like Christmas lights. All gone now, they tell me. So sad. People are wicked: they will do anything to make money. The whole orchid business in Kalimpong is a scam. The nurseries claim to be breeding orchids, but all the flowers are smuggled. Still, with Bhutan desperately short of cash and the wretched Japs willing to pay up to twenty-five thousand dollars a plant, what can one expect?'

Nick waited until she had trailed back into the hotel before continuing. 'I don't like to inquire too closely, Claire. Who knows if the two men dismissed were the only people involved at UNISENS?'

'Could you ask if they left any family here in Calcutta?'

'And then what? You think their families would tell me anything?'

'I could go and ask round UNISENS, if you don't want to. The guys in the lab don't know my face. It's the only way we are going to clear Jack's name.'

'It doesn't need clearing. This is all just vicious gossip, I'm sure.'

But he wasn't that sure, because after a few more minutes of my needling, he agreed grudgingly to spend the next day seeing what he could find out. 'This means you will have to go to the Botanic Gardens alone tomorrow. Will you be all right on your own if I make sure you have a trustworthy driver?'

I shrugged off any anxieties I had about the Gurkha problems. 'I'll be fine. The landlady told me no one would go anywhere in Calcutta if minor commotions like that stopped them.'

In bed that night I picked up one of Magda's diaries from the twelve I had brought to read on the expedition. Understand this, she seemed to be saying, and you will understand your own story; the empty promise of so many historians: I found little here to inform my life and nothing to tie my family to Sally Rivers. Magda's style was alternately philosophical, amusing, encyclopedic, yet behind the cool scientist's prose and the colourful evocations of a vanished century, the woman herself remained elusive. Why? Memory is not a museum, where you have to discard one object to make space for another. It's true that all of us edit our memories to a certain extent; we take out the acts we're ashamed of, the omissions too painful to examine, live our lives in retrospect. But how does a diarist decide what to hide and what to reveal?

I got out of bed and collected what material I had from the Asiatic Society and the UNISENS files and began to arrange it on the rug in rough chronological order: photocopies of nineteenth-century gossip columns, newsclippings, steamer arrivals and departures, reproductions of old postcards of Park Street Cemetery and the opium plantations on the Ganges plain (600,000 acres in cultivation by Magda's time). Before me lay a panoramic collage of Calcutta and northwest Bengal, beginning in 1885, the date Magda and Joseph Ironstone returned to India as a married couple, when Calcutta was still the City of Palaces, an Arabian Nights' spin on regency Bath or Cheltenham. The infamous rickshaws had not yet been introduced by the Chinese as a way of negotiating monsoon-flooded streets, but there were horse-drawn trams, telephones, cars crossing the Howrah bridge.

The Fleetwood archives had yielded one of Magda's cookbooks, left behind with her Bengali cook when she returned to England, and the recipes for pilchard toast and mutton ham – annotated by Magda, 'a capital thing for rough travelling' – were marked with fingerprints (whose?), as was a page with a comment on the 'efficacy of Warren's Cooking Pot and Vegetable Steamer during an expedition to northern Bhutan'. I repeated the Victorian phrasing and the unfamiliar words from Magda's diary (*godown* – a riverside warehouse, *box-wallah* – a pedlar or shopkeeper, *tiffin* – lunch, *factory* – a trading establishment, *pundit* – a wise man or teacher or a native explorer) until I could almost hear her voice and smell the curry puffs her father used to serve at his weekly tiffins for the botanical world.

My photocopied stage was peopled by paper actors with names impossible for my tongue to wrap around. Muttering an archaic incantation: 'Abracadabra! Allakazam! Mahendralal! Praphullachandra! Jagadishchandra!' I conjured from my bed like a genie from a magic lantern (or the fuzzy image projected by the diffuse light of a room-sized pinhole camera, a camera obscura) the lean, white-whiskered Dr Mahendralal Sarkar, a physician of rare vision who sparked Magda's father to study Indian 'green' medicine. By his side was the chemistry professor Praphullachandra Ray, urging me to join him in his search for the missing elements in the Periodic Table, and the saturnine

Jagadishchandra Basu, first Indian professor of physics at Presidency College (at two-thirds the salary of his British colleagues), who demonstrated – right here! in my own hotel room! – the wireless transmission of microwave signals through solid walls. Now *there's* a man who knew about extrasensory forms of communication! As Basu lay down his ingenious instruments for recording extremely small movements in plants, I read the words of his which inspired Magda to copy them out: *It was the watching of a roadside weed in Calcutta that turned the entire trend of my thought from the study of the inorganic to that of organic life.*

These were the stars, but who were the other, anonymous players, Magda's sprawling supporting cast of gardeners and assistant botanists, ayas, indigo planters and opium merchants, with their unheralded exits and entrances? I needed a new twist on Val's X-ray cameras, one that would involve an exposure of a hundred years and reverse the process of turning solid bone into transparent shadows, one that could capture my phantoms on film. My hopes rose on finding a section of the diaries titled 'Rivers', until further reading made it obvious that this concerned the Survey of India.

The best I could do was to assign a letter to each verifiable link with Magda and Joseph (as if these photocopied scraps were the evidence in a trial), filling in the missing spaces with reconstructions I had made by reading between the lines of her self-edited journals. Given that Magda rarely dated these by year, I could only work out the dates roughly from overlaps between her private life and her comments on events of national consequence. But how could I guess whether Exhibit A should be Magda's sketch of a mango grove in Calcutta, done a few days after she and Joseph arrived, or the scrap of paper headed 'Recipe for binding volumes' that fell out of her diary?

Opium dreams, Jack would call the paper narrative I assembled.

## A. Sketches of Mango and Frangipani
### (Magda Ironstone c. 1881–5)

WHAT YOU SEE first is a chain of marigolds sliding down the brown river like beaten egg yolk in a thin gravy. The flowers curl around a jetty, trail in the wake of a sampan, fracture the muddied reflection of a palace at Garden Reach and finally come to rest around a strange bleached white thing half-buried in the river bank. A large soft rubber doll you think, and then the arm moves, beckons slowly in a direction you hadn't considered . . .

*A corpse from a family unable to afford the money for cremation, that is the first thing Joseph mentioned as we sailed up the Hooghly, while I watched the junks and the snakeboats slip by trailing marigolds from the burning ghats above Howrah.*

But we should go further back for a more accurate view, we need to turn over the previous pages, disturb a few leaves in the compost . . .

◆

She was Joseph's second wife. His first had died in childbirth soon after they were married. 'The doctor asked me to choose between my wife and my child,' he told Magda a few weeks before their own wedding. 'If I sacrificed the mother, he swore the child would survive, despite being only seven months in the womb. But I chose my wife. In the end they both died.'

He gave Magda a considering look, weighing up her wiry body and clear golden-brown eyes as if he were reading a profitable bank statement. 'You wouldn't die, though. You are strong.'

*A strong woman, is that all he hoped for? Strong currency to balance his weak stock?*

She had come to England in 1873 to act as companion to her father's aged sister, the same spinster who in 1881 would advise Magda to accept Joseph Ironstone's proposal: 'For at nearly twenty-seven you are no longer young,' her aunt had pointed out, 'and he is handsome and will be rich some day.' Her niece might not be a 'returned empty', that cruel designation for rejected members of the Fishing Fleet who went to India trawling for susceptible European husbands, but Magda's only real attraction for a husband (her father's fortune) had kept pace with the diminishing market for opium. 'You will wait too long, my girl, if you don't accept this one,' her aunt said.

*How do we stray so far from our dreams? Why do we settle for so much less? I remember that my aunt's words made me feel afraid and alone. Any hopes of furthering my botanical studies faded. Thinking back to that time now, I cannot picture myself as the girl who entered into marriage with Joseph Ironstone.*

She did not find him handsome, this small, delicate man whose features would have been almost girlishly pretty had they not been so drawn in on themselves, as if a thread were being pulled too tightly from the inside. 'Bone white,' he joked of his complexion when they first met, not long after his father's company began supplying bonemeal to her aunt's large garden. There weren't many jokes. Sometimes Magda believed it to be no more than a mutual sense of loss drawing Joseph and her together. As children, both of them had lost their mothers – hers to cholera, his in the Indian Mutiny; yet he still seemed attracted to the country where he'd been born, or perhaps to Magda's vision of it. Even after eight years away, India remained in her memory a shifting kaleidoscope of dazzling light, a daily street opera of life and death and rebirth. 'You think we might go back to India and be changed, reborn?' Joseph asked her.

'Reborn, not changed . . .' She couldn't explain. In her India nothing remained the same and everything was unchanging. He brushed her hand quickly with his fine white fingers, and it felt like dry moth wings on her skin.

She didn't love Joseph, Magda acknowledged that, but his sadness moved her. And she was lonely enough to think romance unimportant. Not yet a believer in a world well lost for love, she saw romantic love allied with phosphorus (which is in fish and in the brain), an element that ignited easily on contact with air, often with disastrous results.

It was a marriage marked by ill omens from the start, the servants gossiped. A bout of recurring malarial fever prevented Magda's father Philip from coming to England for the wedding, and her aunt's horror of influenza kept her at home on that day of torrential downpours. The rain continued steadily for the two days it took to move into the Ironstones' house, where the couple went immediately after the ceremony. A dark and gloomy place, every corner held reminders of death's proximity, and Magda surmised that Luther Ironstone, perhaps from having lost his wife and daughter, perhaps from some inner leaning of his own, had developed morbid interests and a disposition to match his profession. Wishing for weather that would allow her to escape into the huge, lush garden (a good advertisement for Ironstone Bonemeal), she stared out the window at plants with leaves too large for the climate, bent under the weight of water. Almost a monsoon rain, she thought, wondering how these exiles from the warmth survived. Some struggled tall and gangly for the light. Some yellowed. Some had been swaddled in brown sacking as if for burial.

*I closed my eyes in the green light and imagined myself anywhere but there.*

In her bedroom the first night Magda waited for her husband to come to her, until she fell asleep, all the lamps still lit. She thought it was the wind made her wake, the curtains swaying and tossing with it like temple dancers. Despite the rain, the room smelled of dust. She sat up and saw Joseph in a chair across the room, watching her, silently, his pale eyes wide and staring. 'They all die,' he said. 'You will see.'

Her skin was cold under the thin white lace. 'What do you mean?'

'All the ones I love. To get away from him.'

'From whom, Joseph?' *What had I done? Who had I married?*

Without answering he stood and left her and she did not see him again for three days. She saw her father-in-law, though. She observed the dislike in his flat estuarine face, sandy and runnelled with deeply etched tracks. In the weeks she had known him he had never expressed any warmth towards her match with his son; neither did he now. He was as squat and spiky as his horned toad of a house. It took all her courage to ask him if he knew where Joseph had gone. 'Gone the way of his mother before him, likely,' Luther Ironstone replied bluntly, and scowled as if Magda were to blame. She wondered if he found her too old, too plain, not rich enough. 'I measured Joseph, you know,' he added. 'He has a different bone structure than her. But it's in him all the same. It's the Congreves, nowt to do with me.'

'What do you mean, sir? What's in him?'

He shrugged her questions off and returned to his apartments above, leaving Magda to wonder how many more unanswered questions there would be before she got to the bottom of this family.

For those three days, Luther left her alone except at mealtimes, and even then he said little. Disturbed by his heavy footsteps on the top floor, his presence hanging over the house like a bad smell, she spent as much time as the rain permitted in the garden, making long lists of its exotic species and sub-species, only driven inside by the dusk and cold.

On the third day her husband's return was heralded by a loud argument with his father. Joseph came to her so nervous that he could not settle in any chair. He did not begin to explain his absence. He paced the room and talked too quickly of ideas he had, experiments that his father did not approve. 'I am taking pictures, cataloguing . . . I am determined to record . . .'

'Record what?'

'The point . . .'

'What point?'

He took her down into the cellar where he kept his cameras and showed her photographs whose subject matter disturbed her. 'Do you think it . . . wise to be so obsessed with the dead and dying?' she asked.

'Your comment indicates the lack of a truly scientific mind,' he snapped.

*But how could these pictures of pitiful souls in the streets – some maimed, some dead, some barely alive – whose circumstances had driven them beyond the point of humanity, how could this be anything to do with science?*

'I am making a study of the link between growth and decay,' he informed her grandly. 'I want to know why one person, one society, fails and the other succeeds. A society grows, becomes decadent – decays – and dies, as this century is doing. What I seek is the point at which negative becomes positive, dark turns to light, rot and decay to new growth.'

When he came to her bed for the first time, Magda kept her eyes fixed on his own tightly shut lids and grimacing features, so that the pictures he had taken would not come between them. Another picture remained, of Joseph's bony white knees as he pulled himself off and the blood she had left on his nightshirt. She tried not to hear him washing at the sink. He did it so carefully, thoroughly cleaning away all traces of what had taken place. *Pollination*, she wrote later, *requires some explanation. Why should it be painful, apparently for both parties?* Although it was over quickly, she assumed that it must have been then that their son was conceived, for it was the only time in those months when Joseph and she were together in such a way. Not an act of love (or of hate, she hoped), but some other emotion which afterwards filled her husband with so much remorse that he could not meet her eyes. This inner turmoil drove him into a black depression, as it would again after Alexandra's conception. He slept for fourteen, even sixteen hours a night and spoke, if at all, with a thick stuporous tongue. Often he did not get up from one day to the next. Neither his work nor his surroundings interested him. He barely ate, he took a great deal of laudanum to kill the pain of persistent migraine. Lonely and filled with anxiety herself, Magda wrote little of this in her diary, preserving it in her memory, an errant catalogue.

The pattern was to be repeated over the next four years: first the restless excitement, the violent arguments with his father, then day after day spent in the cellar with his photographs, finally a silent lethargy almost like death. In those days and nights she would hold him while he told her of his terrible dreams: a spectral woman who pursued him, a murdered girl 'always following', ghosts in the garden's weeds, a black sun. One night, hearing whimpering from his bedroom, Magda crept down the corridor to find Joseph in bed fully dressed. His hands, wrapped around his head, were muddy. So were his trousers, and his fingernails were broken and bleeding, as if he had been kneeling to dig in wet earth. He kept calling 'Mama' and another name that Magda took for his dead wife. He cried louder, 'Stop him! Stop him!' and 'Hilda!' until she shook him awake and held him while he wept.

He claimed to remember nothing of these lost times, or very little. 'Blank pages,' he said.

That is how those four years in London seemed to Magda, who wrote in her journal only of her son Congreve's birth, and of the breathless, waiting nature of that house where even Con walked with trepidation. She stayed partly for her son, a delicate boy born prematurely, and partly out of pity for Joseph. There was no one else to turn to. Her aunt had moved to a health spa in Switzerland soon after the marriage, and Magda didn't like to disturb her father. Philip Fleetwood was having financial difficulties of his own. Yet some of her unhappiness must have been apparent in the regular letters she sent him in India, for not long after Alexandra's birth in 1885 he wrote to offer Joseph the position of manager in his opium business: 'It would be a great favour to me, as I no longer have the energy to perform such a task alone.'

Neither Magda nor Joseph admitted that he was in no fit state to run a business. Both were too elated at the idea of returning to India, of escape. 'It will be a new start for us,' he said.

*12 November: Home at last! I can almost forget the darkness of the last four years. We arrived in Calcutta to find Father at the landing with his arms stretched wide. He proclaimed that our coming had ended the rains and made the flowers bloom. Everything very green, I remember. And our house was as full of light as the Ironstones' had been dark.*

'Too bright, Mummy,' Con said, when Magda walked him down through the bamboos to the mangrove orchard by the river's edge. She hugged him, fiercely glad to be back. He pointed to the gardeners collecting the mangoes' dead branches. 'Look, Mummy: bones!'

'No darling, branches.' *Which the Hindus use to cremate their dead*, she wrote, and later sketched the bamboos throwing up shoots from the shabby older canes. In the same year all the bamboos in the Ironstone garden had flowered and died, while in India they only died down and began afresh.

Returning to the house, she found Joseph striding about the garden with wide eyes, speaking very quickly to her father of all the things he hoped to achieve.

'Yes, yes,' Father said. He exchanged a swift and anxious look with her. 'There is plenty of time.'

Joseph's good intentions did not last long. Increasingly he returned to taking laudanum in the afternoons, a habit he attributed to his mother giving it to him as a relief from his hunger during the siege of Lucknow, and Magda could not claim to be surprised on the day her father came to inform her of Joseph's absences from the factory. 'He has not been seen for weeks, Maggie.' Overdue shipments, pilfering by native workers, a drop in the quality of opium balls produced: all of these problems had built up, and all added to the firm's financial problems. 'If I should die unexpectedly . . .' her father began.

She had suspected that Joseph's nervous problems were held just beneath the surface of a shallow calm on the day he took her to the cemetery where their families were buried. Although it was only two weeks after their arrival in Calcutta, the guardian greeted Joseph like an old friend, leading him immediately to the Ironstone tomb along a path that smelled overpoweringly of frangipani. The trees were planted so that their daily fall of blooms would cover the graves, a waxy carpet Magda crushed underfoot as she walked, releasing the heavy and cloying scent she always associated with death. She watched Joseph at the grave of his mother and sister, running his hand across the words *HILDA MARY* and then that line: *who died on the 21st August 1857 from the sheer want of proper nutriment.* 'Of course, my sister Hilda does not lie here,' he said. 'Her body was thrown down a well at Lucknow with all the others. I saw it.' His voice was chatty, confidential. 'It was because of *him*, you know. Mother made a choice and chose to feed *him*.'

'Him? Whom do you mean?' His father had been in Calcutta at the time.

'The ghost in the woods,' he said, and then laughed as if it were a joke, and shook his head, whether in denial or to clear it she could not tell.

The smell of dead flowers was very strong. 'How often do you come here, Joseph?'

'Often. Not often enough. What does it matter? Every day, twice a week.'

'*More* often, sir,' said the guardian.

Joseph began talking in a rapid, irritable way of his need to find a studio, a place to work, hurrying Magda away before the old man could say any more.

'But you have an office at Father's factory, don't you?'

He twitched his shoulders. 'Not that . . . *clerk's* business; I mean *my* research.'

*I should have realised then where Joseph's strongest contacts lay.*

### B. Teratology (attr. to Joseph Ironstone c. 1885–6)

IT WAS INCLUDED in an album at the Asiatic Society entitled *Forty Photographs of Calcutta Grotesques*. 'Although it isn't signed, as most of Joseph Ironstone's works tend to be,' the clerk had said, 'the images and style do conform to his rather unique vision. They include a dwarf couple with normal-sized children, a man born legless, a blind woman, famine victims and smokers in an opium den. Most were taken in and around the native area of Calcutta known as Black Town.' I felt a jolt of recognition as soon as he showed me the silver gelatine print of a two-headed child holding a malformed poppy. 'Bengali Boy suffering from *Craniopagus Parasiticus*', it was catalogued, and inscribed on the reverse in a familiar handwriting: *Monstrous formations may no more be banished than variation, for in most instances the one differs but in degree from the other. The questions arise: does this irregular form represent the ancestral condition? Is it a reversion? or is it, on the other hand, the starting point of new forms?*

◆

The picture was composed, of course, an icon, a studio shot, as so much of Joseph's current work was. But the child's parents, who were exhibiting it in the marketplace as an oddity, did not mind Joseph taking the boy to his studio to be photographed. They had brought the child, aged two, to Calcutta from a village in the country, as soon as they realised it could be a source of income. It drew crowds wherever it went, and to ensure that no one stole a free look, its parents kept it covered under a cloth, to which might be attributed its pallid skin. The child had been much displayed, Joseph was told by the father, with private audiences before lords and great men of all religions. Asked about the curious purple mottling across one side of their offspring's thin body, the mother replied that the midwife had thrown the newborn on the fire in fear and disgust, trying to kill it. The father had rescued it because the child was a boy, but not before one ear and eye had been considerably burnt away. And had it been a girl? The man shrugged at this question and the woman turned away.

Like the others who saw the child, Joseph was fascinated by its second head. He wondered if the two heads were like twins, unique individuals, or if they shared but a single brain, and if so, did they share as well a single identity?

Where the second head's body should have been there was a short neck ending in a rounded tumour. 'Quite a soft lump,' Joseph said with surprise when he felt it. From time to time expressions appeared to pass across the second head's face. Was this entirely reflexive? Or were such movements of its features controlled by the head's feelings or desires? And if so, by which head? Did the second pair of eyes cry, for example? Could both heads see and hear, despite the mere folds of skin which served as the second head's ears? Could either head speak? No, the parents said, replying to questions that had been asked of them every day for month after month in a variety of native and European languages. Although sometimes the big head made odd panting noises. But not words.

*Ma. Burn fire fear gust killit. Fa. Boy gir? Soflump nek har? preshunzfeelin? smi cry? see ears? Speke? Whasay? Ma. Both heds? Wurdz. Ma.*

The first head's eyes followed Joseph's hand as he passed it back and forth in front of them. But when Joseph tried the same with the second there was no reaction, or none that corresponded to his gestures. He surmised that the second head was parasitic, any movement of its features entirely reflexive.

*Ma fi killt Fa Boygir cry Ma speke Ma fire killt Ma Ma*

*Hilda Mary, beloved daughter of.* Fading away on the 21st August 1857 from sheet want of proper nutriment, as this tiny, wasted two-headed sprite seemed fated to do. One head looking back, one looking forward. While I am always looking back, Joseph thought.

◆ ◆ ◆

### C. A problem with triangulation (Magda Ironstone c. 1886)

'I NEED WORK to take my mind off . . . I need work, Father,' Magda said on the day he came to tell her about Joseph. 'You must teach *me* the procedures of your business.' So it was agreed, and a few days later, at the weekly tiffin party Philip Fleetwood held for his fellow botanists, Magda first saw the man who was to change her life and her family's for good.

She had been talking with George King, then superintendent of the botanic garden at Sibrapur, about a recent addition to the Fleetwood hummingbird collection, a rare and marvellous *Loddigesia mirabilis*. As King admired the skill with which the tiny bird's tail spatulas had been captured, Philip Fleetwood demonstrated how the spatulas were clapped loudly together during courtship, using his hands to simulate their lovesick applause. The new specimen was only one of the hundreds of birds painstakingly stuffed and classified by her father's own hand, as nearly like life as could be affected. Birds, their nests and eggs, even entire young broods, were arranged among dried examples of their preferred habitats in the many glass cases lining the sitting room. 'Living gems, are they not, George?' Fleetwood asked proudly.

Magda had always viewed her father's collecting passion as the scientific offspring of those renaissance artists and natural historians who were governed by naive feelings of awe for anything beautiful or uncanny (for the miraculous, in fact), who displayed in their 'cabinets of curiosity' an arbitrary collection of nautilus shells alongside jewelled Nautilus goblets, meteoric fragments next to astronomical gadgetry. For the first time it struck her that these tiny, jewel-bright birds of her father's were not living, they were dead, as dead as any of the bones and skulls and flayed images in Luther Ironstone's house. To take her mind off the uncomfortable connection, Magda left her father and King and moved towards the garden doors, where she found her eyes drawn to a handsome young Indian sitting stiffly upright on the veranda. He was listening with an expression of forced patience to the harangue of a large military fellow whose florid complexion and puffy features indicated that he was accustomed to consuming a great deal of his own iced wines and mutton pilau as well as the Fleetwoods'. The two men could not have been less alike, she thought, one so pink and loud, the other dark and slim and still.

'Father,' Magda whispered, as he and King approached, 'who are those two rather cross people on the veranda?'

Fleetwood frowned. 'Cross? What? Why that's one of my young botanists – and old Major . . . blast it! Sorry my dear, I can never remember the fellow's name. Indigo planter, terribly keen on orchids, a bit of a windbag.'

George King suppressed a smile under his solemn beard.

'But my good man,' Magda heard Major Blast saying, 'you can't expect us to take seriously the scientific theories of a country where geometry is related to the layout of sacrificial altars, not to scientific principles of geodesy. Your average Hindoo's concept of space is entirely mystic. He cannot begin to grasp the deeper significance of such a thing as our Great Trigonometrical Survey.'

The Indian raised his eyes reluctantly from the cup of tea into which he had been staring. For several seconds he examined his brick-coloured opponent, before replying, in a low, faintly musical voice, 'You believe, sir, that this *Great* Survey can reduce India's mountains, plains, deserts and rivers – not to mention people – to a geometrically uniform imperial space composed of an abstract structure of triangles from whose heights *you*, the active and dominant scientific rulers, may observe *us*, your passive subjects?'

'Well sir, well sir,' the major bridled at the young man's tone, not sure if he was being mocked. 'I believe we have built the skeleton which more detailed geography may flesh out. And our mapping programme would be a sight more accurate had the natives not been so slow to understand its advantages.'

The Indian's smooth brow wrinkled in imitation of someone trying to grasp a difficult concept. 'Each town could then have been assigned a mathematical location within an immobile mesh of meridians and parallels, is that it?'

The major nodded. 'How else can such systems as mail and tax be imposed?'

'And what of nomads, who follow the grazing, attached for one season to this town and next to another? What of tribes who share a single name?'

Magda was impressed by the eager, graceful arguments the young Indian maintained in the face of his opponent, who boomed out imperiously, 'I'm talking of the modern world, sir; you speak of the antique.'

In repose, the botanist's heavy-lidded, elongated eyes and curved lips had given him the look of one of Tibet's serene gods. Blasted by an increasingly bombastic major, he managed to uphold the smile, but not the serenity; it was a smile that narrowed his lips and whitened the skin over his high cheekbones.

The major's voice rang out a stirring declaration: 'I think we must clear a path for the future through the forest of ignorance! Consider poor Everest and what problems he had with the natives when he wanted to fell trees to clear sightlines for his trigonometric surveys in the northern plains. Whole villages came out in battle array, man!' The argument recalled to Magda a British surveyor who had said of triangulation that the surveyor gathered in land like a fisherman casting his net to gather fish, so that eventually the net of triangulation might be thrown over the whole country. The major trumpeted on as if to support that view: 'Whole villages! Simply to protect a few trees which they claimed were homes to their damned heathen gods and spirits.'

'Oh dear,' said her father, anxiously surveying the two warriors. 'I think intervention is called for.'

'So trees are less important than geometry?' the young Indian was asking, his voice not much above a whisper now. Then he took a deep breath and spoke so that everyone could hear, 'And if it had been one of your churches? Would you then have let Russians fell it in the name of mapping *their* empire?'

The major's face had swollen like a red balloon in the heat of the argument. No doubt fearing his guest's imminent apoplexy, Magda's father abandoned his conversation with King and strode over to interpose a polite conversational barrier between the two men.

George King turned to her, laughter evident in his soft Scottish voice: 'That young man has come a long way from the boy who used to write out my garden labels.' He touched her arm. 'Please excuse me, Maggie; I think your father may need some reinforcements.'

The next morning Magda decided to reacquaint herself with the Fleetwood godowns. It was still very early when she set off on the path alongside the Hooghly. A low mist hid the moored rivercraft from sight, their presence conveyed to her by other senses: the soft sounds of a mother singing to her baby, the acrid smell of mustard oil being heated for breakfast. A few steps inland and Magda noticed the mist begin to metamorphose imperceptibly into dust, a triangular wedge of it clearly visible in the open door as she entered the vast, dim space of the main godown. She wondered how this particular triangle differed from its counterpart in England, and whether some future generations of hers might break down such apparent uniformity into exact proportions of red earth, chimney soot, salt of the workers' dried sweat, the ground-up, ground-down stone from a thousand pestles pounding into mortars, the ash from cow dung fires, from burning bones and bodies – and from opium, the fabric of this place: all around her lay deep mango-wood chests of the processed drug. *The smell of our past.* Closing her eyes to take a deep breath, Magda felt something inside her lighten, a weight shift. She recalled her father saying that the workers at the Fleetwoods' Patna godowns upriver were hosed down at the end of each day's labour and the opium-infused water used the following morning as liquor with which to mould and seal the day's output of opium balls. It amused her to think of this distilled sweat of India filling the laudanum bottles of Piccadilly and Park Lane. *And my husband's as well, of course.*

Upstairs in her father's office Magda found a painting of the last sleek opium clipper the Fleetwood family had owned, a boat she could dimly remember: the *Xanadu*, her spread of canvas sail full-blown between three slanting masts. The ship had been sold off after the Second Opium War, when the Fleetwood family began to extricate itself from direct trade with China. They'd become what was referred to as 'middlemen': agents and packers for larger firms, work that Magda suspected her father had never liked. He always preferred medical research to events like the opium auctions, which she keenly anticipated, her memories of childhood visits still clear. The auctions took place in the same high-ceilinged room she remembered, where men came to bid on upwards of 5000 chests of Bengali opium. Tall, powerfully built representatives of the American firm Russell &

Co. of Boston would jostle with slim brown men from Macau, all shouting their bids against stout Indians like Heerjeebhoy and Dadabhoy Rustomjee, whose names made her think of puzzles. There were Chinamen, too, wearing silken coats with wide sleeves (in which, so her father claimed, they kept a breed of dog with a face like a lion).

Attending the auctions as a child, her hand held tightly in her father's, Magda would smell men's sweat from the press of large bodies above her, and hear the rough way in which they treated each other, so different from their manners when they came to take tea at the Fleetwood house. She would try in vain to peer up the sleeve of the Chinaman next to her, half-hoping to meet a lion's gaze, while above them all stood the august figure of the auctioneer, hammer in his hand like a priest in a pulpit poised to strike the Bible.

After one such auction Magda was taken by her father to the docks to see the boats, whippy, narrow-hulled clippers, in use for thirty years by then. He leaned down close and whispered: 'See those, Maggie? They are called clippers. Because they can sail at a fine clip all the way to China – against the wind.'

*Against the wind.* His intonation gave the words a magic which they retained for Magda all her life, so that to do something against the natural trend of things became from then on a venture of significance. 'When they get to China, Father, where will they go?'

He straightened up again and used his hand to shade his eyes, as if he could see further than she. 'When they get to China, they will sail up the Pearl River and into what the Portuguese call the *Bocca Tigris*, the Tiger's Mouth, and there they will sell our black earth to Chinamen from beyond the Great Wall.'

'And what will the Chinamen do with our black opium, Father?'

'The Chinamen will smoke it, dear girl, and it will bring them dreams of sunless seas and fertile ground and sacred rivers like our great Ganges.'

His words that morning were to be engraved on her memory through years of repetition – black earth whose smoke brought dreams of rivers, lions who lived in silk sleeves, ships called *Red Rover*, *Sylph* and *Samarang* that could sail into the tiger's mouth and back.

◆ ◆ ◆

### D. Two clear views of the Fleetwood Laboratories, interior & exterior (anon. c. 1886)

CLARITY IS WHAT we are looking for – or *through*, in fact, for the laboratories are part of the famous Fleetwood glass-houses, said by George King to rival his palm houses at Sibrapur. This is the repetition of an old joke King shared with Magda's father, one that drew a veil over the situation, obscured the clear evidence of how the Fleetwoods' current economic difficulties had left their glasshouses with many broken and missing panes of glass. And we want transparency above all, lucidity, nothing muddied here, no fuzzy-wuzzy nostalgic Victoriana pictures shot with too long an exposure, no darkened rooms, locked drawers, secret compartments. Everything is to be scrutinised under a microscope, labelled by species and assigned its place in the Big Picture.

It starts well, two drawings complete with height, breadth, length; proof that everything at Fleetwood's was built on generous proportions, along the lines of Loddiges' in East London, a nursery once occupying land at Paradise Field (close to Joseph's family home, the as yet unnamed Eden). Not quite the Crystal Palace, but *Big*: it's a time when men like fuller figures. Size counts. Everything is still Great, like Great Britain, and the Fleetwood's great glass paraboloid features a soaring skeleton of iron ribs, its span of glass supported by slender cast-iron pillars that march in tandem with the less ruly living columns of lofty coconut palms.

◆

Growing among these silver-stemmed giants was a luxuriant collection of insectivorous plants, ferns and dainty orchids from Sikkim and Bhutan, and at the far end was a smaller, cooler laboratory devoted to poppies. Magda knew that her father's original aspiration in building the magnificent structures had been to develop a remedy which would be widely available to the poor, in keeping with the homeopathic 'green medicines' advocated by native doctors like his friend Dr Sarkar. What she didn't know was that the Fleetwood fortunes, built on a gummy brown resin which gave the illusion of clarity before permanently fogging the picture, were about to be linked to an even more enigmatic genus.

So preoccupied was the young man in the smaller laboratory with one of his fragile blooms that he did not notice the arrival of George King, Magda and her father for several minutes, and in that time Magda had a better chance to study the combative person she had last seen holding his own against Major Blast two days earlier. She took in his broad, smooth brow and aquiline nose, the profile sharp and clean as a cameo. She observed his long fingers gently teasing earth from the plant's roots, and contrasted them with her husband's small white hands, which she had watched that morning clutching at the bedclothes like the albino crabs you see scuttling under rocks on the seashore.

At her father's greeting the man stood up and she noted his quick shy smile and lanky height and the way his shirt was made even whiter by the copper of his skin. Her father introduced them and Magda extended her hand. The young man hesitated before dipping his head to kiss it, pulling back at the last moment as she started to shake his hand. Apologising for the moist brown earth that had transferred from his hand to Magda's, he tried to brush it off, and succeeded only in sweeping it on to her bodice. This flurry of movement left in the air a faint aroma that she identified as a smell from her childhood, the steam surrounding Bengali sweetmakers when they boiled up their milk and sugar and cardamom very early in the morning. The scent of a promise as yet unfulfilled, she thought.

◆

He felt the beginnings of perspiration under his arms as

Fleetwood's daughter moved closer to examine one of the seedlings. Keeping his eyes down, he studied the flowered cotton covering her thin arm, considering whether this particular white woman was a specimen likely to thrive in the climate of Calcutta. He was amused by the way European women were squeezed into shapes more like cakes or gourds, and suspected it was the kneading effect of their tight clothing that turned the fair-skinned ones either an unhealthy doughy colour or a raw pink, the colour of the slabs of meat they were too fond of. These pink women had a tendency to gain weight and suffer from weak hearts, while others turned yellow and manifested brown spots like those found on paper which had begun to age and catalyse. Prolonged exposure to the extreme Indian light left them brittle, beyond repair, their pigments as faded as English watercolours.

Fleetwood's daughter was not beyond repair, he thought. She was more brown than yellow, and bonier than most of them. Moving his eyes from her arm to her profile, he observed that the barrier of her thick glasses hid pupils that were large and golden, her lids heavy, with lashes sweeping the deep, melancholy shadows under her eyes. Below cheekbones almost as high as his own the skin was stretched tightly over a sharp chin. An obstinate chin, he guessed. But lush, shapely breasts. As if reading his thoughts she looked up and caught him watching her and he felt his cheeks flush.

'I see that you are familiar with the Linnaean system of classifying plants,' she said, reading the notes on one of his diagrams. 'Is it commonly used by native botanists?'

'He learned that with me, Maggie!' George King said.

As a boy, King's former employee had been confused by the Latin binary naming system invented by the Swede, Carl Linnaeus. The allocation of only two or at most three names to a plant – one name for the group of plants it belonged to, the second for a species within that group, a third to define subspecies or cultivar – had led him to assume that the rule applied to people as well as to plants, each Smith or Bannerji a group or species, with properties in common.

'I like the clue Linnaeus gives to a plant's history, Mrs Ironstone,' he answered softly.

'Which our own names no longer do,' she replied. And he thought: Fleetwood, now grafted on to Ironstone and Congreve. How would Linnaeus classify her hybrid offspring, to ensure that their cultivar was evident?

He had long since given up explaining how his own name had come to be lost. Although he joined willingly in his employers' efforts to locate and identify the rarest species of his country, to make orderly and containable its enormous botanical diversity, he was aware that his particular species was an irrelevance to the tireless British classifiers for whom he worked. When he first came to the Fleetwood opium factory and tried to explain the names he was given at birth, the little rodenty nose of the English clerk had wrinkled with impatience long before the final syllable. 'Sounds Jewish to me,' the clerk said. 'But I've got nothing against Jew-boys, not like others in my part of London. Jews have always treated me right. But there's no room for any of this rishfish malarkey. Sign here.'

So he had signed his contract at Fleetwood's with a watery name not his own. 'A new name for my new work,' he thought, and it had pleased him, knowing that his family had come from a place where rivers changed their names when they changed direction. His father, employed by the British to trace the Brahmaputra's principal channel from where it joined the sea to its remote source, had been ridiculed when he returned to say that it often lost its identity altogether; or, after having for some part of its journey lost its original name, was later found with it restored. 'The British are in general unwilling to admit such absurdities,' his father had sighed, 'and thus construct their maps with the same name following the same river from its source to its mouth.'

'And is this not a more logical approach to mapmaking than our own, Father?'

'It will be, when the inhabitants through whose regions this river flows shall adopt the European system. Until then, such an attitude leads to inconvenience and loss of direction by anyone wishing to use the European maps on the spot.'

It had taken years before the boy could see that it made sense for a tributary flowing East to have a different name from one that flowed West. They had different meanings, and meaning was another method of classification, he realised. The holy Ganga, Mother of the World, who began her life as a sky-blue Daughter of the Lord of the Himalayas, altered with each change of course, until, brown and frayed and treacherous as the end of a rope that has passed through too many hands, one of her muddied strands emerged at Calcutta as the Hooghly. Even English cartographers gave up counting the Ganga's tributaries in her last rush to the Bay of Bengal; the number changed with the season. The Ganga was especially dangerous as she neared the sea south of Calcutta, with sand banks whose shapes, shifting constantly, were marked by pictograms of shipwrecks on navigational maps. A hundred and twenty-five miles from the coast, tides still swept upriver and reached Calcutta at six feet high, that long rope of fresh water drawing the sea up over the city's skin, as it had over the coast, where half the land lay permanently under water while the other half, the mangrove jungle, drowned at each high tide.

◆

'Read the bit in your notes about our green poppy,' Magda's father was saying to the young man, 'I've been describing your work to George.'

Her father's employee reached for a small leather-bound book and Magda smelled again his aroma of coconut and sugar. She noticed the back of his neck – like her son Con's, she thought – and then the contrast between that boyish hollow and the broad muscular mass of his shoulders. How old was he – twenty-five? twenty-eight? He cast a slanting look her way, and the slight smile he gave in acknowledgement that she was studying him made her want to touch his fine long fingers again, an urge she attributed to recognition (the sweet smells of childhood, the vulnerable neck so like Con's). Only later did she remember the words of a former president of the Linnaean Society and copy them into her diary as a reminder not to draw hasty comparisons: *The whole tribe of plants in remote countries, at first sight familiar, can prove on examination to be strangers, with other configurations, other qualities. Not only the species themselves are new, but most of the genera. Thus there are few fixed points from which to draw our analogies, and even those that appear most promising are frequently in danger of misleading.*

'My father's notebook, Mr King,' said the young man, looking up from his book. 'One of those you hold in the Botanic Garden's library. Only a copy, sir!' he added, as King's thick brows flew up like two pigeons about to take wing. 'I copied it page by page while I was working for you. In my spare time, of course. My father's book was also a copy – of one that was stolen from him by bandits in Tibet. On his return from that trip he transcribed everything he could remember, including his paintings.'

'Not very reliable, then,' King said.

'Perhaps not, sir. Although my father, his father and grandfather before them – all were trained as copyists. They learned to reproduce every line of Roxburgh's original drawings down to the last watermark.' His smile was less boyish as he reminded King of this, more like the ironic one he had worn while arguing with the major. He explained how his mother's family had come from one of the tribes familiar with a rare green poppy which shared with *Papaver somniferum* the ability both to heal and to condemn. 'A *shaman's* poppy,' he stressed, 'a tonic for the sick in mind as well as body – but to be used only under supervision. They named it the snow leopard, because like that most mysterious of panthers it was dangerous, and so camouflaged that you might stare directly at it from a few feet away and still fail to see it.'

'Read the part concerning growths, man!' Magda's father said impatiently. 'George has heard all the rest from me.'

Leafing through the book in his hand, the young Indian quickly summed up how he had learned from this copy of a copy about the poppy's use in tribal religious ceremonies. He read aloud: ' "not only to call up their ancestors and as an antidote to sorrow and diarrhoea, but also in dosages perilous to the common man, to reduce cankerous growths" '.

'An antidote to sorrow?' Magda interrupted, thinking of Joseph.

King was smiling broadly. 'An antidote to sorrow, diarrhoea *and* cancerous tumours . . . most useful. You have proof?'

'My father found people – borax and salt traders, pilgrims into Tibet, Buddhist monks – who had seen the effect of these green poppies.' Like Jack with his magic beans, the young Indian then pulled from his pocket a rusted tin on which could be read the word 'Century'. 'He had a weakness for English chewing tobacco. These tobacco boxes came in handy for keeping the seeds dry.'

King inquired if the magic seeds had borne fruit yet.

'My father found many examples of what he called the "Tsangpo Green" in your botanical library at Sibrapur,' the young botanist continued, as if he had not been asked a question, 'invariably collected and identified by native botanists. But most of them have since been discarded. All that remains are two dried herbarium specimens so old they have lost the colour from their petals. While they express the prominent fibres and veins, they give only the contour of the dead plant, whereas my father's paintings carry more conviction, are more *real*, than this impression of the thing itself.'

'Fleetwood was telling me that you have managed to germinate the plant,' King objected good-humouredly. 'So why are you stalling us with tales of replicas?'

The Indian's face coloured. Without further comment he led them to a row of pots holding poppy plants in every stage from bud to bloom. The light was dimmer here because of the blinds drawn to shade the young sprouts from direct sun, but even in this low light it was possible to see that there were no green flowers. King, glowering at one washed-out bloom, put into words Magda's own disappointment. 'Is this as green as your famous poppy gets?'

The young botanist shook his head, insisting that his father had described the poppy quite precisely, as if it were a place or a girl he had known and lost. His paintings clearly showed the plant with great rosettes of sea-green velvet leaves, a crown of four large, ruffled petals *like jade butterflies drying their wings*, a sheaf of golden antlers at its heart. 'If you cut open the head just before it bloomed you would find the petals crumpled inside, yet perfect as silk prayer flags, my father wrote, their green intensified to irridescent emerald in the folds.'

It would be found growing among scented primulas the colour of moonlight and poppies the colour of the sky, he said. *Whose* sky, Magda wondered idly. The names for colours were so imprecise. What colour sky was reflected in Homer's wine-dark sea? Was he colour-blind? Most people are to some degree. She had heard that in primitive races one word often sufficed for the whole of the blue end of the colour scale, from green onwards, and her father complained that even the *Iliad* omitted the colours of flowers and sky.

Reports about the green poppy were contradictory, the Indian admitted. Green, yes, on that everyone agreed, although sometimes the green of new rice, other times mossy or faded to an opalescent silver against grassy viridian emerald lime-green leaves. It was said to grow closer to the ground in high places, taller in the valleys. And while it was reported by some tribals to be perennial, others claimed that after flowering once it died. In short, it was a flower whose hallucinatory powers seemed to affect its observers. 'My father hadn't realised that a change in climate often engenders a change in behaviour –'

'So your poppy *might* be greener depending on altitude,' Magda said.

Her reward was another quick smile. 'In a cooler climate – Darjeeling, perhaps, or England. While high altitude is in some respects equivalent to high latitudes, transplanted alpine flora often become monocarpic, as ours have, which means that plants which are technically perennial exhaust themselves producing seeds.'

And so, after flowering once, die, she thought. Was that so bad?

King pointed out that he still had not seen any evidence of the poppy's miraculous powers. His comment elicited a slight shrug from the Indian, who opened the tin of seeds to conjure his father's genie as a witness for the defence. 'Their ability to reduce tumours will not be proven, I believe, until we reproduce the colour. But the alkaloids alone are unique.'

'Alkaloids,' King mused. 'Sertuner's papers showed us that opium with the alkaloid morphine removed had no narcotic effect. What is so new about yours?'

'You haven't read the papers published last year in London about the work on morphine?' Magda's father asked. 'Attempts have been made to find a non-addictive substitute for morphine, first in the early 1870s by boiling it with an acid to create a new substance, then later by experimenting with this molecule to induce sleepiness in dogs. All the papers indicate that the new substance is infinitely more potent than morphine. We have repeated the London experiments here, extracting morphine base from our regular opium plants. The new drug is certainly a heroic painkiller. Indeed, it makes heroes and heroines of all who take it . . . And it is dangerously more addictive than morphine, not at all as it was described. After trying similar experiments with these green poppies, three alkaloids have been isolated.' He indicated the circular paintings produced by his assistant botanist from this microscope work, each one a strange masterpiece, Magda thought, a lens on to the miniature world. She had been impressed by such images ever since seeing the collected work of Franz Bauer, Kew Garden's first artist-in-residence. But the paintings here were of more than usual beauty. Controlled, yet without the sterility of many microscopic studies, they seemed to confirm that order might reign in even the smallest detail of the plant world.

'Two alkaloids I recognise, one is new,' the young man said, 'a narcotic – though not so powerful as my father witnessed. Dogs and monkeys given it show all the signs of dreaming but are still wakeful enough to respond to commands. They are left very calm after this spell of euphoric insomnia, not at all agitated as they are after morphine. As if indeed we had discovered an antidote to sorrow.'

'You're not expecting me to believe that these tribal people isolated the alkaloids?' King's face had resumed its air of mild incredulity.

'No: my mother's tribe simply ate the resin, which is similar to raw opium. There is talk of being infused with the poppy's spirit. I too was sceptical at first. But such poetic definitions are often descriptive of a plant's functions. For example, this poppy's spirit was said to be a youthful one linked to its colour. And only the greenest of the blooms had an ability to reduce the tumours.'

King slapped Magda's father on the back. 'You certainly put one over on me, my friend, when you lured this boy away from us. How did you manage it?'

'Microscopes, sir,' the young man answered. With his own theories no longer under the lens, he was more relaxed. 'Mr Fleetwood was an early member of the Royal Microscopical Society. He commissioned lenses from England for this lab.'

'I suppose you are considering an expedition into Tibet, aren't you, Philip? If not,' George winked at the young man, 'one of these days I might have to lure this talented chap back to Sibrapur!'

◆ ◆ ◆

### E. A Recipe for Binding Volumes (anon. c. 1886)

I CAME AWAKE with a start, the fan over my head keeping pace with the irregular beat of my heart. Beaded with sweat despite the room temperature, I went to the window and opened the shutters on to a hot and silent Calcutta. In the street a reclining cow chewed its cud, a mixed pile of dogs and puppies slept next to a rickshaw-driver's family. I could smell the sickly marzipan scent of frangipani overlaying the tropical stinks of drains and rotting vegetation. What had woken me? A general stickiness in the humid air that no fly-specked Air-Con system could dispel? Or something else, some telling detail I'd missed?

The young botanist's three visitors were about to leave when he heard Fleetwood's daughter say that she needed a little more time to study the poppy. Now there will be nothing but questions, questions, questions, he worried, and the rest of my morning's work lost.

But Magda Ironstone did more looking than talking. She walked slowly past his paintings, laid out next to the plants he was studying, his practice being to add to the images as he discovered more about each specimen. He was surprised to see a woman take so much interest in pictures that were largely scientific. Stopping to pick one up, leaning into another, Fleetwood's daughter made odd little noises, the kind a dog makes settling in front of a fire. She touched a poppy's sexual apparatus with one finger, the drawing of its leaf with another, gently rubbing the paper, reading its surface as a blind woman might. He felt a tingling across his back, the sensation that it was his own skin being touched. Occasionally she flashed a look at him. He noticed that her long eyelashes made her eyes sometimes gold, sometimes deep amber. Not flirting with me, studying me, he reminded himself. Evaluating, more likely; she's my employer now, and at this he felt less like a scientist and more like an unripe mango being weighed for potential as chutney. 'Tell me,' she said finally, 'I understand that for the microscope sections one must use paint – but wouldn't photography be more accurate for botanical studies?'

'Perhaps *too* accurate,' he responded, intrigued by the question. 'For while a painter can manipulate his specimen to isolate and analyse its parts, still representing it as an intact whole, the most a photographer can do is to study a *typical* specimen. He cannot make good his subject's defects or its individuality.'

'Is that a positive thing, then, to make good these defects we find in nature?'

'It is when the defects are superficial. A botanist must be like a plant hunter, searching out family characteristics.' He gestured at two pictures of poppies. 'The fact that one plant suffers from leaf blight does not mean the entire family will produce such blight.'

'But are there not species more prone to rot than others?'

'You asked the question with some *urgency*, Mrs Ironstone – is there a plant family in which you have a particular interest?'

She dropped her eyes to the poppies. 'A particular family, yes,' she replied softly, 'though I doubt you can offer the solution.'

Before he could press her to clarify this, a breath of wind slipped through one of the broken panes in the glass and sent a forgotten recipe fluttering out from between the pages of his old sketchbook: *To ½ ounce sulphate of copper, take 1 pound of binding paste and mix together for binding volumes.*

She picked it up to read, eyes sparkling behind her glasses. 'What alchemist's potion is this?'

'A poisonous solution to brush on books, from the time when I worked at the Botanic Gardens helping the librarian to preserve what remains of their volumes and drawings. The battle against creeping decay was constant.'

'Yes, Father often complains bitterly of the ingenious manner in which India's climate and insects contrive to divide the work of destruction. "One cracks the bindings of books," he says, "the other eats up the inside; the damp turns white satin coats yellow and the cockroaches devour their lace trimming; the heat splits the ivory of miniatures and the white maggots consume the paint. And so they go on helping each other and missing nothing." '

He smiled at her description and nodded. 'This recipe was a formula I found effective in discouraging pests.'

'Yet the formula is *not* so effective, is it?' she asked, the corners of her mouth turning up. 'For you observe that it has not discouraged me from delaying your work this morning!' She started to giggle, and then the giggle turned into a laugh that was not at all what one might expect from such a nice quiet Englishwoman. Not at all *nice*, in the word's original sense of scrupulous, particular – words which until then could have been used to define Magda Ironstone's attitude to him as nicely as they did his own attitude to science. This was a bazaar laugh, generous and irreverent, if a little rusty. It cut through all social niceties. Watching the melancholy set of Magda's features lift, he found himself joining in her laughter, filled with surprised delight that she had seen through his own polite mask.

Later, over dinner with his wife, a kindly but reserved woman whose conversation was limited to domestic concerns, he would consider the binding nature of shared laughter, its sticky, tactile properties.

AFTER BREAKFAST THE next morning, Nick left for UNISENS to find out what he could about the dismissed chemists and I set off in a taxi for the Calcutta Botanic Gardens.

From the start there was some confusion. Between 1885, the date of a guidebook I'd brought from Magda's library, when Calcutta was described as having 'the greatest botanical gardens outside Kew', and the latest edition of the Lonely Planet Guide, the gardens had largely dropped from view. Only one of my three new books mentioned them – dismissively, as the location of the 'Great Banyan Tree' (said to be not that great). My taxi driver nodded vaguely. 'Yes, gardens, yes,' and took me immediately to the cricket grounds at Eden Gardens. When I refused to accept this as a solution, waving my arms like a traffic policeman to the other side of the Hooghly, he turned to give me an unattractive smile. 'This garden is known as B Gardens, Miss. So no wonder I am not knowing it.'

India was full of misread signs and missing letters. Passing slowly through Sibpur, known as Sibrapur in my old book, and endless industrial suburb that seemed to be all outskirts, we entered the Botanic Gardens by the Howrah Gate. There were several signs warning NO VEHICULAR TRAFFIC, but the guard insisted that I keep the taxi. My protests that I wanted to walk were met with his cry of, 'Too far! Too far!', maybe in reference to a wooden map of the garden that stood by the gate, with Africa, Asia, North and South America delineated in pleasant pastels. To reach William Roxburgh's house, marked on the map not far from the Botanical Survey of India (where I had a meeting with the custodian of Roxburgh's 'Icones'), my taxi would have to traverse the entire world – an orderly world, fortunately, the wilderness divided up into categories useful to man. It was not enough for plants simply to grow here, they must be *seen* to grow within simulated natural habitats. They had to be simulated, because no remnant of the original swamp on which these gardens were built remained. One nineteenth-century curator had written that tropical botanic gardens should consist of 'a reduced copy of the virgin wood', the key word being 'reduced'. These were to be Paradise Abridged, less time-consuming to maintain; the jungle confined to a Palm House, an Orchid House or, for those plants stubbornly refusing to grow in captivity, a set of dried specimens in the herbarium. The rule was: Nature is all right, in its place, and its place is under glass.

Like the Fleetwood mansion, Roxburgh's fine three-storey house had been abandoned long since to squatters, and the two-storey arcaded colonial house which served as offices for the Botanical Survey of India, Calcutta Division, appeared at first sight to have been closed up for centuries. Panes of glass were missing from the fanlights above shuttered doors, mildew stained the plaster columns and when I threw my head back to see if there was any movement on the upper storey veranda, two goats thrust their inquisitive Pan faces through the rusted iron railings, twin pairs of yellow eyes peering down at me.

Trying to keep in the shade, I searched in vain for an open window or door. The heat made the crickets too loud, the colours too lushly tropical. Even the small freckles of sunlight allowed through by the canopy of trees were like scalding water where they shifted across my skin.

A man on a bicycle appeared around one side of the building, pedalling so slowly it was a miracle he remained upright. I called out to him but he cycled past as if I were invisible. It wasn't until I reached the back of the building that I saw the notice 'Staff Convention to Discuss Problems of Employees of Centre'. It made me want to cry with frustration. Nick had been right to mock my official letters.

At that point the shuttered door behind me opened, a sleepy

voice asked my business and I turned to see a bare-chested, bare-footed man, his skin very dark against a white cotton lungi.

It was one of those sequences of events that Nick had told me to expect in encounters with Indian bureaucracy. Either you are foiled in your purpose by layers of pointless obfuscation, regardless of the worth of your request, and you wind up with files full of incomprehensible letters explaining why each higher authority to whom you have appealed cannot do what they have spent months telling you might be possible if only you wrote with further qualifications to the superintendent, the vice counsel, the general manager or present custodian.

Or, the boss has malaria, his second-in-command uses the opportunity of a staff convention to enjoy a series of extended lunchbreaks, thus earning the resentful animosity of his underling, who, for a modest bribe, is willing to waive protocol and security and usher the previously frustrated supplicant straight to the source.

Here, once again, I had the feeling that I was following in someone else's footsteps, the vision of a labyrinth, a catacomb containing images of everything I needed to know. Except that in my dreams, my lucid dreams, I enter this room or tomb and the light I bring with me does not illuminate, it dissolves what I have come to see. The pictures or frescos fade to black, a darkroom memory of photographic images decomposing in old chemicals.

I walked into a room shuttered against the heat and could not begin to imagine its height and length. It was so dark that nothing was visible except the ghostly white lungi of the bare-chested clerk as he opened first one great window and then another – no more than three in all, just enough to illuminate the room's vast expanse and throw three dazzling white envelopes of light across the wide dark floorboards on whose surface the clerk's bare feet had left footprints like Man Friday's. He switched on a fan and unlocked a glass case rising into the roof beams, one of many such cases lining the room. He lifted down some large flattish cardboard boxes and placed one after another on the wooden tables under the irregular breeze of that lethargic fan, box after box evenly spaced apart, mimicking the rectangles of sun the windows have laid on the floor down that long dark high room.

When they had all been arranged in a row, he blew the dust off the first box and opened it to reveal a flash of colour, like the first face card turned up in a game of Patience. He paused – the narrator of the play, the umpire, the curtain-raiser – and then, 'The Roxburgh Icones,' he said, indicating the closest of the ten boxes, and waving to the others, 'Etcetera'. He began to take pictures out of the first box and place them in front of me, hardly pausing between each flower: a Madonna lily, an opium poppy, a primula the colour of moonlight, orchids from Sikkim, honeysuckle and jasmine and vanilla-scented clematis and wild Himalayan roses in white, pink and gold. A waterfall of colour and blossom.

I had entered Sally's paper garden.

'Many of these plants are no longer existing in the wild,' the clerk said.

The more transient colours had faded beyond recognition. Green had turned to white. Pictures had cracked and been repaired with tape that had yellowed and left its own pattern of ageing, the repairs now defining the art. I remembered the Kew historian telling me how European paper was sensitive to the monsoon climate, which caused gradual degradation of the structure. 'And strong light makes them very brittle.' He had smiled. 'That too we get a lot of in India. They should really be stored in an acid-free environment.' He explained that the last time he'd seen Calcutta's collection, no such effort was being made, and added apologetically that the paintings were viewed as relics of the Raj. 'So there was – *is* – a great feeling of ambivalence about them.'

'But they were painted by Indians.'

'Ah, yes, but Indians using British paper, British paints, a British style. The vernacular is important, I suppose, whether in art or language, as a kind of code.'

'For Them and Us.'

He smiled at my American bluntness. His was a more oblique approach, a different history, of evasive measures taken against invaders already in residence. 'In this case, paintings using traditional Indian pigments and paper have survived much better.'

'So why didn't Roxburgh get his Indian artists to use indigenous materials?'

'Ah.' It seemed this was going to be his only answer, a faint sigh. Almost reluctantly, he continued, 'The English preferred a less highly coloured effect.'

'Because they came from a greyer country?'

He raised his hands in a gesture to summon that generation of imperial ghosts. 'What a pity we cannot ask them.'

The clerk was reeling off men's names, not plants: a long list of fair-skinned, rosy-cheeked residents of a chill and misty land who in the name of flowers, medicine, adventure had been drawn to this steaming jungle, and who, like so many of the plants whose habitat they misjudged, sickened in the heat and died. Thomas Anderson, director of the gardens, forced to retire because of repeated malaria attacks, dead from the disease within two years of retiring. John Scott the curator, who contracted 'malarious fever of a very bad form' and had to return to Britain in 1879, to die after a short period at home. Another curator who, following an attack by a tigress, was allowed to return to England to convalesce, where he shortly contracted cholera and died. The great William Roxburgh himself, whose state of health, both 'obstinate and nervous' gave him reason to fear that his life could not be a long one.

The catalogue of horticultural mortality was longer, tangled up in my head with the human deaths, because so many plants were named after the men who found them: Farrer and farrerii, Ward and wardii, Forrest and forrestii. One long stuttering list of I I I I I I. As if the men came first and not the plants. Plants collected by sawmill owners in the Himalayas and by the Indian forestry service as they cleared the wild land to turn it into tea gardens. Plants dug up by Victorian botanical artists keen to

have members of their family immortalised. Herbarium specimens removed to England by members of the East India
Company and left to rot for years in the cellars of India House,
where upwards of half the specimens were destroyed by damp,
vermin and coal smoke. Thousands upon thousands of plants
uprooted, packed in Wardian cases and sent to Kew, many that
did not survive the voyage, others that reached their destination
only to weaken and die before anyone could get around to
cataloguing them.

Noting the dates on a few of the paintings in the photocopied
catalogue the clerk had given me, I said, 'I was given to
understand that the icons were commissioned by William
Roxburgh. But Roxburgh died fifty years before many of these
pictures were painted.'

'You are saying to me you want to see *everything*,' he replied,
unperturbed, and gestured to the other boxes. 'Some hold the
bound albums of Roxburgh's original 2542 icons, some hold
Nathaniel Wallich's pictures, some have origins we are not
knowing. And students come here over the years and replace
pictures all higgledy-piggledy.'

I glanced at the catalogue with its false impression of ordered
objectivity. 'So this list is of absolutely no use.'

'Only it is of use to tell you all the pictures which are in these
boxes.'

'But my chances of finding what I want are pretty random.'

He arranged his features into an expression of condolence.
'Depending on who was looking before you and in what order
they are returning the pictures.'

Gently I lifted out of the second box a poppy the colour of the
sky, each petal transparent and crumpled as a newly opened
butterfly's wing. These marks, the hand that painted this, I
recognised immediately. Holding it up to the light I noticed too
late the worm holes tunnelled through the delicate paper, the
mottling of grey-green mould eating into the painted surface.
What happened next took place in slow motion. The paper
began to crack and split and break apart in my hands. Four
pieces fluttered to the floor, crumbling as they landed and

scattering a confetti of colour. They lay there like broken china for a full minute while I stared down in horror, waiting for the command to leave.

The clerk calmly picked up the crumbs and slipped them into the box behind the other pictures. A fragment of the poppy's blue petal remained on the floor, so bright it might have been lapis lazuli fallen from the Taj Mahal's mosaic arabesques. On the paper were the familiar initials: AR, beside some foreign script and the edge of a word – Arun? The beginning of Arunachal Pradesh? Rescuing it while the clerk's back was turned, I slipped it into my notebook, feeling only slightly guilty.

I walked down the row of boxes and lifted each of the lids to search for more work by that remembered hand. One was full of fly larvae and broken fragments. Another's contents were blackened with mould. Between them was a box containing miniatures with colours almost as fresh as on the day they had been done. There was no logic for why some paintings had survived and others not. I have seen burial sites like this. You open up a grave and find one skeleton intact, the bones next to it decayed, crumbled to dust.

'What do the letters IB refer to?' I asked. 'Some of the pictures in the catalogue have IB in front of their numbers.'

'Ironstone Bequest. Married name of Magda Fleetwood who donated these.'

A shiver lifted the hairs on my arms. Why hadn't Jack mentioned an Ironstone Bequest to me?

The clerk volunteered that the four boxes containing the Ironstone Bequest (including a box of photographs he described as 'peculiar') were almost never requested because few people knew about them. 'Which is why these boxes are more orderly than the others. Most people come to see our icons.' He handed me the lid of one box, first blowing the dust off the dates that had been scribbled on its label. 'No one is looking at these pictures for over two years.'

'Do you record names of the people who have looked at the boxes?'

'Some of us do, some not. I have a good memory so I keep all records here.' He tapped the side of his head. 'Last man to look at these Ironstone boxes was most distinguished.' He pointed at the last date, 'That is my writing. I remember him because he particularly requested these boxes and we do not have so many English people. A very tall man, and he is coming back often.'

'What made him seem distinguished?'

'It is not a question of *seeming*, madam. He is one of the Ironstone family whose pictures these are.'

*Jack.* What was he trying to hide?

A grave is just a form of long term storage: it was one of Val's favourite sayings. To uncover the history of a skeleton buried in your closet, I thought, first establish a grid to contain the burial site. My grid was the crossing point of Ironstone and Fleetwood. I walked over to the box of photographs the clerk had described as 'peculiar' and leafed through various mutated plant species, stopping at the eerie portrait of a languid male Ophelia deliberately posed to give the impression that he was the decaying victim of a drowning incident.

'Why would photographs like this be in a botanical collection?' I asked.

'All such pictures are including unusual plants.' He pointed out that surrounding the half-naked man were opium poppies showing stamens metamorphosed into carpels, one of a group of plants subject to such anomalies.

Turning the photo over to read the faded inscription on its back, I recognised the handwriting with a start. Its content was even more peculiar than the image it described: <u>Self-Portrait as a Drowned Man With Poppies.</u> *The corpse which you see here is that of Joseph Ironstone. The unhappy man has drowned himself. Journalists were occupied with his exploits for a long time, but here he is at the morgue for days and none have claimed him. Ladies and Gentlemen, pass along for fear of offending your sense of smell, for as you can observe, the face and hands of the gentleman are decaying like a rotting fish.* Joseph Ironstone: my first real family portrait, but not one I liked. The clerk, assuming I was interested in more of the same, shuffled through the box with no more concern than if it were a deck of cards, pulling out several self-portraits of Joseph. Each one revealed an impotent sensuality that was disturbing, the record of a man who was literally wasting away. 'Mr Ironstone was looking at these pictures too,' the clerk said.

Why was Jack interested? Did he worry, as I did, about the past we shared? Parents, grandparents: they are magnetic forces; whether attracting or repelling, they affect us. What had Jack inherited? What had he learned? 'Did Jack Ironstone go through any other boxes?' I asked. 'I'm his cousin.'

'We can examine the lids to discover which dates correspond to the days of your cousin's visits. But if other people are looking through such boxes since your cousin was here, pictures will be in a muddle.'

Of the approximately 4000 works of art listed in the catalogue, only half were to be found within the boxes meant to contain them. The rest were scattered in haphazard configurations that might have told someone a lot about the general interests of the library's visitors. After an hour I said to the clerk that it would be a good idea for him to replace the pictures in the catalogue order. 'Why, Miss?'

'It would make it easier to find the pictures you want, for a start.'

He pondered this novel suggestion. 'But then, if one goes directly to the picture one is seeking, think of all the others one doesn't see!'

'Whereas in your current system you waste time looking through lots of pictures that don't interest you,' I said impatiently.

'How can this be a waste of time if you are finding something new!'

Shrugging off his logic, I began examining the four boxes containing the Ironstone Bequest. By three o'clock, when the clerk wanted to leave, I had covered twelve boxes fairly thoroughly, glanced through the remaining eight and made a list of all the relevant titles and captions. What *wasn't* here was just as interesting. The absent. The lost or damaged. There were catalogue entries for poppies of every colour from red and pinkish-grey through blue to green, yet no pictures of green poppies had come to light barring one microscope section through a petal. And twenty of the missing pictures concerned the green poppy or the Tsangpo Gorge in Tibet, Xanadu's ultimate destination – exactly the subjects my cousin Jack had shown me at the UNISENS labs in London.

I was beginning to have some idea why my cousin had been so concerned that our shared history remain distant.

◆ ◆ ◆

## F. Self-portrait as a Drowned Man
### (attr. to Joseph Ironstone c. 1886)

THE MAN APPEARED to be dead, eyes closed, face slack under the Ophelia crown of poppies, hands and bare feet discoloured, his limp body slumped against a stone angel. But it was an enigmatic picture, for if the handwriting was that of Joseph Ironstone, as the caption and Gothic photographic style indicated, how could the picture be of his corpse? And if the man in the picture was drowned, how could this be a self-portrait?

◆

He perceived the river now as a vicious brown snake. He saw the pink sky flaked with dirty clouds, a raw skin stretched to dry over the city he had grown to hate, a city sweating and sick with heat. He imagined that Job Charnock could not have chosen a more unhealthful place on all the river for his city, for three miles away was a lake that overflowed every September and then prodigious numbers of fish swam here, but when the floods dissipated those fishes were left dry and with them putrefaction affected the air and caused yearly mortality. Between August and January hundreds of burials were registered in the Clerk's Book of Mortality. We rot here like fish, he thought. He was rotting. His skin was wasting away in opium dreams. His teeth were loose. Soon he would be as thin as his mother had been. He remembered eyes like smoke rings, hands like dry leaves.

He didn't belong in Calcutta, not any more. But if not here, where? Where was the origin of this old desire he had which could not be put into words or even into waking thoughts? *Reborn, not changed,* he thought, as he walked the streets at night searching for someone who could understand the needs that came to him in dreams, someone to make him real, searching for his own reality, his species – on the river banks and in the seething stinking lanes of north Calcutta and the streets behind the tanneries, where the blood ran with excrement and urine between fly-blown carcasses and pigsties and men whose own bodies seemed little better fleshed than the animals' skins they tanned. Like London, he thought, it's become London: black and smeared. The Calcutta he remembered, his mother's green and white City of Palaces, that was the dream. He was born under a black sun. He was the occidental sun, the accidental son. Udderless, rudderless. His camera was the only reality, an extra eye through which he might capture someone he knew was waiting. Then he could rest.

When he could stand the hunt or flight no longer he went to an upstairs room he knew, where the Chinamen met to smoke and dream. He calmed himself with the ritual of it, the list of equipment, the recipe for his only sleep:

a tray
a pipe
a burning taper
the brass thimbles he shared with the others, thimbles full of
that brown syrup thick as treacle into which the wire was
thrust and spun and fired into a single punctuation mark
that put a stop to all his fears

His dear, desired fears:

To slip away.
Waste away.
Decay.

He wrote it down and thought himself a poet.

He was coming to the end of one phase and the beginning of

211

another, for now the opium sleep failed to bring him peace. His sister and the double-headed child were following.

*Ma fire killt Fa Boygir cry Ma see hear speke Ma fire killt Ma MaMaMa*

The child died soon after the photograph was taken, not from starvation (despite its emaciated state) but from a cobra's bite. When he bought the corpse from its mother he found that each skull did indeed contain a separate brain, the chief supply of blood to the upper head being from the membranes of the first head to the second. He cleaned the small skull – skulls – to make the second head's development clearly visible. It grew upside down like a large fungus out of the first child's anterior fontanelle, where the skull had not completely ossified. If asked why he was obsessed with such distorted forms he would no longer have been able to explain. He was silent from one week to the next, and when he did speak he thought it was the second head speaking. *The ghost in the weeds.* No longer lucid enough to see that he was trying to find a way out of this thing he was, this thing he had been trained, preordained to be, he took more pictures of the skulls, but none achieved the pathos of that original shot with the living child. So he went back to the mother to see what he had missed.

◆ ◆ ◆

### G. Dogs in a Landscape: an early Muybridge sequence showing views of the Opium Gardens near Patna (anon. c. 1886)

WHERE WAS JOSEPH while Magda's life was changing in ways she could never have imagined? There were gaps, unexplained absences. Although he seldom talked about his work any more, she knew of the studio he had rented, she had seen a few of his recent botanical pictures, time-lapse sequences which emulated Muybridge's consecutive photographs of a galloping horse. The missing shots she found more tantalising than the frozen images.

'He is very involved with his photography again,' Magda

answered too eagerly, when her father inquired after Joseph. 'He asked for samples of the new poppy species to record . . .' She left it there, unwilling to air any misgivings she felt about her husband's singular interest in the green poppy's recent mutations. Returning home in the early hours of the morning, Joseph would sleep, bedroom door locked, until long after she had left for the factory. At her explanation one afternoon that she was leaving by train for Patna with a selection of the green poppy seedlings, he expressed no emotion. 'To see if they will do better in the drier heat upriver,' she added, but he left her without a reply. They might have been existing on two separate picture planes, their lives diffused and distant images projected on different walls.

She sat alone in first class, her eyes fixed out the train window on a rapid-shuttered view dissecting the Bengal plains. A photograph would have captured her upright figure, neatly bonneted and gloved in pearl grey, the very picture of a Victorian memsahib. It could have revealed no trace of where her thoughts lay – in another coach, a dustier, unpadded compartment, its wooden floors slicked by spit, with a young Indian botanist who was chatting and smoking with porters twice his age. He had an easy command of men as well as plants, and his hand, resting lightly on one of the Wardian cases of poppy specimens, suggested this, giving the appearance of Gulliver grasping a Lilliputian version of the Fleetwoods' glasshouse. A false impression of order imposed on a small, protected world.

*All my life I will remember the drowsy, spicy aroma of the opium fields of Patna. Shall we call those acres of lilac, rose and dove-grey poppies a garden? The bright saris of the women pickers against the grey-green pods were brilliant petals on an ocean of opium and the coloured yarn used by these women to mark the most potent plants brought to mind no more than a childish game, or the ribbons tied in my daughter's hair.*

'How do you know the best time to harvest?' Magda asked the poppy farmers at the first plantation she visited.

'When they wake up every morning with headaches and

nausea,' the Indian botanist answered, before her father's agent could interject, 'then they know.'

Magda was amazed at the grandeur of the business she was taking over. She strolled proudly through the godowns where the bulk of processed opium awaited dispatch to Calcutta. Built like lofty, open-ended railway tunnels to allow the air to pass freely, these riverside warehouses held row upon row of opium globes the size of cannonballs that rose on latticework stacks higher than twenty men. 'For all the world like those curious counting devices which the Chinamen call abacus,' Magda said. Her father's Indian botanist had been deliberately trailing behind, she noticed, dissociating himself from the foreman and the agent. At her comment he spoke up, pointing out that the small boys with the job of turning the balls daily to prevent decay or insect damage complained of the drug's heavy perfume in the hot upper reaches of the galleries. Even on the factory floor it hung like brown sheets, and when the foreman swore that his workers were not affected, the botanist responded immediately, 'Yet I have heard how you can slip into opium dreams simply by breathing the godowns' air, or by walking through a field of poppies after they had been cut with the *nushtur.*'

*The vocabulary of opium stains my lips still,* Magda would confide to her diary. 'Nushtur, *a sharpened mussel shell used to incise the pods. Kurrace, the bowl into which the pod's cloudy sap dripped (or wept, they say here, the pod weeping internally and dying when cut too deep). I can see the factory hands in front of their tiny vessels holding just enough opium for three balls, their basins of water and feathery piles of poppy petals, their cups of* lewah, *inferior opium smeared over the petals as a seal, the brass cup used to shape the opium balls.*

'This is how they become addicts,' *he told me on that first morning in the godowns, but I wouldn't let myself believe him, not yet.*

On her last day in Patna Magda walked down to the river to check that the luggage had been stowed safely aboard the steamer they were to take to Calcutta. The comments made by her father's botanist had cheated her of any joy in this expedition. While reluctantly admitting to herself the odd wish for this young Indian to like her, she still blamed him for causing her to feel guilt instead of pride in her work.

She recognised his tall silhouette under a banyan tree by Takta Ghat, a jetty so named because it was laid with *taktas* or planks, up which shackled prisoners had once been made to carry their packs to the ship that was to transport them to gaol in the Andaman Islands. He was talking to an older man in a narrow rowing sloop that looked as curved and deadly as a scimitar. 'You are not trying to make a quick escape in that decidedly unsafe vessel, are you?' she called out, her attempt at humour sounding forced even to her own ears.

'Escape, Mrs Ironstone? No. I was asking this man whether he would be rowing to Calcutta for the hilsa season.'

'It is a long way to row for fish.' She heard the boatman speaking, but understood only a few words. 'What is he saying about the Ganges?'

'Not the Ganges, Mrs Ironstone. *Ganga*: a generic term he applies to all rivers. He has been telling me that fishing is poor man's work and he wishes that he had taken up a business like his brother-in-law, a funeral photographer who plies crematoriums on the rivers. He works with the funeral priest, the Dead Man's Brahmin. This man says that it is like lightning when the magnesium flare goes off at night to light the corpses for his brother-in-law's camera.'

Magda wondered how much was known in the company of her husband's similar obsessions. Were these two men laughing at her in their own tongue? She waited for the young Indian to show his hand, but his expression remained guarded. How far could she trust him? How far could you trust any people you ruled? 'There is one thing I have been meaning to ask,' she began. 'It has been brought to my attention that there is a scandal sheet reporting lies about my father's business. I found a copy on the godown floor.'

He moved out of the shadow of the tree and the sun fell on his face. His almond-shaped eyes scrutinised her carefully. The effect of this prolonged gaze left her curiously excited. 'Lies, Mrs Ironstone?'

'Perhaps not lies – exaggerations, then. This paper claims my father's trade is responsible for making opium addicts of his workers either by illicit eating or by absorbing it through the skin because they are handling such quantities.'

His chin lifted. 'You think this is exaggeration?'

Magda wondered if that coppery skin was as warm as it looked. She wanted to put her hand up, feel the surface. To give her hands a more appropriate occupation she took a pencil out of her bag and held it like a baton to conduct the conversation along proper channels. 'My father would not allow such injustices.'

'No?' He nodded in apparent agreement. 'Are you aware that the government of Bombay has prevented the government of India from promoting the cultivation of poppies in its region on the grounds that it demoralises the work force?'

'The British did not introduce opium into India,' she answered crisply. 'They merely turned it into a profitable enterprise.' Knowing how pompous her words sounded, she was still unwilling to admit to anyone that the business she loved with the fierce illogic of a first love was so deeply flawed. 'You have been drawing, I see,' she said, trying to turn the conversation in a different direction.

◆

He moved quickly to grasp the album that was propped against the tree. Sheets of paper fluttered out of it and as he leapt to catch them Magda stooped to collect the nearest, bumping her head against his. They both fell back, clutched their heads and apologised.

Laughing, while holding out a hand to prevent a repeat of the incident, Magda reached for the album, which he had clamped tightly to his side. 'Please, Mrs Ironstone, I would rather not –'

'Not *what*?' she asked teasingly, tugging at the album. 'Not show, not speak, not be here?' For a moment their mutual refusal to let go brought her into disturbing proximity with him. He gave in abruptly and made a wordless, reluctant noise as he watched her turn the top sketch over. 'Why . . . it's Father and me!' she said, examining the deft pencil lines. 'How clever . . .' With dismay he heard her voice tremble, her attempt to hide the hurt she felt at his precise caricature. 'How well you have caught our likenesses behind those matching spectacles. Two grey owls.' She tried out a small, ineffective laugh. 'I thought your work confined to the botanical and here I find you straying into ornithology.'

He would have given anything then to have had less skill as a draughtsman. 'I'm terribly sorry, it's not meant . . . it's not –' The drawing, done long before he had met her, conveyed nothing of her beautiful eyes – or spirit, he thought now. But he could hardly explain such things to her.

'It seems you have a dangerous talent.' Eyes lowered, she handed back the album.

'There's nothing finished yet, Mrs Ironstone. Only the beginnings of a series your father has asked me to make of his work on poppies and opium.'

'Along with your research?' she said quickly. 'It must take up all your time.'

'Not at all,' he answered, touched that she would consider his time valuable. *When I paint, I feel my father very close*: that's what he would have liked to say. He wanted to offer her some apology for the cartoon, but couldn't think how to do it without making things worse. 'This is a sample of the standard required,' he said finally, lifting out a picture of two dogs, quite different in style to his own work, though skilfully done. 'It is by an East India Company artist called Shaik Mohammad Amir whom your father admires.' Privately, he thought the two dogs displayed none of the wet-nosed loose-moralled dogginess he associated with canines. They looked very stiff, stuffed even. Suitable for a lover of taxidermy like Mr Fleetwood. 'People say that this artist did not suffer from our native inclination to admire pattern over realism.' He did not suffer from the inclination himself but he knew it was an accepted truism about his race. 'You see how the dogs must belong to English masters, for they wear collars, unlike our dogs. Yet they appear trapped in their well-groomed environment, staring longingly out to the wild country beyond their master's compound. Like those –' He stopped abruptly.

'Like those what?' Mrs Ironstone raised her large eyes above the round glasses, an effect which gave her a vulnerable look, as if she had partially undressed. 'Like those animals we keep walled against their wishes? *Or*,' she persisted, 'like those of us who serve other interests instead of our own?'

*And are no more or less than dogs in a landscape*, his inner voice finished. She held his gaze in a silent exchange and he felt his breath quicken, he felt intensely alive. Is it true, he wondered, is there an uncommon bond growing between me and this woman? Am I imagining it?

Her next question took him off guard: 'Do tell me about your name. It seems so unusual for an –' She stopped. 'Is it not Jewish?'

'A lost tribe, certainly,' he said drily, and could tell that she didn't know whether to take him seriously. 'My name has been Anglicised,' he added.

'Is that why you sign your paintings only with these almost invisible initials?'

'It's not important.'

'Your name? Surely a name must be important.'

'I mean the actual words, the spelling.'

Mrs Ironstone picked one of his pencils from the bench and offered it to him. 'Please,' she said. 'Write it for me. Here, on this painting of the blue poppy.'

He considered writing the Anglicised version, but pride intervened, the desire to test Magda Ironstone further.

'Oh,' she said, her face falling as she watched him sign his father's tribal name. 'How silly of me. You meant that I would not be able to understand the script.'

Once again he'd hurt her. Regretting it instantly, he tried to make amends. 'The closest you might get to an English version of my first name is this, I suppose.' Swiftly he added the shortened name, pronouncing it as he wrote.

'Arun,' she said, 'not Aaron.' Her voice matched his intonation, and it seemed that in saying his name she had dealt him a light but tangible blow.

'Short for Aruncala,' he told her, 'the tawny mountain.'

◆

*I returned from Patna on one of the river ferries that are piloted, so Father claims, by descendants of five Cinque Ports pilots sent out by the East India Company two hundred years ago. The heat had been building up for weeks, but the vessel's swift movement sent a cool breeze over the forecastle where I sat amongst the other Europeans. God knows what it was like in the deck below! I did not see him again until our arrival in Calcutta days later, at dusk. Both shores were lit, as was the Howrah bridge, the glow along that silent dark river throwing into silhouette the rows of black shipping and the long line of godowns like four-poster beds on their piles, while the sky's massed clouds shone with a very lurid and ominous light. Five minutes later, I stepped off the jetty on to firm ground and the vultures and kites began swooping over us in great disorder, evidently beating against a wind that had not yet reached us. In another moment we were struck by a dense pall of dust and darkness so great that I had to take shelter in a commercial coach. Looking out the window after the worst of the storm was over I saw him striding up the bank to the road, a long shawl of white wrapped around his face so that only his eyes were visible. As he passed the coach, he gave us a long sideways glance that sent through me a premonition as violent as the disappearing storm.*

◆ ◆ ◆

### H. A Lost River (anon. Indian artist c.1886)

THE CLERK EXPLAINED that the library's missing pictures might have been sent for restoration after being damaged, 'As you damaged that poppy.' He had an excellent knowledge of the collection's history. In 1861, he said, the Calcutta Botanic

Gardens' custodian destroyed 1500 pounds of old letters and documents, collecting books, diaries and lists of local Indian plant names amassed by native explorers and artists. 'Even more were eaten up over the next thirty years by mould and cockroaches, rats, white ants and the ubiquitous beetle book maggots which are drilling pinholes through even the stoutest pages.' Among the surviving native pictures was a small, unsigned watercolour inscribed *A Lost River*. 'Why the artist should have so titled it is a mystery,' said the clerk, 'for although it is the nature of some rivers to lose themselves, this painting shows a well-travelled stretch of the Hooghly beside the Fleet-wood opium factory.'

◆

'Chatterjee was taken by a tigress on his way from work last night,' Arun announced to Magda one morning in July. 'They think it might be the same man-eater who attacked the curator last year in the Botanic Gardens. You should be careful walking by the river in the twilight and dawn hours, Mrs Ironstone.'

She had watched surreptitiously as he negotiated his way between the opium packers and the sandalwood chests and climbed the steps from the factory floor to her office, a high-ceilinged room where she wrote with a fan in one hand and her pen in the other. Composing her face into an employer's smile for the benefit of the clerks in the next room, she gestured for Arun to be seated. 'It would have to swim the Hooghly for its dinner, this tiger of yours,' she said.

'They are saying it is one of the big cats from the delta land. Tigers who spend their life in the sea in these monsoon months go crazy from the salt. They get the taste of human flesh and then other game is too much trouble for them.'

His anxiety on her behalf made Magda happy. 'We are at less risk here than the curators at the Botanic Gardens, even from amphibious tigers,' she teased him gently. 'They are very isolated out there in the countryside.'

His lower lip tightened and he worked its inner surface between his teeth, a habit he had when he was nervous. 'You shouldn't do that,' Magda said. She raised her hand and almost touched his lip as she would have done with Con, before it came to her with a shock: this is an employee. You must not touch him. 'You shouldn't chew your lip,' she said brusquely, picking up her fan. 'It will give you open sores in your mouth which will be difficult to cure.'

Arun closed his long fingers over his knees until the knuckles turned white.

'My son, Con,' Magda offered as a limp excuse, realising how he might take her comment as patronising, 'he does that with his lips.' In this office, in this context of Please Mrs Ironstone and Not at all Mrs Ironstone, even the word 'lips' sounded too forward. Arun removed his eyes from his hands to fix his stare on the painting above Magda's head. She stole the opportunity to study his mouth. Wide and full, unlike Joseph's, which was pursed as if he were sucking on a sour fruit, a pretty boy's mouth in an ageing face, curiously corrupt.

'Are you admiring the mountain or the artist's skill?' she asked.

'This artist uses too much paint for that landscape.'

Magda laughed. 'Perhaps. Although I like it for the mountain. It makes me feel as if I too am walking there.' Knowing that Arun had worked briefly as one of the Survey's Trans-Himalayan explorers before he joined the Fleetwood company, she told him that she thought him fortunate in his time as a surveyor. 'Had I been a man it is what I would have chosen.' In a warm voice she added, 'Dear Arun –' as if starting a letter to a friend. He flushed immediately. Beginning again, a business letter this time, avoiding the name she called him only in her head, Magda thanked him for the warning about the tiger. 'I will try to be more cautious.'

But she found it easy to lose track of time. It was so dark within the recesses of the factory building that lights always had to be lit. One night, working on after the clerks had left, she looked up from Joseph Hooker's diaries to realise that beyond the factory's open doors all light had gone. She was alone. The rains had stopped for the moment and their cessation had roused her from an imaginary sojourn in the northern hills.

Closing Hooker, she took up a lamp and made her way out past the night watchman to where the river slid past in the moonlight, its waves slapping softly against the jetty. The silence after monsoon rains was a velvet glove cupping the delicate rustlings and stirrings of new growth. In paddy fields you could hear the rice pushing its way out of the slurry. Such a soft, receptive night. Magda undid the buttons at her throat and felt the tickling fingertips of a breeze slip under her dress. The sky had cleared, the monsoon clouds packing down on the horizon like bulky winter eiderdowns, and the moon gave the wet land and the river a steely sheen. A creature slipped off the bank and into the water, leaving a molten serpentine trail. Magda envied it the cool river, although she knew this to be a bad season to be walking near water, because of the fevers it brought. 'And tigers,' she reminded herself.

Slowly, she began to make her way home. Reaching the halfway point between the factory and the garden gate she heard a strange sound, a cough, and her heart jumped. There were padded footsteps coming towards her, then silence, barring the dull thud of her accelerated heartbeat. The footsteps passed her, a figure she recognised, who halted as she called out. She wondered if Arun had been watching over her, and dismissed the idea as a foolish hope. Yet it was odd for him not to have made himself known. 'Are you all right?'

'Thank you, Mrs Ironstone, I am fine. I was . . .' His voice was husky, as if he were coming down with a chill.

The darkness brought a dangerous intimacy, a recklessness that made her want to detain him. She moved closer and saw what looked like tears on his cheeks. 'What is it? You seem very distressed. Have you had bad news?'

He made a move to leave.

'Please tell me what is troubling you.' He would have to be unpicked a stitch at a time like a seam sewn too tight. 'Is it family?'

Without replying he reached into his jacket and produced

a letter for her to read. Magda could almost hear the pompous voice that had dictated it: 'On further consideration we find that we cannot replace the gold medal presented to your father by the Royal Geographical Society in 1871, which you claim to have lost while working for the Survey two years ago. Yours, etc. etc.'

'Which I *claim* was lost!' Arun said bitterly. 'As if I would sell such a thing!'

'Surely you have other mementos of your father?'

He shook his head and appeared to examine the letter for indecipherable signs. 'My father . . .' He cleared his throat. 'You may not know that my father was engaged for many years in mapping rivers, chiefly in northern India and Tibet. Of these, the most important was the Brahmaputra, whose true source he sought.' Or rather, Arun went on, his father had sought to determine which of two rivers – the Brahmaputra or the Irrawaddy – was connected with the Tsangpo river of Tibet. She could hear the river in Arun's voice as he spoke, rolling slipping sliding away across a wide dun valley into the warm night. The Tsangpo, he repeated, that great, mysterious river of the Trans-Himalayas, whose course flowed placidly for many miles at an altitude of 11,000 feet through a shallow trough of gritty, windswept Tibetan plateau and sub-arctic flora; a thick coiling worm of a river unwinding languorously through its wormcasing of sloughed-off yellow sand, as if it meant to continue in this blunt, unfocused way across the plains and forests and out beyond the Himalayas to China, giving no hint of the violent transformation to come, no ripple on its surface, no threatening rapids to indicate that in the east the river narrowed, it bent a sharp knee, forced a deep gorge, plunged through two colliding slabs of the earth's highest mountains. 'And down that gorge carved between near-vertical cliffs the river dropped savagely and steeply, my father reported. A Himalayan Niagara, at its foot rainbows that never faded.'

The Royal Geographical Society had considered this story carefully, Arun went on. It had concluded that the Tsangpo Gorge might indeed include some grand development of fluvial geography, given how far the river dropped between abandoning the Tibetan plateau and entering the lush plains of Assam. But British explorers sounded a cautious note. The only geographical proof of these legendary falls were the surveys done by Arun's father and one other native surveyor named Kintup, they said, both of whom had since been discredited. And no European had been able to retrace their routes.

The lost rainbow falls, the river confluence, the green poppy: these three legends were linked, for the falls were believed to join the Tsangpo and the Brahmaputra, and the poppy was said to grow in that region, especially in a valley whose name had a bubbling sound which made Magda smile. Walking along the river path that night, Arun repeated the word again and again and each time it slipped away from her like a stream over pebbles.

'Your father's survey of the falls,' she said, 'why was it discredited?'

Arun took a moment to reply, his answer coming with some reluctance: 'My father was expected to provide topographic information – to spy, in fact. But to prevent him falsifying data, the Survey never taught him the science of geodesy. Instead he was marched up and down for weeks with the other pundits, trained to measure his strides and to keep each pace exactly the same length as the last, whatever the terrain. Each pundit was given a Buddhist rosary of a hundred beads instead of the usual hundred and eight, and every hundredth pace he slipped a bead along the strand, a rosary equalling not one hundred and eight prayers but ten thousand paces, the total logged on a scroll of paper concealed within a Buddhist prayer wheel.'

Unconsciously Magda had been lengthening her stride to match his. Suddenly Arun confronted her, stopping so abruptly that she had to grasp his arm to steady herself. The contact lasted only a few seconds, but she was very conscious of the warm bare skin she held. 'Thirty-one and half inches: that's the length of stride they taught him,' Arun was saying, staring down at her hand, 'because two thousand of those paces roughly equals a mile. Can you imagine what that was like? To be reduced to a measurement?' Wherever he was, whenever he moved on, that count began again. In the years before his disappearance, his father would often forget himself and move his lips in time to their footsteps through the streets of Calcutta, the boy stretching out his short legs to match his father's measured strides, learning by heart the precise mathematical distance between Black Town and White. A distance we are rapidly diminishing, Magda thought.

'It was not my father's fault that his surveys proved to be inaccurate,' Arun insisted. 'On the road back from the Tsangpo Falls, the party with whom he had been travelling was attacked and robbed by bandits. All my father's calculations were stolen, all his instruments. He was left with his prayer beads and that tin of poppy seeds we have germinated. To pay his passage home, he hired out as a servant to a lama who was travelling to a monastery in southern Tibet. The lama insisted that they both ride on horseback in case the robbers returned. So my father could not count his own paces.' Other men might have given up then. But Arun's father worked out the distance by estimating the length of his horse's stride, the number of times the animal's right foreleg hit the ground. They travelled for three days and nights, the lama dozing on horseback while the surveyor remained awake.

Never to lose concentration, Magda thought, never to let the animal's measured pace lull him into sleep. To count out those cartographic prayers and still take in the land, its rise and fall, rivers and towns. To keep clear in your head a poppy as elusive as a snow leopard, a field of primulas like moonlight.

Even the British officials were impressed. His results, although inaccurate, did credit, they wrote, 'to the explorer's ingenuity and to the horse's equability of pace'. By the time Arun's father returned he was in a condition bordering on destitution, his clothes in rags and his body emaciated. He had been away for four years and had covered 2800 miles, a distance never before or since surpassed in a single journey. All this to find a flower and a waterfall no one believed in. Why? Flowers were not named after natives; nor were waterfalls. Even British botanists died impoverished. The ultimate accolade any explorer could hope for was a gold medal from the Royal Geographical Society, which Arun's father should have been guaranteed for the length of his journey alone. Yet for months the RGS debated whether the medal should go instead to the Survey official who had trained and sent him.

'In 1873, when I was fifteen, my father set off again,' Arun said, 'with second-hand surveying equipment purchased out of his own money. This time he was determined to bring back living specimens of the poppies he had discovered, as well as proof of the falls.'

His padded footsteps marked out several beats in unison with Magda's. 'He was never heard from again.'

They had reached her garden gate. Magda wanted to tell him that she too had lost a parent when she was very young. You could say things in the dark, she felt, on a night like this, to a chorus of drips from the trees and rice growing, things you couldn't say in daylight. Twilight removed the colour, their different colours. She gestured to a bench circling the big cedar like a spoked wheel, where her father liked to sit and watch the river. It seemed safe, not much different than inviting Arun to take tea in the sitting room. After a long hesitation he sat down and she joined him. Two compass points, several degrees away, but facing in complementary directions.

It was Arun who spoke first. 'For years I searched the Botanic Gardens' library and the Asiatic Society for a record of my father's work.' What he discovered was that the records of Himalayan explorations included neither his father's birth nor his death, only his initials, and the words 'Indian surveyor and secret agent, flourished 1867–1873'. 'As if the years with my mother and me did not count as much as their *great* Survey.'

They called it the *Great* Survey, Magda knew, because it was the longest curve of the earth ever measured, like measuring the earth's cheek or its hip, a line of triangles stretching from the toe of India to the foot of the Himalayas. Without native explorers like Arun's father, Tibet and its border countries would have remained off the map, for their rulers were suspicious even of

British botanists, given that botany was often no more than a disguise for espionage. You could hardly blame them, when Hooker himself, later eminent Director of Kew Gardens, was rumoured to have doubled as an agent for the Survey. 'What your father did was to become part of the backbone of Indian maps.'

'Your map, our backbone,' Arun answered sharply. 'And, like all the other anonymous Indians who paced out the subcontinent to provide a base line for this triangulation-strangulation, my father's name never appeared on the map.'

'Fame could have led to his death,' Magda said gently. 'Only when a surveyor has made his final journey can his identity be disclosed.'

'It follows that until there is proof of his death, my father remains anonymous.'

She was struck by an idea. 'Is that why you sign only your initials on your work, because of your father's forced obscurity?'

One moment she was staring into the face of a man who would be good in a fight, and the next it softened. 'Perhaps. I hadn't considered that.' He stood up, and the moon sent his shadow in a long arrow away from her. 'What I wish more than anything in the world is to prove the truth of my father's stories.'

'And I hope *with all my heart* that you may get the chance!' Magda had spoken fervently, without thinking. Shaken by the answering response on Arun's face, she dropped her eyes, trying to regain her composure.

He would have left with a polite nod of the head. But at the last minute she looked up and stretched out her hand to him and he took it in both of his, holding it for a long moment. They parted then as if no more had passed between them than a handshake, although Magda was sure that a man so used to mapping the wilderness must have recognised when he had entered a dangerous place.

She crossed the few yards to the gate with slow steps, wanting to prolong the sensation that she was a free woman. Stopping for a moment, she cupped her cheek with the hand he had

227

clasped and drew it across her lips and down her neck under her dress, leaving on her skin his smell of sandalwood, coconut and earth, trying to recapture the charged feeling of his hand in hers, the warmth and smell of it. She could feel the prickling of fine hairs on her arms and hear the bamboo rustling with a papery sound. The clean metallic smell of approaching rain filled her nose – and another smell, less pleasant, that it took several seconds to recognise. The sickly scent of rotting frangipani. 'But we have no frangipani in this garden,' she was thinking when she became aware of Joseph's eyes watching her from the shadows behind the gate. He began speaking in a low voice that seemed to be directed elsewhere: 'He has been warned about this, the ghost in the weed garden. She pretends to love him but he knows better. She believes him to be a desert, a ruined city. She doesn't realise that the rays of the black sun, the dark sun can scorch her.' *The black son,* she heard, *the dark son.* He was creeping towards her as he recited his mad litany and when he was a few feet away she saw something fly out of his hand and felt it strike her. She cried out as it enveloped her. She was struggling to be free, pulling and sobbing, and then the thing was gone and Arun was holding her, although in her fright she had not heard him approach. 'It's all right, it's all right,' he said as he lifted her up from the ground where she had fallen, releasing her the instant she was steady on her feet. She felt the loss of his support as if he had let her fall again. 'I thought it was a tiger,' he said, 'the way you screamed.' His hand moved towards her face and dropped without touching her.

Her hair was falling loose on her forehead. 'Something hit me. It covered my head. I couldn't breathe.' She straightened her glasses.

'Perhaps it was one of those big brown moths we get at this time of year,' he said. 'They are the size of birds.'

'Perhaps.' Her voice sounded strangely constricted. She still felt breathless.

'Well, if you're sure you are all right . . . Mrs Ironstone.'

She wanted him to use her own name. 'Magda,' she whispered

as she watched him walk away from her. He didn't hear, or chose not to. He walked away and the gate closed and her father called out from the house and in that moment she saw on the ground what Arun had missed: the black velvet cloth Joseph used to cover his head while taking photographs.

The next morning the cloth was gone and so was Joseph.

◆ ◆ ◆

## I. Black Town: from the Calcutta Grotesques
### (attr. to Joseph Ironstone c.1886)

MAGDA FOUND JOSEPH two nights later thanks to the intervention of Ahmed, his driver, who had followed him in the hopes of remuneration. 'Sahib is in trouble in Black Town,' he said. 'Best you come quick.' That was all. She went immediately to the glasshouse and enlisted Arun's help because she could think of no one else so trustworthy, apart from her father, whom she didn't want to worry. Ahmed spoke for several minutes to Arun, and on the strength of this brief conversation the botanist stopped to collect a bag of medicine.

'Is there something Ahmed has not told me?' she asked.

'Precautionary measures only.'

When they reached the place where her husband had been beaten, Magda was told that he had been robbed, as well, although his camera was not taken, only smashed and left beside his body. At first she thought Joseph must be dead, for she had never seen so much blood. She knelt to look at him and came away sticky, her dress soaked and streaked. A man told her that her husband had come here many times to take pictures. 'Too many times,' he added, as if the motive for Joseph's beating had not been robbery. The circle of curious faces closed in and Magda thought she would faint, until she realised that what she had taken for hatred in the faces was only pity. That knowledge gave her the strength to hold her lamp steadily while Arun quickly examined Joseph's wounds.

The man who had spoken to her first pointed to the congested lane of mud huts behind them, separated by the narrowest of tracks. 'There – the widow,' he said, waving at a woman in the grey shadowland furthest from the halo of light. 'He pays her for pictures of her child, the one with two heads. Her child is dead and now her husband.' They murmured among themselves in their own language.

'Arun, what are they saying?' She was hardly aware of using his first name.

'They say that your . . . They say that Mr Ironstone was taking pictures of the woman, who is prostituting herself since her husband's recent death, and of her child before that, who was –' he took a deep breath, 'a child who was born with two heads and was displayed with her to make begging more profitable.'

'But why –' Magda started.

He interrupted: 'I will tell you later. We must get your husband out of here quickly, in case the men who did this come back.'

She stood back while he and Ahmed lifted her husband into the back of the carriage, both men's clothes dirtied by the blood and filth in which Joseph had lain. He must have vomited, as well, for the front of his shirt and jacket was yellow with it, and it had caked around his mouth and nostrils.

She was silent on the way back to the house, wondering if there was a connection between Joseph's beating and the papers she had found in his bedroom, months before when he was in one of his drugged sleeps. She had gone to see if there was anything she could do, only to find the room strewn with scientific texts and photographs he had taken of mutating plants and mutilated people. Perhaps even this two-headed child Arun had mentioned, she couldn't remember. It was a passage written by Joseph that troubled her most: 'The wish to receive or inflict pain is not the essence. The essential impulse is to be completely in another's power, to have lost control and responsibility for one's actions, to be the helpless object of another's will. To be, as it were, before God. Or the reverse, in the case of de Sade. For just as there is no greater power over another person than to make him suffer, so to receive pain willingly is to admit one's guilt and be redeemed. No animal accepts the infliction of pain willingly. Thus, is it not true that to do so is to be more human? More than human. Superhuman.'

Reading these words, she was moved by great pity for the man, as she had been on those nights in London when he had described his nightmare childhood with Luther Ironstone. A sparrow raised in a hawk's nest, Magda pictured it, thinking of the fine bones Joseph had inherited from his mother. He had her looks – and her madness too, Magda suspected. 'She died of a divided soul,' Joseph had insisted. 'The matches simply finished what he started.'

Ahmed and Arun carried her husband with the greatest care past the night watchman and up the stairs to lay him on his bed, at which point Magda paid Ahmed well and sent him away with instructions not to breathe a word to her father. At first she insisted that Arun leave with him. 'I can manage now.'

His refusal was gentle but firm: 'You cannot do this on your own, Mrs Ironstone. He is too heavy for you, and too badly hurt. If you will neither call a doctor nor wake one of the other servants, you must allow me to help. It is important that we treat his open wounds before they become infected.'

Magda would have suffered less embarrassment in Ahmed's presence. Ahmed, she believed, expected the worst of everyone. But she could not bear Arun to see what she lived with, the type of man she had chosen. '*Must* we get the doctor?' A doctor would feel obliged to inform her father about Joseph's degradation, and she didn't think her father's heart could stand such revelations.

'I'll do what I can.' Arun leaned forward over the bed, his hand outstretched. Glancing quickly at her, he asked, 'May I?' And at Magda's nod he gently lifted Joseph's unbloodied eyelid. 'He's unconscious. Let's hope that the opium he has been smoking keeps him so.'

'He has been smoking opium? You can tell that from his eyes? Not simply laudanum?'

'The men were saying that he goes to that part of Calcutta to photograph and then later to an opium house to smoke. Perhaps you did not know that close to the street where we found him is the Chinese quarter where you may find all manner of oriental pleasures, from pork sausages to opium.'

'And Joseph has been seen there?'

He nodded, 'Your driver was sure you knew, Mrs Ironstone. He has driven your husband there many times.' Magda felt his words like an accusation. He looked back at Joseph. 'We must clean him up now, to see if the doctor is necessary.' His eyes asked a question.

'It's quite all right,' she said wearily. 'If you are worried about the propriety of examining Joseph in my company, such delicacy of feeling is unnecessary after what I have witnessed tonight.'

He nodded formally and indicated that they should remove Joseph's clothes. 'Gently,' he added, smiling slightly. 'The man has suffered enough tonight.'

With no further hesitation Arun set to work repairing her husband's battered face and torso. He rolled up his sleeves and washed his hands well in the soapy warm water she had brought at his request, then suggested that she do the same, informing her that the greatest risk in India was from infection. As if I did not know, Magda thought; I have already been infected. She felt faint when they found that the blood had matted and stuck Joseph's shirt to his skin and chest hair, but Arun pressed on, encouraging her with his calm, decisive movements. They soaked the fabric thoroughly in warm water to loosen it and then gently but resolutely peeled the bloodied stuff away while Joseph moaned and muttered. Magda closed her eyes when she saw his wounds open again and bleed.

When her husband was naked to the waist, Arun stood back and told her that they probably need go no further for the moment. 'Most of the blood is from his head, and head wounds tend to bleed badly. Often they look worse than they are.'

He waited without comment for her to get her trembling under control. 'I have put some antiseptic herbs into the water,

Mrs Ironstone, and now we must wash him well, both sides of his body. If I roll him on to his side, do you think you can manage to reach his back?'

At Magda's nod, he placed one brown arm around Joseph's bloodied shoulders and rolled him from her so that the back was exposed. She leaned in and began sponging away the dirt and blood to reveal Joseph's ashen skin. White as a corpse, she thought, white as dead fish, white as bones, white as leprosy. The smell of vomit and filth from Joseph was very strong. The smell of rot. To stop herself retching she tried to force her brain away. She smelled cloves on Arun's breath. His sweat. His shirt wet with it and with Joseph's blood. The three of them closely entwined, locked in an intimate embrace. Her head filled with the images of the dead being washed and wrapped in their winding sheets for burial. Joseph was too white, she thought, his skin too cold. Like the pictures he collected of flayed corpses and bodies made of stone which yet contained soft organs. She swayed, and Arun's calm voice dragged her back.

'There is fresh *paan* in the pocket of my jacket,' he said. 'Spices wrapped in betel leaf. Chew some while you are working. It will keep down the nausea.'

She looked up into his eyes, inches from hers, wanting to lean forward and rest on his warm skin, knowing that tonight they had gone too far, the three of them. Tonight, within this tight little triangle that they formed beneath the swinging lamp, they had begun to complete their own triangulation, their own network of interlocking triangles to spread across the landscape. A baseline could be taken – here, the line of Joseph's white shoulder from the bed to where it is dissected by Arun's brown hand – and from each end of this a bearing taken on a distant point. I am a panopticon, she thought, both telescope and microscope, able to observe the three of us in dangerous proximity while surveying as well the fine pores of Arun's skin, the opiate shadows under Joseph's eyes.

They laid her husband on his back, and together washed his skin so that the hair of his chest, rusty with blood, was black again on his pale chest like ink marks on white paper. Long slow sweeps of the cloth down the length of Joseph's naked chest, their hands measuring together the corpse of her marriage.

Rivers asked her if she trusted him to treat her husband with a native drug he had made from plant roots. She told him yes. 'It is what you call serpentine root,' he said. 'We use it to treat . . . nervous disorders, and for insomnia.'

Behind them she heard the door open. There was a cry – 'MUMMY!' and Con ran across the room at full speed to throw himself into her arms. 'Mummy! Stop the man hurting Father! Stop him! Stop him! Stop him!'

She walked away from the bed holding the child in her arms. 'Sshhh, my beautiful boy. He's not hurting your father, he's helping.'

'He isn't! He isn't! He's killing Father! Look at the blood!'

She put her hand over his mouth. Just for a second to stop the hysterics. Not for more than a heartbeat. Con's eyes widened. And when she took her hand away, shocked at her action, he let out a long high squeal that pierced the house and brought the aya and the night watchman. She heard her father's voice and called out to him that everything was all right, it was one of Con's nightmares.

Con wrenched himself from her to run for his aya, who wrapped him tightly in her arms. To the aya Magda murmured that Sahib had been taken ill and the doctor was seeing to his fever. Her life reduced to a charade that no one believed. 'You may go now. Aya, take Con back to bed.'

Dressed with the herbal poultices, Joseph appeared to need no further medical attention. His breathing was heavy, but no more than was to be expected under the influence of opium, Arun said. They left the lamp alight in case he woke, and stole out silently, both of them formal: please, after you. You have been so kind.

Thinking themselves in control.

Not until she was ushering Arun down the stairs to the door did Magda ask again why he thought the men had beaten her husband so violently. She could see by his face that he did not want to tell her, but she pressed him.

234

'Your husband was beaten because he went back to that part of the city where he had bought the corpse of a two-headed boy,' he said. 'A corpse that should by rights have been burned to offer its soul the opportunity for liberation. And it is said that Joseph has taken pictures as well of the illegal suttee – the wife burnings that still take place among the more ignorant people.'

Magda felt her knees go weak.

◆

She had turned on the stairs with a look of incomprehension, then staggered and swooned. Catching her, Arun was struck by the surprising fragility of her bones under the bulky dress. He picked her up as he would a broken bird, the wing of muslin skirt sweeping to the ground, and saw her pulse beating in her breast. Her skin was very hot against his bare arm. Placing her gently on a chair next to the door of her husband's room, he straightened the glasses on her beaky little nose, noticing the red indentations on either side of it that gave her face an oddly fragile appearance. He had the desire to smooth the marks away with his fingers. The muscles around his heart contracted and he told himself that what he felt for her was pity. He knew from gossip at the Fleetwood Factory that her husband did not stop at opium, but was now taking heavy doses of morphine. Was he right to have given Ironstone the concoction of serpentine root, a temporary solution when what was needed was something more permanent, an *up*rooting?

On the one hand, but then again on the other. He was worried that he was overly wedded to gradualism, as Darwin had been, and admitted that he was an unlikely Darwinian, one who found Darwin's theories not incompatible with *dharma*, the established order of things, law in an eternal sense, neither fair nor unfair.

The colour was returning to Magda's cheeks. With her head thrown back, her dress had slipped lower to reveal a ribbon of pale skin along the tops of her breasts. How white her breasts were compared to the skin where she had been touched by the sun! He felt a stirring between his legs. The sun had given her plump breasts a sprinkling of freckles. Like nicely cooked chapattis. The idea made him smile. He would have liked to put his hand there, spanned those twin curves and discovered whether the white skin was cooler than the brown.

◆

She opened her eyes to see him staring down at her. 'You are tired to death,' he said, fatigue scored in his own face. 'Shall I call your maid?'

'I will be fine. I will rest a moment and then sleep.' Magda thanked him again and bade him good night, resisting all the unsayable things. She stretched her hand out to him. When he bent to kiss it some weakness overcame her and she turned her wrist and pressed it to his mouth, holding it there so that his lips rested against her pulse. His eyes were closed. Magda closed hers and felt him replace her hand gently by her side.

It was her first kiss.

# 8

I WALKED OUT of the botanical library into the late sunshine and headed for Roxburgh's house, where my taxidriver was asleep, his head rolled back against the car's front seat and his bare feet resting on the dashboard. Nearby, one of the squatter families from the house had started a fire. Their dog stretched and gazed at me expectantly, the way Russell used to do when he hoped for a walk. I had no intention of walking this dog, the prototype on which every scrofulous Indian mutt I'd ever seen had been moulded. Sand-coloured, long-legged, curly-tailed, with pointed snout and ears, she wore a knowing, yet apologetic expression I put down to the overextended udders which gave her the appearance of a canine Hindu goddess. 'Shoo!' I said to her as she began to follow me down the path my nineteenth-century map told me should lead to the Great Banyan Tree. 'Go away!'

She wagged her tail and made the motion of moving back without actually doing so, then squatted to scratch her scabby coat. I walked off. The dog – *my* dog now – circled me (out of kicking reach) and trotted ahead, checking over her shoulder to see that I was following, a gracious tour guide fallen on hard times. 'Or perhaps you're moving up in the world, dog, trying for a better incarnation in the next roll call of lives.' Very soon I heard my taxi start up and coast along behind, the driven woken by a sixth sense.

Some things have nothing to do with logic.

Logically, the so-called 'Great' Banyan Tree at the Botanic Gardens should have lost its magic. At 240 years of age it was no longer the dense half-acre forest described in my old guide-books. It had suffered through two cyclones, in 1864 and 1867, with winds that broke many of its branches, exposing it to an attack of hard fungus. Its heart was gone, the main trunk from which the 1800 or so remaining aerial roots grew, rotted through and removed in 1925. Only a central sunlit glade was left, an indication that even at a man's height above the ground the original trunk must have measured almost fifty feet in circumference. But the magic was still here. Peering through the unattractive wire mesh fence protecting the remaining airy thicket of saplings (and the missing, phantom limbs), I was moved by an overwhelming sense of inevitability. I was chasing a genetic ghost story, an illusion. Yet for whatever illogical reason, I was meant to be here, on this day, in this place, with the hawks circling lazily overhead and the ragged boys bowling cricket down the park's long avenue of dove grey Cuban palm trees. I was here to make impossible connections, forge links between the inscrutable past and the overscrutinised present. And this banyan tree – threadbare, hollow at the centre, its remaining roots or branches or trunks clawing at each other like the stretched tendons of old hands – was part of that process.

I thought about the photocopied line drawings of male and female forms on which Val writes the distinguishing features of death with a red felt pen. He keeps a stack in his desk, human versions of the vehicle silhouettes you have to fill in if you're applying for insurance after damaging your car. Sitting down on a bench next to the banyan tree, I pictured three of these forensic paper dolls in my head: one female and two male. Joseph's outline was coloured by the drowned man's self-portrait. For Magda I had to make do with an owlish cartoon the library's clerk had found, which disappointed me, because until then I'd pictured her like Sigourney Weaver with glasses and maybe one of those bad Victorian hairdos (Brunhilda braids wagonwheeled round the ears) which when let down in the throes of passion would reveal her as beautiful. The third figure, my Rivers connection, remained a blank. In his place I had a phantom that Magda referred to as a botanist, a chemist, an artist, a doctor – a master of many disciplines, in the way people before our century were able to be and we are not. I suspect she was a little in love with him, and afraid of it. For want of a name, I called him Arun.

◆ ◆ ◆

## J. During the night all plants are red: a microscopic section (anon. Indian artist c.1886)

ANNOTATED: *Chlorophyll: the Blood of Plants*, the painting was a reminder of the information Jack had given me about the chlorophyll molecule bearing a striking architectural resemblance to the red pigment in human blood. 'Not only that,' he'd said, 'but when moved from light to dark, photosynthesising plants actually emit a red light, although human eyes are too insensitive to the red end of the colour scale to perceive it.' He knew a lot about green stuff, my cousin. Apparently, chlorophyll itself was isolated and named by 1817, but it took another century before there were instruments able to examine its molecular details. And the bloody connection between red and green was not discovered until it was possible to shatter the intact molecules into fragments.

I like to think of those minute chips off the green block as the bone fragments Val sticks under a microscope after he finds them scattered randomly across an old burial site. He has to go through the same process of identification as ordinary anthropologists, using delicate instruments to dust away the irrelevant, trying to connect all the missing shards that have been ground down into a meaningless powder over time.

◆

Magda's father accepted the explanation that Joseph had fallen from his horse, a necessary convention that they agreed to, a social contract. Like the one I signed with my husband, she thought. Physically, Joseph recovered slowly from the beating, even though his mind seemed much eased. Had his brush with death brought this new calmness? Or could it be attributed to the infusion of serpentine root which Magda administered to him three times daily?

At the end of the first week she and Joseph began to take short walks in the garden, his arm resting heavily on hers. They had had no contact of any kind in months, and the physicality of him, the oily-sweet smell of his hair and skin, made her shudder inwardly. She had to force herself not to recoil when he covered her hand with his humid, puffy palm. It made her think of something drowned, or a small and slightly venomous creature. When he tried to describe his work with the two-headed boy she swiftly interrupted with a question to deflect his poisonous vision, 'Yes, Joseph, do tell me about the pictures of poppies you've been doing.'

'They give off light,' he replied after a moment. 'The plants give off light.'

'Do they? How interesting!' A false voice, a false interest.

'It is, isn't it!' he said. 'I've taken long exposures in low light and you can clearly see the luminescence around each plant . . . like the phosphorescence I have photographed from open wounds.' He fixed his eyes on hers with the same moist, clutching sensation that his hand gave her. 'I do love you, Maggie.'

Trying to summon up words of reassurance, the best she could do were a few brittle phrases about how pleased she was to see him looking better.

It wasn't enough. Joseph's face fell. His small pink mouth worked as if he were chewing. She noticed a trail of dried saliva beside his lips like the trail of a slug across leaves. He said that perhaps he would go in again and sleep. 'That's probably for the best, Joseph . . . *dear*,' she forced out, relieved at his departure in spite of herself. Since the night of Joseph's beating she had been neither to the godowns, where in any event there was little work because of the rains, nor to the glasshouses. Between her husband and the monsoon, she felt like a prisoner.

Two weeks after the Black Town incident, Magda's father came to her and suggested an outing to the Botanic Gardens. 'George

King has invited a number of eminent fellows to view the result of these experiments we've been working on,' Philip Fleetwood said.

'What experiments, Father?' By his mischievous demeanour, she judged that he had some scheme up his sleeve.

'Oh, George convinced me a few months ago to let that young Indian botanist of mine work on a project at Sibrapur. But the fellow rather went off the idea, so I have continued, together with a few of the gardens' staff.' Her father beamed delightedly. 'Most fun I've had in years!'

Her heart beat faster at the name. 'You never mentioned it.' Neither had Arun.

'You've had enough to think about, Maggie.' It was as near as he got to commenting on Joseph's condition.

'Is it more poppy experiments, Father?'

'You'll see, Maggie girl, you'll see! And the river outing will do you good.'

The Botanic Gardens' main library, an airy space large enough to accommodate all sixty of the invited guests, had undergone a dramatic transformation into something closer to an altar or a stage set for a magician. In semi-darkness, its tall shutters closed against the watery August sun, the room was lit now only by a few candles at either end of a table covered in black. The centre of the table held two clear glass bowls, perfect spheres of about fourteen inches in diameter, each suspended within the kind of metal stand used to hold rotating globes of the world, and from the bowls or globes came a phosphorescent green glow to which the visitors were drawn like insects around bright lights.

The moment that Magda's eyes had adjusted to the library's theatrical darkness she had been aware of Arun's presence. Occasionally her eyes were drawn to where he stood, a few steps behind King at the long table, and whenever she found his gaze on hers she was gripped by a feeling of faintness. 'You're not feverish, are you, Maggie?' her father asked at one point. 'You look rather pink.'

'No, no . . . I . . . it's the room, it's very stuffy – don't you find it so?'

'It will be worth it, girl, just wait!' His eyes eagerly scanned the table. George King had lifted a leather head harness attached to a microscope that lay between the bowls. He was demonstrating how it was to be placed over the head for increased mobility and secured there like a medieval instrument of torture. It gave King the look of a cyclops or some other fantastic one-eyed monster.

'Come, Magda,' King said, gesturing for her to come forward. 'It was your father who developed this contraption. Why should you not be the first among our guests to peer into the green world he has created!'

Magda pressed forward and observed the water in the two globes to be filled with the brightest of algae, a sparkling emerald tide that appeared to dance in the flickering illumination of the candles. As King adjusted the complex series of buckles and straps which bound the instrument to her head, she felt her whole body become top heavy, all her senses reduced to her eyes. Leaning forward gingerly, off-balanced by her exaggerated viewpoint as much as by the weight of the microscope, she peered into the surface of one of the bowls and saw that what she had taken for an unbroken tide was in fact millions upon millions of minute particles of green, constantly advancing and receding into the depths, receding and advancing, a pointillist painting of an underwater meadow. Increasing the focus, it became apparent that these dancing flakes of colour were in fact tiny creatures, transparent as crystals but for the bright algae they had eaten, clearly evident within their digestive tracts. 'The curious dance which these microscopic planktonic beings perform is simply a reaction to the increase and decrease in light from the flickering candles,' King explained, 'for they are accustomed to feed on the surface of the oceans at night and as dawn approaches to sink many hundreds of feet. They spend the day at depth, and then, as evening draws near, start to come up again. And so it goes, day after day.'

*I was gazing into a green lens on the world – in reverse. For unlike us, these green beings avoided the light.*

King nodded to his assistant, who immediately dropped a cloth over one of the bowls as if it were the cage on a bright green parakeet he was covering. 'Remove the microscope, Maggie, and observe what happens next!' she heard her father exclaim. His voice was full of suppressed excitement at the magic trick they were about to perform. Magda imagined both men draped in black capes, perhaps with scarlet silk linings. Like all magicians, King knew how to build up his audience's expectations. 'First I must give credit to Fleetwood's young botanist here, whose inordinate interest in the colour green led him to discover the properties of these little sea creatures.' At Arun's silence, King continued with his build-up, 'But I must blow Philip Fleetwood's trumpet most of all, the man who suggested the next step.' He whispered to his assistant, 'Light!'

Nothing above a whisper was necessary, for the whole audience was as hushed as a church assembly. The candles were blown out, leaving behind a strong smell of beeswax and smoke. A pale spotlight appeared, shining on one end of the table. No brighter at first than a moon through clouds, the circle of light began to travel slowly over the rippling velvet, much like the moon over a dark river, growing in strength from silver to yellow as it travelled. By the time it reached the bowl it had the full intensity of the noon sun.

Transfixed, Magda had failed to notice the water in the bowl becoming increasingly agitated as the light approached, until one would have thought it was literally boiling.

'Watch closely now!' King's shrill whisper urged them.

It happened very quickly, too quickly for Magda to distinguish what was occurring. Men were crowding forward all about her, eager to peer through the microscope. One after another they pressed their faces into that enlarged world to confirm what all suspected.

*My father and King had managed to break the colour green down into all its separate particles, brought the colour to life – and then they had killed it. The tiny creatures were exploding before our eyes.*

George King explained the trick to his rapt audience. 'It seems

243

that chlorophyll, the green in plants, is responsible. Because these tiny planktonic creatures are transparent, when the light hits the green within them it triggers this violent destructive reaction. The light absorbed by the plants cannot be dissipated.'

A visiting botanist from Wales spoke up, 'Just as well sheep are opaque then. Otherwise my own country would be a horrible mess!'

Magda glanced at Arun and saw reflected on his face a mirror of her own dismay. Her father and King, like the men around them, were too excited to notice. She pushed through to Arun's side, hearing around her the audience's responses, 'Living photographic record . . . photodestructive . . .'

When she and Arun were face to face, only inches separating her hand from his, Magda whispered, 'This isn't what you meant to happen, is it?'

He shook his head miserably. 'I'm sure it's very dangerous, the direction they are going. But they won't listen to me any more.' Abruptly, he turned on his heel and left the room. Magda caught her father's eye and fanned her face to indicate her need for air. He was too preoccupied by the congratulations being heaped on him to do more than nod vaguely as she left.

Outside, she spoke to an old *mali*, who was squatting next to his raked pile of leaves, 'Where sahib go?'

The gardener stood slowly, using his rake as a prop, and waved his arm in the direction of the great banyan tree. 'Sahib go that way, memsahib.' He sank on his hindquarters again, oblivious to the freshening wind scattering his pile of leaves.

Magda could smell the rain coming and feel its cooler air against her hot cheeks. Passing Roxburgh's house, she saw Arun's figure ahead of her. She called out his name in time to the first rain on her face. Each heavy drop landed on the path with a puff, sending up a billowing petticoat of dust. She thought Arun hadn't heard her, and called out again as the metronome beat of rain became increasingly staccato on the ground. She was a few yards from him before he turned and caught sight of her. His expression resigned more than pleased, he said, 'Quickly, Mrs Ironstone! Before you are drenched! It will be dry under the banyan.' They ran side by side through the warm rain, skirting the woods where each branch of the taller trees was hung with the ominous pterodactyl silhouettes of flying foxes.

◆ ◆ ◆

## K. *Ficus benghalensis* Banyan tree
## (anon. Indian artist c.1886)

DESPITE THE STRONG sense of natural movement missing from so many Hindu botanical illustrations, the overall impression in this striking example from the Ironstone Bequest was of mysterious, dark forces – partly to be loved, partly feared, very different from the analytical British outlook. Magda had written on the back: *Banyan. Roots or branches? Artery or tributary? Family tree.*

Val taught me that the names we apply to things can give them a deceptive pattern. Arteries suggest containment, elements that are manageable, tributaries do not. Such metaphors are dangerous though tempting, he said, because wordplay simplifies complexity. For instance, I know that the 'tail' or 'branch' or 'stem' of carbon atoms connected to chlorophyll may break off if the molecule is denatured by heat or acid, along with its core magnesium atom. But even then the ring system remains intact. Even in old fossils like petroleum, the circle holds. Or take the elusive cell scientists have given the near mythical name of 'stem cell'. Buried deep within our marrow, protected by an armoured bark of bone, these are the great great grandparents of all other blood cells. The inner ring on our family tree, they can split and branch out to form any number of new stems. They are described as 'undifferentiated', meaning that they have no distinguishing marks or characteristics, I guess, and 'archival', because these anonymous cells hold the files for our entire blood system.

'The problem with looking for patterns in coincidences is how easily you can find one,' Val said, trying to discourage me – and failing.

245

◆

Magda ducked her head under the banyan's veil of aerial stems and branches and was alone with him in a green room, the drumbeat of rain outside making privacy even more complete. She leaned against a branch that had rooted itself in the ground. 'Isn't this the Hindu storyteller's tree?' she asked, for something to break the thread of tension.

'Yes,' Arun said. His tight smile indicated how uneasy he felt at their sudden intimacy. 'All our stories begin under a banyan tree beside a river.'

Nervously, she walked around the private glade, brushing the roots and branches with her hands. 'A storyteller's tree,' she murmured. 'But how shall we know where exactly a story begins if roots and branches are confused?'

No such problem existed in India, he explained, where all stories were circular. He carried on with barely a pause, as if his next words were a natural adjunct to the spherical nature of their discussion: 'I am going away, Mrs Ironstone.'

She sat down abruptly on one of the tree's low branches. 'Where?'

'To follow my father's route into Tibet. I think it is for the best.'

'Yes, I see, yes.' She started to cry in a way he had never seen a woman do, with no fuss. The tears simply welled up in her eyes, collected along the rim of her glasses and then slid down leaving shiny tracks in the matte powder on her cheeks. She was a thin woman of above average height, but she seemed very small and heavy sitting there. It wasn't fair that she should impose such emotion on him. He wanted to raise her up so that they were on a more level footing again.

'It's these experiments, Mrs Ironstone. They are all wrong, dangerous. You see, I have been trying to identify what it is in this green poppy that might cause tumours to diminish. The old notebook contains a series of drawings of a green paste being produced, which we have assumed to be an extract of chlorophyll. But my father never specified how the paste was

246

to be used, whether ingested or spread on the skin or the tumour. He said only that the tumours would diminish in a gradual way after this treatment, as long as it was done in conjunction with an infusion of the poppy resin and supervised by a shaman. He made this very clear: *It was a question of the whole person being treated, not the tumour alone.* Otherwise the treatment might have the reverse effect –'

'The reverse?'

'It might cause the tumours to multiply.' He was pressing the bridge of his nose tightly, the way Magda did when her glasses irritated her. Forgetting to whom he was speaking, he burst out, 'Fleetwood has got it into his head that we do not need the green poppy, that it is the action of the chlorophyll alone which destroys the tumour. He has brought the poppy research to a halt. Like George King, he prides himself on asking questions, yet doesn't see that these questions are based on human limitations. Scientists too can be near-sighted or far-sighted, they can suffer from peripheral vision and colour blindness. They often ignore the missing element, the unobserved, which may prove to be of more importance than what is seen and contained in a test tube or a glass sphere.'

'What will you do?'

'I have told your father I am leaving to look for the poppy.'

He watched Magda's hands twist on the handle of her umbrella as if it were a microscope she could bring into focus. 'And what if your poppy has vanished?'

'I have my father's surveys. And . . . a story of his, about the poppy's origins being tied to our own. A bit far-fetched, still . . . it's said that my family came from a place he called "the Forest of Air", not far from the Tsangpo Gorge. The name referred to the multitudes of ancient orchids living in the branches of the valley's trees, where they could be away from competition with other struggling plants.'

'Epiphytes,' she said, a child reciting a lesson learned by rote. 'Plants growing on other plants without being parasitic. I've often wondered what they lived on.'

'On air,' he answered, just as mechanically. 'On sunlight.' She knew the answer as well as he. There were two conversations going on, one spoken, the other silent.

'You said something when I first met you about the green poppy being used as an antidote to sorrow. Do you think such a medicine might help my husband?'

'As you know, I have no proof.'

'I could come with you.'

Seeing her in the context of this edited paradise, he imagined what she would make of the roads his father had walked. Magda had the British faith in maps, Arun knew, a faith he had once shared. But a map was not always to be trusted. A map, for example, would show you that the easiest way into the eastern Himalayas must be to follow the river corridor, that narrow, lush span of seventy-five miles or so where the big rivers that rose in the cold heart of Tibet escaped from their dry plateau land and were squeezed between two of the highest mountain ranges in the world to flow out into India and China. The green path of the monsoon. At first sight it would seem easier to pass between mountain ranges than to climb over them. A false impression.

'The gorges are deep and narrow,' his father had told him, 'filled with impenetrable forest, and the rivers quite unnavigable, separated by knife-edge ranges. Not till you get far to the east, to the Mekong corridor, beyond reach of the monsoon, is it profitable or even possible to pass through the breach on to the plateau. But then it is first necessary to cross the rain screen and ascend to the Plateau of Yunnan. No, the easiest way to reach the forest lands beyond the Himalayas is to cross the barrier ranges east or west of the river gap – in military language, *to turn the gap*, before the rivers have dug themselves in.'

The young Arun had pictured those scaly rivers as long green lizards, as dragons flexing their claws in the jungle.

'For there is another consideration, the most important of all,' his father went on. 'In the rain-soaked jungles which cloak the southern slopes of the Himalayas and fill the gorges with leeches and snakes and fever, villages are few and seldom friendly. There are no roads, only rough tracks. There is no transport because there is no grazing; there is no food because there is no cultivation.'

'Let me describe one road you would encounter,' Arun told Magda, trying to deter her with his father's trials. 'It never falls below ten thousand feet and often rises to over sixteen thousand. On it you are passed by mounted Tibetan messengers who pause only long enough to eat and change horses. Their coats are sealed to ensure the secrecy of the letters they carry, their faces are cracked, their eyes blood-shot and sunken, and their bodies eaten by lice into raw sores, sores they attribute to not being allowed to remove their clothes.'

He drew a breath. 'My own condition was not much different when I took that road as a surveyor, and it was a broad highway compared to some roads my father travelled. There were times when I saw no man for days on end. The only living things were leeches no thicker than needles, who waited on every leaf and branch whenever the path fell below six thousand feet, lashing themselves to and fro in a frenzy. If you walk bare-legged your skin soon streams with blood, and even in long trousers you find the things work their way through the eyelets of your boots and they can be detached only with fire, or their bites become infected.'

The colour was back in Magda's cheeks. She looked at him as if he were describing the greatest adventure on earth. 'When we set off to find these poppies of your father's, which route shall we take? Will you choose *to turn the gap* from east or west?'

◆ ◆ ◆

## L. Artificial Horizons, sketches in the Himalayas (attrib. to Magda Ironstone c.1886–8)

THE DIARY SLIPPED out of my backpack and I glanced at the page. My brother Robin, a great believer in the haphazard nature of life, used to play a game with books: let a volume fall open – any volume (car manual, Grade Nine chemistry text, Ripper testimonial) – close your eyes and blindly place your finger on a line to guide your next day's actions. My finger fell on the words *turn the gap*. It meant nothing to me. Magda had scratched out most of the words below this – the diarist concealing what she'd written even from herself? Only a few phrases remained discernible, but one of them was enough: *The map of an unknown country*.

◆

From Kalimpong, Arun had told her, the small trading town where his father had begun his last journey, first you must cross the Sikkim Himalayas, thus turning the river gap to the west, then travel eastwards three hundred miles across the bare wind-swept Plateau of Tibet to find the lost falls.

*To turn the gap.* Writing those only half-understood words filled Magda's head with smoky, half-dreamed ideas from childhood. *You might say that my addiction to illusion, to distant horizons, my preference for the absent over the durable, began there, in the dangerous gap between what is understood and what is hidden, the space between things.* From Joseph Magda had learned the difficulty of pinpointing the start of addiction. Yet she could date hers precisely, and its confirmation months later, when for the first time she watched a bright point reflected off the apex of a distant peak. Kangchenjunga, one of the highest mountains in the world, shone that morning with an intense brilliance peculiar to the surveying device which caught its light, Arun's heliotrope, a darkened mirror Magda kept through all her subsequent expeditions, even in old age, just as a bankrupt gambler addicted to horse races might keep his first winning ticket.

*There would always be this problem of measuring, of inadequate equipment. Artificial horizons is what we called our darkened-glass mirrors and pools of mercury. Artificial because they were used originally with sextants, instruments for measuring the elevation of the sun or stars above the sea's horizon. In the mountains, although you are on the roof of the world, no such horizon is visible and an artificial one must be contrived, in such a way as not to arouse suspicion (for we were considered to be spies, as well as botanists). Heliotropes only work in sunlight, so for night readings we packed*

*mercury into cowrie shells and poured it out into a pilgrim's
begging bowl. Mercury was our horizon. It was many years before I
appreciated all the qualities of mercury, the folly of trusting a
liquid metal.*

*The map of an unknown country: that is what I am.* A woman
who left her young daughter with an aya and sent her son back
to England 'for his own good'. A woman who had her husband
confined to a hospital in Kalimpong. A woman who has lied to
her father to contrive this stolen time with the man she loves by
her own methods of triangulation. *This is how our mapping of
unknown lands always has proceeded. A few lies, a false promise of
perfection. And like the Great Triangulation, this map too is failing
to flatten out all irregularities and errors.*

*We are here in the interests of horticulture. It sounds so
innocent. I am collecting spring flowers like any other maid in
May.*

But the legions of orchids were gone, thanks to Hooker and
men like him. Those blooms which had once lit up the branches
of trees like so many candles had been stolen. The world of
Arun's father had changed, even though Magda was still woken
by the wild music of lamas chanting and blowing their eerie
trumpets from Buddhist monasteries and temples across the
valleys, as Hooker had been. They slept in the open most nights,
where she learned to appreciate a sliding scale of discomfort, the
distinction between a pine needle bed's itchy prickle and the
slow ache produced by hard ground. *One morning he brought me
wild strawberries on a fern plate. They tasted of perfume.* He hung
them over his ears and assumed an exaggerated dancer's
position with rolling flirtatious eyes and hands, making them
both laugh.

In spring they saw poppies the colour of the sky, in autumn
the hills turned to fire with cotoneaster berries. But they found
no green poppies.

*He had studied green the way other men studied classical
architecture. He had tried to break chlorophyll down into its
separate fragments, long before there were instruments delicate
enough to discern its pillars of nitrogen and pediments of carbon,*

*its central column of magnesium. He was my love, my life, my green thought in a green shade.*

When Magda returned to Kalimpong in the early spring of 1888 it was to find that her husband had disappeared from the hospital. A letter from her father, several months old, informed her that Joseph had made his way back to Calcutta, thin and distressed and unintelligible, his clothes streaked with soot. Gossip about his increasingly unacceptable behaviour had seeped out of Black Town and rolled sluggishly through the crowded streets to muddy the pristine neo-Classical buildings of White Town. 'You must come home now, Maggie,' her father wrote. 'I hope this reaches you in time.'

Until death do us part, she thought bitterly. Death or consequences.

# 9

NICK WAS ON his second beer by the time I joined him at the Raj Palace and was looking so much more relaxed that I decided to keep silent about any suspicions concerning Jack's 'acquisition' of the green poppy paintings.

'You managed to see your icons at last?' Nick asked. 'Was it worth the effort?'

'Oh, definitely. I wish Sally had been there. And what about you – did you hear anything more of the dismissed chemists and their connection to Jack?'

'The usual mixture of Chinese whispers and pure malicious gossip, like the drug allegations against the chemists. It turns out that Jack was responsible for having them fired, but nothing to do with drugs. Purely because of sloppy lab work on his chlorophyll project.'

'Really? He was actually working with the dismissed guys?'

'They were keeping track of the samples and placebos and the names of the volunteers.'

I didn't quite manage to maintain a deadpan expression at this news.

'What's that look about, Claire?'

'Nothing. I just. . . Did you happen to find out about the chemists' families? I'd still like to talk to them, clarify the situation.'

'I located one of the families, as it happens. But the situation doesn't need any more clarification.'

'No, I guess not . . .' I carefully peeled the label off my beer bottle. 'Couldn't we phone them?'

'The kind of place that family lives doesn't have phones, Claire.'

'What, it's like a slum?'

'In the wetlands east of the city. Not exactly a slum . . . but the difference is a subtle one.'

'I thought these guys were chemists. Why –'

Nick cut me off: 'Low-level pharmaceutical clerks. And there are plenty of people in India with university degrees who wind up sharing a municipal tap with two hundred other people. This family, remember, no longer has a father to support it. Even before her husband's dismissal the wife used to supplement the family income by selling fish she brought from the wetlands into the city market.' He forestalled my next question: 'No one has seen her at the market since her husband disappeared.' His nervous look had returned as our conversation progressed. 'Why are you making such a big deal of this, Claire?'

'Because Jack's my cousin, I guess. And I don't like to think that people are telling lies about him.'

'People always gossip.'

'Yes, but . . .'

In the end, I wore Nick down again and he agreed to help me spend a couple of hours the next day looking for the chemist's family. 'Just one thing, Claire.'

'What?'

'You must promise to let me do the talking when we get to the wetlands. People there might not appreciate your American accent. Especially after the Gurkha commotion. This is a very strong Communist part of the world, and Uncle Sam isn't known for his benevolent treatment of reds. It's better to leave your camera behind and your notebook. No one will take kindly to forming part of your Book of Lists. There may or may not be any electricity, which means no fans, so wear those cotton pyjamas, the *shalwar kameez*, we got you in the market in Patna, which will also make you less conspicuous. And bring plenty of water – you don't want to drink anything offered while we're there.'

From the taxi it seemed that we were approaching a hilly part of Calcutta, contrary to all the city maps, and about the time that I worked out these were hills of garbage, the smell began to seep through the car's air-conditioning system. Blocking my nose and breathing only through my mouth worked as a reasonably effective filtration system until I began to worry that my inability to cope with the smell of garbage and human shit revealed a sad lack of character. I was breathing through my nose in short shallow huffs, trying to relax into it, when Nick patted my hand with his good one. 'It's not quite as bad as it smells, Claire.' He explained that here in the wetlands, where in 1865 the municipal authorities had acquired a square mile of land for disposing of the city's solid waste, they now dumped liquid sewage and toxic effluents as well. The villagers had devised an ingenious method for profiting by these mountains of garbage: thousands of ragpickers, most of them children, extracted and sold the non-organic material, while the organic garbage – whatever was not eaten by pigs, cattle, dogs – was gradually reduced through time and the weather to humus. When the escarpments of compost got too high, they were levelled by municipal bulldozers, planted with crops by local farmers and the produce sold later in the city's markets.

'They turn this dump into a *garden*?' I asked incredulously.

'More than that. The area also supplies Calcutta with fresh fish raised in the banked-up sewage tanks – *bheris* – you see round here. Sewage is a very rich fish food. And the fish are highly effective in screening out water-borne bacteria, as it happens. The real problem here is not sewage but lack of it. The increased pressure for housing in the city is eating up this network of *bheris*, so the supply of fish to the market is much more irregular.'

'Fish? From these . . . garbage farms?'

'Of course.' Nick was enjoying himself. 'But don't be alarmed. The so-called City of the Future in Florida's Disneyworld recycles its liquid waste in similar lakes.' His amused eyes anticipated every twist and turn of my thoughts. 'And how can one doubt the great god Disney?'

To be horrified or impressed? 'That fish we ate the other night . . .'

'Bound to be! If it makes you feel better, I grew up on fish from these wetlands.'

The taxi deposited us at the edge of a dyke leading between two shallow lakes. 'We'll be about an hour,' Nick told our driver. Unusually for an Indian driver, this one insisted that we pay him what he was owed for the first half of our journey, evidence of a lack of confidence in our safe return that left even Nick uneasy.

We started walking towards a township of grass-roofed houses on the lake's far shore, one of those dream journeys where your destination never gets any closer. I had to keep reminding myself that the most dangerous smells are the ones you don't smell at all. Reaching the settlement, Nick asked for directions from two men who silently directed us further into the sprawling maze of thatched huts, the walls of which were clad and patched in everything from flattened tins to woven grass matting. Reed matting, Nick corrected me: *darma*.

'I thought that meant fate.'

'Different spelling. And it's not fate: it's the social order, the way things should be: *dharma* . . .' Fate: that breathy uncertain sound after the 'd'.

There was something familiar about the village's wary poverty that stirred memories of trailer parks my family had stayed in. Like those slipstream oases, doors here were seldom more than curtains of tattered fabric or thatched bamboo frames bound to the hut with insecure lengths of twine, often guarded by a dog with a long memory of too many boots in the butt, whose lips would pull back from its teeth as we approached. There were people here; we caught sight of them moving to close a door or disappearing around a cramped corner into what Nick called 'gullies', a word from the dry canyon country my family had traversed on the outskirts of Monument Valley, a word suggesting that this was a geological outcrop thrown up by some riverine upheaval of the distant past, not a manmade development at all. Fragile and constantly evolving, yet permanent.

Nick explained that gully was an Anglo-Indian word for a narrow unnamed alley. More of a gutter than a lane. 'I think of gullet, something that closes up when you swallow,' he added. 'Or *gully-gully*, a conjuror's phrase.'

His absent-minded response didn't match his alert demeanour. He was carrying himself differently, shoulders square and scrappy. If he were a dog, his hackles would be up.

There wasn't room between the huts to walk abreast. Nor could we move swiftly while dodging the trickle of open drain that meandered down the middle of the narrow paths, like a dried-up rivulet of the stream that had etched these blighted gullies in the landscape. Dogging Nick's shadow, I had an uneasy, twitchy feeling in my back. I'd had a similar exposed feeling when walking through the streets near Eden after Sally's murder. Watched, followed.

After a lot of weaving and backtracking, one of the paths broadened slightly into a space not much bigger than a small courtyard where a woman squatted milking a cow. Both the cow and the woman cast nervous glances at our approach. Nick approached her politely, his words incomprehensible to me, yet soothing, and I heard the woman mumble a few words in reply. She waved us further into the maze, and squeezed out a few more comments with the milk, keeping her head lowered, unlike the cow, who shook her horns at us.

We walked a little way up the gully indicated by the woman, and then Nick stopped. 'I don't like this, Claire. I think we should go back.'

'Why? That woman sounded as if she knew who you meant. Didn't she tell you which direction we should go?'

'Not really.'

'So she didn't tell you where the guy's wife and family are? Nick?'

'She gave me a rough idea.' He stopped and looked back in the direction we had come. 'She also said that the woman's husband visits from time to time. He hasn't left the Calcutta area after all.'

'That's great! Maybe he'll be there!'

'Not so great. I got the impression that people here aren't at all happy with the way UNISENS treated this family.'

I was reluctant to leave without having accomplished anything. 'Please, Nick: couldn't we just find this woman and –'

'And what?'

'We could say we've come from UNISENS, that they regret her loss of income, offer her some money as compensation. Please, Nick.'

He hunched his shoulders, gave a reluctant flick of his chin in assent and walked on, resuming that tough, bunchy testosterone slouch. I noticed that he had pushed his plastic hand deep into his pocket, concealing any evidence of weakness.

We found the chemist's wife sitting crosslegged at another crossing not far off, outside a thatched cupboard with a single plank as a shelf displaying jars of violent-coloured sweets. There were children playing round her feet and a neat row of the smallest fish I had ever seen arranged on a leaf in front of her. As soon as Nick spoke to her she rose and in one graceful movement gathered fish and children together and started to drift away from us, trying to pull her children with her. But the children would not be separated so easily from the first exciting thing to happen all day. Sucking their thumbs furiously and staring up at me with saucer eyes, unwilling to part from us, they clung to her sari like sea anchors towed in the wake of a sailboat.

From what I could read in her gestures, Nick wasn't making headway with his explanations. In a minute she would disappear down one of those countless channels and we would be back where we started, just a lot hotter.

Moving closer to her, ignoring the hand Nick put out to stop me, I said, 'I'm Jack Ironstone's cousin.' I raised my voice as stupid people often do with foreigners. 'We've come from him. Ironstone. Your husband's colleague. He's very sorry about what happened to your family. We have money for you from him.' I felt in my bag and took out a handful of rupees.

'Are you *mad*!' Nick whispered, grabbing my arm.

The woman started to back away, children still attached to her sari. One boy remained, a ragged clever kid who eyed the money as a hungry wild dog would a bone. It was impossible to tell his age.

'Jack Ironstone,' I repeated to the boy. 'You know him.'

I heard people gathering. Men were blocking the path we had come along. They were muttering to each other and occasionally words like 'Ironstone' and 'UNISENS' rose to the surface before submerging under an angry foreign rumble. Maybe my cousin's name hadn't been a good card to play. I turned to the boy. Suddenly, Nick's hand left my arm. I looked back and saw men around him, jostling him. He was disappearing into the crowd. I could hear Nick's voice talking to them, explaining in a language that must be Bengali because it sure as shit wasn't English and he was gesturing to me or waving me away I couldn't tell.

I tried to press back through the crowd because it seemed I needed to keep sight of Nick. If I kept sight of Nick everything would be OK. Men were in my way, they got in my way, not exactly pushing me but not moving back. Some faces were tough and stiff, some as shabby and shiny as second-hand suits. 'Dead men's clothes': that's what Robin used to call the garments my parents dressed in, and he said that when he was their age he would never wear anything second hand. Except, of course, he never got to their age.

The men closing in on me were wearing clothes that had never been new. I doubted they ever had a label. How can these kind of thoughts cross your mind in less time than it takes to turn your head and notice a man picking up a stone?

And observe that Nick had disappeared. He'd gone.

I felt the money grabbed from my hand and saw the little boy's teeth white and carnivorous with the excitement, the bait in his hand now and not mine.

It seemed like an event that shouldn't be happening under this bright hard sun. One minute it was a Big Adventure and the next everything is happening fast, right now, *present tense.* There's a man picking up a stone. I watch him like it was baseball and look, he's taking aim, the pitcher's winding up.

A hand grips mine and I try to pull away and look down to see the boy, the woman's boy with my money in one of his hands, tugging at me with his other.

The stone hits me. Not hard. Not a big stone, or aimed well. But the blood, I feel that, the tickle of the blood feathering down my leg.

The boy's hand pulling again.

I follow him.

He follows the woman.

We are jogging now and then running.

Another stone hits me, bigger it feels. I don't look back. No time to observe. We turn a corner fast and the men behind us run past, double back, flow through the narrow gully we've taken. Running fast now so there's no time to pick up stones pick up sticks or the current behind will run over you. It's a river game we're playing and the rules keep changing. The banks of the tributaries squeeze between ravines and overflow into wide channels.

What do they call it, the game, what do the English schoolkids call it? Pooh sticks, that's it. After Winnie the Pooh. Robin and I learned it from Dad. Our English Dad. Christopher Robin he called his son in an atypical burst of nostalgia. You drop the sticks one side of a bridge. Run to the other side. See which comes out first.

Which comes out first? In the wide flat curls of river they catch up, in the narrow gorges we leave them behind.

We run through someone's fire and knock over a bucket of milk, a cow being milked, the sheep we kick and push through and with each breath I'm thinking of all those news footages you've watched. The names of cities that spell catastrophe as a list.

I think the pounding is the men following. And the harsh cries to match those faces. It's my heart, my breathing. I have a stitch in my side like someone's stuck a needle there, stitched me up. I've been stitched up. I'm thinking: *Nick*.

Then we're in this dark place, stumbling through a dark labyrinth, only the boy's white clothes to guide me, and I know all the answers, all the images come down to this. The light is going to overexpose everything. Fade to black.

I must have passed out. Heat affects me like that. The woman is offering me something in a saucer, no, a clay cup. Tea, the cup rough as emery against my lip. The best thing I've ever tasted.

The boy – he's maybe ten, maybe fifty for all I know – sticks his head around his mother and asks in a Michael Jackson voice, 'You wanna see me break dance?'

I'm in this tiny dark mud room about the size of a walk-in closet in the States, lying on what seems to be a bench also made out of mud but covered in a striped rug and this kid brings out a ghetto blaster as big as the room, turns it on loud and starts jiving around, wheeling on his shoulder, his head, his index finger. The mother looks at him fondly. His brothers and sisters, all of them virtually naked except for ragged pants, are pretty impressed. It's the first time they've had a captive American, a captive audience. The woman hands me a leaf with rice on it, about a teacup full, with yellow gritty stuff poured over the top. '*Dal*,' she says, I think. It tastes good, and cauterises my mouth with the quantities of chillies.

All the kids squat down and watch me eat.

Why are they feeding me? How long have I been here? Automatically I look at my watch and find it's gone. The Michael Jackson of Calcutta flicks off his ghetto blaster and leans against the wall with his arms crossed, looking pretty cool for someone in a T-shirt with more holes than shirt. He takes my watch off his wrist and hands it back. The face is cracked. Time has stopped.

'So,' he says, 'you wanna know about my Dad.' He lights a *bidi*, the poor man's excuse for a cigarette, made out of one tobacco leaf tied with a piece of cotton. It smells like he's smoking cow shit. He nods at his ghetto-blaster. 'Dad is buying me that. He's gonna get us a TV soon. Wait till he hears about you.'

I choke on the last mouthful of rice.

Turns out his English isn't quite as good as it seemed at first.

It's gathered from rock videos and reruns of *I Love Lucy*. At one point he asks me was Desi Arnaz from Goa, he looks Portuguese, and there are lots of Portuguese in Goa. Cuban, I say, Desi was from Cuba. One of the first Spanish Americans to make it big without disowning his roots.

I can't believe I'm having this conversation.

He's told me his father uses heroin, didn't always, that he hates Jack Ironstone and blames him for his dismissal, although it isn't clear why. He says it's because his Dad has something on Jack, knows something.

'What does he know?'

The mother speaks a few words to the boy and he gives me a crazy translation: 'Their ears fall off, some of the people.'

'Which people? Where?'

At UNISENS, he says. 'They get fed bad leaves and then their ears fall off.'

His little sister wants to know if I have a pen she can use. I hand one over and there's an immediate fight between all the kids to see who gets it first. You would think they'd never seen a pen. Maybe they haven't. My kid takes it from her and uses the back of his hand as a surface, laboriously writing his name, Sunil. 'But you can call me Sonny,' he tells me, 'since you are sharing with us. Like Sonny and Share.' He's made a joke. We check each other out to make sure. Then the whole place rocks with laughter. He was going to a local school until his Dad lost his job. He had to give up school to help his mother and the family. I ask him how many brothers and sisters he has and he shrugs as if it didn't matter. You can see his point. It's hard to count, the way they keep moving around.

A man slides back the thatched door and comes in. Outside it's dark. I'm curiously unafraid. I know it's not Sunil's Dad who has entered because I've been shown a photo of Dad that sits on a trunk which doubles as a table, his arm around the other chemist who was dismissed at the same time. Neither one of them looks like someone you'd trust to help you cross the road. The new arrival is a lot older. He has a tombstone face: long, flat and grey, sitting on a pile of bones. Between my boy and this grave man it seems that I am going to be spirited away to safety under cover of darkness and his rickshaw. Among other things, it has been impressed upon me that I wouldn't be welcomed back to the village with open arms. It has also been made clear that Nick got away, back to the taxi. The tomb-faced man had promised to bring me to Nick. I don't know whether to believe this or not. There aren't a whole lot of choices.

◆ ◆ ◆

### M. Suttee (Ironstone Bequest c.1888)

'ONE OF A SERIES of silver gelatine prints attributed to Joseph Ironstone,' the clerk had said, stressing the rarity of this photograph of a woman burning on her husband's funeral pyre. Committing suttee. Or did he say *entering* suttee, I wondered. In the foreground was the silhouette of a man (possibly European) which stood out against the bright flame that was consuming her. A negative image, an overexposed print, perhaps, the wrong kind of film.

◆

Slack-jawed, a scarecrow, arms by his sides, palms out. An angry crowd behind him. The only thing saving him is his colour: he is white, or would be but for the blood and soot streaking his face. What has he done? What has been done to him?

He doesn't remember. The blood on his face is nothing to the waves of blood beating against the shore of his head. Another head is growing through his left ear. He can feel it erupting from the flesh of his cheek. The colours are dancing. But no one will do anything, no one sees it. A naked woman with haunted eyes, a woman he dimly remembers, is eating *we call them Congreves sir Lucifers sir them what we call Lucifers Luthers.* He conjures another woman *gully-gully* pressed into the shadows of a gully, watching him. He wants her to find him, change his course. She with her clarity, her clear eyes, will see what must be done. He wants to stop but he cannot. He wanted to be a doctor, to heal in others what he could not heal in himself. He is a wizard with a knife, a magician's baton it is in his hands. He tried to cut the second head and found the first dying.

*Ma fire killt Fa Boygir cry Ma see hear speke Ma fire killt Ma*

Where is the cancer is it here between the legs can you cut it out? Locked in the dark, like his sister who stays long after she is cold and smells bad Mummy we're locked in here and outside there is only Luther with his measuring. Be a man. Clip clip clip toenails and hair. Make a catalogue, make a list.

## III BLOOD

# Savage Gardens

# 1

CLAIRE, BODY RACKED by blood-curdling menstrual cramps, forehead pressed to the jeep's cool window as it negotiated the road north to Kalimpong from Bagdogra airport, thought about blood: the hot, sticky-sweet, trailing nature of it; bloodlines: something bloodstock had, good or bad; the difficulty of tracing her own. She wondered: could I be said to have good bloodlines? What did Magda do when she got her period on Himalayan expeditions? Was she hot-blooded or cool-headed? Am I? In France, women who had murdered while in the grip of PMT could be let off. A crime of hot-blooded passion was OK. Crimes in cold blood were less socially acceptable.

She brooded on the coolness – *bad blood* – that Nick had shown towards her since the visit to Calcutta's sewage hutments. Still vivid was her memory of slipping through the village to find Nick waiting for her in the taxi, just as she had been assured he would be by her tomb-faced guide. But Nick's view of events was very different from hers. 'When you ran off, shouting about being from UNISENS, and the men around me went after you, I tried to keep you in sight, but you were too quick for me – and them, luckily. A man who knew where the chemist's family lived – one of the uncles, I think – said you were safe and I would only stir things up again by following you. He agreed to bring you here.'

'Didn't you talk to him about what caused the riot?'

'That wasn't a *riot*, Claire. And the fellow talked a lot of Communist nonsense, frankly. All about the exploitation of the masses by big companies like UNISENS. Said the chemists had been unfairly dismissed, there had been hanky-panky with the test cases – they weren't paid enough or some such thing. Tension is running high at the moment, an offshoot of the Gurkha riot. There are many tribal and Assamese people in the village, all of whom want independence from India. And a lot of men have been laid off recently, which doesn't help. Neither did your American accent and attitude.'

Claire, who had never considered she had an 'attitude' of any kind, let alone American, asked him to define it, but he shook his head impatiently. Even after she had repeated the story given to her by Sunil, Nick refused to take the rumours about Jack seriously. 'Their *ears* fall off? You can't believe such a preposterous tale, Claire.' He drew out his next words one at a time like a man building a brick wall between her ideas and his: 'These were people who came to Jack with *cancer*, you know, simple people who may not have understood what it means to be a test case.'

In the end she dropped the subject, but remained uneasy, and Nick had been noticeably less friendly ever since. Sitting opposite her in the jeep now, he resisted her attempts at conversation by answering with terse, unhelpful replies. Claire concentrated on the climb. The road had begun by following the smooth course of the river Tista or Teesta (depending on the age of the map – higher still, the river would split to become the Lachen/Lachoong, this being a country where names changed with every twist and turn of history), while for the last few miles, it had been a dramatic switchback track through dense cardamom and rubber forest. Ahead was Kalimpong, a 4100-foot saddleback ridge only five hundred feet lower than Rinkingpong Hill, the point where triangulations had been made for the original survey of the town.

'Do all the names round here sound like variations on table tennis?' Claire asked Nick, as their jeep managed the final snarling turn.

He gave her a little smile. Not what you'd call a smile to warm the cockles of your heart, she thought, but a smile, at least. The first in hours. 'Even the Lepcha name for themselves has a playful ring,' he said, 'Rongkup Rumkup.'

'It means "son of the snowy peak, son of God",' added the driver, who claimed to be half Lepcha, half Gurkha himself. He had already warned them of the curfews in force owing to continued outbreaks of Gurkha violence.

Kalimpong was not unfamiliar with dramatic events, Claire knew. In the early 1900s it had been full of British agents spying on Russia, mountaineering reconnaissance teams on their way to and from Everest, Tibetan mule caravans loaded with wool. Roaring through the town's muddy, low-rise streets, Claire was struck by its resemblance to frontier Wyoming, an impression reinforced by the raised wooden boardwalks and the array of pack animals tied up down the main drag. Kalimpong was clearly still the frontier to somewhere. A street from an old Western, she would've thought it, if not for the melange of faces and costumes on the people pushing through its streets, lasting evidence that this small town had once been the crossroads of Asia, a pioneer Hong Kong. 'One of the greatest trading centres in the world, until the Tibetan border was closed by the Chinese in 1959,' said the driver. He insisted that the place was still crawling with spies – Chinese ones these days, since the Tibetan uprising in March, and there were certainly lots of bronze-skinned refugees of the crisis around. Dressed in traditional felt hats and heavy woollens despite the heat, the Tibetans mingled with Marwari merchants whose tweed jackets hung over white lungis, Nepalese ladies sporting nose rings the size of dinner plates, and the sturdy local Gurkhas, whose faces didn't fit the atrocities reported about them in the press.

'Where are the gunslingers and marshals to keep the peace?' Claire asked.

The driver, a self-confessed Clint Eastwood fan, turned his head to grin at her, 'No guns, Miss.' With his left hand he raised a large sheathed short sword. 'Gurkha kukri. Admirably designed for hewing a branch or a foe.' He had been carrying it, he explained, ever since the Gurkha National Liberation Front in Darjeeling had begun calling for their own Gurkha-land, which they wanted to stretch from northeastern India into southern Bhutan. When Claire asked what had started this recent push for independence she was told that it had always been an issue. 'Especially this year, Miss, since census records show that there are too many Nepalese people – especially Gurkhas – outside of Nepal. But this is not a recent thing. My family came as immigrants in the last century. We were recruited to work for British people in timber and tea industries. In those days plenty of land up here. Now there is less land and more of us, India and Sikkim want us to go back where we come from. "Go back home!" government is saying.' He shrugged, momentarily taking his hands off the steering wheel and clamping them back again just in time to make the sharp turn for Hilltops Hotel. 'But this *is* home now.'

Tucked away down a road of orchid nurseries, the old hotel was shaded by the flaming petals of huge poinsettia trees and its doors guarded by stone lions, testament to the owner's Tibetan origins. It was here that Nick and Claire had expected to meet the rest of the expedition. What they found instead was a letter from Jack warning them that he was still in Darjeeling with Ben and Christian, where they had gone to get their visas for Sikkim at the district's central government office. Not only had their visas been refused because of the uprising, he wrote, but the detailed army survey maps issued to the Xanadu expedition in London, maps impossible to buy here, had been impounded, a loss which worried Jack less. 'We have the nineteenth-century surveys and I've recruited guides who know the country better than their own wives' bodies.' Without visas, though, the door to Sikkim had slammed shut, and thus their route into Tibet. Nick, looking up from the letter, said that Jack must have assumed the problems would be over by now. 'He only showed the government officials our maps because he thought they wanted proof we were equipped to travel on our own. But Sikkim is one of the contested areas.'

The rioting had been getting worse, they were informed by the hotel's receptionist, especially in the villages, 'where people are simpler and easily led', and the intermittent curfews would make travelling difficult, if not impossible.

Nick decided to take a jeep to Darjeeling to see if he could speed things up for Jack. 'You'd better stay here, Claire, in case of trouble on the road.'

After an afternoon and evening spent curled up on the deep veranda, leafing through the hotel's library of dusty photographic albums, Claire decided that Kalimpong was a place where anyone who'd ever had something to do with mountains, plants or Tibet might have left traces. As Magda Ironstone qualified on all three counts, it was only a question of finding the right person to ask.

She began the next morning with the hotel receptionist, who regretted his ignorance. 'I am new to the area, Miss. Sadly, the manager is out of town, for he knows everyone.' He recommended that Claire ask around some of the regulars in the back room at Gompu's, a Raj-era tea house now converted to all-purpose bar, restaurant and travellers' hotel. 'It is still run by the same family as in the British days,' he said. 'And anyone with a story to tell in Kalimpong – or one they don't want told – eventually passes through Gompu's.' He cackled briefly. 'Everything passes through fast, like Gompu's food.'

On the road into town she soon caught up with children from the Tibetan refugee school and joined them in a queue at a tea stall run by an old lady wearing the traditional woven striped apron of a Bhutia and a jaunty electric blue nylon ski hat emblazoned with 'I Love New York'. Following the children's example, Claire bought some peanuts wrapped in a twist of newspaper and walked on. About to stuff the newspaper wrapping in her pocket, she noticed its headlines – HEADS OF THREE LOCAL MEN IMPALED ON FENCE BY GIRLS' SCHOOL – and worried about her decision to stray from Hilltops.

But there was no sign of insurgence at Gompu's, a ragged hotel leaning over the dusty cross street with an air of fatigue. Weary at its own past, not only had it seen better days, it had survived to regret them. In the dim light from a selection of low-wattage bulbs Claire took in a back room which in the Raj era must have resembled early English railway waiting rooms. Still boasting its original liver and cream paint scheme (made more liverish by years of cigarette smoke), Gompu's nod at decor consisted of fluttering strips of fly-paper and straight-backed wooden chairs of a discomfort to satisfy the sternest Methodist. It was a place only serious drinkers would enjoy, and the customers tempted by such spartan pleasures were limited to a pair of ancient, wizened hippies, fugitives from the road to enlightenment, and three men with Asian faces more suited to customers in a Shanghai or Macau opium den. A general impression of furtive drug deals going down was heightened when a sudden power cut stopped the fans overhead and reduced the room to black. Within seconds the owner appeared and placed a fizzing lamp on the central table, filling the room with the nostalgic smell of propane gas, and in the intimacy created by its storytelling light the least drunk of the opium trio was prompted to speak. 'Where are you from, young lady?' he asked, in a cut-glass English accent, 'Not Liverpool, by any chance?'

'London.'

His Fu Manchu moustache drooped with disappointment. 'Pity. We ask everyone from England if they live in Liverpool.'

Intrigued, despite her wariness about the wisdom of engaging drunks in conversation, Claire asked, 'Why Liverpool?'

'We're Beatles fans!' his much drunker friend roared at her in an equally upper-crust English accent rendered slightly foggy by the alcohol ('Beatlsh fansh'). He lurched to his feet and attempted a gallant bow, knocking his chair over in the process, 'Conor O'Donnell'sh the name: fifty pershent Irish, hunerd pershent drunkish.'

Claire, surprised at his managing to nod his head without actually falling over, examined his broad copper-skinned face with the narrow Asian eyes and thought: Conor *O'Donnell*?

'Won't you pleash join ush for a drink?' he asked. 'We inshisht.'

As if on cue, the owner's wife, a stout bruiser with powerful biceps and Chinese features to whom O'Donnell's friend referred under his breath as 'the bouncer', appeared with a fresh glass and another bottle of Kingfisher. A chair was pulled out for Claire by the smallest of the three men, who smiled at her shyly and muttered a long name ending in 'lama'. 'But you can call me Tiny.'

'Tiny is famous,' said Fu Manchu. 'He would have been our greatest soccer star but for his size. Instead he coaches future teams all round the region – even into Bhutan, urgently requested by the Queen Mum, who sent him a bottle of her Special Courier whiskey as a bribe.' He turned to the drunk. 'Conor here is our resident poet. Had several books published and read out on Radio Bhutan. He's just rewritten the local girls' school anthem.'

'Not only footballsh but silver prayer wheelsh and other Buddhist artefacsh, Tiny can get you,' Conor said, lagging a few sentences behind. He winked with heavy emphasis. 'He tradesh with monksh.'

'From Tibetan monasteries in Bhutan and Sikkim,' Tiny grinned. 'The monks are smugglers, like half of Bhutan. They use a secret border crossing west of the Ha Valley in Bhutan, and then exchange their goods in the forest where all the smugglers meet.'

'And your business?' Claire asked the moustache.

He waved his hand dismissively. 'Oh, I do very little: a little this, a little that.'

Tiny piped up in a fluting whistle, 'Malcolm is a very rich orchid grower – import-export – and owner of a hotel full of old world charm.'

Malcolm, not displeased with the biography, pulled out some chewing tobacco from a small tin.

'Do you have trouble ensuring that the ones you sell are not smuggled?' Claire asked, remembering her landlady's comments at the Raj Palace. What had she claimed – that most orchids sold as clones in Kalimpong were smuggled from the wild? 'I've heard that a lot of the wild orchids of Sikkim and Bhutan have become rare or extinct through overcollecting.' The hostile silence following her question was exaggerated by a malicious hiss from the gas lamp. Claire broke in nervously: 'Were you born in England, um, Malcolm?' She felt the little bubble of tension melt away.

'No, Conor and I are what you might call tea garden orphans, the product of years of boarding at the Ironstone Horticultural Settlement, now known more simply as Ironstone Homes. Tiny is Bhutia to his backbone, but –'

'Tea garden orphans?' Claire interrupted. At the Ironstone name, she had felt everything come into focus. Even Conor looked less blurred.

'The bashtardsh of tea plantersh,' said Conor.

Malcolm explained that the Ironstone Horticultural Settlements, one in Darjeeling, one in Kalimpong, had been established with a large endowment from a certain Magda Ironstone in 1889, supposedly as an orphanage-cum-school, but in fact as an institution intended for the offspring of local women and the British employed in Darjeeling and Assam tea-gardens.

'She wash shocked, you shee,' O'Donnell slurred his inter-ruption, 'shocked by all the lil blond-haired, blue-eyed, bare-ashed kidsh she shaw running round the tea eshtatesh. A dishgrashe to her proud nashion.'

Malcolm continued, 'The first six children, as well as the subsequent hundreds, were *called* orphans. Truth is, all of them had mothers – usually Lepcha or Nepalese girls – and were largely supported by their distant and anonymous white fathers, whose one rule was that the children should not be told who either of their parents were.'

'At first it was dedicated to boarding and training young boys in botanical science,' Tiny added. Today the Settlement comprised thirty or so well-maintained bungalows, the flower nursery started by Magda, a dairy and a bakery producing what the trio claimed were 'genuine English cream cakes'.

'Not only Malcolm and Conor but many of the graduates have gone on to greatness, despite their lack of parental guidance,' said Tiny proudly. 'I myself have recently coached several future stars of our soccer fields.'

'Do you know anything about the original six orphans at the Settlement?' Claire asked Malcolm, and was told that for a more detailed history she should talk to the retired gardener, an old Tibetan whose name she couldn't catch. Even after he repeated it, the bubbling vowels rolled past her like water. 'Plays the bagpipe jolly well for a Tibetan,' Tiny said. Malcolm wrote down the gardener's name for her on a matchbox. 'Every evening it echoes round the hills. Just like the highlands of Scotland.' He pronounced it 'heelands', with a slight brogue.

She tried unsuccessfully to picture that opium-smoker's face in the context of a highland pub.

'Once we asked if he could play McCartney's "Mull of Kintyre" for us, but he said he doesn't play rubbish songs.'

'If you think of anything else of interest about Magda Ironstone,' Claire said, 'I'll be at Hilltops for the next few days, registered under the Xanadu expedition, Jack Ironstone's party.' About to explain that Jack was her cousin, she decided against it, remembering the reaction she'd had in Calcutta.

'Jack Ironstone?' asked Tiny. 'Well, then.'

'Well, then?' she repeated, interested by the man's conspiratorial look.

Tiny didn't get a chance to answer before Malcolm stood up and insisted on escorting her to her hotel, 'While the curfew may not yet be in force, the natives are still restless!'

'Especially the Gurkhas,' Tiny said. 'Would you like to see the scar on my lower back where I was wounded accidentally by a Gurkha-thrown bomb?'

'An accidental bomb?' Claire asked, after politely declining the opportunity.

'Accidental wound. All the Gurkhas involved came with biscuits to see me in the hospital. They are mostly well-mannered people except they drink a lot sometimes. But if they are rude when drunk they are very apologetic after.'

Claire, keeping to herself the opinion that a bomb was an

extreme breach of etiquette, shook the two men's hands and allowed Malcolm to lead her graciously out of the bar and back to the hotel.

# 2

AS EVENTS TRANSPIRED, Claire didn't have a chance to follow up her lead at the Ironstone Settlements. She was climbing the steps of Hilltops' veranda when Jack, Nick, Ben, Christian and their crew pulled up in a caravan of Land Rovers so ancient and covered in dust that they might have driven out of a World War II desert movie. Over drinks with the four thirsty men she learned just how far the Xanadu expedition had strayed from its course.

The original plan had been to drive by jeep north into the dense jungles of Sikkim along the eastern arm of the Tista river. From there, climbing on foot through the high border passes, they were to have jeeped across the Chumbi valley, a tongue of Tibet lapping the flanks of Bhutan, and travelled by foot, jeep and yak to the Tsangpo Gorge via the mountainous shoulders of Bhutan and Tibet's great plateau. When the visa problem failed to get resolved in Darjeeling, Jack had proposed an alternative plan, as illegal as it was dangerous. He had suggested that the party leave their vehicles northeast of Kalimpong on the Bengal side of Sikkim's border avoiding the jeepable roads watched by the military. Then, minus official permission, they were to proceed by foot into Bhutan, a smugglers' crossing which would take them into the high forests west of Ha and east of Chumbi, where they could re-enter Sikkim at an unguarded pass. All being well, Jack hoped they would be able to pick up some transport further north at a logging camp whose manager he knew.

Claire was amazed to hear that the other three men had already agreed to this plan. 'What happens if we're caught?'

'There are too many remote places to cross for them all to be guarded,' Jack replied, 'and the men we'll be travelling with have done the journey a thousand times. We can play tourists if we run into border guards, tell them we got lost.'

'What about the porters?'

'Some of them are Tibetans, eager to return home, the rest are Bhutias and Lepchas, who are used to ignoring government interference in border crossings. And Ben's delighted by the loss of our maps – aren't you, Ben? The perfect start for a teratologist.'

Claire looked around the circle of men, all of them treating the loss of visas as a big adventure. Jack and Nick she could understand; neither was preoccupied by legal fine points. But Ben surprised her, as did Christian, whose professional future could be jeopardised if it got out that he had acquired plants and seeds without permission from the proper authorities. She pointed out that any specimens they found were liable to be confiscated, a possibility that Christian brushed off. 'Money goes a long way in this part of the world.'

'What are you going to do, bribe the officials to let you steal the green poppy?' Claire's attempt to match the men's relaxed banter cracked on the bribe and came out as a prim-sounding accusation.

'I wouldn't call it bribery,' Jack answered for Christian. 'A contribution to the national economy, say. And UNISENS does intend to set up a research programme here when the political situation is more stable, don't you, Christian?'

'In the meantime, we have no visas,' Claire pointed out, 'and without those we can't get help from the authorities in the event of an accident. What happens if one of us breaks a leg? We get shot?'

Jack grinned. 'You're a doctor, aren't you, Ben?'

'Any of you guys comes down with signs of teratoma, I am perfectly willing to perform emergency surgery on your balls,' Ben said. 'Of course, it's been a while since I've been in an operating theatre, and we might be a little short of trained nursing staff and anaesthetic, but I'm sure we could make do.'

Christian fixed Claire with the long-nosed questing sort of look that she had noticed him apply in London when he was trying to root out her latent opposition. 'I can see you are uncomfortable with this, Claire. Under the circumstances, everyone would understand if you decided not to continue.'

She had been convinced it was a misunderstanding on first hearing of Jack's plan from one of the Bhutanese porters unloading the Land Rovers. The man had confirmed Tiny's comments about the smuggling that went on through the Ha Valley, and seemed more worried about smugglers than he was about border patrols. 'Smugglers won't like it if we are seen to trespass,' he said.

'What kind of smugglers?' she asked, and he explained that Ha was where the Chinese came to exchange gold, Thermos flasks and sneakers for Western watches, pens and saddles from Bhutanese and Indian smugglers. 'Sneakers for watches? Or saddles?' Claire wondered aloud. 'Do India and Bhutan have a shortage of sneakers?'

'Also orchids they smuggle,' the porter replied.

Now she balanced these stories against the support given to her by Val and Nick, financial support in Val's case, reminding herself how lucky she was to be here. 'I . . . yes. I guess I'll come. If you guys think it's OK.' She felt swept up in someone else's story, part of the unidentified detritus accumulating in the dustpan of other, more important lives. No longer the narrator of her own destiny.

At dawn on the second of October the party began to leave Kalimpong, the six Land Rovers departing at intervals of ten minutes in order to appear less conspicuous. Jack was in the lead, the others paired in two jeeps behind him with as many porters as would fit. Driving out on the old trading road to Tibet they passed another two severed heads impaled on the school fence. Claire quickly averted her eyes, but not before she saw the ghoulish trick that someone had played, smearing the dead men's mouths with red lipstick. She *thought* it was lipstick. Whether these were Gurkha victims of the police or police victims of the Gurkhas even the local porters couldn't say. 'A good time to be leaving,' remarked one of the Lepchas.

There was evidence of monsoon damage all along the cliff road above this northeastern leg of the Tista river. Sections of it had been washed away down the hills and the only repair that had been done was to drive a tractor across what remained of the upper landslide areas after the land had stopped sliding, roughly levelling the surface. Over these temporary tracks the Land Rovers, their axles grinding, laboured slowly, giving Claire ample time to speculate on how little prevented them from slipping further into the river. She spent most of the journey with her eyes closed. One of the oldest porters, a Bhutanese Lepcha in his early sixties named D. R. Damsang, was curious about her fear of heights. 'When I was a boy in Bhutan,' he said, 'we had cane suspension bridges so fragile we were not allowed to walk in step across them.' He leaned out of the window and blithely considered the swollen river hundreds of feet below. 'This is nothing compared to the wonders of a Lepcha cane bridge.'

Claire, silently praying to be spared the wonders of a Lepcha cane bridge, almost welcomed the track they took after turning off the main river road. More rock slide than road, paved almost entirely in stones the size of housebricks (with the odd unbroken boulder to negotiate), it was even harder going for the Land Rovers, and along its fifteen or so miles they lurched and swayed and bucked for over three hours, through logged tracts of forest and across streams. 'I think various internal organs have been permanently shaken into a different order from God's original pattern,' Ben said to Claire as they stopped for lunch at the edge of a steep forested slope and were told to disembark.

Here, the first evidence of Christian's leadership qualities was revealed when he produced from his backpack a multi-page inventory listing the contents of each porter's enormous load. 'Every morning,' he informed them, 'I intend to tick off whatever has been unpacked the night before, thus preventing the possibility of "accidental" loss and damage.' Far from resenting Christian's comments, the porters appeared enormously impressed, as they were when he flossed his teeth after lunch (an activity that he performed religiously three times a day, Claire learned). Watching these ablutions, Jack remarked that he suspected Christian of being a secret American. 'Only Yanks are so convinced of the moral superiority of dental persistence.'

'Cleanliness is next to Godliness,' Claire's Lepcha friend said, brushing his own teeth with a frayed twig. D. R. Damsang, like many of the porters, was wearing cheap trainers, while others had the kind of flimsy canvas tennis shoes Claire remembered from kindergarten. Jack claimed that all of them had been issued with boots in Kalimpong. 'Probably sold long since.'

'Doesn't that worry you?'

'It's their business. I've seen sherpas climb Everest in plastic sandals.'

Convinced that such a cumbersome party could never remain unseen, Claire had begun to accustom herself to the idea of arrest and life imprisonment (seeing headlines: AS EX-PECTED, ANOTHER ANONYMOUS FLEETWOOD SINKS WITHOUT TRACE) when out of the woods appeared a herd of sheep driven by four men who were to travel with the group. 'From a distance, we should pass as shepherds,' Jack said.

'Wolves in sheep's clothing,' Ben added.

But Claire was oddly reassured to find herself following in the footsteps of Magda, who had used sheep as pack animals when she crossed Tibet in the 1880s, the desolate, wind-swept tracks being too stony for yaks.

Joining the flock, Claire and Ben trailed the Western members of the party, with the native porters soon far ahead, despite their bad footwear and the heavy loads supported by leather bands around their foreheads. It wasn't how she had imagined the expedition, this undulating caterpillar sharply divided between West and East, and Jack, slowing his long-legged stride to hers as she moved towards the forest, must have read her mind. 'Did you see us more along the lines of a band of pilgrims?' he asked mockingly.

'Well, aren't we?' asked Ben, joining them.

'Absolutely,' Jack shot back. 'A band of pilgrims laden with such things as down sleeping bags, thermal underwear, Arctic tents, the material needed for drying seeds and herbarium specimens and for taking soil samples (including an impressive collection of Ziploc plastic bags in all sizes, enough to stock a California supermarket), the latest in recording, photographic and laser survey equipment, not to mention Gravol, antibiotics, delousing shampoo, water filters and hypodermic packs. All the trappings for civilised travel, as defined by Christian. Carried by porters, naturally. Our leader has the soul of a Victorian explorer, a twentieth-century Joseph Hooker: isolated, but never alone.'

'As long as he doesn't turn into Scott of the Antarctic, I don't mind,' Ben said.

Jack laughed. 'We'll be fine, Ben. Christian has been avidly reading Ernest Shackleton's diaries ever since I told him that American business schools now study the polar journey to learn about Shackleton's leadership qualities.'

'What's the old saying?' Ben asked. 'If you want to get to the South Pole, go with Scott. If you want to get home again, go with Shackleton.'

The men's discussion moved on to Hooker's three-month exploration of Sikkim in 1848, when he had set off with a party of fifty-six. '*Fifty-six!*' Claire exclaimed, and Jack grinned. 'Seven assigned to his tent, instruments and personal equipment,' he said, 'seven more to the papers for drying plants, a porter for each head man, four men to carry ammunition alone, the Lepcha plant collectors, eight brawny Nepalese guards and fourteen Bhutanese porters, not to mention the bird shooters and animal shooters and the trained taxidermists. Console yourself that by comparison with Hooker's team our party of thirty is streamlined.'

'Only because we have exchanged steam for microchip,' Ben replied. 'We're weighed down by a different form of empire.'

Jack cast a quick glance over the teratologist, already red-faced and sweating profusely. 'Do we need a little Buddhist enlightenment, Ben? I'll remind you of that when we hit the first high altitude pass. Ice tends to be hard on bare feet.'

Claire admitted that she was glad not to have to carry her converted X-ray camera, which alone weighed over fifteen pounds, and that didn't include its various tripods and the specialist cameras and lenses and photographic materials she'd brought. Like the other Western members of the party, she carried in her backpack only essentials and a few personal luxuries (a new book of lists along with the carefully edited selection of Magda's journals). Jack had months' worth of tobacco; Nick's pack held his more delicate recording equipment and cameras; Ben carried, among other esoteric texts, the Tibetan *Book of the Dead*, Matthiessen's *The Snow Leopard* and a huge supply of miniature Hershey chocolate bars; and Christian, in addition to Shackleton's diaries, had a cordless electric razor, dental floss, toothpaste for sensitive teeth and a whole Boots range of hygiene products for combating an Asia whose lax tendencies he suspected of being infectious.

Remembering the chlorophyll molecule that had sparked off this expedition, Claire amused herself as she walked by assigning an atom to each of the five Westerners. Was she the fragile magnesium at the molecule's core? Or was that Nick, with his magnesium arm? Before entering the darkness of the woods she took one last look at Kalimpong in the distance, strung out like a necklace around the throat of its hill, and wondered what kind of pressure it would take for the ring and chain of Xanadu's molecule to split apart. As she watched, the northern mountains, the road, the town disappeared behind a bank of woolly clouds and she needed all her energy for the path ahead.

For hours they climbed steadily through a dense mixed forest of conifers and rhododendrons, skirting any open pasture land to avoid being seen. At first the tree trunks sprouted Elizabethan collars of lacy ferns far above, then as the party continued to gain altitude Claire saw that she was level with the tops of trees growing at a steep angle up the path, immense oaks draped in pendulous velvet capes of moss, branches outstretched like giants ready to embrace their dancing partners. Green men of the forest, she thought, glancing over her shoulder from time to time, and was reminded of Magda's words: *By September that shapeless shroud which for months has muffled a lifeless world is blown away to reveal the quick green form reincarnated beneath.* That shapeless shroud, Claire whispered to herself, wondering if reincarnation always felt so exhausting.

Beginning a short steep descent before dark, she stumbled and slid down moss-covered stones until her legs screamed from the effort, reaching a small clearing where the porters had already erected tents. At what point they had reached Bhutan, crossed the boundary between one side of the law and the other, she had no idea or interest.

# 3

CROSSING BACK INTO SIKKIM at dawn two days later, Ben directed Claire's eyes to a range of soaring peaks in the distance. 'Kangchenjunga, third highest peak in the world, nine hundred feet lower than Everest,' Christian said promptly, revealing his confidence in the ability of facts and figures to order the world. Claire heard the juddering syllables of the mountain's name and thought of great boulders and granite slabs of earth colliding together. As if deliberately to prove the limits of their expectations, at that moment a sheet of mist above the peaks ripped across horizontally, and between the torn cloud curtain above them rose a tidal wave of icy white. 'We've been looking too low,' she said.

'That's often the problem,' answered Ben, to the obvious amusement of Jack, the opposing side in an ongoing argument.

'The gods rest there,' a Lepcha porter whispered to her, and she wanted to believe him. Shimmering off to their left like an illusion, a conjuror's trick, the mountain continued to appear only first thing in the morning, before the hot air had lifted from the valleys to conceal it, and at sunset, after the cloud settled into its crevices like a chiffon scarf discarded by some petulant diva in the sky. Unlike Everest, concealed in an archipelago of Himalayas, Kangchenjunga's trinity of white sails floated alone, 'a solitary ice ship rising on the waves of lesser mountains', Ben called it.

### The edge of Sikkim, October 1988

Early this morning I left the tent to have a pee and saw Ben huddled up in his sleeping bag by the cliff edge, a quilted Buddha facing an icy, moonlit Kangchenjunga, while from the pastureland below us drifted the clear toll of mule bells. Up here it's easier to believe Nick's view of Jack and the Calcutta events, which seem less important, maybe because, as Ben says, some things are not meant to be discovered. Of course, he wasn't talking about the secrets in Jack's murky past (which Nick and I have kept to ourselves), he was describing the 1955 British mountaineering team who stopped short of Kangchenjunga's peak as a gesture of respect to the local people who revere the mountain. The team's victory telegram to *The Times* read simply: 'Summit of Kangchenjunga less five vertical feet reached on 25 May. All Well.'

Fortunately, we'll have no such moral dilemmas. The highest pass we have to traverse is under 19,000 feet, which gives me a surprising pang of regret, considering my fear of heights (not something I've admitted to anyone except DR, my Lepcha pal). For the first time I understand why men covet mountain summits. Deserts and rivers flow away from you, engulf you; their landscape is always changing and adapting. A mountain is a fixed point. You can chart a clear course from those peaks, a perfect triangle. The mountains make me want to leave everyone behind and set off alone, to follow Magda's footsteps across the ranges of northeastern Sikkim and western Bhutan, the chain we will climb through to pick up the poppy's trail.

This journey takes us all in different ways. Christian waves his leadership at Jack like a red cape at a bull, assigning us daily tasks – explain this type of soil, Jack, photograph this plant, Claire. Sometimes I think Chris views each of us only in terms of the purpose we serve in his carefully plotted scheme: Nick, with his smattering of languages and his recording equipment, is the expedition's official ears; the porters are legs; I'm the eyes; Ben is our historian and interpreter of myth ('truly a teratologist', as he says); Jack has 'The Knowledge' – he knows the shortcuts of living in these mountains like a London cabbie knows the A–Z.

My cousin has chosen eight stopping points between Sikkim and the Tsangpo Gorge – for the frequency in which they recur in what we jokingly call The Green Poppy Chronicles, the old surveys Jack found in the UNISENS/Fleetwood archives. We are to make a continuous traverse, with no more than two nights in any one place to camp and take samples. That way, even if we don't find the poppy itself, we'll know more about the habitat that spawned it. Or so Christian claims. And there's an outside chance we may find its seeds in the soil, given that poppy seeds can take a hundred years to sprout. Between those brief two-night respites we keep a fairly taxing routine of random sampling of the soil and plants, wherever our journey crosses that of the nineteenth-century Chronicles.

We rise before first light every morning to wash in streams so icy my skin feels embalmed, then set off after breakfast, bright caterpillars in our cold weather gear, emerging from cocoons of anoraks and leggings as the day warms up. Walking for seven to eight hours a day, we experience air like needles of ice on our faces at night, sweet-smelling as some large herbivore's breath after the sun comes up. The walking and plant-collection give a rhythm to this journey that can't have changed much since Magda's time. Like her, we have to dig plants out of glacial debris varying from gravel to boulders, in high winds and snow storms, we have to dry and clean the seeds meticulously whatever the weather. There are still bandits and smugglers here to make collecting dangerous, and tribal people who sell us fresh supplies, although their villages now are within sight of hydroelectric dams. Without visas or detailed maps we are forced into disguise and evasion, as she and Arun were. And while Jack's contacts allow us to traverse stretches by jeep, our need for secrecy, combined with the region's uneasy politics, force us to avoid the main roads and trust in our guides.

When we stop each night, I often use what is left of the

daylight to slip away on my own with Magda's diaries. The only one with a private tent, I am not exactly alone in it while trying to piece together the expeditions she took with Arun, given the continual buzzing and bumbling of large and small moths, flying beetles and earwigs. The worst is a species of daddy-longlegs that persists in sweeping across my face like spider webs, distracting me from sticking pages in my book of lists, which I have been slowly transforming into a long accordion map that eventually should bear a passing resemblance to Christian's nineteenth-century surveys. He calls them *cadastral* surveys, each one the record of a particular native explorer's route march and everything seen from that single perspective. Ben told me that originally these charts contributed to our imagined ability to make a map at a scale of 1:1, a map literally the size of the world. Pretty funny, considering our best map of Sikkim (bought from a bookshop in Darjeeling) is 1:150,000.

'Cadastral: from the late Gr. for list or register; line by line,' Chris explained when I first saw him poring over the survey Jack had found. 'A chart showing the measurement and value of every plot.' He often practises his speaking encyclopedia thing on me, taking the idea of doing stuff 'by the book' pretty literally for a man who continues to break the law. He has a tendency to preach as if from on high, like Moses to the masses. Jack reacts badly when Chris tries this on him, but I feel as if I should be inscribing our leader's commandments on a stone tablet.

Every night, with my tent rattling in the wind, I huddle up with a book, 'the smallest possible tip of one finger exposed to turn the pages', as Hooker wrote to Darwin from a similar camp. Hooker was reading Darwin's Geology of South America, I am mining Magda's schist and shingle, exploring the substratum of Fleetwoods and Ironstones. I share Hooker's interest in the way that a country like this (or a family), combining the botanical characters of several, affords materials for tracing the direction in which species have migrated, the causes that favour migration – and the laws that determine how we mutate.

Today Jack told me I've adopted an antiquated eloquence that sounds as if I've been studying Magda's journals for too long. Everyone knows about them now (although I haven't admitted how closely her journeys with Arun mirror ours). Saying this he ran his hand slowly over the contours of my head, which for convenience's sake I've taken to shaving with Christian's razor, largely for fear of ticks. 'The soul of a nineteenth-century horticulturist in stout tweed,' Jack said, 'but the body of a young monk.' What's he up to?

# 4

ONE MORNING BEN asked Christian if he had considered that the 'Forest of Air', where the green poppies were said to originate, might be based on the mysterious hidden valleys of Bhutan and Tibet, the *beyul*, 'which may be mythical, or may be located in a dimension reached only through meditation'.

'Is that what James Hilton based *Lost Horizon* on?' Claire asked, and continued to mull the idea over as they began climbing after breakfast. She trailed behind with Ben, whose wan face made her suspect he was suffering from the altitude sickness Christian had sworn would not appear until they reached 12,000 feet. 'You read that in a book, did you, Chris?' Jack had teased. 'It hits you at 12,000 feet on the dot? Not a foot earlier?'

'I've got a question for you, Ben,' Claire began, 'as a teratologist.'

Ben stopped, his hand on his stomach. 'I'll answer anything you like, sweetheart, if you tell me what's in those beach pebbles you've been chewing, the lapidary medicine that miraculously put the bloom back in your tomboy cheeks and allowed you to tuck into that cold fried egg and curry over breakfast.'

Out of her pack Claire retrieved a handful of what looked like chalky white fossils with ferns and grasses embedded in them. 'A local remedy bought from a lady in Kalimpong market,' she said. 'It tastes like a mixture of blackboard chalk and root beer.' She giggled. 'The thing is, I wanted a homoeopathic medicine for altitude sickness, but I guess something got lost in the translation because my friend DR, the Lepcha porter – he said she's given me a remedy for vertigo.' DR, hearing Claire's description of the woman, had beamed happily. 'He told me the saleslady was a famous Lepcha priestess who could sing the sounds of wind, rivers and waterfalls "which are very melodious and liberate the dead souls".'

'Useful,' Ben replied, through heavy breaths. 'But it's my body needs liberation.'

'Wait a minute!' Claire walked a little way into the steep alpine woods beside their path, returning with some tree bark. 'Chew this – that's DR's remedy.'

Ben, after examining it carefully, pronounced it to be willow bark. 'It used to be taken for altitude sickness before we developed aspirin. Said to alleviate pain without damaging the stomach.'

'So why did we bother with a synthetic drug?' She felt herself blush. 'That's a stupid question. Obviously, to get more of the stuff.'

'Not so stupid. It was also to stop people wiping out willows, as they almost did with the cinchona tree in the eighteenth century when it was discovered that its bark could cure malaria.' Immediately bombarded with questions by Claire, he held up his hand to forestall any cross-examination. 'Having cured the nausea, my most profound consideration at this juncture is: how long will my supply of Hershey bars last?' He stretched his arms wide and asked her to consider the folly of a short, fat, one-balled ('but big-dicked, big-hearted') man like himself even considering a trek like this.

'So you don't want this other *teratological* question I have?'

'Hit me.'

'I know it sounds crazy, but . . . you know everything about myths and cancer, right? And I wondered . . . have you ever heard of a disease that makes people's ears fall off?'

'The best I can do is the story a Japanese friend told me about it being bad to eat too many abalones because, quotes "your ears will fall off". At first I thought this was an example of inscrutable Japanese humour, but no. Seems abalone filter-feeds on algae and stores up high amounts of chlorophyll derivatives. If you eat too much, this stuff can accumulate in your skin and cause lesions, and because the tops of your ears are the parts of the body most exposed to sunlight, that's where the worst lesions develop. In severe cases, tissue destruction can separate the ear from the head! There's an oriental curse that goes "may your right ear rot and drop off into your left pocket". I wonder if it has its origins in chlorophyll-mediated photosensitivity?'

'I never knew chlorophyll was such dangerous stuff,' she said, considering the implications of Ben's story in the context of what she'd heard about Jack.

'Now, please Claire, can we abandon our university of two for a few minutes and just enjoy the morning and the landscape?'

They had left the open slopes behind and entered a solemn green forest of huge trees with bark wrapped in a caul of interlacing climbers. Descending cables of lianas, flung between the trunks like rigging from the masts of a fleet of boats, gave a nautical effect heightened by the plumed ferns and epiphytes weighing down each branch and causing the trees to creak and tug at their anchors. 'Where have the ghosts of these trees gone, d'you think?' Claire whispered to Ben, stopping to focus her camera on a tree whose heart had rotted away within its rigging of climbers, the hollow now filled with twisting white lianas. 'They look like giant shipwrecks . . . or maybe sinews and tendons. Like those old paintings you get of men with their flesh stripped back to reveal the muscles.'

'What a gruesome idea! I was thinking of a cathedral, myself.'

She grinned at him. 'D'you always prefer to see the best in things, Ben?'

'Not at all.' He shook his head vigorously, denying the accusation of indiscriminate optimism, one that Jack often levelled at him. 'But I always *look* for it. Part of my job as a teratologist.'

'I thought you were supposed to be looking for monstrous forms.'

'And marvellous ones.'

'Like tumours?' she teased.

'Even tumours can be marvellous! Did you know that as a tumour grows it actually evolves? It's one of the reasons I love studying cancer, a disease whose infinite ability to adopt disguises makes it a worthy opponent.'

Claire's gaze had been drawn back to the arboreal pediments and gothic arches above their heads. She reached for her binoculars. 'Up there, can you see? That bald patch? It looks like –' She moved forward into the dripping undergrowth, her grey sweatshirt parting the leaves like a dorsal fin through green waves, and sinking to her knees, picked up what might have been a rubber bathing cap, one of those sea anemone kinds she remembered her mother wearing. Dropped in Ben's outstretched palm a minute later, the tangle of spaghetti roots was easily identified as a broken orchid. 'Claire – you didn't *pick* this!'

'Of course not! There are pieces lying all over the ground and huge bald patches in lots of the trees. Someone has been stealing them.'

'If there are smugglers around, they won't take kindly to observers.'

They hurried to catch up with the rest of the expedition, which had stopped in a clearing a mile further on so that Nick could make a recording. Still breathing hard from the fast climb, Ben immediately began to tell Christian what they had found, his explanation interrupted by Claire. 'It's like . . . vandalising a churchyard,' she cried. Pulling the broken pieces of orchid from her backpack, she noticed that Jack was the only one not to register surprise – Jack and one of the guides who had joined them shortly after they entered Bhutan, the man responsible for leading them back into Sikkim.

'These are plants, Claire, not people,' Jack said. 'And we can't afford to get involved with smugglers, if they're responsible.'

'We're hardly in a position to report them,' Christian objected mildly. 'It's sad, but we're not here for orchids.'

Claire, indignant that the men were taking her story so calmly, turned to Nick for support. He remained silent, but he didn't look happy, even less so when Jack reached for Claire's rescued plant and tossed it into the bushes. 'If the authorities caught us with this there would be real problems,' Jack said, waving to the porters to move on again.

'Very goal-oriented, your cousin,' Ben said. He squeezed her shoulder by way of consolation. 'Surprises me to see him in the position of second-in-command, especially considering that he originally brought the information about this green poppy not to Christian, but to my group.'

'Really?'

'Jack proposed to lead a team of science post-graduates on this very trip.'

'Why didn't you take him up on it?'

'Usual reason: lack of cash. We're a government-funded group at the university. We simply couldn't get the backing. So he went to Christian. As you can imagine, UNISENS is not short of a dollar. Of course, now it will be Christian who scoops the glory.' With his eyes on her cousin's disappearing back, he added, 'Funny how much more in his element Jack seems up here. Could be he's missed his calling, working in a lab.'

'Maybe that's why Christian chose him. I have a theory that Chris sees each of us as just part of a single expedition molecule, the Xanadu.'

Ben laughed. 'A Fleetwood variation on the Gaia theory: the earth and everything on it as a single self-regulating system.'

'It's, like, got its own theory?' Claire thought she'd made it up. 'Cap T, cap G, cap T: The Gaia Theory?'

'Actually it's a hypothesis. Named after the Greek earth goddess.'

'Yeah, well, a *hypothesis*! That makes all the difference!'

'An idea coined by James Lovelock, a British scientist who started off measuring blood pressure under water during World War Two and wound up as a lone conservationist, the guy who first discovered that supposedly "clean" air over the Antarctic was in fact full of CFCs. Lovelock believes that Earth, The System eventually rids itself of any species adversely affecting the environment.'

Claire, still brooding over the orchids, replied, 'Oh yeah? So how come men have been allowed to stick around for so long?' A crow gave a rusty cry overhead as if urging her to press her argument home. 'Tell me, Ben: why did you agree to continue this trip? Without visas, I mean?'

'It's a long story, but the short answer is that for years I've had a crazy desire to see the Himalayan blue poppy.'

'You could've saved yourself a hike through the highest mountains in the world,' she said. 'It's available in English garden centres every summer.'

'I mean growing in the wild, the way Colonel Bailey and botanists like Frank Kingdon-Ward saw it, growing in an alpine meadow surrounded by iris and primulas and the odd yak.'

'It won't even be in flower!'

'Our green poppy might be, though, Jack's snow leopard. And for that I'd do just about anything.' His fuzzy peach of a face squeezed up as if it were being put through a juicer. 'For me, plants divide into poppies and all the rest, all the other plants, the non-poppies. The obsession grabbed me while I was studying at Cambridge, when a friend gave me one of Bailey's blues.' He patted the generous roll of flesh around his middle. 'Ironic, huh? A fat-ass like me falling in love with that tissuey, transparent butterfly of a flower? I had the crazy plan of specialising in rare alpines, starting with a mail-order business from my flat in south London and growing plants from seeds friends had collected in the wild. Reality hit me when forty-foot lorries from Italy started turning up at the front door to collect larger and larger shipments. I'd be saying "There's one of those upstairs in the second bathroom" while juggling three sets of customers. Still, poppies remain an addiction, an "across the crowded room" kind of thing. Like we knew each other in a previous life.'

Claire let him climb a few paces without speaking, his silence punctuated with puffs. 'If we find this poppy, Ben, and it turns out to be as effective as Jack suspects, do you think UNISENS might try to copyright a cure for cancer?'

When Ben seemed reluctant to reply, Claire pressed him, 'Ben?'

'You know, Claire, I have no difficulty imagining you working in forensics. Archaeology would suit you equally well. You're a digger at heart.' He stopped abruptly. 'This is too complex a discussion to contemplate without an injection of Hershey and oxygen.'

Waiting for him to unwrap one of his chocolate bars, Claire stood well back from the gorge that fell away to their left in a near perpendicular series of narrow ridges. 'Cancer is not one disease, Claire, so there can't be a single cure,' Ben said slowly, regretfully licking the last of the chocolate from his fingers, and it seemed to her that he was edging away from the question as she had from the cliff. 'But the realities of our economy force drug companies into pursuing a "magic bullet" to shoot down cancer, even if effective vaccines against malaria and cholera – diseases endemic in the Third World – would save more lives. We come from a gun culture, you and me.'

Claire gave him a small smile for that. 'Christian was talking yesterday about genetically inserting the poppy's essential molecules into daily food. Like – I don't know, putting it in peanut butter or french fries or something. Maybe extending our lives by a hundred, two hundred years. You in favour?'

He put his hand on his heart. 'I'm not the Buddha, Claire, even if my shape indicates a genetic similarity.' He took another deep breath and started plodding up the hill, lifting each foot as if there were velcro attaching his boots to the path. 'Our quest is for the West's Holy Grail, the Evergreen Life, insurance against ageing and death. Unlike the East, a chronically underinsured place where people are preoccupied with spiritual insurance (which costs a whole lot less).'

Claire considered Jack to be a highly unlikely customer for spiritual insurance.

'What really interests *me* in this green poppy,' Ben went on, 'is that it may carry an antibody which blocks the receptors allowing cancerous cells to communicate.' He tried to explain the process in simpler terms. 'Imagine you've got these bad guys who are breeding like wildfire and corrupting the community. Now, instead of killing them off with chemotherapy, you alter their genes so that while they still harbour the genetic mutation that made them bad guys, they can be established in a normal family background where they are forced to behave.'

'Good guys, bad guys, Ben? You aren't suggesting that if tumours can mend their ways, then it follows people can too?'

'I hadn't got that far – but why not? It's possible that this poppy might offer an epigenetic solution –'

'Which is what, exactly?' Claire asked, thinking of epiphysis, the bit of knee bone that is separate from the femur before it begins to fuse.

'Roughly, the action of the environment,' Ben replied as they entered the campsite where the rest of the party waited. 'This poppy could force tumours to behave by fine-tuning their chemical communication with their environment. And if cancer cells can mend their ways, then why the Hell can't people?'

Joining them, Jack cut Ben off with a cool, flat remark. 'Maybe because people are infinitely more complicated than cancer cells, Ben?'

# 5

FOR THE FIRST time in her life Claire was in the company of listmakers and archivists as obsessive as herself. The Lepcha shamans, two small, nut-brown men of great dignity and upright posture who had in their heads every medicinal root and leaf and flower to be found in the foothills of the Himalayas, were literally 'reading' the forest canopy, leading the Xanadu party through this stretch of Sikkim's high country and thumbtacking each colour and shadow to the felt of memory with a name and a purpose. 'The flower of Ketaki – that's *Pandarus*, I think,' Claire heard Nick murmur into the tape machine, responding to their translator's comments, 'worn in the hair by girls to win the love of men. Its seeds cure a wound in the heart.'

*A wound in the heart:* was that a stab wound or a lover's? Claire, listening to the volley and return of the shamans' playful language while she took pictures, tried to grasp how removed Nick's translation was from the original meaning, and decided that this was a landscape where she could believe in almost anything. The air was very thin and sharp, reminiscent of one of those citrusy crisp young wines served with fish, and the light under the huge trees was strange, an encroaching green that only constant movement could resist (stand too long in one place and you'd find lichen on your cheek, a vine wrapped round the tripod). She wondered how it would affect the multitude of photographs Christian seemed to require. Her arms and clothes increasingly streaked with dirt, she marvelled at the geneticist's ability to keep his nails perfectly clean and his clothes wrinkle-free, as if he travelled with an invisible valet.

'How much, if any of the Lepchas' information has been written down?' Christian asked the Lepcha herbalist from Gangtok who was translating for them.

'Very little,' replied the Gangtok man, 'except perhaps in the Tibetan lamaseries, where I have heard that they keep medical scrolls. But largely these secrets are handed down verbally from generation to generation.' Most shamans were secretive about their knowledge, he said, believing that if they passed it on to unauthorised persons, not only would the efficacy of the plants be reduced, but the shaman himself would meet with the wrath of the plants' deities.

Claire suspected that Christian would have happily put the two shamans under bell jars, with tubes letting oxygen in and information out. As it was, he made sure, with his usual sweetly inescapable courtesy, that she and Nick recorded on film and tape as many as possible of the trees, herbs and flowers the Lepcha plant librarians used as remedies. Back in Britain the UNISENS biochemists would decide if a single molecule was responsible or several, and whether the mode of application affected the result. Application and actual preparation of the remedies were things that the shamans, while freely offering names and uses of the medicinal plants, remained cagey about.

'Often they reserve hallucinogens for secret initiation and shape-changing rites that they call "meetings with spirits",' Jack said, to explain their secrecy.

Nick suggested that hallucinogens were something Jack understood. 'Like all old hippies, right?'

'I always wondered what happened to hippies when they grew up,' Claire said, 'and now I know. They change sides and go to work for multinational pharmaceutical companies.'

Filling her lens with a huge lacy herb, she heard from Christian that it was artemisia, a quinine substitute used in China, its active molecule already being synthesised by Western chemists. 'The Chinese refuse to export the seeds,' he said, 'so it's terribly good news to find it here, especially since malaria remains a killer in Sikkim's low valleys.' When she asked him why they needed so many different plant samples if he was

interested in poppies and chlorophyll, he answered her atten-
tively, but with the bored brightness in his eyes that some adults
assume when talking to children. 'I'm interested in the effect of
altitude on plant alkaloids, Claire. Let me explain it in terms of
cinchona. At high altitudes the plant's alkaloids useful against
malaria become more potent and prevalent, until they reach
their highest proportion right up near the frost line. The same
may be true of our poppy, a change in habitat may alter its
molecular structure, as altitude was reputed to alter its
concentration of chlorophyll.'

'What will you do if we find it – synthesise its alkaloids like
we've done with quinine?' She asked the question in expectation
of a full and accurate reply, seeing Christian as a man who never
removed his mental lab coat, a genetic experiment who might
soon manage to reproduce by brain signals alone. Although she
knew he had a wife – Arabella – and two daughters with equally
predictable middle-class names, Claire could never imagine him
with genitals. He would probably have some sort of discreet,
smooth bump, she thought, like Barbie's Ken doll.

'The trouble with synthetic copies,' Ben interjected before
Christian could answer, 'is that they encourage the development
of mutant forms of the disease they've been designed to destroy.
It's happened with antibiotics and weedkillers, but so far *not*
with the natural quinine in cinchona, interestingly. No strains of
the malarial parasite have developed a resistance to the natural
drug, as they have with synthetic antimalarials.'

Jack put his hand out and felt Claire's forehead as if for fever.
'Have you been taking your chloroquine?'

'There's no malaria at these altitudes,' she snapped.

He let the hand on her forehead slide lightly down her cheek.
'Not here, but in some of the valleys. And the parasite can live in
your blood for weeks.'

Survival, Claire decided, was all a question of continuous
mutation and disguise, and no one was better at it than Jack.
Over lunch, her cousin told a story about one of the shamans,
affectionately pantomiming the man's speech patterns and

actions. The theatre of it, the backdrop of mountains and curtain of trees, gave Jack another personality. 'If I am seeing a man who is fat and tired and incapable of satisfying his wife, and who is always thirsty,' said Jack the shaman, Jack the shape-changer, 'then I am taking him to a certain beehive in the forest, and at this place the men are urinating. If then I am seeing bees throwing themselves avidly upon the sick man's urine, so then I know that I must be prescribing these fruit.' Back in his own skin, Jack added, 'The fruit are an antidiabetic, effective with seventy per cent of diabetics. Bees are drawn to the fellow's urine because it's sugary.' His mouth turned down at the corners, the way it did when he was privately amused, an ironic reverse of a smile.

Ben, commenting on Jack's acting ability, remarked that each of them was changing their structure with the elevation. 'Like the cinchona trees.' Behind Jack a trick of hot earth and cold sky was drawing the clouds up from the mountain pastures, transforming the mist into a towering petrified forest in shades of bone white and ash. How long does it take to mutate, Claire wondered, how far from the roots do we have to get before our branches learn a new way of growing? Everywhere she looked she saw omens and portents.

That night Nick took her to a quiet place on the edge of the village where they were staying and placed his cushioned headphones over her ears. 'Guess what this is.' She listened carefully, aware of him making an effort to heal the rift between them, but at first all she could hear was a dry rustle followed by a sound like a seashell over her ear. Then the dry rustle repeated. 'No idea, Nick.'

'The golden eagle that's been following us for days, maybe because our trail is at the same level as his flight path.'

A few seconds later she identified the shamans' musical voices, and then a group of words which all seemed to end in the same whispering vowels. She looked at Nick for an explanation and he said, 'I asked them to recite every different word they have for green.'

Outside the electronic world of Nick's headphones she became aware of real music, the village band serenading their visitors on a strange mixture of instruments, more vegetal than musical. 'Not bad,' Claire said, removing his headset and nodding towards the band, 'if not exactly the Stones.'

They joined Ben, Jack and Christian around a fire in the village square, the porters and guides behind them. With their audience increased by two, the band revved up, beating out a dashing tempo, and at the musical high point Jack suddenly put his arm around Claire's waist and whirled her up and down the village square until she was dizzy, the audience of villagers, guides and porters clapping in time to the music. Faster and faster the beat went, until Jack picked her up off the ground and she had to wrap her legs around him he was so tall. Everyone was laughing. She saw Nick taping the sounds, his eyes checking the sound level, lost in his work, unaware of her. The wind howled around the little square, sending sparks from the fire into the night. Her head was spinning faster than Jack could turn. She was a little girl again, her Dad carrying her like this at a barn dance in Texas. Except that Jack's embrace was not in the least fatherly, and Claire thought she could feel a gun next to her cousin's chest, a shoulder strap under his jacket. 'Is that a gun?' she asked, the question pulling away from her in the wind even as she thought how ridiculous it sounded. But Jack had heard, Jack's mouth turned down at the corners in his ironic anti-smile. He pushed her head into his neck and she smelled sweat and smoke and Palmolive soap. They were approaching a point she wasn't ready for when Ben interrupted and waltzed her off in his ponderous fashion to the last bars of the music.

Sitting by the dying fire, Jack proved to have an amazing memory for bad poetry and worse jokes. He and Ben became increasingly raucous as they passed round a flask of a local whisky called Bhutan Mist. 'Where did you get this stuff, Jack?' asked Ben. 'It would be better used in rubbing down my aching muscles.'

Jack began reciting another poem: 'The Reverend McPherson believed that a nautch, was a most diabolical sort of debauch!'

Claire's cheeks flushed as she saw her cousin check to see if she was listening before he continued, 'That almond-eyed girls, dressed in bangles and pearls, as beauteous as angels, as wicked as devils, performed at these highly indelicate revels.' This time there was no mistaking at whom Jack was aiming the poem. He drank from the whisky, wiped the bottle's neck with his hand and offered it to her. A deliberately intimate act, she thought, passing it on to Christian without drinking. Her cousin's charm left her with a feeling of unease.

Oblivious to the undertones, Ben brought the conversation back to poetry, 'The only poem I've ever been able to keep in my head was by a fellow American, a woman,' he said, stirring the fire with the remains of that day's walking stick and sending up fireflies from the embers. 'The first verse is about a chemist creating a brazen approximation of life. And the second goes: Time to garden before I die – to meet my compost maker, the caretaker of the cemetery.'

Jack threw his cigarette butt into the fire, 'God as a gardener, Ben? It's not a new idea, but it could catch on.'

Ben smiled amiably, 'More of a landscape architect, a Capability Brown, I'd say. A guy who restructures the shape of the land.'

'Without much regard for the tenants,' muttered Claire.

When she and Nick were the only ones left by the fire, she pointed at the tape machine, still running. 'Great sound quality,' she said. 'Pity you can't record a feeling.' Willing him to look at her.

Not taking his eyes from the machine, Nick explained that he was trying to capture the night sounds. 'It's surprising what you hear in the silence, the space between things.' Another form of reading between the lines, Claire thought. The space she wanted to explore lay between her and Nick, but sometimes he made her feel as if she was too tangible, with her clumsy interest in structure and her urgent need to learn as much as she could. He was happier with ephemeral things, the invisible, the absent.

## In the shadow of the Himalayas, October 1988

What secrets is Jack hiding? He could ask the same of me. Everyone has secrets. Look at Magda's diaries, where she tried to conceal her feelings for the mysterious man I call Arun in a haphazard association of triangulation with botany, Victorian photography with the rise of the Indian Independence movement. Her chronology runs all on one plane, past and present inseparable, and her pen and ink sketches are universal, right out of those adventure tales I loved as a child, where fabulous beasts were pursued and slain by knight errants. How did the knights err, that's what I used to wonder. Tonight, reading Magda's condemnation of Sir Joseph Hooker, I got some inkling. He was as guilty as the next man of destroying the landscape he admired, she claims. Sneaking from Sikkim into Tibet against the express wishes of Sikkim's Raja, he plundered the country of flowers – and then had the cheek to complain of Assam's remote mountains being mobbed with collectors, stripped 'as if by wanton robbers', strewn for miles with rotten branches and orchids. He was privileged to see Sikkim's mountains when their flanks were rose-coloured with *Magnolia campbellii*. Only forty years later, Magda found the same magnolia scarce to the point of disappearance, *where once you might look down on them from above as if on a thousand water-lilies floating on the waves of a rough green sea.*

Outside my tent flap now the peaks glimmer under stars brighter than I've ever seen, witness to an entire habitat under threat from population explosion, mining, logging, road-building and hydro-electrical schemes. It's only five years since the valley of flowers in Nanda Devi National Park had to be closed indefinitely even to the grazing of local livestock, yet we are trespassing on an equally fragile environment in search of a flower so rare it has not been seen in over a hundred years. What happens if we find the poppy? What happens if we don't? I keep thinking about Jack (shape-changer, chemist, explorer) and his gun – *was* it a gun? If it was, no doubt he has reasons for needing it. 'Smuggler land,' my Lepcha friend calls the country we are entering.

# 6

CLAIRE MIGHT HAVE let the matter of the gun drop if it hadn't been for the guide Jack picked up at the end of their second week out of Kalimpong, a tough little man with a face she immediately disliked – and recognised, or *thought* she recognised from the photograph at Sunil's shack. If she was right, this was one of the two chemists fired from UNISENS, and he had brought with him four equally tough-looking companions, as well as his own group of ten porters to replace some of the Lepchas. The new party was well equipped, their clothing considerably more modern than the tweed jacket and Indian waistcoat favoured by Jack. The jacket was his father's, he explained when Nick teased him, and useful because it had so many pockets.

'A good jacket for a man with lots to hide,' Claire joked, earning a sharp look from Nick.

On the day the UNISENS chemist turned up, Claire decided to air her suspicions to Nick once again, whatever the consequences. She found him sitting alone with his sketchbook, his back against a birch tree. The wind direction prevented him hearing her approach through the crisp golden leaves until she was a couple of feet from him, whereupon he looked up and smiled, patting the ground beside him with his plastic hand.

Resting her back close to his against the tree, she wanted to talk about anything other than Jack. Although she worked with Nick all day long, they were always surrounded by other members of the expedition. It was rare to catch him when he wasn't immersed in his own world of sounds and abstract green images. 'You're very preoccupied these days,' she started hesitantly.

He picked up his sketchbook, made a few additions to the landscape he was doing and put it down again. She envied him his skill, and had asked him once if he'd studied drawing, at which he'd laughed and said it was a gift, 'a bonus from some long-lost draughtsman in the family', 'I suppose I'm worried about what will happen if we don't find this poppy,' Nick said now. 'We've covered all the sites in Sikkim where it was supposed to have flourished and even the shamans here haven't heard of it.'

'Why is it so important for you, Nick? You're a successful artist; you don't have to prove yourself like this.'

'Don't I?' He lifted his artificial hand and let it fall heavily, then rubbed the junction where it met his real arm. She didn't think it was a conscious gesture, but it summed up his emotions better than any words could have done. He needed to believe in this expedition in a different way than she did.

'You don't –' She stopped, her heart beating fast.

'I don't what?'

'It's just . . . I wonder about these guides of Jack's. They seem . . .'

'Pretty uninterested in botany?' he suggested. 'Well, we'll need more than gentle plant collectors if we run into any smugglers – or Chinese patrols – when we cross the Chumbi Valley.'

'Doesn't it bother you?'

'That we're breaking the law or risking our necks? The law is an ass, as they say, and I trust Jack to know what he's doing up here.'

She hurried through the next words, knowing her how weak her suspicions would sound. 'No . . . you see, I recognised that new guide. He's one of the chemists fired from UNISENS. I saw his picture at the sewage village. At least, I think it was him.'

'If it *is* one of the chemists who was fired, Jack may be trying to make amends. But I doubt it is.' Nick put his plastic arm around her in a quick hug. 'We all look the same to you lot.'

Maybe it was the hug that did it, maybe he'd squeezed out her next clumsy comments. 'I asked Ben about the story they told me in the village, the ears falling off thing, and –'

Nick pulled away from her. 'Not *that* again, Claire!'

Instantly she regretted having brought up the subject. 'But you see . . . there could be a link between Jack's chlorophyll experiments and the ear thing. Ben says –'

'What ear thing?' Jack's voice came from directly behind them, jerking Claire around to face him.

'I – Jack! You scared me! How did . . . I didn't hear you.'

He moved in front of them, standing carelessly a foot from the cliff edge while he lit a cigarette. 'It's the wind. I came down the hill. What ear thing? Something to do with Ben?'

Nick's face was rigid. Claire wondered what else had carried up to Jack in the clear air. Her cousin glanced curiously back and forth between their two tense faces. 'Am I interrupting something?'

Nick once again massaged the junction where his plastic arm met the stump. 'No, of course not. We were just talking about –'

Claire scrambled to her feet, brushing twigs and leaves from her shorts. 'I should – um . . .' Her face was bright scarlet. 'Ben was saying today that I have an ear for language, so Nick has been teaching me Tibetan.'

'Has he, now?' Jack sounded unconvinced. 'Is he having more success with you than the porters had?'

She knew he had been listening to her attempts at learning fragments of Tibetan from D. R. Damsang. 'Nathu La, Jelap La, Donkia La,' she had hummed one day, reading the names off their maps. 'Sounds like a song. La la la!'

'La means pass,' DR had smiled in reply. 'Also a respectful ending to sentence. Jelap La means lonely, level pass. This is Younghusband track.'

'Um. Jelap La . . .' Claire began now.

'Not very useful to teach her, Nick,' Jack cut in. 'It's not a pass we're taking.'

'I was telling her how Younghusband used the route when he attacked Tibet in 1903, and then, appalled at the flood of Tibetan blood he and his British troops had shed, turned towards mysticism.'

Claire felt relief that Nick had backed her up, although she was pretty sure their story hadn't persuaded Jack, who wore the sceptical smile he reserved for Ben's myths. 'That's right, Claire,' her cousin said. 'Up until the Chinese closed the border, Tibetan caravans used to come over the Jelep La into Kalimpong, avoiding Gangtok and keeping their animals in the high country rather than the Tista river valley, where both men and animals died of malaria. The leeches are terrible.' He nodded at Claire's legs. 'As they were on that trail we came up earlier. Did you see the little buggers lashing themselves to a frenzy all over the leaves, ready to launch into the smallest crevice? They looked like bloodthirsty punctuation marks. Have you checked your feet?'

'No. But I'm sure –'

'Take off your boots.'

Normally Claire would have protested at his command. This time she was glad of an excuse to avoid Jack's eyes. Pulling off her boots and socks, she drew in her breath, sickened to see the rigidly swollen black bodies all over her feet and ankles. She began fishing in her pack for insect spray, but before she could find it Jack's hand grasped her ankle. As he took the cigarette from his mouth with his other hand, she jerked her foot back.

'Stop struggling.' He gripped her ankle more tightly, slowly and calmly placing the burning end of his cigarette against the first leech.

'You're hurting me.'

He loosened his grip slightly, while continuing to dab his cigarette against one leech after another, bringing the butt so close to Claire's skin that she felt its heat. No doubt it was the kind of cool precision he applied in the lab. 'I hope you've done this before,' she said, a tremor in her voice.

'Never. But I've always wanted to try the method out.'

'I'm not sure I like being treated as an experiment.'

The air smelled faintly of burning rubber. Nick, watching the procedure with a grimace, pronounced it disgusting.

'But effective,' Jack said, and didn't quite succeed in suppressing a smile.

'Maybe. But I think I'll go and check my feet in private.'

Watching him stride off towards the tent he shared with Christian, Claire was sure that she had widened the rift between them by forcing him to lie for her.

'Why do I have the horrible suspicion that you are enjoying this, Jack?' she asked crossly.

'The power over a helpless female, you mean? I don't think it does anything for me.' His smile broadened. 'Although I'm not absolutely sure.' When he asked her for the disinfectant, Claire told him that she could do it herself. He continued to hold her ankle for a moment longer than was necessary. It was a nice ankle, she admitted inwardly, slim and brown, although marked with red lesions now where the leeches had been feeding. 'Good girl,' he said lightly, releasing her foot with a friendly squeeze. 'Most people are squeamish about leeches.' It sounded like genuine respect on his part, but who could tell? Jack was such an actor. Lighting a fresh cigarette, he cast a long admiring look over her bare brown legs and arms. 'Hasn't anyone told you that sunburns aren't good for the skin, little cousin? You're risking skin cancer wearing shorts and a vest at these altitudes.'

She was quickly on the defensive. 'I go brown as soon as the sun hits me. It's not like I try or anything. Anyway, you're a fine one to talk about cancer.'

He grinned at the cigarette in his hand and held it away from him as if to disown it. 'You should be careful,' he said, 'or you'll wind up looking like a grubby little Neapolitan street urchin.'

'Dad used to go this same dirty brown. Mum always said there must be a touch of the tar brush in our side of the family.'

Jack's mouth narrowed with private amusement. Then he drew his finger all the way down her arm from shoulder to wrist in one slow, languid movement that brought up goose bumps on her skin. 'Perhaps.' He spoke softly, a dialogue with someone inside his head. 'That may explain your *ear* for language.'

Claire watched her cousin walk off, laughing to himself. She decided that the high altitude tan made him look younger and tougher, less of a scientist. His stamina surprised her, given his smoking habits, as did his grace; he did not have the disjointed marionette gait she associated with tall thin men. No, the puppeteer who controlled Jack's movements had his hand closer to the centre of gravity. And she was even more sure that her cousin was not a man to appreciate sharing the glory if they ever found the green poppy.

The next afternoon, after a rugged day traversing a jungle valley, Claire approached Ben on the path winding up into the hills. 'This is a steep hill, Claire,' he said.

'Yes, I'm sorry, Ben. Just one question.'

'You always say that, Claire, and it's always on a steep climb.'

'Sorry. But . . . You know those new guides of Jack's –'

'You mean the Opium Quintet?'

She stared at him, 'Why did you call them that? I mean, I know there's five of them, not counting their extra porters – but why opium?'

'It suits them. No doubt Jack knows what he's doing, but I've never seen such a disreputable crowd in my life. That's not true. I remember once in Mexico –' He lost his breath and stopped to mop his face.

'Are you OK, Ben? You don't look so hot.'

'Funny, considering how hot I feel.' A feeble joke, even by Ben's standards. 'You hadn't noticed it was hot?'

What Claire had noticed was that although Ben never stopped eating, he was losing a lot of weight. Probably from all the walking and sweating, she decided, seeing him mop his face for the fifth time in as many minutes.

◆ ◆ ◆

*Borderlands, October 1988*

Soon we will be crossing the Chumbi Valley and entering Bhutan, once again illegally, thanks to the new recruits' familiarity with smuggling routes. In theory, the frontiers of these 'sensitive areas', the disputed borders between Bhutan,

Sikkim, Tibet and India, are guarded by the military. But, as Jack says, if people want to smuggle things, they find a way – and it's impossible to police every pass in the highest mountains in the world. Still, it amazes me that no one questions Jack's acquaintance with the kind of men who are serving us as guides. Why should botany bring you in contact with such people? I was thinking over a strange conversation he had with Nick today – about legalising heroin, then taxing it the way we do tobacco. Jack said he couldn't see the difference between the export of American tobacco to South America and China and the export of Asian heroin to America. 'Both are potentially lethal drugs of choice, and fine sources of foreign currency. Except that in Asia, where opium is often the only sure means of security, drug barons are heroes.' I've added that conversation to the map of my cousin's geography I've been plotting, a triangulation unconfirmed, but worthy of further surveys:

1  Botanic Library: the missing pix, all related to the green poppy and the route we will be taking into the Tsangpo Gorge region
2  UNISENS: the rumours linking Jack to drugs and fiddling experiments
3  The sewage village: Sunil's stories about Jack, the ears, the reception I got when I mentioned his name
4  Ben's information about the way chlorophyll can photo-sensitise people's skin to the point where they get cancer
5  The guide we picked up on the Ha Valley smugglers' route, Jack's lack of surprise at the stolen orchids
6  The chemist from UNISENS (?) turning up, with no explanation from Jack, the prosperity of his Opium Quintet
7  Jack's gun (?) and his shady friends

# 7

THE NEXT DAY they came to the cane bridge.

Claire had read of such bridges in Magda's journals and hoped them to be an invention of the distant past long since superseded by concrete and steel. *When the proposal of a bridge is decided unanimously by the Lepchas,* Magda had written, *the holy men fix an auspicious date, and on that day able-bodied archers tie threads of cane to their arrows and shoot them across the river. From such beginnings they construct a bridge like the one before us. I know that my friend sat and drew this delicate tracery of cane and bamboo hanging in a single arc across the gap, for his sketch clearly shows the same ravine with banyan trees on either cliff. Swinging out over the racing white water I feel his presence very close.*

Up until they reached the bridge Claire had managed to conceal her fear of heights, largely because it wasn't mountains she had problems with. Mountains she could handle; it was edges she didn't like. And this bridge was all edge: four hundred feet long and not only precarious but rotten, with a stream hundreds of feet below that had swollen to a torrent thanks to the heavy rainy season. In the late afternoon light it seemed that the fragile ropes and strips of bamboo flung across it had no more strength than a broken cobweb. 'Such bridges are lasting no more than two seasons,' D. R. Damsang told Claire and Ben. 'On older, uncared-for bridges like this one the bamboo often tilts and leaves men suspended by the slender canes like human lanterns.'

'How old do you think this particular bridge is?' Ben asked.

'More than three years, this particular bridge.'

'Son of a bitch!' Ben muttered.

Claire couldn't respond because her teeth were clamped firmly shut to stop them chattering.

Having sent one of the Lepchas across to examine it, Jack informed the waiting party that it might not be as bad as it seemed. The bridges were generally quite safe, he said, if extremely simple.

'I don't like his use of the words "generally" and "quite" in this context,' Ben whispered to Claire.

'The two slender parallel canes you see stretched across the river and bound to trees on either side are made of a species of Calamus palm,' Jack explained, his botanical exactitude a meagre buttress for the structure. No thicker than a toe, these parallel canes supported other canes on V-slings made from the same palm, which in turn supported more bamboo canes for flooring. The floor canes were not necessarily attached. 'It's not a problem,' he added. 'You simply hold on to the upper parallel canes, the suspension cables, one in each hand to keep them apart, and then walk along the bamboo flooring.'

Ben winced. 'And if the floor of bamboos is loose?'

'You tilt up horizontally across the gorge, as your Lepcha chum told you.' Jack grinned back at him. 'It's exciting, but best not to let go at that particular point.'

'Oh Jesus.'

The Lepcha returned with a smile to reassure them that the bridge was safe enough if they crossed no more than two at a time. 'And no two must be walking in step, for fear of breakage.'

'For fear of breakage,' Ben repeated. 'Holy *shit*!'

Claire watched her cousin walk part way across the bridge and then crouch down to fasten one of the V-slings more firmly.

She thought she was going to be sick.

The Lepcha porters kicked off whatever footwear they were wearing and tied their shoes to their packs. 'Do this, please, Miss,' said DR. 'Is better for gripping bamboo, which is sometimes very slipping.'

She obeyed him as if in a dream. 'If I take it step by step, I'll be all right,' she thought, squeezing her eyes shut.

'Very *slipping*?' asked Ben, 'Is he *serious*? Very *slipping*? On top of the fact that it looks like it's made out of a lace G-string?'

Jack sent half the Lepchas over first to give everyone confidence. Claire watched them trip across as lightly as if they were on Brooklyn Bridge. She met her cousin's eyes and tried to keep her bottom lip from trembling.

'Al Sirat,' she heard Ben mutter, and, thinking it might be a good luck oath, she repeated his words, but in a louder voice, 'AL SIRAT.'

Ben glanced at her, 'I didn't realise you knew any Arabic mythology, Claire.'

'Is that what it is? I thought it was for good luck.'

He placed one foot on to the bridge. 'Al Sirat: the bridge over mid-Hell, no wider than a sabre, across which all those who wish to enter Paradise must pass.'

'It's just a bridge, Ben,' Jack pointed out, 'not a myth.'

'I prefer myths,' replied the teratologist, taking his second step. 'They're less likely to break half way across.'

'I don't know about that,' Jack said.

'Chicken chicken chicken,' Claire repeated to herself, closing her eyes. When she reopened them, what seemed no more than a second later, all the party was on the opposite bank of the river with the exception of Jack and DR Damsang.

'Now you, Claire.' Jack twitched his hand, beckoning her forward.

'No.' She said it quietly but firmly, knowing that it was impossible.

'Come on! You're holding everyone up.'

'I know.' She was apologetic. 'I can't go.'

'Of course you can,' he said sharply.

'I'll fall.'

'Don't be silly. Follow me. Now.' He turned impatiently and began to move away from her on to the swaying, trembling bridge.

Staring across the canyon at Nick's face, Ben's, all of them watching her, she couldn't explain. This was her dream. Her toes were frozen. She had no grip. *This was how they parted, she on one side of the canyon, he on the other.*

It had started to rain. She heard his warning that the canes were getting slippery, more dangerous. From the canyon below a great spume of cloud boiled up, cutting them off from each other. Through that mist she caught shadows and movements of the past, as if she were in a train with the windows fogged up and all she had to do was wipe the mist away with her hand for the old world, the old dead to be there, staring in. *He waited until she had reached the other side and then he cut the bridge so she could not return.* Her whole body was slick with sweat. She shivered as the bank of mist rising up above the precipice steepened into a high wall in which she could see a shadowy figure, beckoning her to follow, its head circled by a bright rainbow. 'Look!' she said, pointing.

'Come on, you *stupid* girl! It's just a trick of the light throwing your shadow against the mist.' Jack held out one of his handkerchiefs to her. 'Tie this around your eyes and then I'll lead you across. It's an old trick to stop you seeing what you're afraid of.'

She wanted to be able to do it, but she couldn't. She didn't need to have her eyes open. She could picture the drop in her head.

'Please, sir, I am taking her piggy-back fashion,' said DR. 'Is a very small girl and I am not so big. Together we are weighing not so much. If you are following behind then anything wrong will surely not happen.'

Claire was trembling all over.

'Don't be silly, man: look at her! She can't be trusted on your back. She'd let go and pull you over.' Jack shook his head. 'If anyone is going to take her, it's me.' At his words, Claire suddenly knew that this was what Jack had planned all along. He was too smart a man to have missed her fear of heights. His elaborate explanation of the bridge's precarious nature was a device to increase her fear.

'No,' she said.

Jack picked her up in his arms and shifted her on to his hip like a baby. 'Hold on, for God's sake,' he said. 'I have to keep a hand free for the canes.'

He stepped on to the bridge.

Claire felt the slender spidery thing shudder under them. She took one look down and saw the foothold, a single spine of bamboo strips. These were loose, not attached to each other or to the V-slings. She closed her eyes.

'Hold the other cable, dammit!' Jack swore at DR behind them. 'I can't keep the bloody things parallel.'

The sway began very slowly, just a shiver of movement like a skipping rope lightly shaken. Then the whole long suspended fragile web began to tremble and lurch, rolling from side to side and pitching until, finally, the cables tipped up, suspending them over the gorge below.

She felt herself start to let go. As she did, Jack's arm loosened around her.

I am going to fall now, she said, she thought she said. And to herself: he's going to let me fall. It will be an accident. No one could blame him.

And then from close behind she heard DR Damsang's steady voice, naming the bridge, pinning it down, a cable of words thrown across the canyon: 'These two canes we are calling *Saomgyang*, and swinging cane loops are *Ahool*. Bamboo flooring on which travellers walk is *Saomblok*, and two main parallel canes tied so firmly to trees so as to strengthen our passage are *Saomngur*, and two entrances on either sides of our bridges we call *Saomveng*. *Saomgyang, Ahool, Saomblok, Saomngur, Saomveng.*'

He paused, and once more repeated the strange words, singing the bridge to her, weaving its broken canes together with language. A poem against fear.

She thought in some quiet part of herself that if she fell now it would be all right.

'And all together our bridge is called *Saom*.'

Then they were across.

# 8

CLAIRE OPENED HER eyes and saw Jack's an inch from hers and his mouth ringed with white lines of tension. He cleared his throat roughly before speaking but his voice was still husky, 'So, you got all that, little cousin? You will be tested on it later.'

She slid from his arms on to the ground. 'All together our bridge is called *Saom*,' she said. A cheer went up from the waiting men.

With gentle tact, the Lepcha porters pitched camp far enough from the bridge so that Claire would not have to see it. She was even happier when the night folded in and everyone sat by the fire eating and talking about the day as if she had not disgraced herself. Nothing was mentioned until the Bhutan Mist had been passed round several times, at which point Ben remarked in a casual voice, 'I take it then that you're afraid of heights?'

'Terrified.' There wasn't a lot of point in denying it.

'Christian perhaps failed to mention that this little trip of ours was through the highest mountains in the world?' Nick asked.

'It's not so much mountains as cliffs I don't like. And edges.' She paused. 'And suspension bridges, I guess.'

'That's comforting,' said Christian. 'How many bridges are there between here and the Tsangpo Gorge, Jack?'

Everyone laughed. Claire piped up immediately, 'It may surprise you to know that I'm not the first Himalayan explorer to be afraid of heights. Frank Kingdon Ward was, and it didn't stop him doing far more challenging treks than this.' She smiled at the circle of men, 'At least I don't have a phobia about leeches or corpses . . . or guns.' As soon as the word was out she wondered why she'd said it.

Her cousin laughed with the others, but his expression was wary. 'I'll keep that in mind should we come across any corpses,' he said. 'Or guns.'

Ben confessed that guns scared the shit out of him.

'Why?' Claire asked, 'They're just like any other piece of equipment. As long as you follow instructions. My mother taught me and my brother how to shoot.' She noticed that Jack was watching her, waiting for her to make the next move.

'We're not in the wild west now,' said Christian, 'and even if we had a gun . . .'

She hesitated, knowing that she was taking the game further. 'I'm willing to show you. I can use Jack's gun. If he doesn't mind.'

There was one of those silences where everyone rearranges their thoughts.

Jack was staring intently at Claire.

'Of course, if Jack *had* a gun –' someone began.

'I'll make you a wager, Claire,' Jack cut through. 'You can play cops and robbers with my gun, as long as you cross that bridge again. No further than halfway, if you prefer.' He took a drink from the whisky. Everyone listened to the sound of his swallowing. 'But this time I walk *behind* instead of carrying you.'

There was an immediate outcry of protest. Ben and Christian insisted that the idea was ludicrous, that Claire had already been through enough for one day, that there was time to get over her fear of heights later. Nick pointed out that it was dark and Jack had had too much to drink.

'Don't worry, Claire,' Jack said. 'I know it's too much to ask. I'm sure one of us will be happy to carry you across each of the bridges between here and Tibet.'

'Fine,' she said, knowing that he was deliberately provoking her, that she shouldn't rise to the bait. 'I'll do it.' As soon as she said it, her whole body shrank to the size of her heaving stomach and she felt her face wrinkle with worry like a monkey's. To stop herself from backing out, she stood up immediately and began to walk towards the bridge, the light from her torch flickering in

319

front of her like a will o' the wisp. 'From this world into the next,' she whispered.

She heard the men rise and follow, Jack by her side. They reached the bridge, where it swayed gently in the evening breeze. She kicked off her shoes and felt the fear boil up in her like that great plume of cloud had from the canyon. Her teeth were chattering. She thought of Robin, who loved climbing. Keep your eye on the distant view, that's what he'd say. Keep your head up and your eyes on where you're going, not where you've been. She gripped the cables with hands like claws and slid her foot on to the spine of loose bamboo. The sweat started up in her hands, making them slick as soap.

'Don't worry,' said Jack in a loud voice, 'I'll be right behind you.'

Did any of the men recognise her cousin's words for the threat she was sure they were? She slid another foot on to the bridge and then edged forward, inching her hands along the cables in nervous imitation of the clenching and unclenching in her sphincter. She thought: it's not so bad; the darkness cancels out the height.

Jack stepped on to the bridge and the whole structure quivered and recoiled. The sound of the rushing water reached her. She was clear of the bank's stabilising force and the moon on the water far below lit the bamboo clearly.

Jack stepped more quickly and closely behind her, the bridge rolling and swinging with every movement.

He's deliberately walking in step with me, she thought. Unbalancing us.

*Look up look up look up.*

She looked up and saw the hills, seamed with gravel chutes, and in the far distance a ridge of snowy peaks standing out against the clear night sky as bright and hard as polished bone, the vertebrae of the earth. Closer in, a monastery hung from the eaves of a cliff like a swallow's nest. Perhaps it was a nest.

She was almost half way across.

Now, she thought. He'll do it now. If I fall here it will seem like an accident. It will *be* an accident. He can reach out and seem to catch me and then let me slide through his hands. She wanted to look over her shoulder, to let him know that she was ready. But then she would have to catch sight of the leaping water and would have again the sensation that both she and the bridge were running swiftly away.

She heard him step up behind her. Jack was very close.

She began to sing the list of steps that had brought her to this point: *Saomgyang, Ahool, Saomblok, Saomngur, Saomveng*. And all together our bridge is called *Saom*. A calm word from a calm people used to crossing bridges.

She felt Jack's hand grip her shoulder, move down her arm and loosen her fingers from the cable. Pulling her hand away from his, she turned to face him, both her hands once more gripping the cables. His face was very grim, as was hers. Perhaps he had believed that she was going to make it easy for him.

'This is the halfway point, Claire,' he said. 'We can go back now.'

The walk back felt like a dream. One minute her life was in the balance, the next she was beside the fire and someone had put a blanket around her shoulders. Jack was smoking a cigarette. The three other men were congratulating her, Ben almost hysterical with relief, bouncing round her like a tubby Labrador puppy. Nick gave her a drink of whisky. She wiped her mouth on the back of her hand, looked across at her cousin and asked for the gun.

'What is this, Russian roulette?'

'He doesn't have a gun, Claire,' said Ben.

'He has a gun.'

'It's too dark,' said Jack. 'Your hand wouldn't be steady enough.'

Christian gave Jack a sharp look. 'Stop teasing her with your mythical gun, Jack. She's gone through enough tonight.'

She held her right hand out at shoulder height, palm down. There was no movement. She turned it palm up and beckoned with her fingers, the way Jack had at the bridge that afternoon. He stared at her for a moment, then reached under his waistcoat for the gun. After the semicolon of silence that followed its appearance Christian asked, 'What make is it?' Did he hope that putting a name to it, a category, would make Jack's possession more understandable?

'No idea,' she said, glad it was a small one. It felt nice and light in her hand. 'Guns are like cars. I don't give a damn what kind they are, all that matters is that they work.'

'And the colour, of course,' Ben added, to make her smile.

'What will you use for a target?' her cousin asked.

She leaned forward and slipped her hand into his waistcoat pocket to pull out a package of tobacco, smelling the sharp, nervous sweat of him as she did, then walked to the edge of the clearing and wedged the package in the elbow of a branch. 'Could you shine your flashlights – I mean your *torches* on that, please?'

She was aware of the porters and guides joining the group around the fire. She flicked off the safety catch and stood as her mother had taught her, legs apart, knees flexed, both hands lightly gripping the weapon. She fired three times and gave the gun back to Jack. Neither of them bothered to check her accuracy. They stood facing each other, two cousins measuring up what remained of the distance between them, acknowledging the bad blood they shared. The porters ran to the tree. One of them held up the package. Threads of tobacco spilled from the corner where Claire had hit it. 'Not bad,' Christian called back, examining the tree and the package. 'Too far down and to the left, but not bad at all. About an inch between each shot. Nicely clustered, if not quite a bull's eye.'

'Depends what she was aiming for,' Ben said. 'If he wasn't dead after that, he'd probably bleed to death.'

'Of course she knows about guns,' said Jack. 'She's a Yank, isn't she?'

Everyone retired to their beds, except for Jack, who remained alone by the fire, smoking one cigarette after another. Claire thought that his whole body seemed wired with electric energy, a big lean cat not quite ready to spring. In her tent she picked up Magda's diary and tried to take it in. She felt very excited, not at all sleepy. There had been a shift inside her. Something else was going to happen. The last thing she read: *I am a person capable of going too far.* Then she was interrupted.

Claire tried to let herself off the hook for finding him attractive, tried to forget how good it felt, his skin against hers, the smell of him, his hard, long body very white apart from the suntan on his face and arms. Surprisingly white against the black hair at his groin, she noticed, when he turned on the torch in her tent, 'to get a look at my little monk'. Jack was a thorough lover, not hesitant in probing her body's responses, although she felt embarrassed after it was over. She didn't like to associate herself with the tent's barnyard smells, a hot pheasanty reek that made her remember how long it had been since she'd had a bath. She told Jack she was full of regrets, hoping for reassurance from him. All he did was to run his hand over her small flat breasts, his calloused palm rough against her still sensitive nipples, and remark that it seemed a pity. Worried that she'd hurt his feelings, Claire confided quickly that she thought he'd behaved like a hero, carrying her across the bridge as he had. She could hear herself gushing like a kid, 'hero' inappropriate in the context of what had just taken place.

'A *hero*?' Jack, chuckling softly, gave the word an intonation she didn't like. 'A source of heroic elements?' He sounded almost contemptuous (but of himself or her?), and rolled away from her to rest his head on his hand. 'Hero, heroine . . . Did you know that it was a German chemist who came up with heroin's money-winning tradename? It's based on the German word *heroisch*, for mighty or heroic. He was working at Bayer – of aspirin fame – in 1898. Of course, this was years after the first tests were done by Wright in Paddington, looking for a non-addictive alternative to morphine. Bayer made a bundle out of it – marketed it as a new wonder drug, an awe-inspiring painkiller distributed in desirable small boxes with a lion and a globe printed on the label. It was promoted as a non-addictive treatment for the cure of coughs and breathing problems. Non-addictive! Ironic, isn't it?'

Unprepared for irony, she stared into Jack's thin, handsome face and felt humiliated that she had opened up to him – been opened by him, stretched, widened for access in every way possible. This is the man who just made love to me, she thought, and corrected herself, *fucked* me, trying to punish herself for being so weak. 'How did you get to be such a *shit*, Jack?' A futile comment, made to regain a little high ground. He seemed genuinely surprised at her reaction. She watched him process the cause and work out an appropriate response, a man who wore his different selves like a reversible coat. He moved closer, ran his fingers down her cheek. 'Sorry, love, did you want declarations of undying passion?'

Alone again, Claire worried about how you could be lured down with logic and irony, have your faith twisted into a mistranslation of farce, hope into an error of judgement. The fall from grace not so much a dramatic high dive as a series of petty stumbles and small errors of map-reading. She had been suspicious of Jack, but now she was afraid of him in the way she had been afraid of mirrors as a kid: you might glance in their surface and catch sight of your own face horribly distorted – or the reflection of something hiding round the corner to wait for you. She felt very young, unwilling to grow old in Jack's image.

In the next few days she stayed away from him as much as she could. She was embarrassed at the idea that Ben had heard them, and suspected that Christian disapproved, that Nick was ignoring her (what must he think, after all she had implied about Jack?). She thought a lot about Magda's artificial horizons, how easy it was to find yourself heading for one. Later, scanning her own diary for that period, Claire was amazed by its ambiguity. A stranger might infer, might read between the lines, but would find no proof.

♦ ♦ ♦

### The borders, October 1988

Why did I do it? A minor victory celebration for being so brave? I wanted Nick, I got Jack. Dumb dumb dumb. If I'd turned out the light in my tent earlier, if I hadn't stayed up late reading Magda's life instead of seeing to my own, if if if.

When I try to imagine the devil now, he has Jack's face, Jack's grasp of the cut and thrust of international monetary channels, his logic. Jack: the Ironstones' direct line to fire and brimstone. Until I met him, my admiration for scientists rested on firm foundations. Scientists' control of the unseeable universe, that's what appealed to me. These were men with logic on their side. Ask them any question, they had a theory, a *hypothesis*. Ask them why a teapot drips and they'd give you The Teapot Theory, the Second Law of Runnability, Twining's Last Theorem. Of course, at the point it became clear that knowing why it dripped didn't mean that the dripping could be stopped, some people might let their subscriptions to *New Scientist* and *Scientific American* lapse. They might sell their tickets to the next Star Trek conference. Not me. I kept the faith. Until I met Jack. Now my faith is showing signs of subsidence.

# 9

AT A TIME in botanical exploration when the microscope had largely replaced the mule, stories, myths, rumours had become Xanadu's maps. The party had taken an easterly trail out of Sikkim which penetrated the Dongku range to enter a Tibetan valley variously known as the Chumbi (by Christian), Amo-chu (by the Bhutia guides), the Dromo Machu river valley (by the Tibetan Chinese) and the Valley of Flowers (by some of the Lepchas). 'What does it call itself?' Claire wondered aloud, walking at dusk through a fallen constellation of fire-flies. She was living in an imaginary world relinquished with difficulty, a legendary region occupied by Magda and Arun and all the other anonymous Indian artists and guides who had travelled here before them. Jack, dropping back from the leading group to reclaim her, rested his hand on the back of her neck, only to have Claire pull away instantly and check to make sure no one had seen. Her cousin frowned and stuck the offending hand into his pocket. 'You're making it worse, Claire.'

'Making what worse?' She was angry with him for interrupting her internal dialogue with Arun.

'You're making it much more clear that there's something between us.'

'What? What's between us?'

'Nothing worth making such a fuss about. An itch that needed scratching.'

Claire lashed out, close to tears, 'Love has got nothing to teach you, has it Jack?' Immediately she regretted the word 'love'. Another embarrassing concept, like hero and hope.

'Let me see, what did love teach me?' Jack scratched so irritably at the cluster of insect bites on his neck that her question might have been responsible for them. 'I suppose it taught me that bad marriages, like bad hybrids, are prone to vulgar colours and disease. And the lesson of betrayal – I learned that. You love someone and then you betray them. The person who loves you always betrays you in the end. That Judas thing, the lack of faith – in others, in oneself, ultimately. The more you love someone, the more it's yourself you betray.'

Claire noticed that his face, thin to start with, had been reduced to the blade of an axe by bad food and long treks, everything about him sharp and edgy. 'Some girl teach you that?' she asked, her tone of voice gentler than her words.

'The lesson is my father's, taught to him at the knee of your beloved Magda.'

Afraid that he was about to diminish her dreams to the size of a Ziploc bag, Claire marched away from him, preferring to keep her distance now, her own myths intact.

◆ ◆ ◆

*Beyond the Temple of Heaven, Western Bhutan, November 1988*

To the surprise of all of us we made it safely across the Chumbi Valley last week, only to have a narrow escape today on our way to Taktsang monastery, the one they call the Tiger's Nest, which clings to a sheer 3000-foot rock. Beyond it lies Sang-tog Peri, the Temple of Heaven, where Christian hoped to find records of the green poppy, until the guides' sighting of a Bhutanese army patrol on the path forced us to turn away into the forest and take this more desolate route. The mountains around tonight's camp are so sheer and black and devoid of life it's hard to believe anything could survive here. Even the prayer flags are shredded. Yet we have passed several three-house hamlets smelling of wood smoke, and discovered the dwarf Primula *eburnea*, an ethereal gem sheltering from the wind in the rucks and wrinkles of a peaty blanket.

Our problem now is to avoid the military troops who have

been stationed on both sides of the big passes into Tibet since the Indo-China war of 1962. To do this, hampered as we are by the porters' heavy loads of soil samples and the need for stealth, Jack's guides have suggested that we attempt the Yak La crossing, where local Bhutia traders and yak herdsmen still gain access to Tibet's Khangmar district.

◆

'If Chris has his way, we'll carry half of Sikkim and Bhutan into Tibet,' Jack remarked, his eyes on the party's bulky progress. 'Then we can carry Tibet back across Bhutan and Sikkim.'

Christian pointed out that Shackleton had insisted on protecting the heavy photographic glass plates of his Antarctic expedition even after food supplies were rationed. 'And Scott was still carrying thirty pounds of rock samples around and collecting more a few days before his death.'

'Look what happened to Scott,' said Jack. 'Still, I'm sure it was comforting to know his rock samples survived.'

Shortly after this caustic exchange, one of the overladen porters slipped on a path and nearly fell into a stream covered in a thick rime of ice, the liquid underneath as viscous as frozen vodka, an accident that convinced Christian to allow a full day and night of rest before their final arduous push through Bhutan's northern barrier. They were to camp in a valley reached by a climb through the kind of forest Hooker must have found when he first visited the Himalayas in the mid 1800s. Every branch was heavily laden with deep blue orchids, huge blooms that silhouetted the trees like Christmas lights. 'It reminds me of a trip I took to the Venetian glass-blowing galleries at Murano,' said Christian, rarely moved by anything that was not directly related to chlorophyll. 'The same intricate delicacy of those spun glass candelabras.' He turned to Jack. 'I didn't realise they'd be flowering this late. What species are they?'

Jack trained his binoculars on the closest tree and shook his head. 'Some very rare form of Vanda *caerulea*, I'd say. Worth a fortune to the right buyer.'

'Even the common form is rare enough to find,' Ben said. 'Wild populations have been largely destroyed.'

This is the wild garden where all our domestic backyards were born, Claire thought, as she entered the lower end of the valley at lunchtime to push her way through an anchored flotilla of billowing seedheads. Here, Christian proposed that the porters remain behind to rest and set up camp while the four men and Claire climbed another thousand feet for their first view of Tibet. It was a tough two hour hike, but their reward was a horizon of endless mountains, a great spine of bone-white peaks curving away from them to fade into the dun-coloured skin of Tibet. And for that hour on the threshold of what Hooker had called 'the howling wilderness', the party were united as they had not been in days.

Returning to the valley campsite, Claire left the men and went to bed early. She wanted to rejoin Magda and Arun, who had spent a spring night together on a peak near here, watching the snow congeal on their theodolite. *Forced to make our way blind across a treacherous cliff face, before darkness set in we got in a round of angles to the northern snowy peaks where they glittered in the last sun and for one crowded hour as we climbed down through that pale blue forest of orchids we had a vision worth suffering the next six months of rain.*

'If we can look back and catch a glimpse of those old shadows,' Claire wrote, 'can they pierce the mists and see the shade of us as well?' Determined to recapture Magda's imagery on film, she rose at dawn and left a note to explain that she was spending a few hours photographing the orchid forest below.

What Claire found after the long hike down reduced her to tears. The trees that yesterday had shimmered with a flowery blue light had been ripped apart, with pieces of orchids littering the path like the broken glass from one of Christian's candelabras. Small bushes had been chopped down to get to prime specimens, rare ferns hacked apart to free the Vandas growing through their fronds. Almost without thinking, Claire began to take pictures, as she would have done of any other corpses, and by the time she returned to the camp she was filled with a pure white rage that drove her straight to Christian.

'This time we have to stop them,' she began. 'They can't have gone far with the load they're carrying and –'

'Stop who? What?'

With the devastation vivid in her head, Christian's question came as a surprise. 'The smugglers,' she said, and quickly explained what she had found, waiting for cries of outrage to match her own.

Christian rubbed his baby-smooth chin in an adman's mockery of rational consternation. He passed one hand slowly through his shiny brown locks. 'Within Reason' will be carved on his tombstone, Claire thought, as the geneticist repeated the arguments he'd used before: the smugglers would be heading back to India; they would be able to travel fast. Even if it was possible to catch them, the plants could hardly be put back.

One of the Opium Quintet moved close to Jack and Christian to whisper something, and whatever he said stopped the geneticist midflow. 'Ah, I see,' said Christian. 'How many of the porters are gone – three or four?'

There was a lengthy discourse among the men, with Claire as its silent participant. Ben said something forceful about 'a botanical Guernica' and Nick supported him. There was the cut and thrust of Jack's inevitable rebuttal, Christian's demonstration of leadership qualities. Shock, outrage, a closing compromise that reminded Claire of parliament in session. The upshot was that although it was probably the missing porters attached to the Opium Quintet who had been responsible for the damage, the Xanadu party would press on. Monetary recompense by UNISENS to the Bhutanese government to follow.

'Let me get this straight,' said Claire, not bothering to contain her anger. 'It's all right for us to cross the border illegally, it's all right to steal the green poppy if we find it, it's all right that our actions have made it possible for members of our party to hack plants to pieces.' Ben put his hand on her arm and she shook him off. 'So tell me, please: what is it exactly that separates Us from Them?'

'The scouts reported a troop of Bhutanese soldiers on the road we were hoping to travel to the Yak La pass,' Jack said as if she hadn't spoken. His tone was hurried, barely concealing impatience. 'Which means we have a long detour ahead. We have to move fast if we are to cross into Tibet before the snow comes.'

## 10

THE RAIN WAS relentless in the low valleys they passed through – rain, mist, a general fogginess that flattened the light and weighed down both boots and mind. One night Claire washed out her socks and underwear and hung them across the inside of her tent to dry. In the morning it was snowing hard when she got up and her underwear was frozen flat as a paper doll's clothes, so stiff she had to thaw it out in a pan over the fire. Wet inside and out, she listened tiredly to the men analysing alkaloids and acids, and wondered again how Sally's nineteenth-century Indian artists had remained anonymous while plants were delineated so precisely, each name a signpost to history retraced.

◆ ◆ ◆

*A detour between Bhutan and Tibet, November 1988*

> *Falconeri*
> *barbatum*
> *Thomsonii*

*Thomsonii,* named after Dr Thomas Thomson, who loaded up two hundred men with plants, including seven barrels of the azure orchid, Vanda *caerulea,* and watched Falconer's team send down a thousand baskets of plundered orchids in one day, meanwhile cursing the other botanists who followed suit. Very few of the specimens reached England alive. Those orchids that did live often died within weeks of arriving or were killed by neglect. So many died over such a long a period that by 1850 the director of Kew had declared England to be the graveyard of all tropical orchids.

◆

At night Claire lay in her tent and thought about *the graveyard of orchids,* imagining their green poppy in place of the little Vandas, an orchid genus with an endearingly open and freckled face. Uprooted from the damp forest highlands the orchids loved, crushed into the hold of a nineteenth-century ship and transported for weeks through the sweltering heat, they literally boiled to death.

In the borderland between waking and sleeping she was hardly aware that it was Magda's words she was copying into her own cadastral survey: *An orchid is a relic of ancient times. Undisturbed, it may outlive its owners many times over, it may indeed live forever. Half a century after the discovery of the fairy orchid, this once common plant had become so rare that in 1904 an orchid nursery offered a thousand pounds for its rediscovery. What then of our elusive poppy?*

She overheard Jack recounting a story to Nick about an American plant smuggler he knew who claimed to have made more than $400,000 dealing in blackmarket orchids, his prize a fairy orchid poached in Bhutan and subsequently sold for $25,000. 'Even the more common species of lady's slipper he sells for six thousand a plant,' Jack said.

'Why so much?' asked Claire.

'Because lady's slipper orchids resist cloning, and orchids rarely form seedpods,' Nick explained. 'And the seeds take seven years to mature and flower.'

'This fellow boasted that he's never paid the locals more than two dollars apiece,' said Jack.

'How much did you pay for the ones *you* smuggled, Jack?' Claire asked. 'How much could you get on the open market for our green poppy?'

He walked away without answering.

'We're all under too much strain for this, Claire,' said Nick.

'Jack more than any of us. It's not his fault if the men he recruited stole those orchids.'

She wanted to believe in Jack as Nick did, as Nick had to if he wanted to keep going, but she couldn't. 'Why should Jack be more under strain than any of us?'

'Because he was responsible for convincing us to come here in the first place.'

In addition to the sores caused by leeches, scratches and mosquito bites suffered by everyone, each of the Western members of the party had begun to show personal signs of stress. Nick, his headphones never off, continuously rubbed the junction where his plastic hand joined his arm. Christian took to flossing his teeth at odd times, not only after meals. Jack smoked constantly. Ben walked as if he were carrying his body instead of being carried by it. After D. R. Damsang turned back with most of the other Bhutanese near the Tibet borders, Claire felt increasingly isolated. All that remained of their original team were three Lepchas and one Tibetan who had joined them from a monastery in Kalimpong. Apart from the Opium Quintet, the porters and guides were new recruits.

She was losing track of the days. Her skin itched under the bra she could no longer be bothered to remove, her feet were always cold. When Christian, approaching her solicitously, like a doctor showing charts to a terminally ill patient, tried to keep her informed of their position, she scrutinised his inadequate maps with a remote look of disbelief. Nodding politely as he pointed out latitude and longitude, she would tap her index finger in a restless private morse code on the words printed across the Trans-Himalayan region they were traversing: EXTERNAL BOUNDARIES ON THESE MAPS *tap* HAVE NOT BEEN AUTHENTICATED *tap tap tap* AND MAY NOT BE CORRECT *tap tap*. The only geographical records that interested her now were Jack's old cadastral surveys, a tally of individual trees and hamlets and cairns whose loss Claire recorded in her diary along with plant names and Lepcha myths:

*Pilda Mun: Lepcha priestesses who have the power to call back*

*the spirit of dead people into their own bodies and to speak in the
dead people's voices*

For Claire, altitude was charted, not by maps, but by the
disappearance of leeches when they climbed above 6000 feet, by
snow patches appearing like white lichen on the rocks. High
level pasture meant sightings of yak herdsmen's black tents,
alpine forests were heralded by a change to silver birch and
rhododendron from the bamboo and cypress that flourished
between 9000 and 12000 feet.

They entered Tibet on a smugglers' path so narrow that even yak
herdsmen avoided it because they complained that their animals'
horns got jammed between the rocks on either side. Jack's new
recruits managed to pick up jeeps in a town near the border
reputed to be the dirtiest in Asia, hard to believe, given some of
the scruffy towns the party encountered in their journey across
southern Tibet. On the rough tracks the jeeps were forced to take
to avoid military outposts, Claire spent most of the time with a
scarf wrapped around her face against the intrusive dust, an
intimate residue that crept under clothing and roughened every
orifice. In Tibet she learned that places which seemed only a few
miles off might take hour upon hour to reach. The past was much
closer. Sometimes she could dive into it like deep water, dragged
back by the rare moments when they had to pull off the road to
avoid an army vehicle. But more often their journey was through
a landscape travelled only by sheep, goats, mules and yaks, on
unpaved roads that were hard to distinguish from the stony dust.
Closing her eyes, Claire would let Magda's words send her into a
trance: *The idea of a road as a line dividing one man's property from
another's is foreign here, where the land slips and drifts, nomadic as
the men who travel it. Desert conditions of loose and shifting dust
prevent the construction of pukka roads, and tracks soon get buried
or lose their identity, often leaving no trace at all.*
  Robbed of living heroes, Claire fell in love with Arun the way
she had as a teenager with fictional figures like Darcy and Mr
Rochester. 'He occupies me, but not like enemy territory,' she

wrote in her journal. 'I feel that in the ending of his story lies the beginning of mine.' And moved on without a break to copy Magda's words, '*I have come to see that we can preserve things only by stopping life's course,' he said. 'All our botanical gardens reflect no more than the biased nature of any classification system. What is a nation except one more museum forcing a logic where there is none?*' But whether it was Magda or Claire who put down the pen she had almost ceased to care.

'*Each tree has its own way of dying,' he told me on one of our long treks, 'and the architecture of a forest depends on how its trees die.*'

*Like people, I thought; like countries.*

*These patterns he would look for and find in his last few months in England, just as he had in India. 'No man who loves the variety of a wild wood will plant sycamore,' he said, 'for while the native English lime rots through at its base and falls, leaving a stump to sprout and occupy the same place, the sycamore's aggressive habits spread its seeds far, producing hundreds of saplings which multiply at the first opportunity, squeezing out less tenacious native trees.*

'*But an oak dies standing,' he said, 'slowly. It may stand alone as a sentinel for five hundred years, yet in the twenty-five it takes for the roots to rot and collapse the tree inwards, it will have been long colonised by tougher neighbours.*'

'*You mean it rots from the inside out,' I said, 'as a badly governed country does, leaving it open to invasion.*'

*Oak seedlings are rare, he told me, even within oak forests, because they are as intolerant of shade as they are of the caterpillars which infest parent trees, and soon die under another oak's canopy. 'To grow again, an oak needs space – away even from its own kind,' he explained. I found it strange, this oakish need for freedom, considering that in England, oaks are used to mark property, ancient boundaries – between one parish and another, between this world and the next.*

One day Ben came to Claire and offered her his copy of the *Book of the Dead*, explaining that in it she would find instructions for passing through the Bardo, Tibetan for 'between two existences'.

'A hallucinatory period preceding reincarnation,' he said, sounding jittery and nervous, sweat on his forehead as if he had been running a hard race.

'Will I need a compass?' She wondered which of them was crazier.

Jack turned back to see what had caused their delay and she explained carefully that Ben suspected her of being half-dead. 'But enlightened,' Ben affirmed, 'because only the enlightened can recall the memories of past existences, which otherwise are no more than passing shadows, disturbingly familiar.'

Jack gave the two of them an odd look. 'Chocolate deprivation,' he joked roughly, impatient at Ben's determined metaphysics. 'You must have finished all your Hershey bars by now.'

Claire couldn't remember when it became clear that Christian had lost faith in the poppy. 'What real proof do we have?' she heard him ask Nick on one of the long marches after they left the jeeps behind, marches defined by horizons so distant they looked artificial, like the specimen pressed between the herbarium pages they had all believed in, its colour too faded to be proof of anything. 'It has always struck me as strange that no other botanists noted its existence.'

Ben answered with a rare burst of energy: 'Scientific ideas have their time and place, you *know* that, Chris! If you read Bailey's journal for the day he discovered the blue poppy, all you find is a comment to the effect that among the alpine flowers were blue poppies he had not seen before. This is the flower he later admitted was his assignation with immortality, the single thing he would be remembered for when all his military exploits and exploration were forgotten! Yet he had *no idea* at the time! Then you have to consider the thousands of medicinal plants overlooked simply because their use has not been confirmed by Western science, and the eight million sheets of pressed plants at Kew and the Museum of Natural History – a *river* of information drying up: plants which have disappeared, specimens from people whose societies have no written records of their own and whose disappearance takes with them all their knowledge.'

Ben looked around at the silent circle of faces as haggard and weather-beaten as his own. 'OK, I'm babbling. But I think we should go on.'

'So do I,' said Nick.

Christian wearily shouldered his pack again. 'You know the single trait Shackleton valued above any other in his expedition members?'

'Blind stupidity?' suggested Jack.

'Hope,' said Christian.

# 11

THEY STOOD ON the borders with nowhere, Claire thought, 2000 feet above the Kongbo-Tsangpo river, halfway up vertical cliffs as shiny and raw as burnt skin. Into the flanks of this gorge a giant axe had scored raw geological wounds, cracks rent through the stone when the land buckled and split apart.

It was not a good place to suffer from a fear of heights. To the north, the blue Po-Tsangpo sliced its way into the canyon, only to be swallowed up immediately by the boiling grey mud of the Kongbo-Tsangpo pouring in from the south, and every mile or so jagged spurs thrust across the gorge, forcing the doubled river to buckle back on itself furiously, an eel prodded with a knife. Razor-backed and slab-sided, these spurs were cleft by bristling jungle which varied from temperate rain forest of the high gorge at 8000 feet, with its monstrous oaks and magnolia, dropping swiftly through several climatic zones until it reached the sub-tropical jungle, where Christian measured a forty-foot bamboo: two feet from the ground its circumference was forty-three inches round, its leaves ten feet long and three feet across, springing out of a steep grove of similar goliaths. 'Dinosaur grass,' Ben was moved to say. 'You could furnish all the garden furniture in Nantucket from this one plant.'

This was the only time of year when such a trek through the deep Tsangpo Gorge (or Brahmaputra Gorge, as it was known now) could be undertaken, when the river was at its lowest. Exploring part of the lower river basin, the party recorded a boiling point of just above 5000 feet, a drop of 4000 feet from the crust above. 'One of the deepest gorges in the world,' Christian said, 'and perhaps the most biologically diverse.'

Advised by local hunter-guides, newly recruited in the region by Jack's Opium Quintet, they clambered up and around vertical green wedges driven into the bald precipices, negotiating landscape so out of scale with humanity that Claire lost her sense of perspective. She got used to climbing through dense, ancient forest and then passing as if through a green curtain into Tibet's bleak plateau above. On one clifftop, marked as a monastery on the map, all they found were tumbled stones in a great amphitheatre of rock and ice. 'Bloody Chinese!' said Nick.

Claire was aware that her fear of heights had been holding the expedition up, especially in these last ten days following animal trails along the course of the surging rapids in the gorge. The only way to traverse the many spurs of rock that had to be crossed was by means of toe-holds chipped out of the granite. Each time Claire would take one look at the drop of thousands of feet to the river and know it was impossible, and each time she would be encouraged by the porters and then lowered in a rope cradle, helpless as a baby. 'Like Frank Kingdon Ward,' she kept repeating, trying not to feel humiliated.

At the best of times it would have been an extremely difficult trek, and because of Christian's insistence on taking samples the party's hardships were increased. But it was in the gorge that the party heard the first reports of green poppies.

◆ ◆ ◆

*Tsangpo Gorge, November 1988*

The poppy, finally! Or hints of it at least. With the help of the Tibetan from Kalimpong's monastery, one of the porters who has been with us since the start, Nick has managed to translate stories from the few people we've encountered (largely Lhopas and a few Monbas).

It was two weeks ago that we bought the three sheep for carrying our plant specimens and soil samples (the first herd left us in Sikkim), and yesterday one of the sheep lost its footing on the narrow hunter's track we were following and fell over the precipice, breaking its back and smashing to dust the cases it carried. The sight cleared my head again, as well as reviving all my fears.

After that accident we left the sheep at the top when we made our descents. They seemed a lot happier about it. I don't think they are mountain sheep, or not gorge sheep, anyway.

◆

Claire, noticing that Jack's quintet were increasingly restless, wondered if he had promised something he was not delivering. She wouldn't blame them if they were simply fed up with the tedious process of soil collecting, a process made even more laborious without the sheep. 'Soils do not always develop in the same way just because they have the same parent rocks,' Christian said, when there were complaints of carrying yet more heavy soil samples back out of the gorge in their backpacks. 'The world has a subterranean landscape, just as we have. Soils exhibit different properties in layers called "horizons", and the deeper a soil is excavated or eroded, the more it resembles its mineral origins. The poppies might need such a soil to survive ex situ.' The parent rock, Christian called it, and Claire wrote: *Artificial horizons. First excavated by Jack and then eroded. What is left of me is close to the bone, my mineral origins. From soul to soil: a simple slip of the pen. One letter makes all the difference.*

Nick managed to glean information about the poppy's whereabouts from a couple of the Lhopa shamans. At first unwilling to discuss it, they came round after being offered a watch each, but warned that the poppy was poisonous to those who didn't understand its use. It had died out or been hunted to extinction, they claimed, everywhere except in the deepest part of the gorge, in the five impenetrable miles of trail that followed the river's tortured course north beyond the holy cave at Drakpuk Kawasum, gateway to the *beyul* or 'hidden lands' of Pemako. 'Growing in the cliff beside the great falls, that is where you find it.'

Jack watched this transaction with the expression of a person confronted by a charming but shady used-car salesman. When the shamans had moved on, well content with their reward, Christian turned to him: 'Think we've been had?'

'They were cheap watches.'

'The lost falls of the Tsangpo Gorge *and* the lost green poppy?' Christian's voice was as sardonic as Jack's. 'Bit of a coincidence, don't you think?'

'Actually they didn't say green *poppy*,' Nick admitted. 'It was a green flower.'

The four men discussed the shamans' story, Christian worried that the legend of their green poppy, the 'snow leopard' might be attributed to an error of triangulation, a slip in translation. 'Like the one that turned the "Lost Falls of the Tsangpo Gorge" into a Himalayan Niagara, one of the great myths of the nineteenth and twentieth centuries,' he said, 'the focus of endless expeditions.'

Until now, Claire had seen Christian as a man of almost inhuman self-confidence, the kind of person who never had bad dreams, never failed to be picked for the team – whether it was the college debating society or the government's select scientific forum. But this journey had roughened his smooth surface like pumice stone used on tender skin, made it less impermeable to doubt. Listening to him recount how a native pundit named Kintup had sparked off the European search for the falls, it struck Claire that Christian was having difficulties convincing himself as much as he was the others. All of them needed to believe in Kintup's veracity, because his story was in a way their own.

'When you think of how long everyone believed Kintup . . .' Christian began.

'But the "Great Falls" have also been described in Tibetan monks' sacred guidebooks,' Ben pointed out, 'and don't forget that most of Kintup's other geographical details proved amazingly accurate.'

'No explorer after him succeeded in finding the falls,' said Christian. 'Even Colonel Bailey, who reduced the unexplored section of the gorge to less than forty miles, concluded that falls of such magnitude could not possibly exist.'

'What was Kintup's reply?' asked Claire.

'There was none,' Christian said. 'He was believed to have vanished back into the hills, as so many of the pundits had, and died there.' One more anonymous native explorer among many. 'Not until three months before the outbreak of the Great War and thirty *years* after Kintup had returned from Tibet was the legendary figure finally tracked down – in Darjeeling, where he was found to be alive, but living in straitened circumstances as a tailor.'

'A sewer of tails.' Ben's joke crept into the narrative.

'Colonel Bailey interviewed the pundit in the hill station of Simla,' Christian continued, 'where Kintup's memory, even after all those years, proved vivid: it was no monstrous cataract he had seen, but the river falling over a cliff in a series of rapids, transformed into a single Niagara through a combination of the lama who took down his narrative and a bad English translator. Illiterate, Kintup had known nothing of the error, and no one had sought to question him further.'

'But the legend persisted, despite Kintup's statement?' Claire asked Christian. 'It enticed generation after generation of explorer?'

'Until Frank Kingdon Ward managed to penetrate the last stretch of river in 1924,' Christian said. 'All but five miles.'

'Still, five miles that he did not explore,' Claire persisted. 'If it were a missing gene or a strand of DNA you wouldn't take it so lightly.' She saw the mystery being shaved away until nothing was left but a shadow, an unread line. 'Maybe they were looking in the wrong place.'

'She's right,' Nick said. 'After all, Kingdon Ward effectively ended Western scientific exploration of the gorge for three-quarters of a century.'

'Putting aside the question of satellite surveillance photos, which failed to show anything,' Christian said, 'five miles could hardly conceal a second Niagara.'

Not Niagara, Claire thought, but something.

343

'Although, thanks to the wonders of Christian's wonderful laser range-finder,' Jack added mischievously, 'we know now that Kingdon Ward got *one* of his measurements wrong, at the very least. The falls he settled for are seventy feet high, as we proved yesterday. Almost twice the height he estimated.'

Claire's mind travelled down the remaining miles Kingdon Ward did not quite see, into that 4000-foot cleft in the earth's surface where the view was obscured by a rampart jutting out from the sheer cliffs, where the river narrowed from a hundred yards to just seventy feet and the sound off the canyon was of cannons firing. What if the Tibetan myths leading explorers into the most dangerous part of the gorge were a mixture of deliberate untruths designed to confuse or divert all but the true pilgrim? If a 150-foot falls could elude the British empire's best attempts at discovery, how much more easily could a poppy?

# 12

DESPITE WORSENING WEATHER and short supplies, Christian had agreed on one last attempt to penetrate the deepest part of the gorge. Penetration was a guy thing, Claire decided, climbing slowly towards the point judged most advantageous for the descent, a dick thing. It implied a certain amount of resistance from the penetrated (a knife didn't *penetrate* butter the way it did flesh). The weather itself was resisting, gloomy and overcast, with cloud filling the deep valley like a wound packed with cotton wool. And at the point where the animal track they had been following narrowed to a ledge not much wider than a kitchen shelf, Claire had to turn her face into the mountain in her usual fashion, pressing both palms against it with a mossy grip and shuffling her way forward. She tried to ignore the rest of the party forging ahead of her and Ben and imagined herself as lichen, part of the rock, a trick the teratologist had recommended. 'I'll be the only person to have passed through the Himalayas without admiring the view,' she called back to him, not removing her eyes from the comforting granite an inch from her nose.

'That's what courage *is*, you know,' Ben said. 'If you're not afraid, you don't need to be brave.'

About to shout her thanks for his moral support, she heard a grunt from him, the comfortable sound he made taking his boots off at night. There was a rattle of pebbles. She forgot her own fear and slid her eyes round to see Ben on his back, laughing. His eyes widened as he started to slide. He looked surprised by the movement. Then he yelled. He was slipping over the edge, grabbing at the rough grass edging the path, losing his grip and sliding away, the sound of him hitting shrubs and rocks on the way down. She was screaming for Jack and running back to where Ben had disappeared. Crouching as close to the edge as she dared, Claire spied him about twenty feet from her, halfway down a scree slide which ended in a sheer drop to the river a thousand feet below, his arm, at an odd angle, awkwardly wrapped round some broken bamboo.

'Ben!'

'Get help.' His voice was very weak.

'I can't leave you.'

'Get help,' he repeated. 'I don't know how long this will hold.'

She ran, clawing, scrambling her way up the track, oblivious to the drop, until she met the others descending. 'It's Ben. He's fallen. Back there.' She pointed, suddenly shaking. 'I think it's bad.'

Jack, already shrugging off his backpack, gestured to the Lepchas as he did. 'Bring the dandy.' The dandy was what the Lepchas called the rough hammock once used for transporting weak Victorian memsahibs, a device they'd been using to carry samples. Christian picked up the ropes and Claire started to follow them.

'You stay here!' Jack commanded, and Nick put his good arm around her, half comforting, half restraining.

It took the men over an hour to lift Ben up with ropes and a makeshift sling, and by the time they returned, he was unconscious on the dandy. 'Nasty puncture under his arm,' Jack said. 'His feet must have broken the bamboo as he came down and that slowed him, thank God. But the broken bamboo drove a hole into his armpit and brought him up short.'

'Oh Jesus,' whispered Claire.

'Like a side of ham in a butcher's,' Jack added bluntly. 'The bamboo probably saved his life, but I think he may have broken his ankle.'

They laid him down on two sleeping bags and Christian began to examine him with a gentleness that surprised Claire, but at the first probe of his armpit Ben came awake with a yelp, before promptly passing out again.

'He's still unconscious,' Christian said, when he had given Ben a shot of penicillin. 'I don't think it's his head or loss of blood – the arm wound doesn't seem to be too deep a puncture. And I believe his ankle is sprained rather than broken.' He paused to look back at Ben's flushed face, 'But he appears to have a high fever, possibly a result of infection from leech bites, a combination of that and general weakness. It's hard to tell.'

'Ben has been complaining of fever for quite a while,' Claire said in a voice gone small and tight. 'He was worried it might be malaria because he'd forgotten to take his antimalarials for several days after we left Kalimpong.'

'He *what*?' Christian rounded on her. 'Why didn't he say? Why didn't *you*?'

She could feel tears start up. 'He didn't want to make a fuss.' That's why she'd stayed back with him, often pretending to photograph things they didn't really need, taking much longer than was necessary, trying to cover for him. 'He felt bad enough being so slow, holding everyone up.'

'So he should,' said Jack. 'All those lectures on bloody cinchona and the bloody doctor forgets his medicine.'

'Oh fuck off, Jack, will you?' Nick looked as if he might take a swing at him.

'One thing is for certain,' Christian said, 'this man can't walk any further. It's amazing he's gone on as long as he has.' He put his hand on Ben's head. 'We should have noticed. I don't know why I didn't.'

Claire watched Nick search Christian's drawn face. 'It's not your fault, Chris. We're all tired.'

Christian stood up. 'Ben badly needs rest, but this is hardly the ideal spot. We need to get him to a house, somewhere warm and dry where he can rest.' He stared up the steep, narrow path where they had stopped. 'The problem as I see it is that we're about fifteen miles from the last decent village – a good four days' walk even without a sick man.'

'You mean that decent village in the north?' Jack asked. 'The one where we nearly ran into the Chinese patrols?'

'And we're not sure how far it is to the next,' Nick said.

'According to the map –' Christian started.

Jack cut him off. 'According to the map, the last village didn't exist and the one before that, the ghost town, was a thriving metropolis. The question is: do we go on and try to find the next village, or go back, which could take us five or six days at the very least, and risk the patrols?'

'The last village wasn't exactly Tunbridge Wells,' Nick said.

The guides recruited by Jack's Quintet were keeping very quiet, which Claire thought was odd, considering that this was their territory. When Christian turned to them for advice about which village could provide adequate shelter for Ben, they shrugged sullenly and said they didn't know. For the first time, the Tibetan porter from Kalimpong spoke up. He mentioned a village with a good doctor – not so far, he said, maybe four days. 'No Chinese. All Tibetan and tribal people.'

Claire couldn't catch the village name, although he repeated it three times, as well as the name of the valley it lay in.

'Show me on the map.' Christian unfolded it as he spoke.

'The valley I am speaking of is not indicated on such a document, sir.'

Christian scrutinised the map in question. 'I realise it's not detailed. Still, surely you can give us a general idea how to get there?'

'How to get there, yes, but names are not written on this map.' The Tibetan had come from a place where rivers changed their names when they changed direction, he explained, and therefore from his point of view, the Tsangpo/Brahmaputra river on Christian's map looked like an error.

'I don't know . . .' Christian sounded sceptical. 'Can you be sure it still exists?'

'It was my village before the Chinese chased me out from Lhasa in 1966, where I was living as a young monk.'

'That's twenty-two years ago,' Jack said. 'It's probably been burnt by the Chinese or is simply not there any more.'

'Oh yes, it *was* burnt,' the Tibetan replied with the slow courtesy of a man whose only urgent appointment was with his own conscience. 'Yet I believe it is still there.'

But his certainty failed to sway Christian.

'Whatever we do, we should at least find a more sheltered campsite before it gets dark,' Jack said, 'We're like fruit bats stuck to this cliff.'

The rain had begun to fall heavily and the change in temperature brought clouds swirling up from the canyon floor, effectively sealing the group off in a dreamy Chinese landscape, the time of day Claire liked best. Cushioned within the watercolour mists, she could no longer see how high they had climbed.

In the end they moved forward a mile to a wider point in the trail where half the mountain face had been washed out in an earlier landslip, and stopped to wait out the rain. Even here the camping was precarious. In order to prevent themselves from rolling down the steep grade and over the cliff edge it was essential to dig into the flattest space available – behind a tree stump, next to a boulder. The guides and porters huddled down in twos and threes under roughly constructed lean-tos, and the Western members of the party followed suit, with Christian and Nick in one lean-to, Claire, Ben and Jack in the other. Almost oblivious to Jack's presence, Claire fell asleep with the name of the Tibetan's unpronounceable valley in her head, a word that began with a sound like 'R' and rolled away from her, a whispering name as liquid as the rain.

# 13

CLAIRE WOKE TO see Jack resting his head on one hand and watching her across a snoring Ben. 'We need to have a talk,' he said without preamble. 'Nick and Christian have decided to go ahead with one final crack at finding the falls – and the poppy, obviously. They started for the deepest part of the gorge a few hours before dawn this morning, with light packs and mountaineering gear.'

Claire sat upright and hit her head against the aluminium poles supporting their lean-to. Rubbing her bruised scalp, she said, 'What, with Ben sick?'

'Ben knew the risks when we signed up. We're as close as we've ever been to that last unmapped stretch of gorge. If the poppy is anywhere, it will be there. And as you know, this is the only time for a descent, while the water is at its annual low. It might take years to organise another expedition like this one. The rest of us – apart from the two porters Nick and Christian have taken – are to push on to the next safe village and find a bed and medical facilities for Ben. We will be moving on immediately, meeting up with Nick and Christian either at Gyala, or, if worst comes to worst at Pe, where the guides say there is a Chinese compound with medical facilities and a small guesthouse.'

'Why would they have gone without telling me? I'm the one who convinced them of the falls. I wanted to see them too!' She could hear her voice rising, petulant as a child deprived of a promised treat.

'You're afraid of heights. Last night you were exhausted, upset –'

'No more exhausted and upset than any of you,' she said stubbornly, not wanting to believe that Nick would have left without letting her know. 'And how will we meet up again?'

Jack patiently explained that Christian had calculated a day or so for the climb down. 'If the falls are where the old journal says they are –'

'What if they aren't?'

'He wanted an extra day to take samples, if there are any samples to take, and a day to return. Three to four days at the outside. Then four days' march to the village where we will be waiting, giving Ben time to heal a bit. If Nick and Christian haven't arrived after a week, we are to head back to Kalimpong by the southern Tsangpo.' He put out a hand to stroke the side of her face and withdrew it when Claire shook her head.

'I don't see it,' she said. 'Why can't we wait here? Or further up the path?'

'Ben needs rest –'

'In a nice, dry, warm place,' she mocked. 'And you guys think it's better for him to be bounced up and down these mountains for three days?' She touched Ben's forehead, which was cooler than the night before. 'He's still unconscious.'

'I gave him something to keep him asleep so his muscles will be more relaxed in the dandy.'

'Which porters did Nick and Chris take – the Lepchas?'

Her cousin let his eyes slip away from hers for an instant before replying, and in the gap of credibility that opened between what Jack chose to tell her and what he didn't Claire felt her irritation change to apprehension. Something wasn't right. 'No,' Jack said. 'Chris thought the local recruits would be of more use.' He ended any further discussion by rolling out of the lean-to.

A few minutes later Claire heard him giving a shortened version of this explanation to the rest of the party. She was interested to watch the Opium Quintet grinning and chatting throughout Jack's speech, as if they knew that the split had been planned all along.

Claire was astounded when her cousin ordered the porters to unload all their soil samples and most of the plant samples. 'We will make better time without such heavy packs,' Jack said. 'Ben will get to a doctor or at least a warm bed faster.'

The porters, whom she was sure had never understood the point of such a venture anyway, abandoned their heavy piles of Ziplocked dirt with alacrity. 'But we've spent weeks collecting this stuff,' she complained to Jack.

'If Christian and Nick find their green poppy in the gorge, then these piles of dirt will be largely superfluous.'

'And if they don't?'

'Which is more important to you – the dirt or Ben?'

Claire, desperately wishing there was someone she could ask for advice, remembered so clearly Christian's proud comment about Scott having collected rock samples in Antarctica up to a few days before his death. And Jack's response. 'We should at least put the samples somewhere out of the weather in case Chris does want them,' she said, not liking to examine too closely the way in which she had separated Christian's ambitions from her cousin's. When Jack pointed out that the remaining lean-to was too small to accommodate such a pile of dirt, Claire said, with a flash of inspiration, 'We could bury the samples in the ground. Make a shallow trench and cover it with rocks –'

'A cairn?' He compressed an outright laugh into a smile. 'Fine – as long as you're quick.'

Digging a trench in the hard ground was tough work, even with the help of the Lepchas and the Kalimpong Tibetan. She remembered D. R. Damsang being much intrigued by the idea of having collected, packed and identified the earth so laboriously in the first place. He had perceived it as a religious ceremony no less explicable to the unconverted than his own clockwise circumnavigation of Buddhist temples – perhaps pointless, but necessary. 'And now you are moving it to a new location for reburial?' the Tibetan asked. 'Is this the custom in your country?' Bemused, he stared at the pile of plastic-covered earth in its shallow grave. Claire explained that it was because of the seeds that might be in the earth samples. 'We want to preserve the seeds, you see.'

He suggested that she empty the bags of earth into the ground. 'Then the seeds will have a chance to sprout, Miss. For they will not survive inside plastic.'

'Dust to dust,' Jack said.

Ignoring Jack's sarcasm, Claire buried the Ziploc plastic bags of soil under a foot of gravel and then entertained her cousin still more by placing several crossed sticks on top to mark the site of the burial. The best she could do after that was to leave a note in another Ziploc bag, weighted down with a stone next to the tree where Nick had pitched his now empty lean-to.

Any curiosity she had about which plant specimens Jack had considered worth preserving drained away over the next three days' prolonged marches. It became clear to her that Ben, who groaned each time the Lepchas loaded him on and off the dandy, was a bone of contention with the Opium Quintet. Their leader had started arguing with Jack after the first hour of laboured procession back up the trail, Jack equally aggressive in return. Bulls locking horns, Claire thought them, with Jack emerging as the victor – for the moment.

To walk was all she could manage; beside Ben, squeezing his hand whenever he opened his eyes and listening to the odd phrases he mumbled, proof that he was living in a different space than the rest of them. Not long after lunch on the third day, the Kalimpong Tibetan quietly informed her that the party had long since diverted from Jack's stated course.

'Where are we, then?'

'Heading southeast towards the high passes into Pemako. One of our hidden lands, the *beyul*. Recommended only for pilgrims of great stamina.'

'Well, that excludes us two,' Claire said, looking down at Ben's pale face. From what she had read about Pemako, it was not so much hidden as isolated and inhospitable. Predominantly tribal, with no motorable roads linking it to the rest of the country, its virgin jungles were part of a politically disputed region lying one-third in Tibet and the rest in Arunachal Pradesh. Arunachal Pradesh, Claire remembered, home of the second chemist, the Opium Quintet's leader, a state which bordered on Burma, where drug barons like the orchid-loving Khun Sa were heroes.

Jack had been driving the porters on as if they had a schedule to keep or an urgent business meeting to attend, but with the arrival of heavy snow late that afternoon it became clear that there wasn't a remote chance of continuing. They crossed a windy basin between two steep bluffs and were forced to make what camp they could in the shelter of an outcrop of black rock the size of a five-storey building. While the Lepchas and the Tibetan quickly began stowing their packs inside the tents, Claire noticed that the bags containing all her exposed and unexposed film, Nick's tapes and the remaining plant specimens had simply been left in the snow by the other porters. Insisting that they help her to get these under shelter had no effect, and when she went to retrieve one of the bags, the leader of Jack's Quintet jerked it from her so forcefully that the contents spilled on to the snow. She was so stunned by his action that it took her a moment to recognise the shrivelled things lying in front of her.

'Orchids!' she said. With the blood beating in her head, she thought: if they're abandoning these stolen orchids, what's in the packs they are saving? She stood silent and shocked while the man spat phrases in an unknown language, working himself up to a pitch that only stopped short of physical violence at Jack's appearance. 'What is it, Claire?'

She pointed wordlessly at the ground and saw her cousin greet the revelation almost with indifference. The orchids might have been bottlecaps or toothpicks for all the emotion his face registered. He spoke a few terse words to the man in front of them, who stepped forward and started shouting again, even more belligerently. Jack listened for a minute, his face icy, and then pulled out his gun – quite casually, Claire thought, except that he left no one in any doubt that he knew how to use it. The other members of the Quintet had gathered. They watched with sullen faces as Jack pushed her behind him, not taking his eyes off the men, and told her to go back to the tent with Ben.

'But my film –'

'Forget it, Claire. I've had enough of this foolishness.'

She wrenched her wrist out of his hand and started to move towards the pack holding her film. 'Get inside!' he said, grabbing her again and pushing her out of the way with such force that she nearly fell.

*'Hold on hold on hold on. Don't let him see you cry.* Claire repeated the phrases to herself as she walked back to the tent. Ben opened his eyes when she stumbled inside. 'I thought for a minute I'd heard a gunshot.' It was the first lucid comment he'd made since his accident and his voice sounded as if it needed oiling.

She'd heard the shot too. 'Just the tent flapping. There's a helluva storm.' She tried to smile, not wanting to worry him – or herself. *Was* it the tent they'd heard?

Ben's smile was as rusty as his voice. 'Bad dreams again. How about a good escape movie and some popcorn?' His eyes moved to Claire's face, screwed up in an attempt not to cry. 'Sorry, bad joke.'

'I hate popcorn. It reminds me of –' She heard Jack behind her.

'What, no popcorn, Claire?' he said softly. 'I thought all Americans loved popcorn, dripping in butter.' He crouched next to Ben. 'How're you feeling?'

'If it's all right with you, I'd rather not climb Everest at this precise moment in time,' Ben said. 'But better, definitely better.'

Jack laid his hand on Ben's forehead. 'Your temperature feels back to normal. Must've been the leeches and not malaria.' His eyes flicked to Claire as she climbed into her sleeping bag. 'You all right, Claire?' She didn't respond. 'Well, sweet dreams, you two.'

It was the butter, Claire thought as she heard him leave, the smell of butter. That's what put me off at UNISENS, when Christian gave us all a ride on his Woody Allen nose machine. The smell of butter reminded me of popcorn and popcorn is the smell of death, Robin's death. If Jack had seen me then, he wouldn't be so sure of me, he wouldn't think he could manipulate me so easily. He has no idea how strong I am. She closed her eyes and remembered her last night with Robin. The liquid in his lungs was editing his conversation by then to an odd urgency, but he managed to raise his eyebrows at the hospital's 'care' visitors, the Catholic sisters with their bland expressions and matching platitudes. Claire could see him struggling to summon a caustic phrase, his grimace misinterpreted. One of them dropped to her knees to pray for the angels. Robin winked at Claire and she knew that he wanted her to send the woman away. How can I do that, Claire asked herself. Who am I to decide whether molecules hold precedence over angels? He whispered, 'Praying mantis.' That sent the woman packing. 'Does it make them feel good?' he asked. 'I mean: does it make them feel GOOD? Holy. Alive, in the face of all this rot.' Behind his head was a moving tableau of the AIDS patients still mobile, pushing portable IV units like department store dummies.

It shamed her that after the second night sleeping in a chair beside Robin she couldn't take any more, not with the young man next to him moaning, 'Don't leave me, Mom! Don't leave me!' and Robin's restless morphine sleep that kept him tossing and crying, in turns enigmatic, comic, tragic: 'There's going to be lots of blood!' Or 'Lipstick!' or 'Count the nappies! Count the nappies!'

The nurse told her that he had worn disposable diapers for the last two months. 'Your brother's so sweet! He calls them "nappies", like the English.'

The way their English father had, Claire could have said.

During the day he would half wake and before he got himself together hiccup out a list of wants:

I want –
I want –
I want –

A puzzled look on his face, as if he were trying to remember a name or a face. Then, 'I peed my pillow' or 'My nappy needs changing. I want the nurse.'

The hospital was very short staffed. Budget cuts, the nurses told her.

By the end of the week Claire was no longer convinced that the routine recording of temperature, blood pressure, amount of urine passed actually constituted the preservation of anything one might consider life. Saving life! Like a bank, a bloody blood bank. Saving it for what?

The last day, when her mother went home to sleep, Robin and Claire managed to convince the doctor that the IV and the drugs it administered were no longer palliative. Robin could be unplugged. Almost immediately he started to swell up with the liquid that was no longer being drained off by the drugs. Claire took off the plastic ID bracelet when she saw it was cutting into his wrist. He joked that he didn't need an identity any more. There was a fight even then, long hours on the phone pleading with other faceless doctors to increase the morphine. They explained again and again the results of such a decision. Effectively killing him. Manslaughter, she thought.

'You do realise that if we increase the morphine as much as you are asking, it will suppress his breathing until, eventually, it stops.' That phrase repeated with minute variations until she did indeed feel like a murderer, until she dragged the doctor in and made Robin answer the questions as if he were an unwilling bridegroom at the altar or a witness on the stand and she his prosecuting attorney:

'Robin, do you understand that if they keep increasing the morphine, it will eventually shut you down completely?'
'I do.'
'You'll die.'
'Yes.'

'You want that?'

'I do.' You could see the strain in his face, the effort to remain conscious, to give the impression of alertness so that she could not be blamed.

'In effect we are killing you, Robin.' I am giving them permission to kill you.

'No.' One syllable responses were all that he could manage.

'No?' asked the doctor, eager to avoid the decision. 'You don't want that?'

'Not killing,' said Robin. 'Letting me go.'

Claire was crying now, unaware of the tears running down her face. 'Oh Robin. But is it what you want, are you sure?'

His chin came down, and for a moment she thought it would stay down. Then he took a deep breath and said, 'What I want. Morphine.'

Oh, nobody could say that Claire Fleetwood had not absorbed the bitter taste of this particular alkaloid.

She sat with him from five in the afternoon, watching the nurses come and go with the shots of morphine in increasingly large and frequent doses, hearing that last enigmatic reference to lipstick. Some time around 2.30 in the morning he gave a deep rattling sigh. She leaned close to whisper, 'Still there, Robin?' And thought: how strange: I can smell popcorn. Is this what death smells like? 'Death as a bad movie, Robin,' she whispered, wondering if he was still alive, and if so, what he could hear or understand. 'I know you'd laugh.'

She laid his cool puffy hand on the sheet and went out to the nurses' station, where the smell of popcorn was stronger. 'I think –' Claire began.

One of the nurses interrupted her, the fat lesbian one in the hockey T-shirt, 'We're making popcorn – want some?'

'Actually, I think –' Claire said. She didn't like to say it, disrupt this happy gathering with the news that her brother was dead.

'Sure, honey: have some!' The friendly nurse heaped it on to Claire's hands before she could protest. 'Night nurse food: popcorn, pot noodles, cup-a-soup!'

Claire, stared down at the popcorn in her hands. 'Actually, I think my brother just died.'

'Naaahhh,' the nurse responded brightly. 'It's the morphine. They do this morphine thing: short breaths and then a long silence to get you scared and then this big deep sigh. It can go on for days.' She walked in and looked at Robin. 'You haven't left us, have ya angel?' She snapped on a latex glove, picked up his hand and pressed her nail hard into his thumb. 'If they're still around that always gets them!' she said to Claire, the words coming on a wave of buttery popcorn.

Robin took a huge breath. Ready for a long dive into deep water, Claire thought. The nurse smiled and left.

When Claire had finished her popcorn, she brushed the salt off and again took Robin's hand. It was very cold, as was his forehead, cool as stone. She called the fat nurse and told her that this time she thought her brother really was dead. The nurse didn't seem annoyed, but she had trouble finding a pulse. She kept putting the stethoscope on different parts of Robin's chest. The popcorn she was crunching probably didn't help her to hear.

'Thing is,' the nurse said, 'I don't like to wake up the doctor who's on call unless I'm sure your brother's dead.'

'No, I can see that,' Claire answered. It seemed reasonable. You can't wake the dead; why wake the living?

Finally the nurse called one of the interns from the cancer ward on the floor below. He was a Chinese boy, really cute, Claire thought. He didn't appear to be more than about seventeen. He stood in the nurses' area eating big handfuls of popcorn and said, 'So where's the stiff?'

The nurses looked embarrassed. Claire waved her thumb towards Robin's room and the young intern gave her an interested smile. 'You new? Off duty now?'

Claire nodded. 'Off duty, I guess. He's my brother.'

The intern's smile slipped from his face. He dropped the popcorn back into the bowl, wiping his greasy hands on his hospital green pants. 'Oh. Um. Sorry.'

'That's all right,' Claire was sorry too, for upsetting him. 'He liked popcorn.'

He came out of Robin's room a few minutes later, pulling the transparent latex gloves off his hands and nodding bashfully at Claire. 'Yup. Sorry. Your brother is um has um passed on, um passed away . . .'

Claire was aware that they were all watching her. She wished that she didn't feel so dried up. 'So he's dead then?'

'You want to stay with him for a while?' asked the fat nurse. 'After all, he is your brother, honey.'

Not that in there, Claire thought. That's not Robin.

'I guess you guys weren't so close,' the nurse said. Her expression indicating disillusion with the AIDS patients' relatives who didn't want to get dirty hands.

'I should call my mother,' Claire said.

It was light by the time she got back to the hotel but her eyes were hot-wired open. Suddenly hungry, she switched on the television and sat for an hour watching reruns of sitcoms and eating stale cheese snacks from the minibar.

It was not until two days later that she started to cry.

Claire held herself together this time long enough to pull the sleeping bag over her head. Then she let the tears run silently, the way Robin had told her to do when she was being bullied at yet another new school. 'Never let the bastards see you cry,' he would say. Robin, I really miss you, Claire thought. And could hear him tell her to keep her chin up. No – her *chins*, that's what he said: 'Keep your *chins* up, Claire!' Robin, whose theory about old souls and new ones got him through the bad places where his form of sexuality incurred mockery or aggression: 'It's the new souls you've got to watch out for, Claire. The old souls, the ones who have been around a long time, they're the tolerant ones.'

'Are you all right, Claire?' asked Ben.

'Fine.'

She had nightmares, of course, as she'd had for weeks after Robin's death. This time she dreamed of a house that was and was not Eden. She was in the cellar watching water rise up through the floorboards. However many times she emptied the water it continued to rise, black and slimy, until she was swimming in it. A stone angel hovered above her, and she wasn't sure if it had wings or arms raised over its head. She wanted to warn it: dive into that well and you'll never come up, you'll enter that garden to dive forever. But there was someone else in the room she had to help, a woman sitting in a chair and pointing with one hand through a window to what looked like unplanted flowerbeds, mounds of earth that she insisted were graves. 'Beds for the dead,' she said, reaching out with her other hand to Claire, and when Claire grasped it she felt but could not see a third hand there, a sticky, clinging hand whose flesh came away in her own. A latex glove.

In the night, Claire rose up out of her bad dreams whimpering, and before she was fully awake she was aware of someone holding her, stroking her sweat-soaked face with a cool hand and whispering that it would be all right, she wasn't alone. 'Arun?' she said first, yet even as she whispered his name she knew that it couldn't be true because history never smelled so real, of male sweat and tweed jacket and the hot acrid odour of cigarettes. 'It's all right, sweetheart,' Jack whispered. 'I won't let the nightmares get you.' She wanted to tell him that her father had done that too, split the word so that it sounded less frightening, a herd of dark horses, no more, but she fell asleep before she could, Ben's loud snoring blotting out all other sounds.

She woke shortly before dawn desperate for a pee. Peenis-envy, she thought. If Freud had only realised. Everything to do with convenience, not sex. How had Magda managed in all those Victorian layers?

She eased herself outside into the night. It was very dark, but not as cold as she'd expected, a soft, dreamy darkness. At first all she noticed was that the wind and snow had died down completely. She edged down the slope, wishing she had remembered to pick up her torch. After a few footsteps there grew in her a feeling of unease at not seeing the tents of Jack and his guides. They had seemed much closer when the porters set up camp. She left her mark in the snow and shuffled a bit further in the direction of the other tents, where Jack's tent should have been and wasn't.

# 14

JACK WAS GONE. So were all her cameras, the heavier scanners and survey equipment that Christian hadn't taken with him, and all but the Lepchas and the Kalimpong Tibetan. The Opium Quintet and its band leader had moved on to more profitable venues. Claire, drained of all adrenaline, returned to her tent and lay sleepless until the blue dawn gave her enough light to set off across the broad, flat basin towards a ridge overlooking the next valley. New snow squeaked under her boots and gentle gusts of breeze blew the white powder up in dancing ghosts that followed her as she walked. Feeling weightless, her mind empty, she scrambled to the top of the ridge to find its black surface wind-scoured clean as a teflon frying pan. A sweep of her binoculars revealed no sign of Jack. The snow had covered all trace of paths, removed footprints, erased the past. She wondered if she would ever see Christian or Nick again, and considered the likelihood of her own and Ben's survival. Her life spread out before her like a clean white sheet of paper on which to write a new story.

She climbed slowly back down off the ridge and on a whim lay down on her back in the fresh snow, sweeping her hands across its surface until they met above her head, then back again. 'I have turned the gap,' Claire thought, rising carefully so that she wouldn't mar the perfect angel left behind.

Retracing her steps to her tent, she dipped her head in to find Ben awake. He grinned at the sight of her head amputated by the zipper like a big game trophy hung on the nylon wall. 'Where's that popcorn?' he said, as if the night had been only a minor interruption in their earlier conversation, 'I'm starving.' She told him she'd rustle up some eggs, hoping inwardly that such a thing was possible.

There wasn't much food left, the Lepcha porters informed her – no eggs, but some flour not worth the bother of transporting. 'Do you know what time the others left?' Claire asked, and was told by the Kalimpong Tibetan (the only one with a watch) that it had been about three in the morning. He had his mouth full, as did the Lepchas, and at her hungry look, the Tibetan withdrew from his pack a bag of wizened yellow cubes and offered her one.

The football sock taste of old parmesan rind was immediately recognisable. 'That stuff! I think I've got some in my bag too.'

The porters smiled and nodded as she emptied the books out of her backpack to reveal a long forgotten bag of yak cheese, bought at the same time as the Lepcha medicine. 'Very good on long marches,' the Tibetan told her. 'Enough to get to my village from here.'

'Your village? Is that why you stayed behind with us?'

'We couldn't leave you, Miss,' replied one of the Lepchas, 'and anyway those men were not wanting us.'

'I guess not,' she said. 'You're not really their types.' Along with the cheese, Claire had uncovered a forgotten disposable camera given to her by one of the secretaries at the office. Her only remaining camera, she realised, amazed that she'd carried such a primitive device all the way from Kalimpong. She returned to her tent with nothing better to offer Ben in the way of breakfast than yak cheese.

He was waiting for her impatiently, sitting on a rock outside the tent. 'I've cut my hair,' he said. 'How do I look?'

He looked like death. His steel grey hair was now cropped close to a head that was more of a skull and he had lost so much weight after the weeks of climbing and illness that he was almost unrecognisable. 'Um . . . like Paul Newman's shorter Jewish brother?'

'Newman *is* Jewish.'

'Oh well, then. Maybe he's shorter, for that matter.' She held up the bag of yak cheese. 'Hope you like square eggs.'

'What is it?'

'A real challenge. Even for a latent Buddhist like you.'

He bit into one of the orange cubes and winced in distaste. 'Know what a Jewish Buddhist says when faced with something like these? Oy! om Oy! om Oy! om.'

'You must be feeling better. Your appalling sense of humour has returned.'

'So where are Jack and the other porters?' Ben asked, valiantly attempting to chew the cheese into something more malleable.

'They're . . . um . . . gone.'

He swallowed with an effort. It took a long time. She imagined the cheese travelling down his gullet and through his guts in fits and starts to be excreted with its geometric shape virtually undiminished. 'Gone where?' he asked finally.

'I'm not really sure. Pemako or Arunachal Pradesh, the Lepchas think.'

'But what about Jack?'

'With them, I guess.'

'Under pressure?'

Trust Ben to give Jack the benefit of the doubt, Claire thought, and decided to leave him with his hopes intact for the moment. 'They didn't actually leave me a flowchart of their movements.' Briefly she ran through their situation (no guides, no maps – not even Christian's – no food), omitting her suspicions about Jack, and watched as Ben tried to summon up his old smile, even though his once peachy face was now as puckered as sun-dried fruit. She told him how little remained of their weeks of hard work, the cemetery of plant samples and specimens and seeds left behind, the erosion of their expedition. All she had were three exposed canisters of film from the gorge, along with her notes.

'Let's talk to the Lepchas,' he said.

'The Lepcha porters don't know this area any better than we do. There is one man – you know him, the Tibetan from Kalimpong monastery, who claims to have been born in a village not far from here. But . . .'

'But what? He sounds ideal.'

'He sounds it, but . . . he left Tibet twenty-two years ago, as a sixteen-year-old. Plus, he couldn't point out this village of his on Christian's map.'

Ben stared bleakly at the remaining yak cheese in his hand. 'Still, he sounds our best bet.'

'Our only bet, you mean.'

They set off for the Tibetan's village two hours later, Ben leaning heavily on one of the biggest porters. His still swollen ankle forced him to swap his boots for the man's worn sneakers and from Claire's viewpoint their progress looked like a three-legged race for cripples.

Most of the provisions were used up by the next day, with the exception of yak cheese and the Tibetan barley staple known as *tsampa*. The effort it took Ben to walk drained all his energy for conversation, and he fell asleep as soon as they stopped each night. Claire suspected him of being halfway to another incarnation. What kept her going was the thought of this dreamlike place called the Forest of Air, the mythical home of their green poppy. She pictured it in Cinemascope or early black and white, filled with men who talked like Ronald Colman and lots of those old-time actors – Alec Guinness, Yul Brynner – with their skin painted bronze, not looking even remotely Tibetan. Sometimes during their long marches through dust and rocks and snow she would start to hallucinate Arun walking next to her, bringing her grace and strength as he had done earlier, and in those hours when the past seemed too close, she would focus her attention on the Tibetan porter, a man who was certainly strange enough to serve as their guide from this world into the next.

It took them five days to reach the Tibetan's old home, where any remaining hopes that Claire had had of finding Arun's Forest of Air were shattered. This treeless valley with its village of mud and turf and wind would not serve even the relentlessly optimistic Ben as a model for paradise. Claire watched as people more ragged and grey-brown than the land around them scuttled across the river, paddling circular coracles of skin and

366

waving their arms in greeting. The gesticulating passengers resembled the legs on upturned beetles.

'You mentioned a doctor for Ben?' Claire asked their Kalimpong guide, when he had settled their packs inside a dark and smelly wooden guesthouse – one of the few wooden buildings, the largest in the village, nevertheless. 'A good sign', as Ben pointed out to her.

'Already you have met him, Miss. My father. He will shortly be coming to take your friend to our hospital.'

Claire realised that he was talking about the bald shaman or monk from the beetle coracles. Almost overwhelmed by a tide of fatigue the same shade as her surroundings, she held herself together by summoning up her rage against Jack. The thought of his desertion stiffened her resolve to do more than just survive. She would keep Ben alive and she would get back to London as a witness. What was that romantic line Ben used to hand out? From one of his antique Indians: *No need to go outside your house to see the flowers, my friend. Do not bother with such an excursion.* Inner resources, she thought, that's what you've got. Mine those North Sea reserves, those sticky black deposits of hope.

'Who's that mystic poet guy you're always quoting?' she asked Ben, now ensconced in the scrubbed little room that served as a hospital. 'When you're not telling me I'm halfway to the next world, that is.'

'Misquoting, probably,' he said, with a tired smile. 'Get some rest, Claire. I don't think these hospital facilities could cope with another patient.'

Her walk back to the guesthouse proved that the village wasn't all mud. There were thriving vegetable gardens, a bakery producing barley bread and luridly iced cakes, a small but flourishing orchard of apricots and walnuts where she was offered a handful of the wizened products as a gift by the shy man who had grown them. Grateful for any change to the eternal diet of yak cheese, Claire sat down in the sun outside the guesthouse to eat. She considered lighting a fire with her personal cadastral survey as a gesture of penance at failing to feel sufficient gratitude for being so warmly welcomed here. She mocked her wasted time, all the nights in her tent spent sticking pages together. On her worst days' marches she had imagined that if she died, someone might find it, 'and know that I existed, that I, Claire Fleetwood, passed this way and left a record'. The futility of this impulse to transcend anonymity did not prevent the methodical listmaker in her from wanting to add a few more details, and the Tibetan porter found her still writing half an hour later. 'You seem sad, Miss.'

'Not sad. Not really. I'm very tired. It's probably the altitude.'

'This is always a problem for people who are not used to climbing so high.' He sat down and examined her accordion survey with interest. 'This is a holy book?'

She laughed, 'Holy! No, no, although for all the work I've done, it should be.'

'It is very like our holy books, which are folded like this. You would like to see them, Miss?'

Ben was sleeping, the whole village seemed to be joyfully preparing for this evening's celebratory feast to welcome home their returned son (Claire wondered what culinary highlights were left to hit with the combination of *tsampa*, yak cheese and dried fruit); what did she have to lose? 'Sure, why not?'

'Since the Chinese came and burnt the town and the monastery, the monks are living in a cave higher up valley. This is where they are hiding our holy books. It is a little climb – that is all right for you with your fear of heights?'

'Fine.' There wasn't much further to fall, so far as she could see.

On the way out of the village they passed the burnt-out shells of wooden buildings and the remains of a ruined monastery where Claire's guide had studied before going to Lhasa, the path to it still marked with the ragged remains of prayer flags on thirty-foot bamboo poles. Two village dogs veered off from where they had been playing in the wreckage of the monastery and followed Claire, one of them nipping at her heels in a friendly fashion as if to keep her close to the Tibetan, who, while not seeming to walk fast, had a long regular stride that covered the ground with great speed. The path's incline got steeper with the narrowing valley, forcing them into single file, and the distance between them widened. Claire wanted to ask him to slow down, but still couldn't pronounce his lengthy name. The dogs, padding along in his wake, turned back and barked, drawing his attention so that he stopped to wait for her. 'Excuse me,' she said, 'but is there a short form of your name?'

He said it very quickly and like the name of his village, this valley, all the words in the strange dialect his people used, it ran past her like water before she could catch it. She thought she'd missed it in the gunshot sounds of the multicoloured silk prayer flags that had billowed and cracked all along the last winding mile. 'Could you repeat that?' Once again the sounds – all vowels they seemed, like Italian – bubbled away. The man started to laugh at her attempts. 'I'm sorry,' Claire said, laughing too, 'but it's a very slippery sort of name.'

'Slippery?'

'Like a fish – hard to catch.'

He nodded, pleased with the image. 'My name means something like rivers, Miss. The name of my village is the same, what we call the meeting of the three rivers or tributaries, which are not far from here.'

'Rivers? How funny. I have – *had* – a close friend called Rivers.' She hesitated, 'Would you mind if I called you Mr Rivers?'

'That is what most people called me and my cousin in Kalimpong. Those who could not pronounce our tribal name.'

'You have a cousin in Kalimpong?'

'A very distant cousin, yes. That is why I went there after escaping from the Chinese in Lhasa.' He turned and started walking again, the narrow path preventing more questions.

# 15

IF NOT FOR the rough, unfinished stone over her head and the mountain's cool mineral breath blown in from natural fissures and orifices in the rock walls, Claire would have found it hard to remember that she was in a cave. Every surface inside the monastery was painted with clouds, conch shells, gods, devils and dragons, a mosaic of all that the artists could imagine in this life and the one to come, and rows of niches built into the walls sheltered a selection of metal buddhas who reposed on silk cushions, some half lifesize, some no bigger than mice, their beatific expressions in contrast to the array of demon masks scowling down from above. The monk who had greeted Claire at the entrance led the way in an unhurried fashion towards the library, seemingly unsurprised by the visit, although Mr Rivers whispered to her that he had not been informed of their arrival in the valley. 'He has been expecting us, he says.'

'How?'

'The priests here know such things,' Rivers answered her, accepting such contradictions as easily as he did the idea of a fat bald man being able to float crosslegged on a celestial lotus blossom.

The library consisted of row upon row upon row of deep, open cubicles, each holding a single parcel wrapped in orange or yellow cloth, and from one of these bright parcels the monk extracted a neatly stitched leather bag. 'Very old map of our valley,' said Rivers, removing the bag to reveal a narrow book, its pages bound between thin lathes of wood small enough to fit across the length of Claire's hand. She unfolded it to discover a continuous black and white line drawing of mountain silhouettes, with notes written in an immaculate but inscrutable script. After a few minutes of opening and closing the pages as if she could squeeze music from their accordion pleats, she handed the book back to Rivers, who showed her that the pages were folded from a single piece of paper, 'once wound round a prayer wheel'.

'Very interesting,' she said flatly, failing to keep the cold and hunger out of her voice. She felt like a tourist stumbling through someone else's marvels. Follow the wrong branch of your family tree for long enough, Claire told herself, and you're bound to wind up out here on a limb with nowhere to go.

'Yes, very interesting.' Rivers nodded, taking her at her word. 'This is how spies for British people were once hiding their maps and geographical notations, disguised in Buddhist prayers.'

'I've read about that.'

He placed his finger on a nest of calligraphic squiggles under one of the mountain silhouettes. 'This I think is the map of a journey.' Running his forefinger along the tops of the peaks. 'This is our country, our mountains.' His finger stopped. 'Here is Mount Namjagbarwa, the citadel, which you see from this monastery on a clear day.' He moved his finger to the left. 'Here is Gyala Peri, in its nest of icebergs. Here are the lost falls of the Tsangpo.'

'Which don't exist,' Claire thought, his words rolling over her as if they were spoken in a language not her own: 'enlightenment . . . mountain range . . . Aruna, charioteer of the sun god Surya . . . orchids . . . forest of air . . .'

'Excuse me – did you say the forest of air?'

His finger stopped. 'Yes, here: our valley. A name for the old forest.'

'But there is no forest here.' She was helpless in the face of such illogic. 'Is that the reason for its name? Because the forest is imaginary?'

'No. Once this valley was filled with first-growth forest. When the Chinese invaded Tibet in 1955 they were logging the whole valley, cutting down all our trees. What was left went for firewood. People now have started to replant fruit trees. But you cannot replant such trees as we had, not in our lifetime.'

'Why was it called the forest of air?'

'Because of the orchids which were living in the forest here years ago. They lived on air, on sunlight.'

'No green poppies?'

'We have stories about these poppies, yes, but they have never been seen here, not in my lifetime or my father's.'

'But you must have heard us talking about the forest of air and the green poppy. Why did you never mention these stories of yours to one of my party?'

Mr Rivers shrugged. 'No one asked me.'

Kintup could have said the same thing. Claire touched the tiny map. 'Where did this book come from?'

Her guide turned to question the old monk, who was watching their exchange with interest. 'He says that this book is actually made here many years ago.'

'Ask him who made it.'

Again she had to wait while Rivers and the monk conversed slowly in their own language. Even her guide seemed puzzled. 'I am sorry, but he uses an old dialect, which is after so long somewhat foreign to me. I believe he is saying that this book itself was –' He opened it out and tapped the cover, searching for a word.

'Bound? The cover, the pages put together?'

'Yes, the book was bound here by the monks. Pages are from another place.' He turned to the monk again. 'Yes, from a frozen man they found.'

'A *frozen* man?'

'Sorry, he meant from a man who they believe froze to death,' he corrected. 'Many years ago. So many, even this monk, who is very old, cannot tell, although he has visited the place, which lies not far from a narrow pass leading into this valley from the south, near where the three rivers meet. The story is that the frozen man was a spy, because although he was dressed in the clothes of a pilgrim, with a prayer wheel and a rosary, his rosary had only one hundred beads, not one hundred and eight. This wheel and rosary the monks brought back, and inside the prayer wheel they found this map.'

She was aware of a pulse beating hard in her temple, a little red worm of nervous excitement.

'The monk insists they took his things only to preserve them against bandits and thieves,' Rivers said quickly, looking concerned.

'Is he still here? The bones, I mean? Have they kept the skeleton?'

'To have a dead body in a holy place like this would be a desecration. And they would not disturb his bones.' The monk was muttering something.

'What's he saying?'

'He says that he does not know if the body is there or not, but it is on a very lonely, isolated track where foresters used to go many years ago, when there were still big trees there. There is a cave near the skeleton. But I'm sure –'

'Take me there!' said Claire. 'Or tell me how to get there.' How could she explain this sense of urgency that was driving away her earlier fatigue? The implication of Rivers' words was impossible, a teratology, the one big story containing within it elements of all the others.

'You will not like it,' he said. 'This place is very steep and much higher.'

'Is there time to get there and back before dark?'

Rivers's graven eyes examined hers intently for signs of morbid interests. 'Yes,' he responded slowly, drawing the word out like a tenuous silk thread that might snap if she pressed too hard. 'I think so.'

'Please, Mr Rivers. Can you – *will* you take me there?'

They climbed into a desert winter. A scouring sandy wind clutched at them with persistent fingers all the way up the river path, rattling the stripped bushes, driving eddies of grit into their faces. As they gained altitude, the path gradually narrowed to a faint animal track and wound between enormous boulders of rock and ice that had been rasped by the prevailing winds into pyramids and monolithic obelisks. A vast Zen garden of raked granite and dry stone streams, it was a place Claire could not imagine ever held trees, until Mr Rivers pointed out the stumpy silver discs pressed into the ground like reflected moons, all that remained of their felled trunks. 'It's funny . . .' she began, 'I have this strange feeling that a distant relative of mine might have been here.'

'That would explain why the monk knew you,' Rivers said blandly.

Claire smiled at the way he included her eccentric beliefs within the realms of his own. 'Her name was Magda Fleetwood. At least, that was her maiden name.'

'Oh yes, a most distinguished woman who set up the Ironstone Settlements.' Mr Rivers nodded sagely. 'Honoured to make your acquaintance.'

'You know of her? I wish . . . I wish I could be sure if she came this way . . .'

'So you must talk to her old guide when you get back. My cousin,' he continued, oblivious to Claire's intake of breath, 'who before he retired was gardener at the Ironstone Settlements, where I too was working for a while.'

'Her *guide*? No, that's not possible . . . Because he – of course he –' She stumbled over the words, '*Surely* anyone who guided Magda is long since dead?'

'No, Miss. Mrs Ironstone's last trip is in 1920, with my cousin who was a young man of twenty-one. Naturally my cousin is a very old man now, but still living – on the Darjeeling side of the hill crowded by the Ironstone Horticultural Settlements. They call his house Magda's Hope.' A chuckle. 'Because always they hope it will one day produce good tea.'

'Can you stop a minute?' Claire asked, 'I want to find something.' She fumbled in her pack. Of course it was still there. All the random things remained. She showed Gompu's matchbox to the Tibetan. 'That name – is it your cousin's?'

He glanced at it briefly. 'Yes, Madam. My cousin and this valley. We are all called by the same name here.'

'And this?' Her journal flapped in the wind as she opened it to the page where she had taped the fragment of blue poppy from the Botanic Gardens.

The Tibetan ran his finger uncertainly along the looping sinuous script. 'Second word, I think so, yes – although it is very strangely written. But this is very old script. First word means Aruncala, the sacred tawny mountain.'

*Aruncala.* Arun Rivers. Claire felt light-headed. It's the altitude, she thought, and then: to come all this way, to have everything come down to this accidental meeting in a muddy valley on a muddy, muddled tributary. She had been playing chess with her imagined Magda and Arun and Joseph, moving them from black square to white and back again. Now the power balance had reversed and the old story was taking over.

'You must ask my cousin to perform on his bagpipes when you meet,' said Rivers with the conviction of someone who knew such a meeting was inevitable. 'But not Auld Lang Syne. He hates that.'

If they hadn't been told exactly where to find the skeleton, they could have walked past a hundred times without seeing him. He was pressed into a shallow impression between a triangular rock and the mountain face where he had waited, Claire saw, in the position all people suffering from cold are told to adopt, as if for imminent rebirth (or burial), his legs pulled up against his body, his arms wrapped round his chest to gain as much warmth as possible. Although this foetal crouch had gradually collapsed as his skin and clothing fell apart, the narrow V of rock into which he had closely wedged himself had preserved his position remarkably well. Claire knelt and touched the delicate tracery of his hand and then his leg, noticing as she did that he was missing three toes on his left foot. Standing, she tried to think what the site reminded her of, the pyramid-shaped rocks blasted by sand and wind to the bleak tan of an Egyptian landscape. The burial place of a pharaoh, she decided, or a martyred saint.

She turned to Rivers. 'There's something I have to do. It won't take long.'

'You will not desecrate his bones?' Clearly he found her behaviour disturbing.

'I won't touch him. I want to . . . I want to say a sort of prayer for him.'

He nodded, still unsure of her, then turned and pointed back down the trail. 'If you don't mind, I will go a little way downhill where the wind is not so hard.'

'How will I find you?'

'There is a natural geyser there, behind more rocks shaped like these.' He nodded at the sand-coloured rocks sheltering the skeleton. 'You will find me by looking for the volcano of mist swirling up from the geyser.'

When he had disappeared, Claire removed the little disposable camera with its meagre twenty-four shots, nowhere near enough to make the kind of catalogue she would need, and began to work, paying special attention to the skeletal left foot with its missing toes. She tried to be methodical, to keep excitement from clouding her judgement, but these were the first bones since Sally's that made her want to cry.

There was nothing to indicate this man's race was Indian or European. He wore no rings or crucifix, carried no pocket watch or coins. An anonymous pilgrim, his robes long since rotted away in the years of frost and spring thaw, on whom, Rivers's monk had insisted, no surveying equipment other than the false rosary and the prayer wheel with its hidden map had been found. Worried that the quality of the film she was using would be woefully inadequate, she knelt again, hesitating for only a moment, and then carefully removed a fragment of toebone from the damaged foot and put it in her pocket. A relic from a martyr's shrine.

It was in leaning to remove the piece of bone that she caught sight of something under the skeleton's left hip, a small object the size of a matchbox. She worked her hand under the bones and removed a little box, rusted shut, that rattled slightly as she dropped it in her pocket with the bone, as if it were filled with tiny ball bearings. Or seeds. With the sensation of having found her way to a familiar place, the way you do in a foreign country on unexpectedly meeting someone you know from home, she thought of Nick's words: whatever you go looking for in the East you will find, and what you find is a reflection of yourself.

# 16

EVEN HIS WEAKENED condition couldn't stop Ben staying late at the welcome home party for Mr Rivers that night. 'I wish I had your energy,' Claire said. She wrapped her friend up in blankets and propped him on a bench next to the fire.

He smiled at her. 'I didn't go on a pilgrimage today.'

Ben's trusting, tired smile made Claire feel slightly guilty. For reasons that she hadn't clarified yet even to herself, she had told him about the monastery and nothing more. She'd kept secret the skeleton and the forest of air and the seeds, swearing Mr Rivers to silence as well. 'Until Ben is feeling better,' she offered, a weak excuse that the Tibetan didn't question. As she left the party to walk back through the deserted village, she heard Ben happily confiding in Rivers, 'Great shindig! Reminds me of my bar mitzvah.'

A faint triangle of moonlight from the open door to the guesthouse gave Claire the illusion that she could find her way to her bed without a torch, and she was starting the long process of exchanging several layers of dirty clothes for others that were marginally less dirty (or worn less recently, at least) before the cigarette smoke filtered through all the other smells in the house's pungent interior. '*Jack!*'

'You didn't think I'd leave without saying goodbye, did you?' Her cousin's voice came from the direction of the dark shape that she knew to be Ben's bed.

She switched on her torch and let its beam play over the room. A foot from where she stood was her cousin's backpack. Beyond it, Jack himself lay shivering on Ben's bed, swaddled closely in a sleeping bag. 'You don't look good, Jack. Yellow, like an unwrapped mummy.'

He held up a plastic vial of tablets, almost empty. 'I've been taking something for the last few days to kill the hunger, just as great grandfather's workers used to at the bonemeal factory. Useful stuff, morphine.'

She could see how jumpy he was. 'I figure you're alone, Jack, or I'd have spotted your friends in the vicinity. How did you find us?'

'By following your footprints.'

'When did you get here?' Jack must have arrived after dark, Claire thought, or someone would have remarked on his presence.

'Depends what you mean by *here*.' He drew deeply on his cigarette and coughed. 'Damn! I'm almost out of fags.'

'Why did you come back?' She was pretty sure why he'd left. 'How *could* you leave us like –' She bit off the words, furious at the way her voice revealed her feelings. How could he, when he'd held her like that after her nightmare? She answered her own question: betrayal. He'd admitted his capacity for it days ago.

'Not so much of a hero any more?' The bitter laugh that followed his comment broke into another cough, a long wrenching sound that hurt to hear. 'You've done all right. I knew you would.'

'No thanks to you, you *shit*! We had no food, no –'

'It was time you tried out the delights of *tsampa*.' He retched and spat on the floor. 'Anyway, my charming business associates didn't leave me a lot of choice.'

'What was it, Jack? Drugs? The heroin your pals had been making in Calcutta?'

There was a little silence before he spoke. 'You found out about that, did you?' He sounded almost admiring. 'The heroin production was nothing to do with me, of course. All their own clever work. But I made a few other promises I couldn't keep. Chris wasn't the only one with high hopes of finding this bloody poppy!'

'Don't tell me that Opium Quintet of yours was interested in a cancer cure!'

'What did you call them?' He laughed and coughed again. 'The Opium Quintet? I like it. But you do them an injustice. They *were* interested in a cancer cure – as long as it promised them more profits than heroin. And they were even more interested in the idea of an opium poppy that could be grown at unusually high altitudes, as my research suggested this one might be, a poppy they would be able to grow in isolated mountain regions away from prying eyes. Trouble was, they never quite got it into their heads that there would be no "money up front", that there *could* be no question of money at all, in fact, until the poppy was actually located and the theories proved using alkaloids extracted from the real plant.'

Claire wondered why he was telling her all this. What had he to gain? 'So the orchids they stole along the way no longer satisfied them?'

Jack made a noncommittal sound and let his eyes stray around the room. 'Nice to see they've put you up in the best place in town. Not much of a paradise, though, is it?' She watched him take in the guesthouse's long ceiling beams carved with dragons and clouds, the massive supporting posts, still showing faded traces of what must once have been brightly painted patterns. 'Odd, these wooden beams, considering this valley is virtually treeless. Quite a few of the older houses have them, the ones that weren't burnt. Did you see those dug-out canoes behind what's left of the monastery? Forty feet long, from single logs.'

'Maybe they aren't canoes.' Before the words of denial were out she started to worry about what a man like Jack could do to this place if he made the same connections she had done. She could see what would happen, the Chinese reclaiming this valley they had abandoned, the monks exiled again, the villagers and their orchards uprooted, the earth combed and sieved for seeds. Either the Chinese or other profitmongers moving in, men with the pretext of benefiting humanity, and meanwhile money and aid going to everyone except the ones who needed it the most.

'Of course they are canoes,' said Jack in a knowing way. 'You can still see where the oars rubbed on the wood. Funny, given that these people are now reduced to leather coracles.'

'There's nothing here, no plants, just mud,' Claire could hear the tension in her own voice. Why had she mentioned plants? 'No drugs. Nothing *you'd* want.'

'There must have been a forest of big trees near here at some point,' Jack mused, ignoring her protests. 'Maybe still is.' He stubbed his cigarette out, tapping a beat, and quoted, '*Forests ancient as the hills . . .*'

It was Jack who had first told her about the green poppies in the forest of air. She had to stop him putting the pieces together, at least for the moment, until she had time to think, consider. Dropping her gaze to the pile of heavy clothes Jack had left on the floor next to his backpack – the old jacket of his father's, the Indian waistcoat he'd worn that night they'd danced together; *danced* together, she reminded herself, with her chest hard against his, feeling what might have been . . . A month ago she would never have contemplated the next step. She wasn't a gambler, a chancer. Not like Jack. A month ago she had nothing to protect, she was a different person, softer, less desperate . . .

She shone her torch directly into his eyes, kept it there until he put up his hand to protest that she was blinding him, then switched it off, knocked it deliberately against the floor and said, 'Damn! I've dropped the flashlight!' In the dark, her fumbling search through his backpack seemed to take forever. Maybe it wasn't there after all. Wouldn't the Opium Quintet have confiscated such a useful tool? Or was that how Jack got away?

When she switched the torch on again she was pointing the gun at her cousin. She felt slightly ridiculous, not even certain if it was loaded. What would she do if Jack called her bluff? But it was the only diversion she could think of. 'Very fetching,' Jack's teasing voice made it clear he thought she was joking, 'although you make an unlikely armed avenger. A little too petite for the role, I'm afraid. And what exactly is this in aid of? Because you think I abandoned you? I had no choice. I was the insurance for my associates. As soon as possible I slipped away.' He sat up and swung his legs over the bed. Given that he was still wrapped in Ben's sleeping bag, the effect was comical rather than threatening. 'Come on, Claire! Put the gun down.'

'I'd like to clear a few things up first.'

He raised his hands, palms up, a mock gesture of honesty, while trying to disentangle himself from the sleeping bag that had wrapped itself even more tightly around his legs in his first sudden movement. 'Tell me about your chlorophyll experiments, Jack, the ones that didn't work out, the ones you managed to cover up with the help of your friendly chemists.' That would do for a start, keep him busy while she thought of an alternative to this stupid gun. She was pleased that her voice was steady, unlike her legs.

It was so clearly not what he was expecting her to ask. The carefully constructed facade of assurance slipped off his face, peeled off like old wallpaper. Slowly he reapplied his confident mask. 'You don't need to play at judge and jury, Claire. Ben will be grilling me later. Why not leave it to him?'

He hadn't mentioned Nick and Christian. Had he made sure already that they weren't here in the village or did he know that they wouldn't be coming? 'Ben can have his turn later. I'm waiting, Jack.'

She saw him searching his brain for a plausible lie. 'This is silly, Claire. You're not going to shoot me.'

'Maybe not. Then again, in my fear at discovering a strange man in my room, the gun might go off accidentally and hit you in the kneecaps. Or the balls.'

Jack tried to stand up. The twisted sleeping bag caught him round the ankles and unbalanced him so that he was forced to sit down again abruptly. 'Bugger!' He kicked savagely at the bag.

Claire released the safety catch on the gun. At the almost inaudible click it made, her cousin stopped dead. 'Start with the bit about how chlorophyll's photodestructive tendencies made your test cases' ears fall off.' She expected him to laugh, but even in the flat light from the torch she could see the lines around his mouth and eyes deepen until they might have been carved by a scalpel.

'Who told you about that?'

'Never mind who told me.'

'Let me see, it was six or seven years ago, I think, shortly after I came across the green poppy documents.' Jack spoke slowly, his eyes never leaving the gun. 'I started investigating the photodestructive habits of chlorophyll as a possible cancer treatment.' His eyes strayed briefly to Claire's face. 'I suppose you know that the antioxidants in green vegetables are there to protect against any lethal free radical cascades initiated by chlorophyll?'

She tried to shrug that one off in a knowing sort of way, long past the point where he could divert her with his encyclopedic knowledge.

'Anyway,' he continued, 'my idea was to load a tumour with one of these photosensitisers, then zap it with laser light and stimulate a burst of free radicals that killed the cancerous cells. After Christian came on board, he put a lot of effort into designing chlorophyll-like molecules that could be targeted to tumours, accumulate there and very efficiently absorb laser wavelengths to produce maximal cell destruction.'

All this overload of technical information was doing something similar to her. 'Get to the point, Jack!'

He tried on one of his rueful smiles, a little ragged round the edges, like a shirt with cuffs worn thin from overuse. Her cousin had charm when he needed it, Claire thought. Conmen, salesmen, actors had to be charming. 'It's not very interesting,' he said, 'a sordid little tale. You see, we weren't getting anywhere close to the results the Fleetwood files claimed that Tibetans and Bhutias had achieved with their highly primitive methods. And the tribal shamans had always stressed that they used the poppy's extracts to treat "the whole person", so I kept trying different angles – perfumes, skincreams, food. I started extracting leaf juices from high-chlorophyll plants, separating the protein fraction and turning it into edible products, and I found that leaf protein is always green because chlorophyll sticks to it. That didn't worry me until I began working with two chemists in Calcutta, doing feeding trials with rats.'

He paused and patted his hand on the pocket of his shirt. 'I really need a cigarette. You couldn't roll me one, could you?' Her look answered his question. 'I guess not . . . Anyway, my great sin was . . . I didn't go slowly enough . . . I was impatient to achieve something before Christian did . . . I didn't wait to find out what happened to the rats . . .' The confession, jerking out of him, came to an obstruction and stopped. 'Don't you *see*, Claire? I'm forty-four years old – forty-one at the time . . . I was looking for a way *out*!' His voice cracked and he had to start again. 'I was looking for a way out of all the pettiness in my life, the stink of other people's bodies, the creams to smooth rich old women's vanity.'

She knew he was trying to close that distance between them he had once been at such pains to maintain, willing her to understand his point of view (*we're alike, we're cousins, I've been part of you, inside you*). 'Don't expect me to feel sorry for you, Jack.'

Her cousin dropped his eyes and his face turned a dull shade of red. 'I went ahead and ran a few illicit tests on people. Then one day . . . Then one day,' he resumed woodenly, 'I noticed that the rats had started to develop horrible skin lesions. The chlorophyll derivatives were accumulating in the skin and photosensitising the creatures. Lab rats are albinos so they have particular problems with this.'

Claire thought about the point in developing photographs where you realise that the picture has been overexposed and positive becomes negative. 'And it turned out that people are prone to the same problems the rats had,' she finished, sure that she had to put it as if all she needed was confirmation. Claire's voice was flat calm, but it was a false calm; she was only just holding on. Confirmation of her worst suspicions about her cousin was the last thing she wanted.

384

And suddenly it wasn't the gun forcing Jack to speak. The gun was a toy. The gun was a block of wood, a finger cocked. Like a cheating husband desperate to confess his infidelities to his wife, Jack *needed* to confess. He'd come back for absolution. '*Some* people – those with very fair skin. If they eat this high-chlorophyll diet, exposure to sunlight can result in skin cancer. In men with short hair, even the dark-skinned ones I worked with, it affects the tops of their ears, the parts of the body most exposed to sunlight. And tissue destruction can actually separate the ear from the head.'

'Their ears fall off!' *That's* what the chemist's kid had meant! 'Nick didn't believe me when I told him. He thought I was crazy, vindictive –'

'Nick? You told Nick?' His blade of a face sharpened from resignation to wariness, no longer quite so much like the lovable but seedy uncle caught in a minor misdemeanour.

Claire, who had been relaxing her hold on the gun, raised her arm to its former horizontal position. Had she made a mistake telling Jack how much she knew? 'That's not the end of your sordid tale, is it? Where did it go from there? The two chemists decided to blackmail you?'

Tentatively Jack moved his feet, still trapped by the sleeping bag. 'Not exactly. But I couldn't tell Christian about my problems with the leaf protein experiments or he'd have fired me immediately, and it was difficult to cover up what had happened.' He coughed again. 'So . . . I agreed to pay off the poor bastards who were stuck with no ears, and in return for a reward, my two chemist friends took the blame, said it was an accident, they had mixed up the lab tests, the people with the ear problems already had cancer when they came to UNI-SENS. The trouble was that the circle of people who knew about the mess kept widening. I simply didn't have enough money to pay them all off.' He pressed his fingers into his forehead. His hands were shaking. 'I tried to borrow from my bitch of an aunt –'

'That's why you quarrelled with Alex?'

'I hoped the green poppy discovery might get me out

of the muck, but in the meantime I needed some ready money.'

'If you admitted to UNISENS what you'd done, the cancer victims could've got recompense –'

'No. UNISENS has a liability limitation clause that all their employees and test cases have to sign. The victims could've sued me, but not the company, and I would've gone to jail, in which case there would've been no money for anyone.'

'So instead you agreed to shift a little heroin under cover of UNISENS.'

He tried to smile and failed. 'I prefer to see it as giving the independence movement in Arunachal Pradesh a financial leg-up. Helping out the local economy. A few packages here, a few packages there.'

'So Derek Rivers passed on a few bits and pieces for you?' It was another wild guess, one of the many theories she had been considering in the days since Jack had abandoned them. A *hypothesis*, Claire thought. But Jack lowered his head and spoke to the floor with a baldness that stripped away all his charm. 'I had to find someone quickly. Drug-pushing isn't exactly my field of expertise, whatever you may think. I knew through Nick and Sally about some of her father's less savoury contacts.'

'Tell me about Sally. That's why Derek beat her up, isn't it? He'd got her involved in the drugs somehow and that's what got her killed.'

Jack's eyes came up and he stared at her, genuinely shocked. '*No*! Not at all! At least . . . Listen, Claire, you've got it all wrong. It was . . . a stupid mistake.'

'A *mistake*!'

'I'm sorry, I don't mean that the way it sounds. I mean the beatings . . . Sally was a sweet girl. I wouldn't have done . . . I got to know her through Alex – they'd always been close. For a while Sally even acted as a kind of go-between for me with Alex. I was looking into the background to Magda's ridiculous will and found out some things about a connection between the

Ironstones and the Rivers. I said as much to Sally. She was foolish enough to tell her mother, I guess, and Derek got on to it. The bastard cornered me one day, had the wrong end of the stick entirely, thought there was money in the connection for him. That's as far as his limited imagination went. He told Sally to nose around your house for proof.'

'Did she . . . nose around?' Say no, Claire thought. Please say she didn't.

'At first she went along with it, but when she got to know you better she'd only pretend to look. She flatly refused to do more, even after Derek found out and started knocking her around. She came to me for help. I went immediately to Derek and told him it was all a mistake. That he had no legal right to Eden, there was no buried will, or whatever foolish idea he had dreamt up in his thick head. I tried to explain that his connection was to an Indian doctor who'd worked for Magda and –'

'An Indian doctor?' Claire tried to wipe the interest from her face.

'All Derek said was that he "wasn't related to no fuckin' Paki". So –'

'Why didn't you go to the other trustees, the solicitor? Because Derek would've ratted on your little drug transactions?'

'I . . . It was . . . complicated. But I don't think Derek had a hand in Sally's death. At least . . . he was a bastard, but he wouldn't have arranged his own daughter's murder.' Jack hurried on, his voice rough with emotion. 'No one was sorrier than I that Sally got . . . that she died.'

Claire had many more questions, but she was sure that if she pushed Jack to fill in the gaps in his story he would only begin to lie – if he hadn't already. What did he have to gain by telling the truth? In the end, everyone lies when they are up there in the witness box. For whatever reason, they stand up and swear – on the Bible, on the Koran, on their brother's grave. They say yes, that's the man, Number Three, yes, I'm *absolutely* sure he is entirely to blame.

And some tiny part of her still wanted to let her cousin off the hook.

'You were interested in the Indian doctor, the connection between Magda and the Rivers?' Jack asked, catching Claire off guard, dangling the one irresistible bit of bait.

# 17

IT WORRIED CLAIRE that Jack had regained all his composure. Gone was the raw, scraped sound in his voice and the shuttered eyes. 'Let's put the story together, shall we?' he said. 'We might begin in late April, 1888, when Magda and her husband set sail from Calcutta for England.'

She didn't need Jack to paint a picture. It was there already, lacking only a year to place it in her paper narrative – Exhibit 'O'. She could see the river in its old age, tall-masted ships jostling for space with the flotsam of sloops and steamers, sampans and ferries. And corpses, Claire recalled: five thousand corpses were thrown into the river one year, so Bengal's sanitary commissioner complained – fifteen hundred from the General Hospital in Calcutta alone. There would have been monkeys, as well, troops of them poised on the steps of the ghats like sightseers waving off the ship as it passed close by the King of Oudh's palaces, a river so still that the woman has a clear shot of the King's birdhouse, the palace of the chief queen, the peacocks, her pictures only a little fogged around the edges, maybe from the rising mist or the out-of-date photographic process. She is thinking about her husband, how long the serpentine root will continue to work. *Until death do us part. Death or consequences.*

'The ship passengers remembered Magda on the journey,' Jack continued, 'but Joseph was not to be seen on deck except once, when he appeared in a wheelchair pushed by his Indian doctor – "a tall man", one passenger reported to the police, with the copper skin of a Tibetan. Hypnotic eyes, said another. Handsome but suspicious, they found him. Reserved, "very haughty for a native".'

'What police?'

'The police investigating my grandfather's – Joseph's – disappearance.'

'Why would the police interview the ship's passengers so many months later?'

'Because they were still trying to trace the whereabouts of the Indian doctor, who vanished at the same time as his patient. I found the story years ago in old police files and newspaper reports of the period.'

The gun was heavy in her hand, drooping now. Suddenly she wanted to stop digging up the past, leave whatever was buried in its grave.

'The sea voyage seemed to have revived Joseph,' Jack said, keeping up the suspense, refusing to name names, 'for on arrival in London he once more took up photography, overruling his wife's protests that he should rest.' At Claire's own protests that he couldn't possibly know all this, Jack smiled. 'You have Magda's journals, I have Joseph's – not so wordy as hers. I found them in the cellar.' Jack willingly admitted that he had been looking for evidence to get his family house back. 'It's an ugly old place, but why should you have it? And your daughter and daughter's daughter? Not to mention all the other people living illegally at Eden who have managed to fool the trustees over the years. Did you know that in the end Alex left everything – all her money – to the Eden Trust?'

She watched him studying her grip on the gun, assessing her for chinks in the wall, weak places he could chip away at, and she managed to summon up a note of indifference: 'What's an Indian doctor got to do with anything?'

'Patience, Claire, patience. Years ago, Alex showed me the copious notes kept about their home life by Joseph's and Magda's London housekeeper, Mrs Byng. She recorded everything, including the weather (and its influence on the relative lightness of scones – she was a scientific woman for her class) and her employers' departures to and from their country home during 1888.' For a couple of months the family remained in London, Jack said, before moving to the small estate Luther

Ironstone had left his son in Suffolk. 'Mrs Byng makes several mentions of the Indian doctor. She notes her disapproval of his wife, "a dark-complexioned, under-educated woman" who was installed with her two children at the back of the house, in a cottage that would eventually become Number One Eden Dwellings. Here the family immediately set about establishing a vegetable garden to compete with Mrs Byng's beloved dahlias. The lushness of its produce the housekeeper put down to "filthy Hindoo practices", as she did the smells of garlic emanating from a kitchen that was "just what one would have expected from those dirty heathens, full of seeds and bits of bark and strange powders. *Rivers*, those Hindoos call themselves, and have not the grace to look chagrined by such an unjustified assumption of a good Christian name." ' Jack clearly enjoyed his mimicry of the bigoted housekeeper.

*My Dad has always lived at Number One.* That's what Sally had said.

'Nick and his grandfather are also related to Dr Rivers in some convoluted way,' Jack said. 'The Indian doctor was very prolific, unlike my family.'

From the first of August to November the Ironstones and their Indian doctor spent about one week a month in the city, the rest of the time in Suffolk. Claire heard the pattern forming long before Jack. 'No reason is given for the visits,' her cousin mused. 'I suspect Joseph had to stock up on more morphine – he was almost certainly an addict by this time, if he carried on in the style he had begun in his first year in Calcutta, when his diary entries were still more or less coherent.'

'They weren't later?'

'Crazy as Nijinsky's. Joseph, poor soul, suspected the Indian doctor of trying to poison him. In fact, Rivers was treating him with serpentine root, a perfectly acceptable medicine for manic depression and –'

'Divided souls.' Claire, repeating a phrase from Magda's diaries, wondered if this was all a person's life came down to, this odd collection of prescriptions and postcards and servants' gossip. Exhibit P: *One day he asked Arun for a more permanent cure than this serpentine root he was taking and my friend, saying nothing, simply laid the tin of poppy seeds in Joseph's hand.* That's what Magda had written. *Poor Joseph. He wanted a cure for what he was.* 'But the Indian doctor couldn't cure him?'

'Joseph's diary, combined with the photos he took, shows an increasingly alienated mind. An unsavoury collection, those pictures. I found some of them at the botanic library in Calcutta.'

'Part of the Ironstone Bequest. Interesting what was missing from it.'

Jack resumed as if her comment meant nothing to him: 'The Ironstones were in town for Bank Holiday Monday on the sixth of August. Joseph remained in the darkroom he had built in the cellar while Magda took Con and Alex and Mrs Byng by coach to Alexandra Palace, where they stood in the persistent drizzle ("characteristic of this gloomy summer", wrote Mrs Byng) and watched an intrepid Professor Baldwin ascend in his balloon to a thousand feet before finally parachuting to earth. "The family left for their country home early the next morning, too early to read the newspaper reports compiled that day, the seventh of August." '

'Newspaper reports?' asked Claire.

'Your father never showed them to you? I'm surprised. Maybe he had given up on his crazy theory by your time.'

'What theory?'

'I remember him working out all the dates, trying to establish which one was to blame – Joseph or his Indian doctor.'

'What dates? Responsible for what?' Her cousin was enjoying keeping her in the dark, being the one in control again, despite the gun. He was teasing her with his withheld power to inflict pain, the way he had with his cigarette on the leeches.

'Your father was always proud of that file of clippings he had. I think they were collected by the stout Mrs Byng herself. His theory was possible, of course, but no more so than a hundred theories that have baffled the police since 1888.'

1888: *Jack's year, Jack of all trades, especially murder.* She felt that all of her time at Eden had been spent trying to put these

392

pieces of bone together. *Jack's Back!* Newsprint swimming before her eyes, details lost, Claire had the salient words imprinted on her mind: WHITECHAPEL HORROR. Martha, Polly and Dark Annie, Long Liz and Catherine and (the bloodiest of all) Marie. She asked her cousin to repeat the dates of the Ironstones' visits to London – the first of August to the eighth, the thirtieth of August to the tenth of September, the twenty-eighth of September to the second of October, the thirty-first of October to the end of December – matching them up with the old childish mantra of Ripper victims and dates:

*7 August: Martha*
*31 August and 8 September: Polly and Dark Annie*
*30 Sept: Long Liz and Catherine*
*9 November: Marie*

'I'll let you in on the family secret about Magda and her husband,' Jack said. 'One that particularly concerns their relationship with her handsome, mesmerising Indian doctor . . . Dr Rivers, who had relatives in Kalimpong – where Magda went in the spring of 1889 to set up an orphanage for mixed race infants, one of them a William – Billy – Fleetwood, no more than a couple of months old.' He paused. 'Your grandfather. Officially, a distant relative of Magda's.'

'And?'

'Magda was an only child. Her father's sister had died years earlier. There were no other Fleetwoods, distant or otherwise.'

'Maybe he was a foundling,' Claire said quickly, trying to evade Jack's conclusion. 'She wouldn't have called him Fleetwood if he was hers . . .'

'Perhaps not.'

'If it's true, if what you are suggesting is true, why wouldn't Dr Rivers have claimed William?'

'Perhaps he didn't know, perhaps there was a good reason Magda didn't want her offspring raised by Rivers, by Dr Rivers . . . who vanished so mysteriously at the time of Joseph's murder.'

'Disappearance: Joseph disappeared,' Claire said, Jack's voice echoing in her head. 'There was no body.'

'Wasn't there? And what was that you found in your garden?'

'You don't know it was murder.' But Claire could see the bullet holes in the body's thigh bone and hands. Her father's garden, *Jack's* garden: that's what he'd meant. All her reserves, all her poise was twisting backwards out of her control in one last funfair ride. *Divided souls.*

'It was murder. My father saw it. Or at least he saw his mother crouched beside his father's body on the ground. The ninth of November, 1888: he was only seven, but it's hardly something you forget.'

Both Joseph and the Indian doctor disappeared on or around the night of the Ripper's last murder. Joseph and *Arun.* Either man might have been, might have done . . . Claire didn't finish. Backing away from Jack and his words, shaking her head to reject everything, all of it, she felt sick, dizzy. 'That isn't Arun. Or Magda. I know them, Jack.'

'Arun? Who is Arun?'

She wanted Jack to stop talking, stop his voice going on and on and on until she could think more clearly. She needed to be *clear.* How could she make him stop? His feet were free of the sleeping bag now. She wondered if years later people would worry at this story like Jack Russells at a rat, the way she was worrying at Magda's. What would Ben think? The truth was that she had always had the potential to go too far, and so did Magda. As Claire watched her cousin kick the sleeping bag away and begin to move towards her (his story giving him the time he needed), she could see it all, how history repeats itself . . .

Outside, it was clear and cold, with stars that burned through the screen of the sky. His body was black against the light. She was afraid of what he could do, of what he had done already. Would he hesitate to kill her? He was whispering something. The gun was in her hand. Later she would call it a waking nightmare.

His eyes were more accustomed to the dark. He froze, asked

what she wanted from him. 'A confession.' Justification for what she intended to do.

Her hands were shaking and she didn't think she could do what was necessary.

He started to plead for understanding. She didn't want to understand any more.

He turned to run as she squeezed the trigger, closing her eyes against her own action as she had been taught not to do. A bad shot, through his thigh, pulling him halfway round to face her again. He fell awkwardly, putting his left hand out to break the fall. She had seen deer fall like that, plunging one side of their antlers into the ground. For her next shot she kept her eyes open. He raised his right hand, the palm outwards. As a deer will turn its eyes on its killers.

'It began in a garden and ends in one,' she thought. 'Jack is dead; I killed him.'

The same bullet passed through his upraised hand and into his skull and as it did she heard a long thin wail, an unnatural sound like a rabbit caught by a fox and turned to see Con's small figure, her son's figure silhouetted against the back door light. He was screaming and screaming and she told him to run inside, Mummy has shot an intruder, a murderer, a kidnapper who has taken his Daddy away. 'Run! Run!' she said. But it was a full thirty seconds before he did and in that time Alexandra joined him and Magda had no choice but to push them inside, slam the door and lock it. She had things to do. *Jack* she called him as she dug and hacked at the earth and roots. Not his own name with its biblical roots, but *Jack*, the anonymity he'd given himself, a name that dissociated her from her actions.

It might have happened like that, Claire thought, not the way her cousin had pictured it, not that other, worse possibility . . . *Arun (They say I'm a doctor now ha ha!)*.

The room had been getting darker. Claire, shaking the torch, realised that the battery was going and glanced down for an instant. That's all it took. Jack lunged for the gun and she heard the crack of it going off, the dead sound of a bullet hitting flesh, before she hit the floor and felt the numbing dream take over.

# 18

BEN, HELPED BACK to the guesthouse by Rivers, entered too late to see the shooting. 'It was an accident,' Claire said when she regained consciousness, a lie she maintained throughout Ben's brief questioning. Stunned by her fall but suffering no more than a bruised shoulder, she didn't really know why she'd lied. To gain time? 'I'm very tired,' she said when Ben attempted once again to get the details, the motive. 'I want to sleep now.' She didn't watch as the village men summoned by Rivers carried Jack out, refused to admit what she was capable of in the name of a muddy valley and a long-dead man.

Her night was full of the bad dreams Jack had planted there, including the one that must have obsessed her father all his life. She saw an old map that had been pinned up in the Fleetwood trailer when she and Robin were children, a 'Descriptive Map of London Poverty' published in the 1880s, which showed streets that she now knew lay south of Eden, marked in black to denote their occupation by the vicious class. Overcrowded, labyrinthine, the dirty alleys and blind courts between Petticoat Lane and Brick Lane were a maze through which a man could move like a shadow. (But not the Indian doctor, not Rivers, Arun Rivers; he wouldn't have known the streets well enough to elude the police the way the Ripper did. Claire held on to that.) She saw the cellar in which Joseph spent so much time, the drawers full of toenail clippings and teeth and locks of hair. To those grisly pieces of evidence in the case against Joseph she added his endless visits to his sister's grave, his obsession with the two-headed boy, his crazy mother, the laudanum addict, dying by her own hand, chewing on the matchsticks called Congreves or Lucifers.

But wouldn't Joseph have taken pictures? People would have noticed a photographer at the crime sites. People had noticed many things, including an Indian doctor. She was able to push that thought away until a witness stepped forward, the laundress, Sarah Lewis, who tesified after the last murder to seeing a man carrying a black leather bag at the scene of the crime: 'About twelve inches long. A doctor's, perhaps.' Or a photographer's, Claire insisted, falling asleep to dream of bloodstreams, all the blood, Jack's blood.

Early the next morning Ben arrived with Rivers and his father to check on Claire's condition, bringing with them a plateful of the baker's square little cakes in lurid shades of magenta and acid yellow. Ben discussed bruises, aching shoulders, the possibilities of concussion and fracture – anything other than Jack and the gun.

It was Claire who brought the subject up. 'How is he?' she asked, when Rivers and his father had left them alone with the confectionery between their knees like a psychedelic chessboard.

'It was a good clean shot. He'll survive.' The smile Ben gave her was a pale version of his usual efforts. 'Was that what you intended?'

'I told you last night. It was an accident.'

Avoiding her eyes, Ben picked up one of the cakes. 'Have you tried these? In time I think they might even take the place of Hershey bars.' He put the cake down untasted.

'Does he say differently?'

'Jack? He says nothing at all.'

Any further discussion was forestalled by her cousin's arrival. He stood well back from her bedside, twitchy, probably desperate for a cigarette. 'What would you like me to say, Ben?' he asked.

'Is it bad?' Claire asked, nodding at Jack's shoulder.

Jack shrugged an unconvincing negative, flinching slightly when the movement jarred the side through which her bullet had passed. 'The magician bandaged it last night with a compost of his mysterious leaves and twigs.'

Ben stood up, to give himself authority, Claire imagined, although his authority reached no further than Jack's shoulder. 'I think it's time one of you guys explained in more detail what happened last night. You could start with why you deserted us, Jack, and move on from there.'

Jack repeated a similar excuse to the sketchy one he'd given Claire the night before, 'Those fellows – the Opium Quintet you called them? – they thought I was keeping the green poppy's location a secret deliberately, to get the money for myself. As soon as they realised I didn't know a damn thing, they let me go and continued on into Arunachal Pradesh, where some of them have links to an independence movement . . .' His eyes flicked nervously to Claire, waiting for her to confirm or deny his story.

'Can you leave us alone for a few minutes, Ben?' she asked.

'Are you sure that's wise?'

'I just need a little time to clarify some things with Jack, to ask him a few family questions.'

Rather unwillingly, Ben agreed to leave. 'But I won't be far away.'

'I can't believe there's anything left you haven't asked,' Jack said to her as they heard Ben's footsteps retreating across the gravel path, 'or demanded to be told. How many other skeletons do you want to dig up?'

She shook her head, not sure herself how much more she wanted to know. 'I just . . . I wondered if your father ever discussed what happened the morning after the shooting?'

He shrugged. 'Alex was too young to remember and my father had a lot of mental blank spots about that night, not surprisingly. He remembered Magda locking them in the house and swearing them to silence, then the police coming the following afternoon. Maybe Rivers helped her to bury Joseph, who knows? My father and Alex were considered too young to be questioned.'

'And after Magda moved back to India, what happened to them?'

'She visited Alex and my father a few times, while they were still in school. When it became clear that their mother wasn't coming back from India again, they went through the house systematically rooting out and destroying every picture of her. Nor surprisingly. Whatever way you look at it, Magda is either a murderess or an accomplice to murder. Your great grandmother, my grandmother.'

She tried out a weak smile. 'It doesn't necessarily make us bad people. Nothing stops murderers having kids. I mean, just because someone's Dad was a surgeon doesn't mean the offspring are quick with a scalpel and a surgical needle –'

'Or guns.'

'Even if it's true, that's not all she was, it wasn't her defining moment.'

'Wasn't it? Murder seems pretty definite to me.'

Claire thought that if she refused to believe it was murder for long enough, an alternative slant on those old events might emerge. In her head she argued self-defence for Magda, manslaughter at the worst. 'I mean, she was other things as well. She moved on. She became a sort of demi-saint in Calcutta, she set up charities for orphans and widows –'

'She abandoned her own children to a series of expensive boarding schools, summer schools, finishing schools, tutors,' Jack said acidly. 'My father was always a cold, unemotional bastard. You can hardly blame him, with parents like his. He was probably watching for signs of madness in every move he made.'

Did Jack watch for similar signs in himself? 'Your father should have – *you* should have read her diaries.'

He smiled wearily. 'Believe me, I tried, when I was looking for a way to break her will. But Magda kept a journal for fifty years! You've only read a tiny proportion of her dreary magnum opus. In the time it took to read all her life I would have used up my own.'

Instead of using it up in the way that you have, Claire thought.

'What are you going to tell Ben about me?' Jack asked roughly. He'd had enough of history.

That was the million dollar question. Was it exhaustion that had stopped her telling Ben the whole truth last night, or her realisation that once she told him, events would be in the hands of men again, as this whole trip had been?

◆ ◆ ◆

*The Forest of Air, February 1989*

Ten days after we got here I went with Mr Rivers, Ben, Jack and several of the villagers back to the Tsangpo Gorge to look for Nick and Christian. We found the lean-to and my Ziploc bag with its note still in place under the rock, nothing else. No rumours of any European trekkers among the tribal people we met. The Tibetans said they could find no marks along the cliff edges to indicate where Nick and Christian might have made their descent. Mr Rivers suggested that our friends might have been caught by a Chinese patrol. 'In which case, perhaps it is better to wait until you are back in England before approaching the authorities.'

'Otherwise his village may get blamed for Xanadu's unauthorised visit,' Jack said. All I could think of was to leave another note under the rock, explaining the location of this valley, and dig up some of the soil samples we had taken from the Tsangpo Gorge on the off chance that they may contain something of interest.

We have been in this valley for six weeks now, waiting – on Ben's insistence – in the hope that our missing friends might miraculously turn up. He continues to believe in miracles, despite the fact that we are leaving for Kalimpong soon with two of the village monks, who will drive us as far as the Bhutan border, where the Lepchas can take over. Ben suggested that Nick and Christian might have taken a different track out of the gorge and thus missed my note, 'Or met up with a Chinese patrol,' added Jack, and Mr Rivers has promised to keep a lookout here for them. Personally, I don't really expect much any more. For days now I have been dreaming about Nick, always the same dream: that plastic hand of his with its magnesium core growing out of the snow like a strange pink tree or a flag planted on a mountain peak.

Ben has spent most of his time helping out in the clinic and taking notes about local medicines from the shamans and priests. He told me he would've been quite happy to remain in the village for good, had Tibet's political situation been different. It suits him here, both in his capacities as teratologist and as amateur botanist. 'Maybe I could help them with their replanting schemes,' he said today, and winked at me, lightly tapping his backpack, where he keeps samples of Tsangpo and valley dirt. I still haven't told him about that rusted box of seeds I found beside the skeleton. 'Who knows what we might find in this valley?' he said. 'Randomly. Like so many scientific discoveries.'

'Ever the optimist,' Jack answered. 'It's been picked pretty clean by the Chinese.' If my cousin has asked the villagers any questions about old forests or green poppies, none have been repeated to Ben and me. Jack seems to have lost interest. Maybe, like me, he was shocked by what almost happened to him, what I almost did, could so easily have done.

◆

'You are the one who inherits Eden after me, aren't you, Jack?' Claire had asked her cousin on the morning after the shooting. 'I'm the last one, right? It's so obvious. I should've guessed it months ago.'

Her cousin let out a single heavy sigh that underlined his family's weary history. 'You're welcome to it, Claire. You would have years of legal battles to get rid of all the leeches and hangers-on who live in the almshouses. I should know; I *wasted* years wining and dining that boring old fart Frank Barrett before I managed to get out of him the information that when the female heirs finally ran out the estate reverted to me – but only the part of it you're now living in.'

'But you'd still like that main house, right?'

'It was never the *house* I wanted.'

'Then what were all those references you made to breaking Magda's will?'

'I wasn't talking about the house. Not exactly. It was . . . breaking her *will*, her intention. I wanted a different inheritance than she'd left me.'

Surprisingly, Claire found she could forgive Jack lots of things. It came down to family, she thought, and she was as guilty as Sally had been of wanting to protect her own. Rationalising Jack's crimes, she saw how the drugs had started as an effort to fix his mistake. And drugs were a fine moral line; she was too much a child of her parents not to admit that there was an element of free will involved in their use. She suspected – she hoped – that Jack was essentially a petty criminal, pushed further by circumstances. He might fail to help her, as he'd failed to help Sally, but he wouldn't harm her directly. Probably wouldn't. Although the indirect harm Jack and his kind could do to the people in this valley was incalculable.

The plan she came up with was a risk. Claire had tested its weak points out in her head like a cripple with a crutch. She knew that even if she told Ben the whole truth about what Jack had done in Calcutta, her cousin could still deny it. There was no need for Jack to remind her that the two chemists involved in the chlorophyll fraud were long gone, or that most of his cancer victims were either dead or had been paid off enough to keep their mouths shut. She was gambling entirely on the petty nature of Jack's criminality and on his desire – despite all his protests – to take over Eden Dwellings.

'This is the deal,' she said to her cousin. 'It's kind of corny, but it's the best I can think of right now. We write one statement in which I sign over all my legal rights to Eden, and in a second statement I make notes about what you've told me and you sign them. Then we put your confession with my diary into one of those envelopes like you see on TV – "to be opened in the event of Claire Fleetwood's death or disappearance", that sort of thing – and we send both statements special delivery or whatever to Frank Barrett. This way, if you decide to –'

'I've got the picture, Claire.' He sniffed warily around the idea. 'What guarantee do I have that you won't get back to

London and change your mind, turn me in, tell Barrett to open this dreadful confession of mine?'

'None. No guarantees. You just have to trust me, Jack. You've got more reason to trust me than I have to trust you.'

'I still don't understand . . . what do you get out of such an agreement, apart from a stick to beat me with if I make a single step from the straight and narrow?'

'You're not the only one who never liked Eden Dwellings, Jack, and for you at least it has some sentimental attachment. As far as I'm concerned, it's too big, too . . .' *Full of dead men's clothes.* Robin's phrase. 'But I love that garden. Part of our agreement is that I get to be head gardener. And your confession gives me some leverage if anything goes wrong again.' But not much, she thought. Not if Jack decides he doesn't want to return to England under those terms.

They didn't have to trust to the mail, because Mr Rivers' father had contacts with a tour guide in Pe who thought he could get the packages out of Tibet with a courier. Claire told Ben it was a report of what they'd found on the trip. Passed off as a trekking route for tourists and pilgrims, Claire's cadastral survey and Jack's confession left for London in a tourist bus a week before the departure of the remaining Xanadu party. Eight of them – Ben, Claire and Jack, with the Lepchas and two drivers – were travelling in two hybrid vehicles on loan from a neighbouring valley. One-part Land Rover and one-part village bus to five-parts Tibetan dirt (and immediately dubbed the Dust Rover and the Autodidact by Claire), they bumped and rattled across a pilgrimage route out of Tibet which skirted most of the large towns and military camps along the borders. It took three weeks before the drivers were able to leave the group in the capable hands of a nomadic Bhutia yak herding community travelling southwest into Bhutan.

Spring hadn't come yet to the routes they walked from there. Following yaks along paths that had to be abandoned because they petered out in headachy ridgetops or were buried under avalanches, the party climbed through a vast pelt of evergreens still in the white fingers of glaciers, and left the yaks and their minders behind in high grazing lands studded with early alpine flowers as bright and dense as the enamel base of an Italian crystal paperweight.

Waiting for Jack to make his next move, Claire felt his eyes rarely leave her. They both knew that there was every likelihood of his confession never reaching London, in which case their cat and mouse game would begin again. If she went to the police, there would only be the question of why she hadn't spoken up sooner. Even when she was falling asleep to the grieving language of thawing ice, Claire didn't relax. She woke with stiff, aching muscles, often in exactly the same position she had dropped off, by her side Jack's gun, which Ben had agreed to let her keep only because she had a tent on her own. Convinced she wouldn't have the nerve to use the gun again, she still kept it, hidden next to her, in the series of buses and gypsum trucks that carried them across Bhutan. She noticed that her cousin was always the last person on to the bus and the first off. If he could, he chose seats behind Ben and her, pressing his wakeful face into the window and radiating tension like static electricity. He let his long chin go grey with stubble, and when he did shave he counted out the strokes of the razor one to ten like a ritual. With clairvoyance, considering subsequent events, Claire decided that Jack had the look of a convict steeling himself for one last bid for freedom.

# 19

IT WAS FIVE months almost to the day after first leaving Kalimpong by the time Jack, Ben and Claire arrived back in the little frontier town. One of the porters was weak still from a foot which had become infected during the six weeks since leaving Rivers's muddy valley, so Jack and Ben decided to take him to the big hospital in Darjeeling while Claire organised their flight connections to London. Before doing that she had one more connection to tie up. Closure, she thought of it, a part of her slammed shut and buried for good.

The driver she hired in Kalimpong veered his jeep off the road to the Ironstone Settlements, taking a switchback track that wound steeply down and down through miles of tea, dropping 3000 feet in elevation before they forded a shallow river beside an abandoned tea factory with the faded words 'Magda's Hope' still discernible on its paint-scabbed sides, and turned sharply to climb again on a narrowing track that went from gravel to dirt to a rutted surface that was more root than road. The green hummocks of tea here were bald with neglect, worn velour cushions on an overstuffed sofa, and the jeep's tyres left claw marks on the final, near vertical stretch, where Claire had to shut her eyes against the sheer drop to her left.

The house was surprising after such a hair-raising drive. It might have been transplanted from Aberdeen, so solid and grey were its sullen granite walls. India had contributed only a corrugated-iron roof and a magenta bougainvillea wrapped round the stone veranda where an old man with the placid features of a Tibetan monk waited. He was not much above average height, but his military posture added inches, as did his ancient blazer and striped tie. Claire stumbled over his unpronounceable name before giving up: 'Mr Rivers?'

'So I have been known for many years, except to close friends and family.' He gestured for her to enter the house. 'You will take tea with my wife and me? It is, I'm afraid, mandatory in these parts. And our coffee is very bad. For good coffee in India you must travel to the south.'

The house, he informed her, was owned by a Mrs Gupta, who rented a single room to him and his wife on the second floor. 'You must excuse Mrs Rivers,' he added softly, leading Claire into a hall filled with dark colonial furniture. 'She suffers terribly from arthritis, or we should have given you tea on the veranda.'

To their left Claire noticed a large aquarium in which a fluorescent plastic skull opened and closed its mouth in pantomime laughter.

'Mrs Gupta keeps Siamese fighting fish,' Mr Rivers said. 'The skull aerates the fishtank. It serves to frighten off the cat.'

The unlit hall upstairs did smell strongly of cats, intensifying as they approached the end room, a dim, odorous cavern no more than twelve feet square. Claire was glad that Rivers had mentioned his wife, otherwise the surprisingly forceful voice suddenly shrilling a welcome from its recesses might have come as a shock. A bill from Liberty's of London, yellowed with age, fluttered to the floor at Claire's feet as she moved forward through the gloom, followed by a flurry of more pressing financial statements. Still she could not discern the voice's source. Apart from the huge unmade bed which occupied most of the room, and two broken chairs (one containing a commodious wicker rat trap, the other a stack of files and an apple core), the remaining space was furnished in wooden tea chests overflowing with books, newspapers, yellowing journals of the Royal Geographical Society, dog-eared cardboard files. Shelves, holding more journals and files, rose from floor to ceiling on three walls and stretched across the window, allowing in only corrugated stripes of light, enough to see that half of the

407

fourth wall was covered in a huge map of Central Asia. Long ago, when these shelves had reached the limits of their capacity, space had been cleared on the bed for the overflow of files, and to these had been added a domestic collection of toilet rolls, batteries, old Maglites, garden magazines, flower bulbs and stacks of seed catalogues.

It seemed too small a room to contain this weight of antique information. Not until Rivers cleared the rat trap so that Claire could sit did she finally discern a frail bundle of bones lost in the iron bed. 'Excuse the mess, dear,' said the bones, in the highly bred tones of the Queen's Christmas speech, 'but I've lived entirely in this room for thirty years.' She gripped a zimmer frame next to the bed and leaned forward so that Claire could see her birdlike features for the first time. 'My husband tells me that you may be related to Magda Ironstone.'

Claire was peering curiously at the woolly ski hat covering most of Mrs Rivers's sparrow head. The old woman tapped the hat and bellowed, 'Keeps the cockroaches out of my ears. Terrible things. Had one in there a month ago. For days I could hear it munch munch munching away. Got the Lepcha doctor in. Terrific man. Now, about Magda . . .'

'I'm not sure about our relationship . . .' Claire began hesitantly. 'At least . . . I am William Fleetwood's grand-daughter and I think Magda might have been . . .' She paused. 'My grandfather may have been Magda's illegitimate son. But I have no proof.'

'We're all bastards round here, dearie!' the old lady boomed. 'It's the tea.' She picked up a Maglite with her claw and shone it on Claire's face. 'Good God, girl! You're as black as a Tamil! Bad as my brother.'

'I've been in the mountains for a long time,' answered Claire, wondering why she was apologising. 'The sun was very strong.'

'My wife is half Lepcha, half Yorkshire,' said Rivers, as if that explained a lot.

Claire jumped and squealed as something furry landed heavily on her lap.

'That's Gladstone,' Mrs Rivers said calmly. 'Inherited him

408

from an old Parsee woman next door who died. Named after some damned Hindoo movie star.'

'The Parsee woman?' It was hard to keep track of the relationships here.

'The cat. Until we told her it was a tom.'

Gladstone dug his nails into Claire's thigh.

'Fling the bugger off if he annoys you. Can't abide the damned cat, myself. But *he* likes it.' She waggled her ski hat at Rivers. 'Bloody useless ratter.'

Claire, trying not to giggle, wondered slightly hysterically if she meant the husband or the cat. She gave Gladstone a good hard pinch and he hissed and hurled himself under the bed, where there was an immediate crash of breaking bottles followed by the strong smell of alcohol.

'The bugger's knocked over our bar!' said Mrs Rivers. 'I'll kill him if he's broken the brandy!'

'I think that's gin, dear.' Mr Rivers sniffed appreciatively. 'Got it from the Queen Mum of Bhutan by way of payment for the daffs.'

'My wife used to breed champion double daffodils.'

'Time was when everyone round here longed for my daffs,' Mrs Rivers sighed, then rallied. 'Come on, old boy! We must remember that the girl's not here to discuss my bulbs!'

'No, no . . .' He rustled ineffectively through the folders around the bed. 'Let me see – yes, I have it!' An instrument containing both a telescope and a movable mirror was passed to Claire. 'Heliotrope,' Rivers said. 'From the Greek. The name for something which turns to face the sun. I have a flower of that name in my garden –' *The exiled sunflower*, Claire thought.

Mrs Rivers cleared her throat.

Hastily, her husband went on: 'It's an apparatus that was once used for signalling, especially in geodesic operations. The mirror, reflecting the sun's rays, acted as a form of artificial horizon. It was my grandfather's, sent to me upon Magda Ironstone's death, with a note and some pictures.' The paper chase continued until Rivers stood up, waving a letter in one hand with jubilation. 'This is what you'll be wanting! You see, my grandfather was Aruncala Rish – let's call him Rivers. His son – my father – was ten when the family went to London, England. Eighteen eighty-eight, I think it was. Grandfather was the Ironstones' doctor. Father came back here and fell in love with a local girl . . . and I was born in 1899 –'

'Another bastard to join the gaggle in the Ironstone Settlements,' his wife said.

'Sowing his wild oats, dear. Anyway, Father found that India did not suit him, so he returned to London, where he subsequently married. An Englishwoman. We always kept in touch, at least until the war. They had lots of children – grandchildren, even. Some of them married local Indians, some of them married English. All of them stayed on at Mrs Ironstone's estate, Eden Dwellings.'

*Sally, Mr Banerji, Nick.* Claire added them up. And Derek Rivers, of course. What was he – Arun's great-grandson? Another distant cousin?

'Get on with it!' Mrs Rivers was clearly used to being the accelerator on her husband's stuttering engine.

'Yes. Well. This note, as you will discover, comes from a certain William – Billy, we called him – Fleetwood.'

Claire held the envelope in both hands, afraid to open it. My *grandfather*, she thought. Her throat felt tight.

Mrs Rivers passed her one of the Maglites from the bed. 'Use this, dear. It will be easier to read.'

'Billy sent me this letter a few months after Magda died. She had dictated it to him, as you will see, but she wanted me to know the story too.'

'My dear Rivers', the letter from William 'Billy' Fleetwood began, 'Apologies for using the English name, but so I knew you when I taught at the Settlements. I write this from a desk overlooking the crowded streets of Calcutta, imagining that high cool place where we were born. I regret to inform you that our dear Sister Saraswati – Mrs Ironstone (as I still think of her) – has passed on to greener pastures.'

He didn't call her his mother, Claire thought. So we were

wrong, Jack and I were wrong. Magda is not mine after all. You let your guard down and that's when it happens: history jumps up in the shape of a laughing fluorescent skull, grabs you by the throat and wrings a yelp out of you.

◆ ◆ ◆

WILLIAM STOPPED TO stare at the heliotrope on his desk, thinking of Magda's words, *my only wordly goods, the only one whose loss I could not bear.* Then he began to write again: 'As a result, I myself will be going to England, for my dear mentor has left me an art gallery in Whitechapel, can you imagine? Apparently, she wished me to carry on the work she began. It seems that I shall get my view of the Tower at last, just as you and I imagined all those years ago!

'Mrs Ironstone had few belongings at the end, and this heliotrope, given to her by your grandfather, Arun Rivers, was very dear to her. She wished you to have it, along with the testimony which follows (most of which you know already, of course, having played so central a role as her guide on the last expeditions).' No one had realised quite how old Magda was, William thought, remembering how she had walked and ridden like a young woman until a few months before being struck down for good. Her guides in the high Himalayas had seen her spend days in the saddle with no more to eat than a handful of *tsampa* and a cube of yak cheese. She appeared to live on air and sunlight alone, like the ferns and orchids she admired.

Re-reading what he had written, William added, 'And so, in confirmation of all those tales you used to tell me of your grandfather's courage, I send this story, as dictated to me word for word by Magda Ironstone a few weeks before her death.' A story which is mine, as well, William thought, although she told it back to front, against the prevailing wind, as she did so many things.

◆

After my brief visit to Kalimpong in 1889 (when I did not meet Arun, who was guiding a botanical expedition in Tibet) it was

411

five years before I returned to India. I had waited impatiently until Alexandra was old enough to be sent away to boarding school – and by then, the fog of England had worked its way under my skin and Arun had faded back into the mountains. But although he never wrote directly to me, he had distant cousins in Kalimpong whom from time to time he would visit – and gossip gets passed on in a small town, as you know. Thus news of him had arrived irregularly, as everything did from India, in mail packets concerning your progress at the Settlements.

Returning to Kalimpong in 1894, I sought out Arun's cousins and learned how he had taken up the old search for his father and the green poppy. I traced him to a village on the borders between Sikkim and Bhutan, where he acted as a guide for various botanical and political missions, and there we met, no longer the same people who had parted six years earlier. I was a middle-aged widow and Arun . . . Arun, whom I remembered still as young, had the face of a man who has renounced almost everything.

So we began our travelling again and witnessed extraordinary sights, extraordinary events – perhaps more so than in our earlier journeys together. I believed that he still loved me, as I loved him, yet between us lay a rift – the unforgivable action which had cost us both so much.

*That husky, slightly imperious voice had failed her for a moment here, William remembered.*

It was the winter of 1895. For four days we had been riding our ponies parallel to the icy pyramid of sacred Chumolarhi. Late on the third day it began to snow and we could no longer make out the tracks of our porters, who had gone ahead as usual to make camp. Soon the glare from that bright blizzard enfolded us in its grip and we were truly lost. Had there been but a particle of blue sky, we might have found relief, but a dazzling mist enclosed us, our eyes filled with a featureless brilliance. Snow blindness was nothing to this! What could we do but wrap our faces in scarves and trust to the ponies? Just as we began to fear we should have to spend a night in the open, we heard a shout and two men appeared out of the driving snow holding aloft a torch: our head porters, informing us that there was no shelter in this wild place. But further on, they said, a bridge led over a river canyon to a place where we would find protection from the storm. We had to let the ponies go, hoping they would find their way to shelter.

You know how these Lepcha bridges frighten me, William, however many times I encounter them. On this one, much in need of repair, we were the last across, Arun and I. And as I stepped forward I felt a premonition, a tenuous connection loosening and shuddering in a way to make me pause.

'Go on,' Arun said. 'Quickly. The cable is loose.' He passed me the bag in which he carried his heliotrope and other surveying equipment. 'Take this.'

'I'll wait for you.'

'Go on! I will stay just long enough to fasten the cable. It will be safer for me if you are off the bridge.'

I looked back only once and saw that he was there, crouching behind me on that icy span, securing the cable to preserve the passage for the next traveller, as all men in this mountain region are taught to do. Then the effect of the glare upon my sight was greater than I have power to describe, and the effort of keeping my streaming eyes open was torture. Once again I covered my eyes, lunging blind as a dreamwalker along this treacherous bridge, trusting only in Arun, who called out to me the Lepcha names for those bridges as I floundered on, an old game of ours to give me courage.

*Saomgyang, Ahool, Saomblok, Saomngur, Saomveng. Claire repeated the words in her head.*

Or so I imagined. In truth, it was the wind that spoke, the bridge's creaking and complaining.

Reaching the other side, I pressed my head almost to the ground, trying to discern a path ahead of me, and after some searching, I could see traces of blood in the snow left by some poor fellow whose feet the ice must have cut. I plunged on, uncovering my eyes only to be sure of the way forward and for an instant made out two baggage porters ahead, before all again was darkness. Thank God, out of that snowy void came the voice of our head porter, and he took my arm and led me to our party, huddled away from the wind several hundred yards from where I had thought myself lost.

I told him then that he must go back to look for Arun.

The man's face was as blank as the snow. 'He gone, memsahib.'

'Gone? What do you mean?' I cried, waving back to the web of cables hidden behind a wall of white. 'He's behind me, repairing a cable on the bridge.'

'Bridge gone too, memsahib.'

His calm acceptance made me want to scream. 'Don't be a fool! I was on it.'

He nodded. 'Bridge gone now, memsahib.'

And that is the last I saw or heard of Arun Rivers for twenty-five years.

# 20

CLAIRE LET THE room come back into focus, hardly aware that she was crying. She had read somewhere about quantum memory, the ability of every particle that has ever touched another particle to remember this association and carry it forward. This was what I felt on the bridge, Claire thought, even as she shook off the implausible idea: it was *Magda* calling out the words I heard. This was how they parted, Magda on one side of the canyon, Arun on the other. He did not fall. He waited until she reached the other side, then he went back across the bridge and cut the cane ropes so she could not return, cut that long tenuous spiral of twisted strands linking two stories.

But *why* would he do such a thing if he loved her, as she said he did? Because of *her* unforgivable action – or his?

Mrs Rivers was watching Claire eagerly. 'Have you got to the part about my husband and Magda's last trip, the one she took with him to find Aruncala?'

'No.' Claire had difficulty getting the word out. 'How did she find him again?'

'By following his father's trail!' Mrs Rivers beamed with pride, her nose almost touching her chin. 'My husband was only twenty-one, but already he was famous as a guide. For years Magda had searched those mountains without success, return-ing to England between her expeditions.' She swept her arm in the direction of the wall maps as if to gather up the whole of the Trans-Himalayan region in her crooked little fist. 'But it was not until my husband helped her that Magda found what she wanted.'

Mr Rivers remonstrated gently. 'In the process of her earlier trips Magda gained her reputation as a botanical explorer, of course. You've heard of the Rhododendron *fleetwoodii* and the Primula *arunii*, Miss Fleetwood?'

'No.'

'You must know of the various Himalayan poppies Magda discovered (though none of them approaching green)? She was in her sixties then, but still very strong, fit as any man.'

Claire shook her head humbly. 'I'm not much of a botanist, Mr Rivers.'

'But the last journey: that began in 1919,' Mrs Rivers pressed, 'with my husband! It was *his* idea to start from the Tsangpo Gorge, then work southeast into the mountains between Tibet and Assam, following the routes of Arun's father.'

'It took us a year to find him,' said Mr Rivers, 'because Aruncala travelled in disguise, you see, as a monk, an artist, a salt trader, a doctor, rarely under his own name. They were dangerous times – the Russians did not appreciate the representatives of imperial Britain trespassing on their borders – and like him, we were often forced to take remote routes to avoid arrest. For days, Magda and I would climb without seeing a soul, ascending, descending, creeping like ants along river canyons on paths that were no more than the scratching of a giant's fingernails across a blackboard of sheer cliffs. We searched out all the places where Arun's father had seen the poppy, the snow leopard, but always it eluded us. There were no green poppies – and no Arun.

'Waiting for the mountain passes to clear of snow, we discovered a village where Arun had gone from house to house reciting sacred books, and heard people there describe him as a holy man with a knowledge of medicinal plants. "A great skill in taking likenesses," one man said, and he introduced us to the families with whom Arun had exchanged sketches for food. A middle-aged woman brought out a painting he'd done of her father, who had died when she was eleven. "Of course, my father was much bigger," she said, "and this picture is small. He looks so far away." She was ignorant of the European way with perspective that Arun had been taught, you see.'

He resumed the story, bringing to life the letter in Claire's hands. 'In a monastery downriver from Pemakochung Magda recognised paintwork and frescoes my grandfather had helped restore to earn his passage onwards. The monks retrained him, that's what they told us. For them, all life is *maya* or illusion, and since art is by its very nature an illusion, it is valid only as a vehicle to clarify man's relationship with God. The antithesis of what my grandfather had been taught at the Calcutta Botanic Gardens. From the monks he learned the art of gilding Buddhas twice his height, and by the light of burning butter lamps was encouraged to abandon accuracy and instead to paint clouds curling like waves in crimson skies and blue-faced gods who rose up out of giant lotus blossoms.'

'How can you be sure it was his work,' Claire asked, 'if the aim of Buddhist art is that the artist's ego must not intrude?'

Rivers smiled. 'This was my grandfather's problem. His lotus flowers were too botanically accurate. The monks complained. Too realistic, they said. Also we found that he had begun to leave his notes behind with the more trusted monks, long strips of paper he had secreted in the drum of his prayer wheel and on which he had recorded tiny landscapes and botanical studies, and these we used as maps to guide us.'

'Why would the monks give his notes to you?'

Rivers shrugged. 'They trusted us, Miss Fleetwood, perhaps because I was able to interpret my grandfather's words, which even they could not. He had gone back to writing in his father's language, you see.'

*A wild bog garden of rhododendron is less anonymous when each varietal has been identified, but what does that tell us? Is a man defined by his height, skin, colour, name? How shall we decide which species to save? Shall its practical use to man be the only criterion? What of this forest of oak trees, trunks an inch thick in green moss, rising straight as bamboo prayer canes to a height of four hundred feet, above which spread the branches trailing creepers hundreds of feet long?*

Rivers could quote his grandfather almost word for word. 'In the likeness of fluted columns,' he told Claire, pointing at the page where Magda had reiterated Arun's words. 'That is what my grandfather wrote. Pillars holding up the sky.'

No murderer could write like that, Claire was sure – almost sure, and she understood how a woman might struggle her whole life to preserve the memory of a man who saw the world in such a way.

'At one point Magda and I followed Arun's detour from the main river, when he was forced back almost to the Bhutan border to avoid mounted robbers of the sort who had left his father for dead years before. For several weeks Arun had lived in these border villages, supplementing his funds by teaching the shopkeepers a Hindu method of arithmetic, still in use when we got there.'

It was here that Arun's spirits failed, Claire read. 'Have lost nearly all hope of finding the poppy,' he wrote. 'Yet I am determined to overcome my despondency and make one effort more to find out what happened to my father.' With that monastery, Magda said, Arun left documents summing up his belief that the green opium poppy was a freak, an accident of vegetable teratology adapted only to its own realm. It would not survive transplanting.

'By the time we left the last monastery, winter was approaching and the bandits of the Tea Road to Lhasa were desperate,' Rivers said, his old voice quavering. 'To escape them we crossed the swollen and ice-rimmed rivers on inflated bullock skins, where two of our porters died. One morning we woke to find that the yaks, for lack of good fodder, had been reduced to eating our tent.

' "Perhaps we should leave him in peace," Magda said to me one day. I think we were both considering that in the end neither Arun nor his father wanted them found, these green poppies, this great waterfall, this lost valley.' Rivers glanced across at his tiny shrivelled wife and she stretched her fingers out to him. Claire marvelled that they could feel so moved by a man they had never met, by these events that took place almost seventy years ago. Staring down at the letter in her hand, she heard the voice she had travelled with for months: *In the high*

*Himalaya we saw natural geysers hurl boiling spumes of water
from the frozen ground. Sixty feet into the air, and so intensely cold
was the air – the mercury not rising out of the bulb until nine or ten
in the morning – that the arcs of scalding liquid from the centre of
the earth froze as they fell and formed great monoliths and
pyramids of ice.*

*When we found him, he was a frozen pharaoh in an icy Egypt.
Long dead, crouched as if for rebirth. A frozen pharaoh – and we
were the archaeologists plundering his tomb. Our triangulation
was complete.*

'But how did you know it was Arun, Mr Rivers?'

'She knew. On one of their expeditions he had lost three toes
on his left foot from frostbite. And then, you see, we followed
the path from the pass down into the valley and the monks
showed us Arun's map, his notes.' He smiled fondly. 'In those
days, before the Chinese came, the valley was filled with trees
and flowers.'

'And poppies?'

'Oh yes, there were poppies, though we saw none in bloom.'

The Rivers were silent while Claire read the postscript
William had added: 'As you can imagine, Rivers, I was still
keen to have some confirmation of what you and I had always
suspected, and for the first time, knowing there might not be
another opportunity, I dared to ask Mrs Ironstone what I had
never asked before. "You are mine, dear William," she answered
immediately. "Please forgive me if I have never told you so. I
swear to you, I thought it for the best to have you raised to
manhood at the Ironstone Settlements instead of with me. It was
a decision not easily undertaken, but your birthright was not my
only secret, and for many years I was afraid of other questions
you might ask were I to confess." '

*To explain properly, I will have to tell you about the last night
Arun Rivers spent in London . . . Oh, I was crazy myself that
night. I can hardly bear to think of it. My own diaries reveal a
woman I do not recognise, so many secrets does she keep even from
herself. Again and again I have asked why I chose to marry Joseph,*

*a man from that strange, decaying family, a man whose mind was twisted and turned in on itself by his father, by the tragic circumstances of his mother's and his sister's deaths. But I can only guess now at the motives of that woman, who thought, perhaps, that her love could change a man's character, turn back the course of his life. I learned that childhood's wounds continue to trouble us all our lives, like a broken foot that has healed badly and. on which we have learned to walk with a limp.*

*All I can say in justification for what I am about to tell you is that I had come to think of my husband as a monster. I had followed him to the lowest places, seen the savage things he photographed. Violated women, drowned women. More and more savage they became, pictures I later destroyed. I was worn out from his madness, afraid for myself and the children. Then, you know, there had been all the newspaper reports about the Whitechapel horrors, dates which exactly matched our monthly visits to London. And on the last night . . . on the last night, when I saw him in the garden, his hands and clothing bloody . . . on that night I took a gun and committed the action for which I have spent so many years atoning. After such a deed, how could I consider myself a fit mother for the children I had already, let alone the one I carried within me?*

*You are not the only one to have suffered as a result of what I did. My terrible action cost me the love of my other children – and of Arun too, in the end. There had been foolish talk of an 'Indian doctor' being involved in the Whitechapel murders, perhaps because Arun had been known to treat some of the poor residents of that quarter, just as he had treated Joseph. I begged Arun to flee the rumours and the revenge that would seek him out as an easy target. He did not want to leave his wife and children, but I promised him they would always have a home. And so he left, returned to India and took up his old name.*

*I know he doubted my motives that night; I think he died doubting them. Arun maintained that Joseph was not a violent person. A sick man, yes, mentally unstable, certainly – perhaps because Joseph had forced himself to look where others turned away; Joseph took himself down to Hell, then tried to climb back up again. Father would have said that both Joseph and I sailed into the Bocca Tigris, the Tiger's Mouth, and then could not navigate our way back out. And if I was wrong about Joseph, as Arun believed, why did the murders stop after my husband's death?*

*Oh, but when I look at what a fine man you are, I see that this triangular tale that began in one garden and ended in another altogether cannot have been for nothing. You must believe that I have loved you best of all my children, perhaps because of your own sweet nature, perhaps because of the love I had for Arun Rivers, who never knew you were his son.*

'Is this what you came all this way to find, dear?' Mrs Rivers asked.

'I guess so,' Claire answered. To think that she had left Eden to get away from all the bones and melodrama! But *had* Magda told the truth? Where was Arun while she was killing Joseph, burying him?

'It's a terrible story,' murmured Rivers.

'Strange that she would wait so long to tell William that he was her son, Arun's son,' Claire said to him. 'She didn't *have* to tell him then, after all. Or you.' What if William Fleetwood wasn't Arun's child, but Joseph's? What if Arun wasn't as innocent as Magda insisted? People always tried to put the best slant on their own actions, even in their diaries. How could you know the truth? The most advanced computer program in the world, with a complicated graph showing exact rectal and environmental temperature and comparing it with body weight, clothing, humidity – still, even that could only tell the time of death within 5.2 hours; it couldn't give you a motive, or measure the actions of those people from a hundred years ago. Claire had come to the conclusion that history was a loosely strung net and what slipped through and swam away was the truth.

'She had a few small strokes in the months before the fatal one,' Rivers explained, 'enough to give her a premonition of death. Until then we had all thought her immortal. I think that before dying she wanted to exonerate my grandfather from any suspicions regarding his actions at the time of the murders and Joseph's disappearance.'

'Even here in India people had heard about Jack the Ripper!' said Mrs Rivers with relish. 'I've always been a keen reader of all the theories. You know that there has been increasing talk of this Indian doctor as a possible suspect.' With no hesitation, she moved from murder to ask if Claire would like another cup of tea before getting back to Kalimpong.

'Thank you, I would,' Claire said. 'Was it tea from this estate?'

'That muck?' Mrs Rivers snorted. 'Kalimpong's never been good for tea. We use second flush Castleton. Best there is!'

With the tea, they finished off another round of stale Bourbon biscuits served on chipped Wedgwood plates, and then Mr Rivers walked Claire downstairs past the laughing skull. Shaking her hand at the door, he declared that it had been a delight to meet her. 'Do drop by again, Miss Fleetwood, any time you are passing this way. Mrs Rivers is not over keen on visitors – because of her joints, you see – but . . . we're always here to family.' Together they contemplated the almost impassable road below the veranda, and the unlikely possibility of another random visit.

Sitting between Ben and Jack on the flight home Claire kept in her mind that picture of Mr Rivers on his veranda – double-exposed, triple-exposed on to one lost river after another, beyond him the cast of Tibetan villagers with their phantom forest and the great blue curtain of the Himalayas dissolving into the morning like one of Turner's paintings. *The dissolution of earth into light*, Claire wrote; her own voice, not Magda's, a new voice learned from a landscape of permanent horizons: *In Japan it would be called a 'borrowed view': a distant scene deliberately framed within the close-up of a garden's planting. And wherever I go from here, whatever Jack does, that borrowed view will be part of me.*

# IV TRACE ELEMENTS
## Sally's Garden

# 1

EVENTS MIGHT HAVE gone differently for Claire if Derek Rivers had not vanished with his wife in December rather than continue to 'help the police with inquiries' about Sally's murder. With Derek around to confirm her story of Jack's drug connections (provided he *had* confirmed it), Claire might have been more tempted to let Barrett open that package from Tibet, let responsibility for her cousin's future rest in someone's hands other than hers. As it was, Jack's confession, which had arrived back in London three weeks before she did, lay unopened on Frank Barrett's desk, a potential time bomb. The two cousins sat with their eyes fixed on it and their hands rigidly gripping the arms of their fake walnut chairs like a pair of hostile sphinxes.

'Would you like this back, Miss Fleetwood?' As Barrett offered Claire the well-travelled package she felt the side of her face nearest Jack grow hot. He must have been wondering at that point how far he could trust her, and for how long. 'No,' she answered, 'you keep it.'

The solicitor picked up the second package, Claire's letter passing on her share in Eden Dwellings to her cousin. An exorcism, she thought of it – wasn't that what was required when someone was possessed? An exorcism, the only solution to their shared history of possession and dispossession. She understood now how her father must have felt. 'Your offer is an extraordinary one, Miss Fleetwood. Don't you agree, Jack?'

'We are an extraordinary family, Frank,' Jack replied, with the tight-lipped expression of a man forced to testify against his better judgement.

'You told me so yourself the first time I came here, Mr Barrett,' Claire said.

'Still, to give up your inheritance like this . . .' Hastily Barrett added, 'Very generously, of course.'

The past I'm heading for is a different one, Claire thought, then pressed him: 'It's legal, though? You've told me that I'm the last woman in line.'

'If you step aside, the property automatically reverts to the next male heir.' Barrett nodded at Jack. 'For good.'

So it ends with me, Claire thought, shrugging off whatever legacy of guilt Magda had meant to pass on to her female descendants. 'And you will try to get the trustees to agree that I can lease the Rivers's house now that they've gone?'

'I'll see what I can do. Given your family background and your generosity in handing over the main property, along with Mr Ironstone's endorsement . . . I can't see what objection they could have unless the Rivers return.'

Nosing around the Rivers's abandoned house on her first morning back at Eden, Claire had found nothing to indicate that their departure was anything but permanent. Number One, Eden Dwellings was empty bar the usual detritus of lost lives: old copies of the *TV Times*, a cheap Walkman still holding a tape of Tom Jones's greatest hits, a couple of pairs of dirty Y-fronts in the corner of a cupboard. She had learned about the Rivers's disappearance from Fatbwa and Mustafa, who warned her that the murder suspect she had identified had been brought up before the Crown Prosecution Service in January, only to be released on an unspecified technicality. He couldn't be tried again, at least not for the same crime. A local newspaper had proposed the theory that crucial witnesses had asked for anonymity, and when the CPS refused to grant it, the police couldn't guarantee witness safety. One more inconclusive result, like everything to do with Sally's murder.

Claire and Jack rode together down the lift from Barrett's office, reaching the street in silence, each wrapped in their own private hopes and resentments. Her cousin was the first to speak: 'You do realise that if anything untoward were to happen to you, that package would be opened and I might be blamed, even if –'

'Anything *untoward*, Jack? Good word. Untoward how – like murder? Falling under a bus?' Half-joking, she added, 'Then I guess it's in your interest to see I don't accidentally electrocute myself on the toaster, right?'

Jack replied tersely that smugness didn't suit her. 'It isn't unheard of for solicitor's offices to be burgled, you know,' he said, sowing a seed of doubt before striding off, his narrow Goya figure framed in a cloud of cigarette smoke. She thought it was a brave comment for him to make considering that there was nothing to stop her heading straight back inside and having Barrett open the package. But Jack had always been a gambler, after all. Hadn't he gambled on her silence and won? What more was there to risk? They were co-conspirators of a sort, anyway, united in the story they had told first Ben and then UNISENS about the disappearance of Nick and Christian. And I don't know that Jack's story *isn't* true, Claire thought. There had been no report on the missing men from the Tibetan authorities. Nothing more could be done, short of creating an international incident.

It took some lengthy paperwork from various solicitors and trustees before it was agreed that she could take over the Rivers's house, which she did happily, despite the memories of Sally it held. 'I am a transplant that has successfully mutated, adapted, taken on protective colouring,' Claire said to Mustafa. No longer a volatile fugitive.

Neither was Jack. He didn't hesitate to pack up most of Eden's dusty relics and store them in a warehouse, quickly replacing them with sleek furniture as angular as himself. Then, not long after moving in, he gave up his job at UNISENS to make another bid for freedom from his past, the response to a TV producer who had read about the Xanadu expedition in the science press and asked Jack to present a short series of popular science documentaries. Demystify genetics for the public: that was the brief. Attending a preview of the first two – the dangers of genetically modified crops, the possible existence of a gene for violence or homosexuality – Claire had to admit that they weren't bad. She was glad to see that with his own stake in Eden partially confirmed, her cousin had begun to lose his convict's air of desperation. His only worry, Jack confessed to her in an atypical moment of intimacy, was that Derek Rivers might spot him one day and try a little blackmail.

Of course, Claire didn't expect that she and Jack could be friends, not while that package remained in Barrett's safe, but for a long time they did manage a guarded courtesy. Jack even watched her drastic transformation of the central garden with a tolerance which led Claire to the hopeful but not very realistic belief that by changing her cousin's environment she had actually managed to change his character, a belief supported by the last entry found in her journal, one final list for her Book of Lists.

◆ ◆ ◆

### Spring 1991: *Epiphyte, Epiphysis, Epigenesis*

This garden belongs to everyone at Eden Dwellings now, a sort of community allotment dedicated to Sally, Nick, Robin, Arun and all the other lost seeds. You don't have to look any further than our shed, the hull of a 1930s' Hebrides herring trawler donated by Percy, the Scottish ex-fisherman who runs 'Bag-it with Maggots'. Roofed in thatch by a Yorkshire friend of Jack's, the trawler is still painted with the Gaelic name, *Carn Du*, which Percy told me means dark cairn, a pyramid of stones raised as a memorial or landmark. Something to guide you home across rough and dangerous seas, says Mr Banerji, who is still waiting for Nick's return. Around the cairn he has planted oil seed rape because it is cheap and colourful and makes a good manure crop and I've discovered that walking-stick cabbage, chosen for the beauty of its two-foot sprays of spring flowers, also attracts green fly away from other plants. An informal organic layout reflects the boundaries between family plots, with Mr Banerji's patch almost entirely devoted to green herbs (greens being the only thing Bengalis like more than fish). Fatbwa, surprisingly, has turned out to be a strict weeder, his pumpkins, corn and

428

beans highly regimented in a deep-mulch common to West Indian allotments that is only disturbed by Russell's burial of the odd bone. Slug pellets are banned. On damp days, Mustafa gets his nieces and nephews out with buckets to collect the snails and take them to Mill Hill cemetery. Mrs Patel and Mrs Whitely do most of the propagation on their windowsills and I'm the architect, in charge of the *bones* of the garden, you could say. Fatbwa is helping me with new methods of grafting that promote sustainability. Together we have pioneered the garden's most spectacular feature, what Jack calls my 'mutilated' fruit trees: Himalayan crabapple, whose trunks are woven into living hoop fences to prevent spring scorch, and wild mountain cherry grafted into wind-resistant silhouettes like Giacometti sculptures.

It seems I have a real knack for fantasy. Take Arun's toe bone. Instead of running a DNA test on it to see if that skeleton in Tibet was part of me, I made a collage of the bone with the snaps of his burial site, a reminder of all those stories I thought I'd invented which did turn out to be true. A teratologist in the making, Ben calls me – and who knows what's possible? Listen hard enough and the trees might talk. Maybe that's why I have such faith that my epigenetic experiment on Jack is going to work (good words, the epis: in the names of chemical elements, 'epi' denotes the bridge in a molecule). Wrong or right, it's the best I could do. Any attempt to work out a different plan only brings me back to the elements revealed when I dug down into my family compost:

Arun Rivers
Joseph Ironstone
Magda Fleetwood

Hero?
Martyr?
Murderess?

Martyr?
Murderer?
Saint?

Fish, blood or bone?

Which order is the right one? What did each one contribute to me, Claire Fleetwood, to Jack or Sally? How far back do we have to go to find the stem cell? It's a thought that struck me while examining a handful of Fish, Blood & Bone (which pretty much resembles Robin, post cremation, the uniformly gritty couple of pounds they euphemistically called 'ashes'). Reading the contents of the box of fertiliser, I learned that along with traces of magnesium, calcium and sulphur it contains roughly equal proportions of nitrogen, for stimulating green growth, phosphorus, for the production of seedlings and a good root system, and potassium, to promote flowers. I have no idea how it all breaks down. In fact, the way I look at it is this: there's a little Jack in all of us (as Magda learned), and who's to say which Jack is to blame? No one can analyse the effects on us of his presence or absence. Not so far, at least. Species identification is always difficult, as Ben explained when he came with a progress report on the poppies he has managed to grow from the Tsangpo seeds I gave him. He reminded me that botanists like Linnaeus defined one species from another by such things as whether they produced dry carpels or fleshy berries. Incorrectly, as our ability to sequence genes often proves. Berried specimens from Asia can be closely related to dry-carpelled North Americans, the very species which were originally used to separate the two genera. In the case of our poppy, the first batch of Tsangpo Greens were closer to grey, and they were monocarpic: after flowering once, the plants died before seeding. But we've still got the second box of seeds, the one Val found next to Joseph's skeleton. We'll be more careful with those. After all, to judge whether a species has become extinct or not, to judge what we've lost, first you have to know that it existed:

*From:* Friends of the Earth
*To:* Claire Fleetwood
*Subject:* THE RED LIST OF EXTINCTS
Abronia *umbellata Lam. ssp. acutalata* (Nyctaginaceae),
    common names: pink sandverbena; rose-purple sandverbena:
    Brit. Columbia, Oregon, Washington

Acacia *kingiana* Maiden & Blakely (Leguminosae): Western Australia

Acacia *murruboensis* Maiden & Blakely (Leguminosae): NSW

Acacia *prismifolia* E. Pritzel (Leguminosae): Western Australia

Acacia *volubilis* F. Muell. (Leguminosae): Western Australia

Acalypha *rubra* **Roxburgh** (Euphorbiaceae): St Helena

Acanthocladium *dockeri* F. Muell. (Compositae): NSW, South Australia

Achyranthes *mangarevica* Suesseng (Amaranthaceae): Tuamotu Is.

Acianthus *ledwardii* Rupp (Orchidaceae): NSW

Acmadenia *baileyensis* I. Williams (Rutaceae): South Africa – Cape Province

Acmadenia *candida* I. Williams (Rutaceae): South Africa – Cape Province

Adenia *natalensis* W. J. de Wilde (Passifloraceae): South Africa – Natal

Agalinis *stenophylla* Pennell (Scrophulariaceae), common name: narrow-leaved false foxglove: Florida

Amperea *xiphoclada* (Sieber ex Sprengel) Druce var *pedicellat* R. Henderson (Euphorbiaceae): NSW

Amphibromus *whitei* C. E. Hubb. (Gramineae): Queensland

Anacyclus *alboranensis* Esteve Chueca & Varo (Compos): Spain (Isla de Alborn)

Angraecum *carpophorum* (Orchidaceae): Reunion, Mauritius

Angraecum *obversifolium* Frapp. (Orchidaceae): Reunion, Mauritius

Anthurium *leuconeurum* Lemaire (Araceae): Mexico

Arabis sp. 2 (Cruciferae), common name: rock-cress: Utah

Argentipallium *spiceri* (F. Muell.) Paul G. Wilson: Tasmania

Argyreia *soutteri* (Bailey) Domin (Convolvulaceae): Queensland

Argyrolobium *splendens* (Meisn.) Walp. (Leguminosae): South Africa – Cape Province

Argyroxiphium *virescens* Hillebrand var. *virescens* (Compositae) synonym: Argyroxiphium ***forbesii*** H. St. John; common name: greensword: Hawaii

Armeria *arcuata* Welw. ex Boiss. & Reut. (Plumbagina):
Portugal

Artemisia *insipida* Vill. (Compositae): France (south-west Alps)

Asclepias *bicuspis* N. E. Br. (Asclepiadaceae): South Africa –
Natal

Aspalathus *variegata* Eckl. & Zeyh. (Leguminos): South Africa –
Cape Province

Asplenium *fragile* K. Presl var. *insularis* C. Morton
(Aspleniaceae): Hawaii

Aster *blakei* (Porter) House (Compositae), common name:
Blake's Aster: New Jersey

Astiria *rosea* Lindl. (Sterculiaceae): Mauritius

Astragalus *kentrophyta* A. Gray var. *douglasii* Barneby
(Leguminosae), common name: Douglas' thistle milk-vetch,
ex: Oregon, Washington

Astragalus *pseudocylindraceus* Bornm. (Leguminosae): Turkey

Astragalus *robbinsii* (Oakes) A. Gray var. *robbinsii*
(Leguminosae), common name: Robbins milk-vetch:
Vermont

Badula *ovalifolia* A. D. C. (Myrsinaceae): Reunion

Barleria *natalensis* Lindau (Acanthaceae): South Africa

Begonia *cowellii* Nash (Begoniaceae): Cuba (Granma)

Bertiera *bistipulata* Bojer ex Wernh. (Rubiaceae): Mauritius

Beyeria *lepidopetala* F. Muell. (Euphorbiaceae): Western
Australia

Bidens *eatonii* Fassett var. *major* (Compositae), common name:
Eaton Beggarticks: Connecticut

Bidens *eatonii* Fassett var. *simulans* (Compositae), common
name: Eaton Beggarticks: Connecticut

Bidens *heterodoxa* Fernald & St John var. *monardaefolia*
(Compositae): Connecticut

Blutaparon *rigidum* (Robinson & Greenman) Mears
(Amaranthaceae): Galapagos (Santiago)

Bonania *myrcifolia* (Griseb.) Benth. & Hook. (Euphorbiaceae):
Cuba (Guantanamo)

Botrychium *subbifoliatum* Brackenr. (Ophioglossaceae),
common name: makou: Hawaii

Brachycome *muelleri* Sonder (Compositae): South Australia

Brachystelma *glenense* R. A. Dyer (Asclepiadaceae): South Africa – Orange Free State

Bromus *brachystachys* Hornung (Graminieae): Germany

Bromus *interruptus* (Hackel) Druce (Gramineae), common name: interrupted brome: U.K. (south and east England)

Bulbophyllum *pusillum* Thouars (Orchidaceae): Mauritius

Bulbostylis *neglecta* (Hemsley) C. B. Clarke (Cyperaceae): St Helena

Bulbostylis *warei* (Torr.) C. B. Clarke (Cyperaceae), common name: Ware's Hairsedge: N. Carolina

Byttneria *ivorensis* Hall (Sterculiaceae): Cote d'Ivoire

Caladenia *atkinsonii* Rodway (Orchidaceae): Tasmania

Caladenia *brachyscapa* G. W. Carr (Orchidaceae): Victoria

Caladenia *pumila* R. Rogers (Orchidaceae): Victoria

Calamagrostis *nubila* Louis-Marie (Gramineae), common name: reed grass: New Hampshire

Calanthe *whiteana* King & Pantl. (Orchidaceae): India – Sikkim (Choongthang)

Caliphruria *tenera* Baker (Amaryllidaceae): Colombia

Calocephalus *globosus* M. Scott & Hutch. (Compositae): Western Australia

Calochortus *indecorus* Ownbey & M. E. Peck, common name: sexton Mt Mariposa-lily: Oregon

Calothamnus *accedens* T. J. Hawkeswood (Myrtaceae): Western Australia

Calothamnus *blepharantherus* F. Muell. (Myrtaceae): Western Australia

Campanula *oligosperma* Damboldt (Campanulaceae): Turkey

Caralluma *arenicola* N. E. Brown (Asclepiadaceae): South Africa – Cape Province

Carex *aboriginum* M. E. Jones (Cyperaceae), common name: Indian valley sedge: Brit. Columbia, Idaho

Carex *repanda* C. B. Clarke (Cyperaceae): India – Meghalaya (Cherrapunji; Shillong)

Carmichaelia *prona* T. Kirk (Leguminosae): S. Island (N.Z.)

Cassytha *pedicellosa* J. Weber (Lauraceae): Tasmania